Dull Hearts

BRIANNA WOODS

has context menu

To *Mom* for gifting me the art of writing…

to younger *Bri* for keeping that passion alive…

and to my *unborn*—praying you don't grow up too fast.

Acknowledgments

I want to acknowledge and thank God, first and foremost. Not only for giving me the miraculous energy and imagination to complete an entire novel, but for blessing me with the gift of writing.

I want to thank my mommy. You introduced me to writing and sparked a passion inside of me. Thank you for always letting me read your stories (and constantly correcting my English).

I want to thank and acknowledge my best friend, Ebonee. Where in the world would I be if I didn't have you there to bounce ideas back and forth? Thank you for always being down for a good plotting sesh.

I want to acknowledge my Amazon (SAV4) fam. You know who you are, and I'm so thankful for your support and encouragement to finally publish this bad boy. But seriously, thanks for the lil' push.

Lastly, I want to thank the Amazon Publishing Center for making this process seamless. This is an amazing opportunity and I'm so grateful for the instructions and aid of the editors and my project manager, Erik Peterson.

Table of Contents

"For this people's heart has grown dull…but blessed are your eyes, for they see, and your ears, for they hear."
(Matthew 13:15-16 ESV)

1

If I said I liked the rain because it reminded me of my mother's funeral, would that be weird?

I traced the clear droplets with my eyes as they squiggled down the cold glass of the nook window. The hardwood bench hurt way more than the crimson lines across my left wrist. I winced, adjusting my rear on the seat. The worn thing responded with an eerie creak.

Oh, mom. "You would have never moved us into this stuffy old house."

I closed my eyes and saw her face. The secret technique I kept to myself. She nodded at me in agreement, freckled eyes smiling—a shade the color of fall leaves. *Wow.* She looked even better than the last day I saw her. I couldn't help but smile back.

"Elonie."

My mom suddenly dissolved into the dark. She always vanished when he came around. I peeled my eyes open and faced my father. Presley Davis. Pushed out of a Thai prostitute (no doubt wearing that same disapproving leer on his face). It's no wonder the woman flew across seas to return him back to my grandfather. Things I had in common with Presley Davis:

1. Abandoned by mother

2. Dislike towards father

3. Our last names

I'd also gotten his biological mother's eyes. The only facet that connected me to the paternal side of my family.

"Your behavior is unacceptable." He'd never outright mention the cuts, but it'd been the wince that'd given his acknowledgment away. "How many times do I have to tell you the world does not revolve around you?"

"It's just too—"

"Don't.

I attempted comfort in the small space again. Curling even further into a ball of brown (my favorite color) plaid. My dad sported his earth tones as well. Opting for a dark olive suit to go along with his leather briefcase. His usual lawyer attire.

"I'm grieving." I continued my irksome performance. "Perfectly normal. Perfectly sane."

He only shook his head. The look weighing down his tired, stoic features. The look spoke to me, saying he wished it'd been him instead. He wished he hadn't been left to put up with me for the rest of his life. I know it's what he thought about me... and, well, I thought the same thing. I wish it had been him instead. I guess we had that in common, too. He knew not to entertain me, walking out of the new bedroom without another word, but his presence remained where he'd stood. Haunting me. Yelling at me to get up, get dressed, and get out of this house.

My eyes burned with tears that didn't mean much. I cried often. Sadness being an emotion that I'd been cursed with from a young age. I felt no other emotion as strong as I felt sadness. I wanted to throw a black pity party that matched my mood, but truly, I just wanted attention, and, at this point, Presley had made it his mission to deny me any of his.

So I got up. I got dressed. I got out of *his* house.

The dark gray sky poured down on my umbrella. I silently wondered how it'd feel to twist my ankle on the brick steps I bimbled down. Dr. Portis, Ph.D wouldn't have condoned those types of thoughts. I know he secretly loved when I called him that no matter how many times he insisted I stop. I missed him and refused to believe that he'd encouraged this move.

He's a doctor, not a dummy. But nice try, Presley.

"Put them on my desk. I'll look over them when I get there." I pretended to tune him out as I drew on the car window. "Just a small delay…I'll be in shortly."

H-E-L-P

"Will you do your best to cooperate at school today?" he asked me after hanging up his phone call. "I have a new client."

"Another homewrecker?"

"Don't start with this."

"You're still married."

"Marriage ends in death, Elonie."

"Says who?"

He sighed from his chest. The topic had been discussed many times before, but I knew he couldn't resist the opportunity of defending his female company.

"Do the others know about her?" I continued.

"Not another word." The spark to his flame. "I don't want to hear another word out of you."

He hated hearing the truth spoken out loud. My father preferred his damage covered in dust and cobwebs filed away in the storage cabinet of his mind. No one had the key except for him. I, especially, had never been granted entry—no matter how much I tinkered with the lock. Mom had been allowed a peek every now and then when she'd been alive, reporting things back to me when I grew curious enough to ask. She'd been secretive, too. But me… I wore everything right on my wrists.

I drew a heart around the four-lettered word on the window. Behind it, a dreary blur of dark brown caught my eye. I'd barely paid the neighborhood any attention since arriving to Aylesbury a month ago. Today being the first day I'd actually left that bedroom. Presley's incoming phone call fell on deaf ears this time as I became absorbed by the passing houses. I'd never seen so many stand-alone homes in my life. Daunting as they peeked through the thick trees. Massive in size. Depressing in color. Suddenly, I realized I had been too harsh on this little village of a town. I wanted to blame the move for my problems. I wanted to hate this place. These people. I wanted to…but I had already accepted it all. I, very suddenly, wanted whatever hid behind those menacing oaks and elms.

"I think I'll manage," I answered the question this time when he'd asked again, unable to rip my eyes away from the brick building our driver pulled up to. "Is it private?"

"None of the private schools would accept your record."

A job well done, I'd say.

Presley's phone began its third vibration of the morning, and I swept up my leather knapsack from the floor while he busied with the thing. "It's my client. I have to take this."

"Anyone I know?"

My dad almost looked as if he'd smile at my glib remark—a rare phenomenon—but then I blinked and realized it'd only been my imagination. Presley hadn't smiled since mom. Even before her death, it hadn't happened much. She'd been the only person in the world who'd have possessed that superpower.

"I miss her," I said. "Do you think she's—"

"Go on," he replied, albeit gentler.

And I did. I went on on my own, but I stayed to watch the car successfully turn the roundabout. A pout having returned to my face as I sunk my chin low.

2

I once saw those dark blue orbs roll back in his head. His body shuddered so hard it brought me to tears. I swore I'd never do it again, apologizing over and over, truly thinking I'd hurt him.

I'd never wanted to hurt him.

"Tighter, Brynn…"

My heart throbbed in my throat. One small hand around his neck. Fingertips pressing into warm, sticky skin.

Focus.

Do what he said. Squeeze harder.

"Tighter!"

I moaned in fear, but my nails pierced skin as I gripped him. Feeling that hard lump jump against my palm. I watched his head jerk back, and my eyes bled out involuntary tears again…he held me.

"Hey, girl." He sounded as if he'd run a triathlon, but he could still manage a laugh. "You're too sensitive."

I sniffled, leaking out like a faucet onto the ball of his shoulder.

"Come on." He blew against my damp cheeks. That voice of his calmer than a river. "You just made me feel so good."

I lifted my chin, raising my dead weight from his heaving chest, noticing the red crescent moons on his neck.

"Look at you." I sulked.

I didn't like seeing them blending in with the old scars. I touched his skin again. Soothing them with the same fingers that'd created them. But my fingers weren't good enough. He needed me to make it better. I dove in without thinking, painting over those marks with gentle kisses, a silent apology wrapped in each one.

"You always know how to treat me." He dragged his fingers like a feather down my spine. It made me kiss harder. Wanting to drown him in my affection.

Hard and repetitive knocks shattered the intimate silence between us. The hands on my waist suddenly tightened in his grip as they shifted my stiff body behind him like a shield. My hands went towards my tights without my consent, but I kept a steel glare on the beady black eyes peeking through the fog of the window.

"Mr. Cohen!" The pounding knocks continued, triggering the beginning of a migraine. "Come out of there right now!"

I huffed as I yanked the nylon up my thighs. "But we're not even on campus. He can't—"

"Shh. Just let me handle it."

I shifted backward against the car door and watched him roll down the window, revealing a man's invasive face. Though, my attention had been seized by the faint bite of Jean's tone towards me.

"Jean Cohen," the security guard scolded with a gruff voice that sounded offensive amongst the soft patter of the rain. Those binocular eyes immediately cut to me. "And Miss Walsh."

Jean asked casually, "You mind waiting while I get dressed?"

"Out of the vehicle now. Both of you."

Crap.

I mentally chanted this as I walked up the brick steps, holding my black leather jacket over my head. I'd only wanted some alone time.

One last bit of normalcy before entering back into that nightmare of a school. Where the parasites of my past lingered, and old memories always came back to haunt me.

I instantly regretted leaving Paris.

"Sit down."

I sat by Jean on the wood bench, dripping wet fingers interwoven with his, the chipped fingernails of my other hand scratching through the hole on my inner thigh, longing to hold a cigarette. I hated the ticking sound of the clock in the principal's office. It always made me anxious.

"We are not going down this road again this term." Principal Singh stood over her desk with palms pressed flat. "Jean—five days out of school suspension."

I flinched next to him. "Are you crazy?"

"Excuse me, Miss Walsh, but you are treading thin ice already. You will be given a week off in school suspension only because I've considered your brother's sudden—"

"Don't you dare bring him into this." I shot up from the bench. "Give me the same consequence."

"There's no need to be dramatic, Brynn."

"Please," I then begged.

"A week of in-school suspension starting tomorrow. Today, you'll be sent home for dress code violation." She shifted her black marbled gaze down my ripped attire with a shake of her head. "I'll send letters in the mail to both your parents requesting conferences."

"They're in the city," Jean stated, "and they won't be back until the end of the week."

"Thank you for that information, Mr. Cohen. I'll be sure to contact them by phone Monday morning."

I noted Jean's chuckle. He harbored the same scorn for this place and the people who inhabited it. The main reason why he stayed away standing right in front of us.

Other people.

He hated everyone.

Except me.

"Can we go now?"

Principal Singh crossed her arms. "Together?"

"Well, I did drive her here." Jean finally stood up from the bench and gave his long limbs a stretch.

I lowered my eyes to the coffee mug on Singh's desk. A plum lipstick stain curved the edge. Some cheesy principal slogan written on the front. But I focused on it…and not the painful ringing in my ear.

"Brynn," Principal Singh spoke again. "Is it possible for you to contact your mother for a ride?"

"My mom," I uttered, scratching my neck now, a deep frown weighing on my lips. "No, she's—she's still in bed."

"Is there anyone else who can pick you up? Perhaps your father?"

My chest felt like it'd collapse from the mention of him. I knew I couldn't be here much longer.

"Look, Principal Singh." Jean moved forward, placing me behind him again, and I naturally rested my forehead against his soaking coat. "I'll get her home, and I'll drop her off again tomorrow. Don't worry about it, alright?"

"You don't seem to understand the meaning of suspension, Mr. Cohen. You are not allowed on Aylesbury premises or in the nearby radius considered to be its school zone."

"And what's considered to be its school zone?"

"Wouldn't you like to know?" Principal Singh nearly smirked. "It's better if you just stayed home, but do understand that if you choose not to you will be charged with criminal trespassing. Is that made clear?"

Jean didn't answer, but she didn't seem interested in waiting for him to either. "Brynn," she continued, "I'm sorry, but you will have to find another means of transportation for the remainder of the week."

Funny how easy those words slipped off of her tongue. But she couldn't be sorry. Not really. Otherwise, she would understand how terrible the next five days were about to be.

"I understand that you used to be close with Allan Turner…"

That's it. I'd officially grown tired of hearing her stale voice. I wanted out of this claustrophobic office. I looked up at Jean, tugging on his threads.

"I'll see you in a week, Singh," he said as he backed towards the door. A crooked smile indenting his face.

I rushed back down that narrow hall. The ringing sound only grew louder in my ear. My cigarettes were in his car. In my bag. Under the seat. If I'd been thinking straight, I would've remembered to grab them. Why couldn't I ever think straight anymore?

"Watch out—"

Jean's warning had come too late to stop the collision. I ran right into the person rounding the corner. I stumbled backward and, before hitting the ground, had been caught by Jean's quick arms.

"Are you okay?" he asked, guiding me up.

"I'm so sorry," the girl standing there spoke, her amber eyes as liquid as her tone, "I swear I didn't see you."

"Clearly," I muttered, yanking down my pleated skirt. "Freak."

I shoved past the girl. Ignoring her startled gaze. She didn't get it. No one did. I couldn't take any more of these obstacles. I never should have come back. I never should have left France. Everything felt good there. Just me and Jean. No cares in the world.

I just wanted that back. I just wanted a smoke.

3

At least I'd tried, right?

I'd attempted the positive route, and look where it got me. Crying on the bathroom floor. Knees jabbed into my chest. Tears staining my cheeks. I closed my eyes again. I needed to see her emerge from the darkness and convince me that it would all turn out fine. But I could only see their faces. A girl, a guy, and me—the freak.

Why do I let it bother me?

I care too much, not about humanity or world peace or saving the whales in the ocean. I care about perceptions; I care about what I look like on the outside. We all secretly do, don't we? Wondering how we'd come off to ourselves if we'd met us. I would absolutely hate myself…I just know it.

The door to the bathroom opened on the other side of the stall and I'd holed up inside. High-pitched giggles ruined the mellow atmosphere. I pushed up from the freshly mopped floor and began pulling out a long strip of toilet paper for my draining nose. Meanwhile, the chatter increased as more girls entered the restroom.

"My parents surprised me with a new car," one mousy tone said. "They put a ribbon on it and everything."

"I got festival tickets for this summer," another chimed in. "Should we all take a road trip cross country?"

"No thanks," an interesting rasp bowed out. "I plan to spend the entire summer in the city. My dad's letting me stay in his brownstone—no transportation necessary."

I kicked the toilet handle with my boot and rushed out of the stall. A fog of beauty products hitting my nostrils as I quickly rinsed my hands. Hopeful that maybe I'd make it out of this lion's den unscathed.

"Hey, you're not a senior." That first voice—the mousy one—shattered that hope into a million pieces. "Only senior girls are allowed in here."

"Alright," I mumbled, wagging my wet fingers as I headed for the exit.

"Wait—"

The aged, raspy tone. A voice that said, 'I'm older than you and can tell you what to do, and you'd let me.' I turned around and, all at once met the gazes of a fairly large group of girls. Some of them weren't necessarily surrounding the one who seemed to stand front and center, but they were all visibly on the prowl.

I immediately recognized this film.

Those other girls were just onlookers thirsting for a little bathroom brawl. And could I blame them? Sleepy town. Nasty wet morning. Hushed hallways. A trio of mean girls beating up the poor old' new girl would be the cup of crack everyone needed at this point.

"What's your name?"

"Elonie."

"Are you a freshman?"

"Junior," I answered as if on trial.

"Well, that's no fun."

I knew I looked confused because she giggled. Then everyone else did. Classic unison for a classic scene.

"You must be new, or else you would've known the rule," the mouse spoke again—a petite girl with a peachy cream skin tone and a black French bob.

"Are you new?" Hazel green eyes kept me frozen in place. Eyes that belonged to the raspy voice girl with the warmest skin and bounciest head of curls I'd only ever seen on baby dolls. The gingham headband looked as if it'd break, attempting to pin them down.

I only nodded. Regretting crying now. I watched them looking me up and down. I could only imagine what I looked like to these girls. What conclusions were they jumping to? What judgments had they already made?

"Why are you dressed like that?" the third one questioned. She stood a little taller than the others. Model tall. And pale as a fish's belly with a face dusted in freckles. "You look like a walking thrift shop."

"Don't be rude, Sophie." Hazel eyes casually shook her head. "Forgive her. She's tactless."

"I'm supposed to meet the principal." I took the only opportunity I could get to make a better impression. "Do you know where his office is?"

More giggles from the background. What now?

"Principal Singh is a woman." The curly-haired girl seemed the most intrigued by me, the smile on her face exposing a great set of teeth. "I can show you to her office if you want."

I nodded again. "Thanks."

"Wait, Danielle, what about lattés?" her mouse friend whined, a pair of neat eyebrows tugged high.

"I'll meet you girls there." Her suede kitten heels tapped against the vinyl towards me. "Shall we?"

I walked silently alongside Danielle. The lengthy hall acting as a dust-speckled tunnel we moved deeper and deeper into. It had a sort of musty wet odor now from the influx of soggy students piling in from the downpour. I focused on them—some passing by us and others grouped in the corner pockets of the gloomy halls. The few that had actually looked our way barely noticed me as they were too busy staring at the girl next to me. I didn't know why, but I inched closer to her. That's when they noticed me. Confusion perking their slumped postures and drowsy eyes.

Hang on. I knew that scent. "Opium?"

Danielle caught my eye. "How did you know?"

"My—" I paused. No, I shouldn't mention my dead mother on the first day of school. "The vanilla notes. I have a bottle at home."

"They don't sell it here. I have to go into the city every time I run out."

I smiled a little.

"Are you from the city?"

The question stunned me. It'd been so sudden. I hadn't thought about what my answer would be. I could say yes... I'm technically from there. At least, that's what the birth certificate says. I could say no... emotionally, I'm detached. I've been sheltered all my life and home-schooled for most of it.

No...I definitely could not say no. "Yes."

"I knew it," Danielle said, green eyes sparkling. "You barely bat an eye at Sophie's insult. People from the city really do have thicker skin."

My hand found my wrist and squeezed. "I guess."

Danielle slowed in her steps as we approached an office door with a glass cut out. "If you were a freshman, I'd make you clean the girl's bathroom for a week. It's the consequence for breaking the rule," she said with hands tucked into her burgundy wool overcoat. "Lucky you, you're not. Have a nice meeting with Singh."

I watched her wink, but something forced my voice up my throat again before she'd fully taken off.

"Danielle—"

"Hm?"

"I was wondering what the consequence is for juniors who break the rule?"

Her smile reached her eyes this time. "A warning."

4

Jean wanted to go home. The first bad sign. He hadn't eaten anything at the café. I chain-smoked over my cappuccino and stared at him the whole time. He hated when I did that, but how could I look away? I could feel everything he felt. I could taste what festered inside of him.

"Brynn?"

I blinked. Suddenly, exiting my head. "Yes?"

"Did you plan all of this?"

"Of course not, Jean—" I pleaded with bulging eyes. Barely able to keep my leg and the hand that held my cigarette from shaking. "Please don't think that. I can't take it."

He leaned so far back I thought he'd break the frail wicker chair. My body suddenly felt as though it were that wicker chair. So close to breaking underneath his steady gaze. Those eyes cut deep, and they dug a hole right through my chest. "You can't take it?"

"It's because I would never—" As soon as my voice cracked, he stood to his feet, and so did I, high-tailing after him. "I'm sorry, Jean, wait—"

"It was your idea to hook up there, Brynn." He didn't fail to remind me as I followed him to his truck. "You and your confidence—what in the world made you so sure it wasn't school property?"

"I don't know, I just thought—" I leapt back as he swiftly turned to face me. "I don't know what I was thinking."

"After everything you said in Paris about being over him…"

"I am over, Allan." I inched towards him but kept my hands up as a barrier. "I'm not riding to school with him. I'll walk all the way if I have to."

"Why'd you wear that skirt?" He swiftly switched his glare to my attire. "It makes you look stupid, and it's embarrassing."

My brain had fully scrambled, sliding past my lips like goo. "In—in Paris, you—you said—"

"Come on, Brynn. You know how I get when I'm inside of you. You know I say a lot of things."

I nodded my assurance. "I'm sorry. I'll get rid of it, okay?"

The rain started again. Softly sprinkling my already crumbling face. Jean didn't look at me. He never could when I got this way. Desperate, like a dog for a bone.

"Take a walk, alright?" He began to turn, but then, suddenly, he stopped—running a tense hand through the dark, stringy mess atop his head. I waited with a throbbing heart that felt like it'd burst at any moment. "I want you to know this really hurts me, Brynn. You know how much I hate doubting you."

I wiped the rain and salt from my cheeks as I watched him climb into his truck anyway. My body knew no boundaries as I stood at his window.

"I'll walk to school every day until you come back," I assured him again, fingers curled over the glass. "I won't ride with him. I'll prove you can still trust me, Jean."

He stared forward, nodding a little, but I could tell it didn't matter much to him. Words never did. I slowly backed away and watched him leave the parking lot.

Without me.

I knew today would suck. I just knew it. I should've trusted my gut. I should've stayed in bed when I'd heard the rain. I should've stayed in France when he'd joked about it, and I'd given the lousy excuse of not wanting to abandon my mom and upset my dad.

I kicked pine cones as I walked alongside the road. The image of my mom curled up in that bed made me shiver, but the sudden blaring honk of a car horn made me literally jump out of my skin.

"You're walking into the road," an older man shouted out of his window. "Are you alright?"

I quickly nodded, warmth rising up my neck.

"Do you need a ride, honey?" The old woman seated in the passenger seat called out.

I swallowed the knob in my throat. "No, thank you."

"Are you sure? The rain isn't stopping anytime soon."

"I live right on the corner." I pointed before tucking my hands back in my jacket. "In the apartment complex."

"Oh?" The woman seemed to squint her eyes as she peered at me. "Is your father, Pastor Dwight?"

I rubbed my eye, more droplets falling on my face as I just stood there, sensing the conversation had gone on too long already. "Yes," I muttered.

"You look so much like him." Suddenly, the woman beamed from ear to ear. "I'm so sorry for your family's loss."

"I'm late for school—"

"Wait, are you sure you don't want a—"

I took off in a brisk jog. Still able to feel that woman's eyes on me. Filled with a sick sparkle after she'd connected the dots.

I hated this town so much I could die.

"Mom?" I gently called out, hanging my bag on the wall hooks before venturing down the hallway in my slippers, knowing my dad hated mud tracks on the floor.

I found her in the same position as she'd been in when I'd left. I kept my distance, remaining put by the door, staring at her through the moody gray filter of her bedroom.

"I got sent home," I said to her.

She only stared. Not at me. At the fireplace mantel that had once been covered in family pictures. She lay frozen stiff beneath those heavy blankets. Nothing there behind those bold eyes. Eyes that matched my own. I looked just like him, too. Somehow, I'd gotten the best of both their looks. But the treatment of the red-headed stepchild instead. I slid to the cold floor and rested my forehead on my knees. Tired from the walk. Soaking wet from the rain. My eyes began to droop…

That's not true, and you know it.

I gasped, raising my head.

My eyes darted around the room. My mom still lay there, but I felt something else. Something colder than her dead stare. My heart picked up as I reached for my cigarettes and pulled them out.

"N-no," I stuttered, pushing up from the floor, leaving my mom and rushing down the long hall toward my own bedroom.

Nothing about the space eased my tension. The only place I could remotely gain comfort happened to be the closet. I'd slept there for weeks after the accident. I curled up in the corner now, cigarette wobbling between my fingers, defeated again by the pain crawling throughout this house.

5

Principal Singh—definitely a she—had welcomed me into her school with less than open arms. I knew she had mulled over my records for quite some time before I'd arrived, and everything about the woman spelled no nonsense. But I sensed that she had to be.

Principal Singh had been popular, too.

I could tell as I'd sat across from her. I'd never seen a principal look so…poised. She didn't have to try too hard. She'd perfected her demeanor long ago. She'd been that girl. The cool, exotic girl in school. The one with the hot boyfriend. The die-hard friends. The great hair.

I'd complimented her hair—jet-black locks like fine silk falling over tall shoulders—but she hadn't liked that. No nonsense. I could still see the stern will behind her onyx eyes. I'd decided right then that I wanted to be her best pupil. I would make her like me.

"One, two, or three?"

I blinked. Fragments of Principal Singh disappearing only to be replaced by the lady returning my stare. Her eyebrows shot up, and someone from behind me vocally urged me to hurry up. I looked past her towards the dry-erase board. The breakfast menu displayed in a neat black font.

"Two," I blurted out.

"Blueberry or banana?"

"Blueberry. She handed me the appropriate recycle-friendly container and held out her hand. "Lunch card."

I froze again. "What?

More exasperated sighs were heard, probably from the same complainer from before. Though, the lunch lady didn't look too thrilled herself.

"You need to pay for your meal with your lunch card. Do you have one?"

Principal Singh had mentioned it. I'd just been so wrapped in my thoughts I'd forgotten to ask the relevant questions.

"No," I began explaining, "I'm a new student."

"Come on." A male voice heightened above the low murmur of the cafeteria. "What's the hold-up?"

I couldn't help it. I finally glanced over my shoulder. A sea of crucifying eyes locked on my face. No doubt taking screenshots for their memory bank of reckoning.

"Ackert," the lunch lady scolded. "How many times will I have to tell you to quiet down in my cafeteria?"

Ackert.

The ebony-haired boy walked towards me, ignoring the outpouring of complaints from the several students who stood in front of him in the line. My heart flopped around like a fish out of water as he neared closer.

"Good morning, Miss Lewis." He gripped the slab of white block that formed the food station, leaning against the plexiglass. "What's going on?"

Her caterpillar brows furrowed tightly this time. "Excuse me, Mr. Ackert, but this is wildly inappropriate—"

"I don't have a lunch card…" As soon as I spoke, his eyes fell on me and I figured it smart not to say anything else, knowing some sort of alien language might come pouring out.

He, however, had barely looked at my face before he'd lost interest.

"I'll pay for it."

"Mr. Ackert—"

"Miss Lewis, my dad wanted me out on the field half an hour ago."

"I won't allow it. Now get back in line."

Oh no. The vomit burst up my throat again. "Just let him pay for it."

I knew I'd gripped his attention. I could feel those eyes. But mine were currently being devoured by the lunch lady.

"Excuse me?"

"I-I mean. If he wants…"

"Detention." Her unmoisturized skin stretched against sharp cheekbones, resembling some kind of witch I'd watched in an old cartoon show. "Both of you."

I began shaking my head. But, surprisingly, my voice stayed wedged in my throat. Apparently my nerve had curled up in fear as her words computed in my mind. I'd already done it. I'd already messed up everything. I slammed the container onto the counter and took off. Swallowing down what had to be a lump the size of a boulder in my throat. I knew my dad would be pissed.

Who cares what he thinks?

I did. I couldn't help but obsess over what I predicted he'd say to me when he found out I'd—

"Hey!"

I suddenly came to a halt. Noticing I stood on that huge staircase. The one I'd planned to explore after finishing my scope of the cafeteria. I'd planned to sit and wait. Maybe I'd meet somebody. Maybe I'd run into Danielle again. But I hadn't planned for this. I glanced down at the hand on my arm. I hadn't realized how far I'd gotten or that he'd been chasing after me. He seemed happy to see me this time. Those delighted eyes nearly absorbed me.

Brown—my favorite color.

"Where are you going?" he asked me as he laughed. "No one's allowed up there until the first bell."

My eyes hadn't blinked yet. I knew what would happen if they did. "I'm new here."

"Well, that explains everything."

My wrist still tingled beneath my sweater sleeve after he'd let it go. I knew I'd have to replace the bandage soon. Right then I realized the entire cafeteria had seen what had happened. The warmth on my cheeks had to be visible.

"I'm Liam."

The mumbling grew foggy as his voice brought me back to the surface

"Elonie," I replied.

"You're a little crazy, Elonie." He grinned down at me. "She'll probably give you another day for that."

"Another day?" I couldn't have looked more confused. "I didn't do anything."

"If chucking a muffin at Miss Lewis is nothing…"

"But I didn't—" I looked around him and noticed the contents of the container I'd slammed had ended up all over the floor. My eyes widened with guilt. "I didn't mean to do that."

"Look, my dad might actually kill me this time. He lives for rainy mornings like this, and I'm already missing warm-ups." He started backing down the steps and I seemed to tower over him now. "Give me your number. I'll text you the directions to the office so you can get a lunch card."

I pressed my lips together just in case they betrayed me and told him the truth. That smile he gifted me made me feel special. I wanted to give him my number. I wanted to wait for that text message with nervous anticipation. It'd probably arrive during my first class. The class, I'd planned to steal a seat by the window and waste the hour watching the rain…and maybe fantasize about what mom would be doing right now if she were still alive.

My hands barely wanted to return his phone after I'd finished with it. "Thanks."

"No problem." He slid the device in his back pocket and chuckled. "See you in detention, crazy girl."

6

My brother would have stayed here forever. He'd loved his life. His family. His friends. If it hadn't been for me, he'd still be with them. He'd be making my father proud and putting a smile on my mother's face. If I'd never been born, he would still be alive.

You don't mean that!

My chest collapsed against my lungs as I jumped away from his voice. A murky image of my bedroom suddenly placed in my view. My skin sizzled underneath the heavy jacket I hadn't taken off. I felt suffocated.

"Ethan?" I heard my mom cry out. "Is that you, Ethan?"

The ringtone of my phone buzzed against me, blending with the ding of the doorbell that hit my eardrum like a punch to the face. I groaned and began peeling off the leather, working to calm my nerves by taking deeper breaths. But the attempt grew sour as the noise continued in my ears. I quickly dug the cell phone out of my pocket, blinded by the glow, though quickly gutted by the missed phone calls on display.

"Ethan!" The heavy stamp of my mom's feet running down the hallway quickly snatched my attention. "Mommy's coming, Ethan!"

"Mom," my hoarse tone called out as I pushed up from the carpet.

"Mommy's coming!"

I abandoned my phone as I rushed out of my bedroom and after the woman, who stood not much taller than myself. "Mom!"

I watched her fighting with the door knob before I reached her and threw my arms around her shoulders. A wild flame sparked in her eyes. I knew she didn't recognize me as her daughter right then. Only as someone currently standing in her way.

"No!" Her voice climbed to a stunning height, as she'd barely used it since the funeral. "He's my son!"

"No, mom—"

"Ethan!" Her fingers gripped into me, shoving me into the wall. My back burst with pain, but she showed no recognition of what she'd done. She didn't care about me. She didn't want me near her. Still, I sprung forward again. "No! He needs me! My son needs me!"

"Mom, it's not him—he's not—" I fought back tears as I gripped the doorknob, taking a stance in front of it, my chest heaving up to my neck. "He's not here, Mom. He's not here anymore."

My mom fiercely shook her head, gripping the frizzy curls fanned about her screwed face. "Ethan!" she cried out.

I clenched my jaw. Staring at this monster, she'd become. Remembering how she'd been before. Knowing it had been all my fault. I'd done this to her. I'd created this mess. And I didn't want him to see it. I didn't want him to see what I'd done.

A firework set off in my head. The aftermath of its heat settling on my cheek. My mom stood there, a watery blur, stroking the weapon pressed to her chest. I knew she hadn't meant to do it. It wouldn't be the first time she had. After all, I'd done, I deserved it.

The doorbell rang again in the resounding silence that followed. I swallowed my pride, realizing what I'd have to do, and turned around. Opening the door up for him.

My mom dropped to her knees once she realized her son did not stand on the other side, releasing a sob so heavy it made me shudder where I stood. I closed my eyes to it all just as his arms wrapped around me.

"Brynn…"

Jean's voice melted over me. Easing the tension as, droplets dotted my face.

"I didn't want you to see this." I hugged his waist as his fingers massaged my scalp, the sound of the slow rhythm beneath his shirt comforting me. "She hates me so much."

"Shh, shh." His arms gently rocked me. "I don't hate you. That's all that matters, right?"

I breathed in his scent, tightening my embrace. "I'm glad you came back."

He tilted my head up, brushing his thumbs against my cheeks. "You're okay."

I nodded, laughing as he pinched the corners of my mouth. "I can't believe you're in my house."

I really couldn't believe it. He'd never been inside. I'd never wanted to invite him in. I'd never wanted him to see this side of me. The other side. The ugly side. I felt better around him, in his home. It felt like I could survive a little bit longer. But when I came back here—surrounded by the silence and guilt and shame—

He chuckled. "Ethan would've hated me coming in here."

"Ethan," my mom whimpered.

I'd forgotten her lying there for a moment. My only concern being him. I needed him all to myself.

"Let's take care of your mom," he murmured.

My eyes peeled open, and I took a deep breath, nodding in compliance. "Mom?"

"Ethan," she whispered, "my baby."

I crouched down next to her. "Mom, please, get up."

"Where's my baby?"

My eyes fluttered, and I quickly glanced up at Jean. He slowly joined me on the floor, placing a palm on her robe-clad back, beginning a rubbing motion.

"Mrs. Walsh, Ethan was my friend." The lie sounded so smooth, slipping off his tongue, and instantly, my mom's eyes settled on him.

"You…you're friends with my son?"

Jean nodded as he slipped his arm underneath her legs and began lifting her up. "Ethan used to tell me about you. He loved you a lot, Mrs. Walsh."

I rose in tandem with my mother, noticing the small smile adorning her petite lips, encouraging her with a smile of my own when she stole a glance at me.

"I love my boy," my mom assured us. "He's such a good boy."

I led Jean down the hall as he carried my mom in his arms and then turned to face him once we reached her bedroom. "She usually just sleeps it off."

"Fill the bath first," he said, cocking his head back.

I glanced down at my mom, who'd rested her head on Jean's firm shoulder, eyes already drooping. "My dad usually does—"

"It's just your mom, Brynn."

I rubbed my fingers at my side and forced my feet to move towards the bathroom, ignoring the piercing feeling stirring in the pit of my stomach. My hands acted on autopilot. Turning the knobs. Lukewarm water rushing out and beginning to fill the tub.

I stood up again at the sound of him entering the bathroom, watching him place my mother on her feet, her eyes fluttering open to look at me. Weary eyes staring directly at me. I wanted to rush over and wrap my arms around her. Tell her I hadn't meant to ruin her life. I hadn't meant to take away her only son.

Stop doing that. I frowned and lowered my gaze to the floor. Stop blaming yourself.

"I'll leave you to it," Jean said before leaving me alone with her.

It's just mom. My heart throbbed in my chest as I inched towards her. It's just… "Mom?"

Her lips formed another smile. She looked as if she recognized me this time. "Brynn…"

"I ran a bath for you," I told her, taking her hands into my palms. "Do you want to get in?"

"A bath?" she asked.

"Mhm."

"I'd love a bath." She nodded and planted a kiss on my cheek. My heart sank. "Thank you, dear."

I struggled to let her hand go but eventually did as she walked past me towards the tub, beginning to undress. Then, I watched as she sank beneath the water. Her head rested on the porcelain edge, and her eyes peacefully shut. I thought back in time. Sifting through the memories of my mom back then. She'd never been the most confident. Always neat and put together, but definitely self-conscious. The mere thought of seeing her like this made my cheeks flush. I allowed her privacy, closing the door behind me before joining Jean at the edge of my parents bed.

"What's that look for?" he asked me.

I simply shook my head. Though, immediately, I realized the small act had offended him. How many times would he have to tell me? We belonged to each other now. Even when I'd catch him staring at me with those penetrating eyes, I'd still get that same feeling. The feeling that I belonged to him.

Mind. Body. Soul.

And I liked it. The feeling of giving up myself. No longer responsible. No longer held accountable. I had absolutely no say in what happened now. Only Jean did.

"It's just a strange feeling," I offered a response, reading his expression to see if it'd suffice.

He took a deep breath, deciding to overlook the slight, and generously dangled his arm around my shoulder. "Come here."

I curled myself into his side and rested my head against his chest. The silence of the gloomy bedroom surrounded us. I closed my eyes when he tilted my head back with his palm. Feeling his lips meet mine. Catching hints of the last cigarette he'd smoked and the rain shower from earlier. Then we sank down onto the bed. Our breaths blending…

breaking that all-encompassing silence. Involuntarily, I caught a whiff of my mother's scent on the blankets. It'd been so long since I'd been in this bed. That chilly fall morning had been the last time. I'd never imagined in a million years I'd be in it with Jean. He'd been right before. Ethan would have never let him past the threshold if he were still here. My brother had never liked him. Though he'd never gotten the chance to tell me before he died, I used to wonder... why? Now, I didn't care. I no longer understood how anyone could not like Jean.

The sloshing sound of water caught my attention, causing me to part from his lips as my head lifted from the mattress.

"Jean?" My eyes became fixed on the bathroom door. "I think my mom's getting out."

"You're hearing things."

The quick sound of more splashes hitting the floor caused me to flinch upwards. "Mom?" I called out. The blubbering sound that replied turned my stomach. "She's drowning."

"Hey," I felt Jean grab my arms, stopping me in my haste, "everything's okay."

"No, I heard her, she's—" A heavy pang weighed on my chest. "I can hear her, Jean!" I did hear her. Struggling behind that closed door. Alone. My voice escaped me in a wild cry as I fought to get up. "Please—we have to—"

He finally let go and darted ahead of me into the bathroom. I ran after him on wobbling limbs. My eyes squinted as the blinding white light flooded in. But when I saw her, my heart shattered. Watching him pull her lifeless weight from underneath the water and onto the soaking floor.

No. I refused to believe it. My eyes were only playing tricks on me.

Jean laid her on her back and pressed against her chest with firm hands. Meanwhile, my head spun as fast as my heart thumped around in my chest. I couldn't hear anything but that loud ringing tone. The same sound that wouldn't leave my head after I'd left the hospital that night. And now it'd returned to haunt me. I couldn't tear my eyes away from my mom. Her lips parted as he breathed gusts of air into her body.

What did you do? More breaths. Push. Push. Push. She's our mother!

Breathe. Breathe. Breathe.

But I couldn't.

My chest had completely given out. And, suddenly, I just collapsed.

7

I'd been able to get out of serving a second day of detention. I'd explained the entire situation to Principal Singh when I'd gone to the office to retrieve my lunch card. Seemingly convincing her that it had all been a huge misunderstanding. She'd conceded, though left me with a firm warning about associating with students like Liam Ackert. I'd actually been surprised to hear a principal speak so candidly about the students in her school. But Singh didn't strike me as just any normal principal.

"What else did she say about me?"

I glanced over at Liam. We had study hall together. I'd arrived at the room earlier than my classmates and sat in the back, allotting myself the opportunity to watch as everyone poured in. Our teacher didn't seem to have a real job other than walking around every so often to make sure we were being productive, so conversations had naturally ensued. I'd chosen to get started on my French homework, already having an assigned paper due at the end of the week, but Liam's pondering had made the task difficult. Eventually, I'd given up altogether, becoming locked in those deep brown eyes filled with excitement. It surprised me how he looked at me now, especially when he'd been so dismissive this morning. I'd almost begun to doubt I'd ever receive a message from him as I'd sat in my first period. Waiting to feel that small buzz beneath the frumpy material of my sweater where I'd hid my phone. But when it finally came... I just knew I looked like an idiot grinning to myself beside that dew sprinkled window.

"That's all," I said, smiling far less than I had when he hadn't been around. I didn't want to look too eager or come off too desperate. I just wanted him to like me. "So, is it true you're defiant?"

"Ah." Liam shrugged, though still chuckling. "I'm not too bad. Maybe a little entitled."

"Isn't every coach's kid?" I only guessed.

He hid another boyish laugh with the neckline of his black sweater. "I'm just surprised she let you off the hook. Singh never gives anyone a break."

"Never?"

"Listen, I've been here since ninth grade and not once have I heard of her cutting someone's detention."

I tapped my pencil against my notebook. Delighted to hear those words, but still in need of more information to really affirm myself. I looked at him again and noticed he'd been staring, though he quickly averted his gaze with the clearing of his throat.

"I bet it's because I'm new." I fished for more, yearning to hear his thoughts. "Special treatment, maybe?"

"Taylor's been here less than a year, and that little brat's still afraid of her after getting sent up for a dress code violation."

"Taylor?"

He appeared to roll his eyes, and I leaned in slightly enough to keep him interested in talking to me. "You've probably seen her around. She comes in an annoying pack of three."

Of course. How could I forget? "The whiny girl from the bathroom."

He laughed and, this time, it caught the attention of our teacher. But Liam didn't seem to care as he shifted to face me. "That's the one."

"I met her this morning," I went on, reciting the names off hand, "and Sophie and Danielle."

"Hm. I bet Danielle gave you a warm welcome."

I felt my brows knit. Reading through his sarcastic tone. "She did."

"Listen, don't feed into their crap. They're not your friends."

But how could he say that? I mean, no, I didn't think they were my friends…not yet, at least. But for him to say that. For him to rip the rug right from under me. It made my eye twitch in irritation.

"Are they your friends?" I still asked.

Liam turned his lips down and shook his head. "We were never really…" He looked as if he'd wanted to say something else, and I sat on the edge of my seat, almost urging him to continue with my eyes fixed on him. "That stuff's all in the past now."

"Well," I picked up my pencil, pretending as if I'd suddenly become interested in my paper again, "I believe in letting things happen naturally, you know?

Or as naturally as I could get things to happen. I'd known meeting new people would be no easy task. I'd known I'd have to take a few extra steps to ensure a comfortable position in this school. A position that would at least get me noticed in this dark woods of a town.

"I get it." He nodded in respect for my obvious stance. "You're the type that likes playing with fire."

My smile returned. No one had ever caught on so fast before. "Sometimes," I answered shyly.

He seemed pleased at my confirmation of his guess. I could tell he found me interesting. His eyes glanced down every now and then to my mouth and then sometimes further, clearly as curious about me as I'd been of him.

"You like playing with fire, too," I said.

He cracked another smile, though he couldn't deny it as he nodded. "Sometimes." Still, that inner doubt crossed his face. "But I learned my lesson about playing near the big flames."

The big flames…I wondered who, in particular, were the big flames. And why were they such a threat to him? Liam didn't seem like the type to be easily intimidated. He oozed a strong sense of pride, courage, and, as he'd put it—entitlement. Nothing about him screamed fear. If anything, he seemed to enjoy stirring up the pot just enough to make it bubble but not boil over the edge.

"So," I sighed, choosing to end that conversation for now. I had a feeling I'd have more than enough time to dig out the meat of his words. "I guess I won't be seeing you in detention today."

"Why not?"

"Singh agreed to let me serve it tomorrow since this is my first day. She also assigned me a tour guide for the rest of the week."

His brow lowered while the other remained raised in suspicion. "A tour guide?"

"I guess to keep me out of trouble." I reached into my bag and pulled out the white slip she'd given me. "His name is Allan Turner. He's supposed to meet me here when the bell rings."

Liam groaned and threw his head back, dragging his large hand down his face. "Of course."

"Do you know him?"

The question had been purposeful. Liam's tightened jaw and narrowed eyelids basically spelled it out.

"Listen," He suddenly lifted from his once relaxed posture, "I think it's best if you just stick with me. I know the ends and outs of this school. It's not that hard."

"Is there something wrong with Allan?"

"Like I said before, you just don't need to mix yourself with that group." He knew I didn't get it. That much seemed clear from the widened gaze he pinned me with now. "You're an interesting girl—"

"I thought I was a crazy girl? I teased, naturally.

"That too." He chuckled, his defined muscles slightly releasing the tension my questions had caused. "I just know how they are. And I know this might sound like too much, but could you just trust me on this?"

Of course, Liam. "Sure."

His warm eyes blinked as if surprised that someone would actually trust him. Someone who'd just met him, at that. The shrill bell blared its obnoxious warning that the end of this class had arrived. I began closing my materials and stuffing them back into my bag.

"Where did you say you moved here from?" he asked as he pulled his backpack over his shoulders.

I hadn't, and I thought I wouldn't have to talk about it anymore today. "The city."

"Really?" He slid his palm down his low fade as he shot me a glance of disbelief. "You don't have much of an accent."

Another job well done. "Thanks."

I teased another grin, and he caught on in good timing, grazing me with another one from his endless collection.

He definitely liked me.

I hugged my arms as I followed him towards the exit, making our way out of the freezing room. The entire building seemed to be freezing, an odd choice to blast the air on a cold, wet day like this one. But, then again, nothing about the school had felt necessarily comfortable so far. I recalled this morning, remembering the faces of my peers. Not one had looked particularly content. Oddly similar sizes and shapes moving rather languidly through the hallways in their respective cliques. Some had given me a glance. Others hadn't even bothered. But I'd expected nothing less. I had to earn that recognition—I knew that.

"Good afternoon, Mr. Jones." A boy entered the classroom just before we'd reached the door, causing me to slow in my steps, the base in his voice resounding. "I'm looking for Elonie Davis."

Little did he know, I had already been staring right at him. Quickly realizing what had become so plainly obvious.

They were twins.

"I'm taking over as her guide," Liam spoke up before I did. "She wants me to do it."

Identical hazel eyes fell to me. A less enticed gleam in this pair. What I noticed could only be labeled irritation. I knew the expression all too well. I'd been raised on it.

"Principal Singh doesn't care what she wants, and neither do I," the boy replied, still staring at me as if I'd been the one to say it…or maybe he just didn't have the tolerance for Liam today. "I'll be waiting in the hall."

Liam turned around as soon as he'd left. "He's bluffing."

"Still," I nodded, glancing towards the door, then back up at him, my fingers squeezing my arms nervously, "I promised Principal Singh I'd stay out of trouble if she didn't call home about my detention."

His face softened. "Mom?"

"Dad," I muttered.

He blew out a heavy sigh. "I guess I'll have to let you go then."

I attempted to save face. "Maybe we can meet up for lunch."

"I usually go out to the fields and practice my kicks during lunch break." He winced as he scratched the good bit of scruff on his chin. "The bleachers will probably be wet, but—"

"I don't mind."

He liked that answer, chuckling to himself. "Crazy girl…"

I followed him into the hallway where Allan Turner waited in front of a set of mahogany lockers. One hand tucked in the pocket of his trousers and the other tapping swiftly away at his phone.

"She's all yours," Liam announced, to which Allan lifted his head only slightly. "Tell Singh I said hello when you drop by her office to deliver that daily report of yours."

"Touché," Allan simply replied.

Liam rolled those brown eyes of his away from his seemingly unfazed opponent and turned towards me one last time. "See you in the bleachers."

I nodded as I chewed into my lip, those nerves that had disappeared when Liam had laughed only moments ago returning in full force and making a home in the pit of my stomach. Allan abruptly stepped towards me, just as forward as his sister had been this morning, and made a beckoning hand gesture that furrowed my brows.

"Let me look at your schedule," he demanded, his voice no higher than it'd been before but still able to shake my core.

I swung my bag from my shoulder and began digging for the paper Principal Singh had given me. Clawing around the dark depths as an exasperated sigh slipped out of his mouth. I dropped to my knees—the only thing I could think to do—and diligently began pulling out my things.

"What grade are you in?" The judgment sounded ripe in his tone and rained down from above me.

"I'm a junior," I answered just as I'd found it and stood up again. "Here's my schedule."

He accepted it, though he still peered down at me, clearly studying me. Dissecting me like a frog on a lab table. "When do you plan on picking your bag up from the floor?"

I felt my eyes flutter, something I couldn't control, similar to the heat flushing my neck and face. I lowered and grabbed the forgotten thing. Wishing I could climb inside of its depths and disappear forever. That feeling had returned. The feeling from this morning when I'd cried my eyes out behind that lonely bathroom stall. They'd seen right through me then. And now, so did he. I followed him down the vast hall through the scattered students, not even checking for watching eyes this time. Did he know everything? Could that even be possible? My eyes threatened to well up as I entertained the baseless thoughts in my head.

"So, you're smart after all," Allan's voice penetrated my skull and forced me back to reality.

I folded my arms across me again. "What do you mean?"

"You've qualified for advanced classes," he explained as he led me up a flight of wooden stairs that creaked loudly underneath our shoes. "One happens to be on the senior floor."

"Which one?" I asked, clearly proving just the opposite of his observation as I had not probed over my schedule as he did now.

"Statistics."

Figures. I'd inherited the mathematician gene from my dad.

"It's where we're going now," he continued, and then he said, "I'm a teacher's aid for that class."

"No kidding," I mumbled under my breath but quickly masked it with a cough after he'd glanced at me. "I guess that makes you smarter than me then."

"Of course it does."

I noticed the way he'd said it. As if he had to vocalize it. Leaving not even a sliver of room for doubt. I didn't dare steal another look at his face, but it had fully etched itself into my brain anyway. He had the same honeyed complexion as Danielle. Appearing somewhat out of place in this gloom of a town. Same sandy brown curls. Keen hazel green eyes. Of course, he soared far above her in height, and his features had more of a masculine edge, but there'd been no use in denying it. They were each other's spitting image.

"You're Danielle's brother, right?" I went for it.

He made a small, amused sound as we turned a left corner. "I wonder what gave it away."

"You both have beautiful eyes."

I knew he wouldn't appreciate the compliment, and that theory quickly proved to be true as another less-than-thrilled sigh slipped out. "Turn around."

My eyes grew wide, noticing he'd stopped in front of a classroom door, but the expectant arch of his brow made up my mind for me. I turned around.

"I'm saving you the embarrassment this time." He unhooked the flap of my bag and slid my schedule back inside. "I won't need it again until after lunch."

I faced him after he'd finished. "When is lunch?"

"Next period. I assume you've retrieved your lunch card by now?"

Good. He didn't know about the mishap this morning. Principal Singh hadn't told him that much. I nodded and formed the words I wanted to say to the best of my ability. "I actually know where the cafeteria is. Liam—"

"Didn't Liam get you into trouble this morning?" he asked, and I noticed a subtle smirk sitting in the corner of his full lips. "Detention on your first day of school."

My hope shriveled into dust as a frown weighed down my face. Principal Singh had betrayed me, after all. But could I really call it betrayal? It'd been clear Allan held a higher position in this school and, inevitably, in the eyes of Singh. Liam had so much as stated that with his joke earlier. And Allan hadn't denied it. He knew he held power, and he wanted me to know it, too.

"Liam has a habit of getting himself involved in things that don't concern him," Allan explained with a sudden blasé shift in tone, only making me more curious. "It'd benefit you to steer clear of him."

"Funny," I found my voice as I followed him into the classroom, "he said the same thing about you."

Allan only nodded, saying, "I couldn't agree more."

8

The voices started before I'd gone to France. Small at first, then gradually becoming louder the more I resisted. Now, I couldn't get rid of him. It pained me to think like that. For the longest time, I'd wished I could speak to my brother. Just to see his face…feel his warm hug…hear his laughter. No one had a better laugh than he did.

But I couldn't take it anymore. They weren't real. I knew exactly what they were. Every time, they spoke to me, yelling at me to make the right choice, begging me to stop my internalized hate. I knew what it really meant.

Guilt.

My guilt. So overwhelmingly overbearing that it came in the form of Ethan's voice and randomly tormented me throughout the day. I never listened to it. I wanted it to leave and never come back. I didn't deserve its pity. I knew what I deserved, and soon, Jean promised we'd do it. Soon, it would all be over. But I hadn't wanted that for my mom.

"No!" I screamed at the image of my mom still lying on the bathroom floor, except now a crimson puddle surrounded her. I twisted my face in confusion as a cold shudder racked my bones.

My eyes skittered over, bringing a larger image into my view and, at that, I began sobbing. "Ethan?"

He lay next to her, bleeding out from his head, one hand attempting to reach out and grab me. I instantly brought my hands up for him to hold on to, but as soon as I did, I noticed the same shade of blood covered my hands and dripped down my arms. I took one long, terrified look at myself and screamed in horror.

"Ethan!" I cried out, springing up from a hard surface, only to be quickly muzzled by a firm grip. Fresh tears spilled out of my eyes as Jean's face filled my view. The expression he wore was somewhat relieved…but overall pissed.

"Listen to me," he began, his breaths clipped short. I abruptly nodded. Giving him my undivided attention. "Your mom's out of her mind. She's got your dad on the phone—she almost called the cops, Brynn. You need to go talk to her. Calm her down."

My eyes practically lit up upon hearing his words. She's still alive. I didn't kill her. My mom had survived. I nodded fiercely, and he released my mouth, helping me stand to my feet before allowing me to walk on my own. I slowly managed to wrap my head around what had happened. I'd clearly fainted, and what I'd seen had clearly been a terrible nightmare. Still, I felt unnerved as I wandered into our living room. The high ceilings with its long beams looked down in judgment at me as I hurried, as fast as my feet would allow, across our white marble floor. My bare feet stung from the cold surface. I could hear my mom's worried voice trailing out from around the corner of our kitchen, and I paused in my steps, quickly facing Jean.

"I think you should wait on the terrace while I talk to her," I suggested.

He glanced past me. Hearing her talking about him to my father. Grimacing at the words she used. He slowly brought his hands to my face and smeared the wetness from my cheeks. "Lie your butt off."

"I will," I assured him with another urgent nod of my head. "I promise."

After he left, I continued towards the narrow hallway just past our kitchen. The area that hadn't been touched in over a year now and only hadn't collected dust due to the housekeeper my father kept on duty. Nothing about this house seemed worthy of living in anymore. My mom barely left her bed, only to be bathed and force-fed meals, depression having taken the worst toll on her. My father, well, he didn't work in the city, but he never used to be as absent as he'd become now.

I knew he couldn't stand seeing his wife in her state. He would never voice it, but I saw the effect it's had on their marriage. Another thing that I took the blame for.

The only thing you are to blame for is what you almost let happen today.

I shook my head as if I could shake the voice out of it. My fingers nervously seeking my scalp and scratching hard. "Leave me alone," I quietly snapped.

"She's dead!" I heard my mom wail as I rushed into the dining room, looking around frantically before noticing the door to the pantry closet. "He killed our daughter, Dwight! He murdered our baby girl."

My forehead sprouted with sweat as I stood in front of it. No time to register my mom's genuine cries of concern for me. It'd been so long since I'd heard her speak about me with endearment. It just made the circumstances that much more upsetting.

"Mom," I called out, and my voice cracked involuntarily. "Please open the door, mom."

I heard something topple over and then more stumbling as my mom sobbed my name. The door immediately opened up and I nearly fell over as she threw her arms around me. My body froze. Tense from the weight of the hug. My eyes wide and unblinking. Somewhere on the floor, I heard my father's voice shouting my name through the house phone no one ever used. I figured she hadn't remembered where she'd put her cell phone and had grabbed the closest thing next to her.

"Oh, sweetie." My nose sunk into the robe she wore and stayed there for a long moment. Inhaling her scent. Remembering the flowing dresses she used to wear and that warm vanilla scent, she'd spray on her neck. That mystic twinkle in her eyes that had always made me question her realness as a little girl. I lightly pressed my palms into her back and for a moment, I did feel young again. "Did he hurt you?"

And here I went, betraying her once more.

"Mom," I said, peeling back from her chest and meeting her teary gaze. "I need to talk to dad."

"Of course." She sniffled, wiping her tears away with her fingers. "He's still on the phone."

I knelt down to the floor and retrieved the cordless phone, pressing it firmly to my ear. "Dad, listen to me."

I watched my mom's face as I started explaining to my father what happened. Her once relieved smile slowly shaped into a mask of disbelieving horror.

"And then when we found her," I continued, blinking out genuine tears now, remembering how the true events had unfolded. "I just—I just fainted. I thought she was—"

"No, honey, don't." My mom reached for my arm and pulled me into her again. I naturally rested my head. "It's fine. I'm here. I'm not going anywhere."

I nodded, listening to my father's tone soften, truly out of character for him. He told me to ask my mom if she remembered getting in the bathtub. I asked her, my chest constricting a bit. She only shook her head as she rubbed my arm. A startling juxtaposition from the harsh touch of her hand earlier.

"She doesn't remember," I said to him. "But she's been out of it ever since I got home."

He asked me why I'd come home, and apparently, she'd overheard. "Dwight, please don't interrogate her. She's shaking."

Still, my dad wanted to know. "I got sent home for my skirt. It was too short."

Then he asked about Jean. The one topic I had dreaded. But Mom had had enough. She snatched the phone from me.

"Dwight," she said my father's name with more force than I'd ever heard her speak his name before. "If our daughter and her friend hadn't been here, I would be dead."

It amazed me how she'd come to my defense. That would have never happened before Ethan's death. But my father hadn't changed at all. If anything, he'd only become even more intolerant. Even more demanding. My stomach began its usual cartwheels every time he started yelling at me. He hated two things more than anything else in this world:

1. Lack of control
2. People undermining his authority

He grounded me before I got a single word in. Apparently, Singh had already done her due diligence and phoned him with all of the details that occurred this morning. I stood with warm cheeks as my mom stared at me after relaying the message.

"Dwight—" She paused and sighed, rubbing a tired hand across her forehead. "Yes, I understand that, honey. I'm not condoning anything."

And, just like that, she'd caved. I swallowed the knob of pain in my throat and rolled my tears back, leaving her in the pantry to talk to him alone. I don't know why I'd hoped for a different result. It's not like I'd told the truth. The story had been completely twisted with dishonesty, and yet, I still wanted my father to acknowledge the brave thing I'd just done.

I saved his wife's life.

I could have let her drown in that tub. But I didn't. I wanted her to live. I begged Jean to let her live.

Still, he did not care. Nothing I did nor could ever do would fix it. Saving his wife wouldn't bring back his son. He only wanted to punish me. And I deserved it. I deserved to be punished.

I ran out to the terrace where Jean sat smoking a cigarette. One foot propped on the knee of his other leg—shaking wildly. But when he saw me he quickly stood up and chucked the cigarette away, grabbing me into a tight embrace.

"I want to do it now," I begged, pressing my forehead into his chest, fingers desperately clinging to his jacket. "I want to go away."

His fingers crawled into my hair. "What happened?"

"I just want to go, Jean."

"Shh shh." He attempted to console me, rubbing my scalp urging me to calm down. "We will, I promise we will."

But I couldn't be consoled this time. I soaked his clothes with my tears. Sobbing louder. "They hate me—they hate me for what I did to Ethan."

"Brynn, listen to me, okay?" He lifted my head with his hands and slid my hair away from my forehead, exposing the ugliness I know covered my face now. My nose drained, mixing with the salt of my tears down my quivering lips. I wanted to look away, but he held my jaw firm. "It doesn't matter what they think. They don't matter."

I squeezed my eyes shut. "I don't want to be here anymore—"

He gave me a hard shake. "Hey, listen to me."

My teeth clacked and cut through my tongue, a sharp iron flavor covering my taste buds. I noticed his impatience with me. A very bad sign. Jean had more patience than any guy I'd ever met. It's one of the things I loved most about him. He'd told me how long he'd waited to finally talk to me. How often he'd watched me sitting in the lunchroom. Becoming more and more isolated from them all until, finally, I'd made my way outside. Away from the chaos and pleasantries. Away from all of the people that used to love Ethan.

And right into the arms of the one my brother hated the most.

He held me in those arms now. Whispering into my ear, "Soon... it'll all be over soon."

9

By the time lunch hour rolled around, my wrists were practically on fire. I'd excused myself towards the end of math class, ignoring Allan's wry glance, and had been in the girl's bathroom since, attempting to create a makeshift bandage to stop the sudden bleeding. I'd promised Dr. Portis, Ph.D., that I'd never do this again, and I'd kept that promise. Mostly to prove it to Presley. I would no longer be a screw up. I could get better. I'd taken the colorful pills, filled up the countless decomposition notebooks, and went on the self-reflective morning walks. Forcing myself to forget last year and everything I'd done.

But then they'd shown up.

Together. Sending my make-believe world crashing down around me.

The bell sounded, and I flinched, looking down at the toilet paper wrapped around my wrist. The blood already seeping through the thin material. I knew I'd have to see the nurse, or else someone would notice soon. When I walked out of the bathroom, I hadn't expected to be met with both pairs of piercing hazel eyes staring back at me.

My chin dropped slightly, catching Allan's eye first. "Sorry, I was just—" Then Danielle's light giggle captured my attention. "This is… a senior bathroom, isn't it?"

"Allan told me you have a class on our floor," she replied, gracing me with her pearly smile. "That automatically makes you an exception to the rule."

"Thanks," I moved aside to make room for a few girls to walk into the bathroom. Allan unveiled my bag right then and handed it to me, "and thanks."

"We were wondering if you'd like to sit with us at lunch," Danielle mentioned as the three of us headed down the hallway, her delicate frame snug in the middle of our trio. "Weren't we, Allan?"

"Hardly," her brother voiced his mild protest.

"I actually have to go see the nurse," I informed them.

Danielle glanced over at me. "That explains why you were in there so long."

"Just cramps," I quickly clarified before her mind ran wild.

"I guess you aren't so tough after all." Allan suddenly chuckled at his sister's statement, the sound completely catching me off guard. "What? She's from the city. You know how people are there."

"You're from the city?" he asked, doubt already caressing his deep tone.

I'd been exhausted from this topic since it'd first been mentioned. What does it matter now? Here is where I lived, and here I would apparently stay. "Yes," I still casually confirmed.

"I can take her to the nurse, Allan." Danielle quickly offered as we took another short staircase to the main floor, our shoes all tapping in unison. "No need to tag along."

Allan appeared slightly conflicted but obviously choosing not to voice his concerns as he simply agreed and parted ways with us at the bottom. I can't say I hated to see him go. I felt odd around him. Almost exposed. I didn't like it at all. But I kept these thoughts to myself, having an inkling that Danielle wouldn't appreciate me talking behind her brother's back. The girl walked next to me again, moving with ease through the lunch rush, returning greetings as she received them.

Danielle's popularity had become more than apparent to me. She had this school in the palm of her French-manicured hand. And she knew it (much like her sibling). I stole a glance at her as I had done before. Noting more things. The faint dimple in her cheek that Allan did not have. The sparkling diamond stud tucked in her ear. No other jewelry besides those in sight. An unspoken trait of her personality: subtle charm.

"How are you liking it here so far?" Her voice demanded my full attention. Another similarity between the two of them. "I assume Allan is doing his job well."

I nodded. "He's fine." But feeling as though that had been too vague, I continued, "It's probably irritating having to babysit the new student all week."

"Don't let my brother fool you." Danielle waved my words away with her hand. "He absolutely loves it."

Well, consider me fooled. "Does he volunteer?"

"It's kind of his duty as student body president."

"Oh." I had obviously underestimated the amount of power he held. "That's pretty great."

"Not as great as my role as senior class president," Danielle went on, "Re-elected three years in a row. This term, I'm in charge of spring fling and our prom theme."

Of course. How did I not suspect a little sibling rivalry? "What did you choose?"

"It's a surprise, silly." She laughed as we cut the corner down a hallway opposite from the nearby principal's office. "But you should definitely come to both. It's going to be amazing."

I thought about that invitation. Wondering how far off those dances were and if I'd be completely blended in by then. Would I walk these halls as purposely slow as my peers? Would I talk in that same upstate snooty accent? Would I wear chess blazers and overcoats and A-line tennis skirts with stockings, too? No, I didn't see myself that way. Something told me I would not turn into a Danielle this time.

I just smiled at her, and she smiled back. We then entered the nurse's office. I followed her inside and stood silently next to her while she informed the nurse of my issue. The woman had blonde hair, all tucked up into a tight bun at the back of her head. Her pale blue irises examined me behind thin glasses as Danielle spoke.

"Take a seat over there," the woman said to me, and I instantly noted a faint accent. "Do you have the paperwork filled out?"

"Yes," I answered, taking a seat on the blanketed cot, fidgeting with my fingers now. Danielle looked as if she were more than happy staying in this room with me, but I desperately needed her out. Finally, she met my beckoning eyes. "These cramps are definitely getting worse, Danielle. Do you mind getting a bottle of water for me?"

Nurse Miller motioned towards the corner without looking up from her clipboard. "Water from faucet. Cups in cabinet."

My gaze shifted to the sink I hadn't noticed before, heat coursing up my neck. "I-I meant soda water."

Danielle giggled. "That's a myth, but sure. I'll get one from the vending machine down the hall."

I gently released a breath of air when she'd finally gone. But with it came the pain of my wrist, and right away, I remembered the true reason I'd come to visit Nurse Miller.

"Your parents did not authorize the ibuprofen," she stated, scrolling through the documents of my file.

I knew this. Presley wouldn't have trusted me with that type of freedom. "Actually, Nurse Miller, I came here for a bandage."

The woman's blonde eyebrows joined. "Show me."

My fingers gripped my wrist, my chest picking up as my heart awoke with a maddening thump. Nurse Miller didn't seem fazed as she waited patiently. I swallowed and began lifting my sleeve to reveal the bloodied tissue wrapped around my skin. She sucked her tongue in a disapproving manner and shook her head.

"I'll get you something for it," she said, then pointed towards the trash. "Go throw that away."

I pushed myself up from the cot and rushed over to the bin. Hearing the door close behind me. The tissue had matted together and completely stuck to my skin now. I removed as much as I could. Lightly brushing my fingers across the red cuts. I hadn't realized how many I'd done. I just remembered wanting that horrible feeling to go away.

The door opened again, and I looked up from where I'd returned to the cot. Expecting Nurse Miller to walk in with that same disappointed stare and a multitude of bandages. But Danielle had come in toting a cold can in her hand, though her eyes had quickly settled on my outstretched and exposed arm. My throat dried up like a desert, and I had to swallow hard to be able to form any coherent words.

"It's-it's not what you think—" I could feel the tears rim my eyes as I pulled my sleeve down and stood to my feet.

Danielle hadn't gotten a chance to say anything before Nurse Miller appeared behind her, passing her by with ease.

"Sit, sit," she said to me, flapping her hands down against the air.

"Nurse Miller," Danielle quickly intervened, heading towards me as I sat back down. "Can I have some ibuprofen? I have the worst migraine."

"I'll get it for you right after—"

Danielle discreetly nudged my shoulder, and I, even amidst my confusion, got the memo. "I can do it myself."

Nurse Miller pursed her lips, gazing at me doubtfully, but she relented and handed me the supplies. "It'll burn at first, but clean them good, then apply the bandage."

I nodded and said that I would, then watched the nurse leave out once again. Immediately, I turned to Danielle. "You can't tell anyone about this."

"Hey." Her voice wrapped around me like a hug as she sat next to me, shoulder to shoulder, face to face. "Your secret's safe with me."

I sniffled as tears streamed out, and she laughed a little, using the sleeve of her coat to wipe them. It seemed so strange to fall apart like this in front of someone I barely even knew. But I couldn't help but trust the warmth that radiated from Danielle.

"I used to have a friend—" Danielle cleared her throat and, oddly, tilted her head, thick curls falling down her right shoulder. "She would...scratch."

My chin lowered. "Please don't think I'm a freak."

"Never," Danielle insisted, slipping one arm around my shoulders. "Maybe not as thick-skinned as I thought, but that's fine, too."

The school bell rang throughout the building once again, causing me to stiffen and rise out of her embrace. "What bell is that?"

"The lunch bell."

I shook my head, hearing the door open behind me, Nurse Miller making her final entrance. "Take two with water, Danielle."

Danielle accepted the small paper cup holding her pills. "Will do, Nurse Miller."

"I'm so late." I hurried with the bandage. "I was supposed to meet Liam in the bleachers."

"Ackert?" Danielle laughed a little harder than I'd heard thus far. "Why on earth would you want to do that?"

I slowed in my actions. Thrown off by her question, a little embarrassed suddenly that I'd mentioned him in the first place. "I just promised I'd eat lunch with him."

"Word of advice," Danielle stood up and walked up to me, placing a gentle palm on my shoulder. That perfectly even smile sorted on her face. "Don't."

10

―――――――⟨∘⟩―――――――

I'd dreaded coming back here. More than I'd ever dreaded anything in my entire life. I hated everything about this town. I'd left Paris with so much resentment. Wishing I'd had a little more time to feel slightly normal again. It's not like my aunt wouldn't have let me stay. Shar would've enrolled me into a school herself if the decision had been left up to her. She never grew bored of my holiday visits. She actually enjoyed having me in her flat. Except this time, I felt like I'd barely seen her.

I smiled to myself, gripping my huge umbrella, fresh memories surfacing in my head. Shar had been so excited that I'd met someone. Usually, I stayed to myself when I came to visit her, only getting out on weekends when she'd drag me to the breakfast café right below her place or the times she'd talk me into attending one of her class lectures. But this time, I had a role to play: moping. I moped around the place until the time came for our plan to be hatched. I went out to the shops to grab items from her grocery list and came back with Jean in tow. Idiotic grins on our faces as we fooled my aunt into thinking we'd just met. We knew it'd work out perfectly. Jean fit right in with the people there. Not the fashion-forward ones or the artsy types. More like the sun-beaten farmers in the countryside. Still, my aunt hadn't questioned it. I figured it'd been the guilt of telling me no that kept her enthused enough to entertain my late-night outings and early-morning barge-ins. But I had never felt as free as I'd felt strolling the wet winter streets of Paris with Jean at my side, almost forgetting that large voice that lived in my head...

Almost.

I tightened my hand on the curved tail of the umbrella, a frown chasing away the smile just as quickly as it'd appeared. My morning had already been ruined by that incessant ringing and Ethan's objections cluttering my mind. Or mine… I couldn't tell the difference anymore. I knew the voices weren't really him. But I didn't want to believe they were me either.

I'd sat on the shower floor and smoked a cigarette in complete silence before my mother knocked on my door to say goodbye. She'd been different ever since yesterday. She definitely hadn't gone back to bed. It's as if she were too afraid to close her eyes now. She'd stayed in the kitchen all night, cooking up whatever she could find until my father had finally made it home and convinced her to lay down. I knew he wouldn't yell at me again. He'd done enough of that on the phone. But I'd turned over my cell phone to him and hadn't even attempted to ask when I'd be ungrounded.

"I'm taking your mom to see Dr. Patel tomorrow," he'd said, standing like an obscure statue in my doorway last night. "You'll drive to school with Allan Turner. Your principal notified me that he's more than willing to oblige you for the rest of the school year."

I wanted to protest, but the solemn expression on his face caused me to bite my tongue. I'd laid in bed after he'd left with the worst insomnia I'd had in a while. Thinking of a multitude of ways to avoid waking up this morning, but before I'd known it, dawn had arrived.

The rain started up harder again, and I moved closer to the woods. I walked alongside, watching as another car passed by me. My heart palpitated every time one did. Breathe, I told myself. I could do this. I could make it to school without—

The sudden loud honks from a vehicle driving towards me with blared high beams caused my feet to become frozen to the wet pavement. Both eyes glued to the boy getting out of the car, a navy hooded parka the only thing shielding him from the buckets pouring down from the sky.

"Come on!" Allan shouted at me, motioning with his arm.

I struggled to move my head, but my voice came out clear. "No! I'm walking!"

He slammed the door, "Don't be ridiculous!" and began trudging towards me. I hurried in my movements and, for a split second, thought about using my umbrella to fight him off. But his will and intolerance gave him the strength he needed to easily hoist me up, shoving my flailing body into the passenger seat of his car.

"No!" I pushed his shoulder, watching him flick on the child lock. "What are you—"

He firmly grasped my wrists, both eyes stilling me in my efforts. "Quit behaving like a child, Brynn."

I blinked wildly, that old familiar sensation settling in as he released me. Slamming the door in my face as he returned to the other side. I drew in breaths. Desperately needing fresh air to combat the suffocating scent lingering in the vehicle. Too many memories attacked my head, bringing me back to a time I'd thought I'd escaped. I couldn't take the overstimulation.

"What were you thinking?" he asked once he'd gotten back on the long road.

I shook my head. "Don't even think about lecturing me. I don't have to answer to you anymore."

That seemed to make him uncomfortable as he adjusted in his seat, the squeak of the windshield wipers blending in with his heavy sigh. I stared ahead. The umbrella he'd snapped shut, laying across my lap and soaking my gray sweater tights. I pushed it to the floor and began squeezing the damp material, attempting to calm my nerves.

"I was supposed to pick you up." I noticed a slight rasp edging his tone, indicating that I'd made him more frustrated than he'd let on. "Didn't your father—"

"He told me," I bit.

"Then what were you doing walking in the rain?"

I let another short silence pass between us, my head beginning to throb with a headache. "I need a cigarette."

"Don't you dare."

I inhaled sharply, averting my eyes out of the window, panic settling in. "I shouldn't be here."

"Him," he uttered grotesquely. "Did he tell you to walk?"

"Shut up," I snapped, finally giving him my attention. My hand gripped the head of the seat as I twisted to face him. "Don't talk about Jean like that."

He muttered under his breath—very unlike him—and glanced at me. "If only you could hear yourself."

"Let me smoke," I demanded.

"This is my car, and it will be kept clean."

I grit my teeth. "Then let me out."

"I will do no such—"

"Let me out!" The scream shot out of my mouth before I could stop it, causing him to swerve the vehicle hard. My body flung back into the door, and my head knocked against the window. The pain from the thud blossomed at the back of my head and brought tears to my eyes. "Let me out—let me out, Allan."

He'd pulled the car to the side of the road, and before I could stop him, his arms were around me. Pressing me against him. Forcing my face onto his shoulder. His fingers grasping the back of my neck.

"Calm down," he said into my hair, stilling my trembling body with firm hands, that scent that clung to the seats of the car now enveloping my nostrils. I couldn't help but relax into his embrace. My body knew him too well not to trust it. "It's just me…"

But that's what terrified me the most. Him. Allan Turner. My first kiss. My first love. My first everything. He made me so nervous…so in fear of what he might do…how he might try to creep his way back into my life.

You needed him once.

But not anymore.

My fingers curled into fists. I'd fought too hard to distance myself from him. I couldn't go back now. I pushed against his shoulders and he slightly pulled back. Peering down at me with those paralyzing eyes, I'd thought I'd never see this close up again.

"Take me to school," I mumbled.

His gaze roamed my face as if mentally noting small features to keep in his mind for later, but when he dropped his eyes to my lips, his frustration returned in the form of a deep frown. I would've been embarrassed if I hadn't been so relieved that he'd decided not to kiss me.

I sat a bit calmer in my seat now as he got back onto the road once again, heading straight towards our school—both of us remaining dead silent the rest of the way. When we arrived, I hurried to get out, forgetting the child lock still kept me caged in. I watched him walk around the hood of the car, my eyes catching the glances of a few students passing behind him, no doubt whispering about us. The suffocating feeling returned, and I nearly fell out of the car, attempting to escape the small hell.

"Brynn—"

"Just stay away from me, Allan," I insisted, gripping my useless umbrella at my side as the rain showered me again. "Please?"

He only stepped closer. "You know I can't."

"When will you get it?" My eyes squinted as I stared up at him. "It didn't happen to you, okay? You and your family don't have to worry about anything."

"Of course, it happened to me," he hissed, though quickly composed himself with fingers gripped on his mouth as if stopping the words that sat on his tongue. "It was ours."

I suddenly took off. Ignoring the sound of my name, he shouted it above the rain. I ran away from those words he should've just kept on the tip of his tongue, away from that boy and his opinions and our memories. None of it mattered anymore.

None of it.

11

I could not trust her.

I knew it as soon as she'd spilled her secret. The girl who had once been her friend. I'd wondered instantly why the past tense. What had happened between Danielle and the girl who scratched? My curiosity would definitely kill me this time if I didn't play it smart. But I wanted to know more. I needed to know her secrets. I just couldn't trust her with mine. No, Danielle had made that very clear. I could tell she'd been pleased by the way I'd easily skipped out on lunch with Liam and followed her like a lap dog to the cafeteria instead. I'd sat across from the girls in the snug diner-style booth. Pretending to focus on the strawberry salad I'd settled on as I completely absorbed their conversation.

Taylor had done more complaining as she'd calculated the calories on the nutrition label of her sandwich before deciding to go back and grab a salad, too. Sophie had arrived at the booth a few minutes after Taylor had returned, unloading with stories right away. Danielle hadn't seemed too interested as she'd been jotting notes in her planner while sipping on a warm brew, her own lunch going untouched. Sophie's endless chatter hadn't done me any good either. I'd recognized none of the name drops that had left her mouth. But the stories had been entertaining—nothing compared to my reveal in the nurse's office— but still worthy of gossip.

"Mademoiselle," a thin but soft voice trickled into my ear as an encompassing presence hovered over me, and I gasped, forcing my eyes away from the rain that fell outside, "eyes on le plateau."

"Je suis désolée," I apologized.

My French teacher left my desk and moved further down the aisle, continuing with her lecture. I could feel the stares of my classmates. Probably wondering. Or maybe they weren't. Maybe they didn't care about the new girl who sat next to the window—zoned out in her thoughts again. The same thing had happened yesterday, too. But Madame Etienne had been understanding. I doubted it'd continue, though. I glanced up from my textbook and noticed the woman seated behind her desk now. I then dared to look at my surroundings. Tucking my hand under the coiled drape of my hair, my eyes drifting from one focused face to another. Just as I'd suspected. Not one of them noticed me beside the window. Their pencils scribbling and their pages flipping almost in unison.

They didn't care.

No one ever cared.

I gently gripped the back of my neck as I lowered my eyes back down to the book. Reading the directions of the assignment everyone had already begun working on. But the blare of the bell interrupted my slow perusing and immediately I looked up at the clock. Had the hour really gone by that fast?

"Rappelez-vous," Madame Etienne announced, standing up from her seat, "all papers are due à la fin de la semaine."

I stayed seated as I watched my classmates gather their things and head for the front door. Some briefly spoke to Madame Etienne before walking out. I waited until each and every student had left the classroom before finally standing up and making my way towards the teacher.

"Bonjour, Madame." I adopted the most convincing tone in my tool box as I etched a smile onto my face. "Can I talk to you for a moment?"

"En français s'il vous plaît," Madame Etienne insisted, shifting to the edge of her desk, palms clutched in front of a black pencil skirt.

I nodded and repeated the question again in French. She obliged me with awaiting eyes.

"Well," I continued, speaking the language. "I wanted to apologize for letting myself get distracted. It's not like me at all."

I couldn't tell if she actually believed that part, but she seemed enthralled by something. Her eyes nearly smiled at me with delight.

"You speak so well," she complimented me. "Much better than most of my seniors. Stay focused, and you'll do fine."

I grinned at her words, thanking her again before exiting the classroom with a little more pep in my step. At least until Allan's disgruntled face greeted me outside of the door.

"You seem to misunderstand the concept of time."

I frowned as I followed behind him through the crowded hall. "Sorry, Madame Etienne wanted to speak with me." He replied with nothing, and I chewed my lip, thinking of something that would ease the tension. "She wanted to compliment me on my French. She said I'm better than the seniors in her classes."

I noticed a slight curl on his lips once I'd successfully scurried alongside him, his slower pace finally allowing for it. "Apologize in French, then."

I knew that smile couldn't have meant anything good. Crossing my arms, I said, "Je suis désolée."

"I know my lateness offends you," he continued.

My eyebrows furrowed. "Je sais que mon retard vous offense—"

"But I promise it won't happen again."

"Mais je promets…" He glanced down at me, awaiting the rest of the sentence, "Cela ne se reproduira plus."

"Hm."

My eyes shifted downward. "Do you speak?"

"I've taken classes here and there." He kept his gaze forward, though he didn't seem focused on the students we passed by, suddenly appearing to go inside of his head for a moment. I wondered what had crossed his mind, and I almost asked until he began speaking again. "It's not a particularly useful language unless you plan to live there."

I avoided making further conversation for the remainder of the walk to class. Allan struck me as the tense, brooding type. I knew I'd get nowhere attempting to get inside of his tightly bound head.

"Au revoir," he teased dryly before leaving me at the front door of the study hall classroom.

And just like that, Allan had become the least of my worries, a deep set of brown eyes holding me in place as soon as I'd walked into the room. I'd expected this. After all, I did stand him up. The way he stared… it's as if he knew I'd been avoiding him all morning. I'd refused to even venture into the lunch room, passing the time in the school's library instead. The area had been large enough for me to hideout amongst the humongous bookshelves of alphabetically sorted literature. I'd even found a few books to check out before hurrying to meet up with Allan.

"Hey," I greeted Liam once I'd sat down, my damp palms gripping my elbows as I leaned forward on my desk.

He chuckled, but I couldn't tell if he'd done it out of spite or amusement. "Hey?"

"I'm sorry," the words spilled from my mouth like vomit. "Please don't be mad at me."

"I'm not mad at you," he replied, and his soft features expressed how genuine his words were. His body rose from its comfortable slouch. "I expected them to drag you into their demented inner circle."

"Demented?" I questioned.

I could tell I'd caught him off guard, and easily, his face hardened again. "It's too much to even begin to explain."

Those words disappointed me. More of our peers entered the classroom, and the room slowly became louder. Drowning out this dire discussion between us. And it did seem dire now. I had absolutely nothing on Danielle, and she had everything on me. Vulnerable didn't do the feeling justice. Exposed didn't even cut close. But it had been my fault. If I weren't such a basket case. If I weren't so emotional and impulsive. If only I didn't wear it all on my sleeve.

"If you can't explain," I failed to hide the irritability in my tone, "then I don't see the point in commenting at all."

He seemed taken aback, and I figured he'd seen right through my act. I began shifting my body away from him, prepared to accept that I might not get what I wanted. Then I noticed the expression that crossed his face. It'd been so quick, like a light switch flickering on. His eyes fell to his lap—regret—then back up to mine again. He would speak. I could tell.

"What happened to trusting me?"

"It just seems unfair."

He sighed, bringing his hand down his face, an act I'd seen before. "Just forget it."

No!

"No," I snapped. If he hadn't looked thrown off before, he definitely did this time. "I-I mean…"

"Look," He suddenly scooted forward in his seat, "it's not something I can just explain. Besides, you wouldn't get it. You weren't here last year when everything happened."

"You want to protect me," I finally said, fixating a sincere expression back onto my face as I dared to place my hand on his forearm. He wore an emerald mountain fleece today, though I could still feel the definition of his arm underneath the thick material. "Then protect me."

Liam shook his head as if he wanted to shake the secrets he so obviously harbored out of his mind.

"My friend, he—" He paused for a moment, and I watched his shoulders roll back in an attempt to roll the pain that so evidently glazed over his darkened glare. "He was killed."

"Who was your friend?"

He blinked, unable to stop the tear that trickled out, though he quickly brushed it away before dropping his eyes down again—shame.

"Ethan… my friend was Ethan Walsh."

12

The ticking…

I glanced up at the clock from behind my oak cubicle. Only one more hour left. Still, I clenched my teeth in stubbornness as I dragged the hand that clutched my number two pencil across my notepad, writing out the next word from the long dictionary list I'd been assigned.

Dull.

I wrote down each letter in my bubbled handwriting, then returned my focus to the definition. Lacking interest or excitement. I remained fixed on the word. Tapping my eraser to the rhythm of the ticking.

I hated that ticking.

It'd just been me and Miss Ingram. Clearly, no one else in this school dared to be served an in-school suspension. No, everyone else did as they were told (or at least pretended to). I used to be one of those pretenders.

You were always good.

I rolled my eyes at the voice, beginning a scribble on the corner edge of my paper. I had pretended right alongside them. I used to be studious, just like them. Bright-eyed and bushy-tailed. Hair tied in silk ribbons with a demeanor dripping with liquid gold charm. I had bathed in the mess of it all, and I'd enjoyed it.

Snap.

My eyes blinked out of their distant gaze and took in the broken lead of my pencil. Fourth time today. Immediately, I stood up, but the door opening seized Miss Ingram's attention before I could. I didn't sit down, though. I remained standing to see who'd come to crash our party of two.

"Good afternoon." Allan strode in, making a swift beeline towards Miss Ingram's desk. "I need a signature on a detention slip—junior class."

"The detention must be completed first," Miss Ingram informed.

"Principal Singh is making an exception this time. She's a new student and is still adjusting to where everything is. I've been instructed to drop off her verification slip to the office for her."

"Oh." Miss Ingram accepted the slip. "Take a seat anywhere you'd like, dear." She then shifted her attention to me. "Did you need something, Miss Walsh?"

Allan looked over at me—clearly startled—and down I went. Hidden by the upright dividers of the cubicle. I heard his footsteps once he left. The thud of the door resounded in my ear. My fingernails lightly scraped my palm, but I pushed the urge away, finding the clock with my eyes again.

Forty minutes left.

Another set of footsteps grazed my eardrum, causing me to discreetly glance around the edge of my cubicle. I watched as the girl who'd come in with Allan seated herself in the chair next to me. A million other available seats, and she chose the one closest to mine. I shifted as far over as I could and leaned forward with my arms firmly planted on the desk table. Pencil in hand again. Though, I'd quickly been reminded of my dilemma as soon as I'd prepared myself to write.

I sighed and stood to my feet again. "I need to sharpen my pencil."

"You've been up to sharpen your pencil several times today," Miss Ingram stated the obvious, one hand tucked underneath her cleft chin. "Maybe you can try using a pen instead?"

"And if I mess up?" I asked, urging her to rethink her moronic suggestion.

"Your assignment will not be graded, Brynn."

I couldn't help but roll my eyes away before I sat back down. What kind of a psycho copies down definitions in pen? I rolled the shortened yellow stick between my fingertips as if to roll away my growing frustration.

Thirty-five more minutes.

"I have a mechanical pencil you can borrow," another voice suddenly debuted in the silence that followed.

That tone. Weirdly enough, I recognized it. A single, but still fresh, memory resurfacing. The girl invaded the privacy of my cubicle as she stood up, holding my gaze, and I could already feel the cold metal of my invisible armor building around me.

"Breakable lead every thirty seconds? No, thank you," I muttered a reply.

"It's this or a pen." She stepped out of her cubicle and inched towards me. "The latter is kind of torturous, don't you think?"

"I'm sure I'll survive."

"And if you don't?"

I closed my eyes and exhaled. "Just give it to me."

She handed over the pencil and returned to her seat. I sat grumpily in mine, though I forced myself to mindlessly copy down the next definition on my list—tuning out the shuffle of her supplies.

"Excuse me—" Her voice burst through my forced concentration, and internally, I seethed. She'd stood up from her seat again. "What exactly am I supposed to do?"

Miss Ingram, the person she'd directed the question towards, cleared her throat. I couldn't see her face, but I guessed that she'd slid off those reading glasses she'd been wearing since this morning. I hadn't been able to get a good look at her novel on my pencil-sharpening journeys, but it had to be a page-turner to keep her so engaged. A sordid romance, no doubt. Ingram had to be pushing sixty. Anything to keep from becoming frigid, I guess…

"Are you confused about where you are?" Miss Ingram wondered, her voice as frail as the pencil shavings that lay underneath the sharpener. "This is detention, dear."

"I've never...I'm sort of new to this."

Those few words told me everything I needed to know about this new girl. She wouldn't be one of the pretenders. She had no reason to pretend.

"Oh, well, it's certainly good to hear you aren't a repeat offender." Miss Ingram giggled at her own joke. "You have the option of completing any homework assignments you may have or copying definitions out of one of the dictionaries stacked on the bookshelf."

"I finished my homework in study hall today."

"Any upcoming exams you'd maybe want to study for? Quizzes, perhaps?"

"I guess I could work on my French paper."

"That's a very good idea," Miss Ingram affirmed. "The dictionary is only meant to be a last resort for those students who run out of assignments to work on." I rolled my eyes as she rambled on. "However, Brynn did mention earlier that she was struggling with her French assignment. It's been so long since I've taken French myself, I'm afraid I couldn't be of much assistance..."

My jaw clenched, annoyed that I had to engage once again. "I already know someone who can help me, Miss Ingram."

"I don't mind," the girl butt back in.

I cracked a wry smile, not even bothering to glance the girl's direction. "It's pointless. We're in the same grade."

"You have Madame Etienne?"

"No—" My brow rose as I scribbled in the margin again. "Madame Etienne teaches advanced French."

"I know, I'm in her class."

My hand froze, and I finally turned my head, mending my eyebrows. "Good for you."

"Well, isn't that lucky?" Miss Ingram said. "You can take the remaining twenty minutes to quietly work on the assignment together."

"Actually," I drew in a deep breath, "I was planning to double-check my math homework."

"I'm also in advanced math," the girl spoke again.

"So, why don't you put two and two together and leave me alone?"

The expression she'd worn on her face yesterday when I'd bumped into her in the hallway settled on her features now. The sort of look that instantly made me feel like a wild animal, causing a fit inside of my cage. And, her, the innocent visitor on the other side of the glass.

I hated the way she looked at me. As if I shouldn't be pissed off. As if my response hadn't been warranted. But she didn't know me at all. She fluttered those long eyelashes and took her seat. She didn't dare speak to me again. But that odd feeling remained like an itch I couldn't quite scratch. I adamantly watched the clock until, finally, the last bell rang. I waited for Miss Ingram to sign off on my detention slip, laser-focused on her penmanship as the beginning of another downpour started up outside.

I threw on my hood before walking out into the hall. Making a left and leaving behind the ruckus my peers caused in the background. Realizing, suddenly, that the pretending hadn't really stopped. It'd just taken a different course. Now, I had to pretend like everything still felt normal. Like that summer hadn't happened. Like Ethan still existed.

It wasn't your fault.

Of course, it'd been my fault. Everything had always been my fault. I'd been born with the defect. Not him. He'd been the perfect one... the perfect friend... the perfect student... the perfect son. And the best brother I could have ever asked for.

I'm still here.

"Not true," I muttered, pushing through the double doors, an exit that led me outside on the far side of the school building. I fumbled with my umbrella before taking the narrow ramp down onto the sodden grass, caring less about the drenched state of my leather boots and more about distracting myself away from my thoughts.

My mind had become my worst enemy since he'd died. Always shuffling through the details of that night. Wondering what would have happened had I made different choices. Torturing myself day and night with re-enactments of the choices I had made.

I hated it.

Jean hated it more.

He could always tell when I'd go away. That's what he called it. He didn't like it when I got lost in my own head. Jean had been convinced that everything had happened as it should have. He'd have dreams about me, he'd said. Even before it happened. I remember when he first described those dreams to me. I'd been scared to hear what he'd thought of me—to find out my brother had been right all along—but it'd been the complete opposite. Jean showed me the real me. The me that he'd dreamt. Afterward, I could never go back to her again.

But those memories tried to pull me in every time, and that's why he hated them. He knew what it would mean if I ever let myself go away for good. I didn't want to do that. Not yet. Not without him by my side. I didn't want to hurt him. I could never hurt Jean. Not like I'd hurt Ethan.

My shoes tapped against the concrete I'd finally reached, the sidewalk marking the path that led me off campus. I distanced myself from the honking vehicles that waited in the roundabout in front of the school. The parking lot on the other end was packed as parents arrived for the PTA meeting. A year ago, my mom would have been amongst the flock of women who were frequent attendees, debating on frivolous social events and coordinating committee gatherings. Ironic how priorities had shifted. Even more ironic how entire lives had instantly changed.

I allowed the rain to create somewhat of a calming effect around me as I worked hard to micromanage my thoughts. I'd made it to the other side of the street, choosing to forego the quicker route in hopes to avoid being kidnapped by Allan again. But this way would be longer, and it annoyed me that I'd even been forced into this predicament. I would have called Jean if I'd had a phone. Part of me had hoped he'd be there waiting just outside the school. Showed no regard for Principal Singh's threats and made-up rules. But I knew my luck had run out a long time ago. Things like that just didn't happen to me, and I'd grown to accept that small fact of life.

"Hey!"

My heart pounded as it had this morning, though I quickly recognized the voice hadn't belonged to Allan this time. Still, I stood frozen stiff on the sidewalk.

"Do you need a ride home?"

Her.

The girl from detention stared at me from the inside of a black SUV, her body slightly raised from her seat with one hand curled over the edge of the window. I shifted my jaw in swift contemplation before a lightning strike followed by a loud crack of thunder quickly made up my mind for me. I dodged across the street and slid my small form onto the seat, folding my umbrella closed before shutting the door.

The warm interior of her vehicle enveloped me, and I released a silent breath of relief, grateful to be out of the impending storm. I knew I should have thanked her, but naturally, I placed my attention on her driver first.

"I live at the end of Heath," I informed him. "The huge apartment building on the corner. You can't miss it."

He acknowledged me with a nod, and only then did I fully relax in the seat, inevitably feasting my eyes on the girl next to me. "I thought I told you to leave me alone."

I watched the slight jump of her neck as she swallowed, the act bringing a tiny smirk to my face. Those piercing eyes wandered down to the small hands that rested in her lap. "I just saw you walking and figured I'd offer you a ride."

"So, you're stalking me now?"

"Of course not," she quickly denied, meeting my gaze again, seemingly terrified at the mere thought alone. "I just wanted to help."

I looked away, biting my inner lip as I placed my elbow on the armrest. I couldn't help but question her intentions as we both sat in silence, my focus mostly on the dreary scene outside.

"Do you always walk home from school?" Suddenly, her voice trickled itself back in, lassoing me out of my thoughts.

"Never," I simply answered. Then I faced her, noting the look on her face that spelled sout her peaked interest. "It's only temporary."

"For how long?"

"A week."

She nodded as if she understood. "I won't mind."

"Excuse me?" I cocked a brow in disbelief.

"It's going to be raining all week."

"So?"

"So, I wouldn't mind giving you a ride to and from school for the rest of the week. I mean, it might be out of the way, but that doesn't matter to me."

I felt my eyes narrow. "Why would you want to do that?" I couldn't seem to wrap my head around her offer. "You don't even know me."

"You're Brynn. You're a junior who takes French like me. And you think I'm a freak." She smiled and shrugged a little after the last part. "I know some things about you."

Warmth settled across my cheeks to the tip of my ears, recalling my rude remark in the hallway yesterday. "I'm—I didn't mean—"

"Forget it." Her hand metaphorically swatted the memory away as if it hadn't happened. "I expected my first day to be rough."

I folded my arms across my stomach and stared forward. "Clearly. How did you end up in detention anyway?"

"I accidentally threw my breakfast at the lunch lady," she replied.

My laugh escaped me before I could stop it as I glanced her way. "Miss Lewis?"

"It was a huge misunderstanding." She shook her head. "But Principal Singh gave me a day in detention for it."

"The perks of being a new student. That would have easily been a solid week for anyone else."

"What about you?" Her question caught me off guard, and I stiffened a bit. "How did you get detention on the first day?"

"Just a misunderstanding, too," I said and quickly looked away again, hoping she'd be satisfied with my answer and wouldn't press it any further.

She seemed to get the drift as I noticed her shift to a more comfortable position in her seat, though her attention had left me. "Is this the complex?"

I took in our surroundings, reminded of the reason why I'd gotten into her car in the first place. My head nodded in reply before I blurted out a yes. Her driver pulled up right onto the blacktop of the Tudor-styled residence while I reached for my umbrella on the floor.

"How's seven-thirty?" I heard her ask me just as I'd placed my hand on the door handle.

I glanced over my shoulder, noting the faint gleam in her hopeful eyes. "What's your name?"

"Elonie."

I fashioned somewhat of a smile onto my face. "I'll see you tomorrow, Elonie."

13

"Are we friends?"

I stared back at my reflection in the slightly fogged mirror. Stretching the corners of my mouth. "Are we friends now?" I spread my lips, revealing my teeth, attempting to push my dripping wet coils behind my ear. "Can we be friends now?"

No, that didn't sound right.

I lowered my eyes to my hairbrush resting on the edge of the pale pink sink—the retro decor still a major eyesore for me—and grabbed it. I drug the bristles through my scalp in order to tame my curly mane. A giant grin replacing the mild version from before.

"Maybe we can be friends now?"

I cleared my throat.

"I want to be friends," I said, immediately cringing at the way my voice sounded. Annoyed, I threw the brush into the sink and flicked off the light switch on my way out of the bathroom. The floorboards of the bedroom were cold underneath my bare feet as I approached the small wooden desk directly across from my bed. The pad of my fingers tapped against my lips as I stared out of the large window, watching the rain pouring down like the inside of a car wash. I saw her walking alongside the street again. I had almost let her be. Let her continue on with her life. A life without me in it. But curiosity wouldn't let me.

Curiosity wanted to know why she'd been walking in the rain to begin with. Curiosity wanted to walk in the rain with her.

"You should want to be my friend," I whispered, sinking into the chair, my damp head rested on my palm. "Shouldn't you?"

Maybe we hadn't talked much during those car rides. Maybe she hadn't opened up in the way I'd expected her to. But couldn't she tell how close we were going to be? My eyes narrowed, remembering the way she'd gotten out of the car for the last time. It'd been slightly different than how she'd gotten out that first day. She still wore that awkward smile that didn't quite fit her sober features, but she didn't say she'd see me tomorrow. The week had ended, and she'd no longer needed my assistance. I knew that…but I couldn't accept it. And neither did she, I could tell.

I pushed up from the chair and walked over to the brown shopping bags on the nook bench. All last week, I'd observed each outfit she'd worn. Noticing how she differed from the other girls at school. Her clothes were surprisingly ordinary. They didn't scream for attention, nor did they flaunt her family's wealth. She didn't want to be seen. She wanted to hide and did so very well behind that huge jacket of hers.

I stared down at the one I'd bought over the weekend. I hadn't even worn it in the store. I'd just paid for it and left. Now, I dragged my fingers across the leather sleeves where I'd set it out. Imagining showing up to school with it on. What would she think? Would she call it desperate? I frowned a little. Maybe I wouldn't…not yet.

I pulled on fishnet tights, then black socks, and finally, the skirt. The brown midi I'd found among the racks of a thrift store the weekend before I'd moved here. One of my favorites now.

"Will you reconsider the dinner?" Presley asked, seated next to me—in her spot.

He'd returned from the city last weekend, though he'd spent a large majority of it working in his office, only coming out to distribute checks to the house staff. His workaholic tendencies didn't affect me anymore. I'd accepted that he used his job as a coping mechanism to deal with mom's death. He had his ways, and I had mine.

"I can't meet her." I tugged the sleeves of my sweater over my hands. "It wouldn't be fair."

"Your mother is not here, Elonie."

I closed my eyes, a wave of nausea passing through me. "Please don't say things like that."

"For goodness—" His ringtone cut him off, and he deeply sighed, taking the phone call instead.

I waited for him to hang up, watching the dense woods and wondering what exactly he'd do if I just unbuckled my seat belt, pulled the door handle, and rolled right out onto the gravel. We weren't moving at that fast of a pace. Would my body just tumble and bounce until it reached the grass, or would I meet my fate underneath the rear wheels of this SUV? How would they scrape the skin I'd lose off the road? Would Presley actually cry at my funeral? Would I even have a funeral?

"That was her." He distracted himself with the flap of his navy blue tie so that he didn't have to look at me. "She extends a hello to you."

"Does she live there now?" I stared at the side of his face, watching his jaw flex after I'd asked the question. "Is that why you moved us out here? So that she could..."

"No," he began, smoothing his hand down the length of the material now, "I sold the property like I said I would. It didn't feel right to—" He finally looked at me, eyes unblinking at first, as if he'd seen a ghost on my face. "But we did purchase a hi-rise in the city, a couple blocks down from the firm."

My neck tightened as I tried to nod. "So, what are you hiding all the way up there?"

"Elonie," He shifted towards me, "understand that I never intended for this to happen." I'd never seen him look so sincere. "This couldn't have come at a worse time, I know, but I can't ask her to abort it—and she doesn't want to either."

I seemed to blink in slow motion as I turned my head and noticed we'd entered the roundabout in front of my school building. The only sense of security I felt I had right now.

"I guess that's game over," I replied, a broken laugh trickling out as tears pricked the corner of my eyes. He didn't appreciate the witty remark in the least and adjusted himself back into his usual stern posture.

"Don't use this as leverage to misbehave," he said as I slid out of the vehicle before our identical pair of eyes met again. "Remember everything you've accomplished, Elonie. Don't mess this up."

The knob in my throat had only hardened as I entered the building, the echo of his parting words teasing its way underneath my skin, touching every sensitive nerve in my body. I yearned to cut it out. But I could barely focus in the midst of the cluttered bodies I passed by. I needed to get away from the chatter… a place where I could be alone. The senior bathroom from that first day came to mind, but my feet were just as confused as my brain felt. Pausing every few seconds to let someone pass. Halting abruptly when another zipped by, cutting right across my path, suddenly making me too dizzy to continue.

I drew in a deep breath and inched closer to the wall, gripping myself in a soothing embrace. Maybe this direction would lead me there. I told myself to believe this as I kept walking, tuning out the voices around me until they all sounded muffled. Like I'd suddenly gone underwater, and all I could hear were the ragged sounds of my own breathing.

"Excuse you—"

I rushed past the commenter as she came out of the bathroom and threw myself into the closest stall, releasing my stomach into the toilet without hesitation. Tears poured out right along with it.

A baby!

I exhaled and rested back on my hind legs, staring at the wall, then shutting my eyes to reality for one small second.

Screw you, Presley.

Screw you and your baby!

Knocking erupted on the other side of the door, causing me to flinch out of my short-lived serenity.

"Elonie?" The voice belonged to Danielle. "Are you okay in there?"

Heat flooded my face. "I'm f-fine."

"Are you sick?"

"Just—an allergic reaction." I quickly flushed the toilet and rose to my feet, opening the unlocked door. "Sorry, I just need to rinse my mouth out."

"Here," Danielle reached into her large canvas bag and pulled out a travel-sized version of mouthwash. "I use it after I drink coffee. You can keep it. I have an extra."

I accepted the small bottle. "Thanks."

"I've never seen an allergic reaction like that before," she continued on, as I ventured over to the sink to freshen up. "Usually, students just get hives or their throats swell up."

I busied myself with rinsing my mouth so that I didn't have to talk much, though I nodded as I swished the liquid around before finally spitting into the sink.

"Anyway, I assume you won't want to eat breakfast then," Danielle said as she walked over to the paper towel dispenser and cut off a piece for me. "But you can still come sit with us, can't you?"

"Sure," I agreed. Anything to shift the attention away from the make-believe allergy. "I'll join you."

I wiped my face and tossed the paper towel away, turning around only to find she held out another small bottle for me. "Our favorite."

I sprayed the perfume on my neck and handed it back to her. "Thanks, Danielle."

"Good as new," she complimented with a bright smile.

I followed her out of the bathroom and back into the hallway, surprised that time hadn't stood still for the rest of the school as well. No, once again, they appeared disinterested, walking the hallways without a clue as to what had just occurred only moments ago. But not everyone appeared so oblivious to me and it quickly became apparent that someone had been watching as I walked out of that bathroom.

Those eyes were like magnets as they pulled my attention in. Stopping me dead in my tracks, which I only noticed shortly after had been a huge mistake as this allowed him the chance to head straight for me.

74

Move, you idiot.

But I couldn't. My ankles were frozen. My legs felt as though they'd been liquified. My body stood completely paralyzed. But a quake awakened inside of my chest. The sick sensation from earlier returning two fold. And, suddenly, no other person existed except for this boy. This boy who looked as though he were about to kill me with his bare hands.

The pathetic squeal that fell out of me sent a surge of heat across my face again, but that embarrassment didn't compare to what I felt as he grabbed my jaw and forced my head back, exposing my ear to his lips. I stared into a void of pitch black and bursts of color. Unable to utter a word through my sewn lips. The warmth of his breath sunk into every crevice of my body and I felt every muscle involuntarily relax.

"Stay *away* from her," he growled at me.

My eyes leaked out tears as I fiercely nodded to something I couldn't quite comprehend. But it didn't matter. He'd only wanted my understanding. My chest finally fell once he released me, and I stumbled backwards into arms that only made me flinch away. Sound rushed back to my eardrums, and my hands clasped my head in excruciating pain. My eyes still tightly shut. I heard everything. But I didn't want to. I wanted to turn it off.

"Oh, man," someone said, "that's embarrassing."

"Look, right there…on the floor."

I would've given anything to turn it all off again.

14

Something had happened.

I could feel it as I paced the wet pavement. Holding my lit cigarette discreetly at my side. The other hand clutching onto my cell phone for dear life. It hadn't buzzed yet. That's how I knew that something had gone wrong. Jean would've been back by now. He'd promised he'd come back. And he'd never lie to me. Something had happened to him because of me. Because I'd screwed up.

I sucked in a drag, forcing myself to calm down, though it barely helped this time. I glanced up from my phone, watching the front doors open, only to be let down again when I noticed it hadn't been him coming down those brick steps.

"Calm down, calm down." I rested back against the bed of his truck, inhaling from the stick again, though my hand trembled now.

My phone's vibration alerted me, and I quickly dropped to a crouch, putting out the cigarette. Then I opened up the text message and read what I'd already known. I couldn't have raced towards the steps any faster than I had, bursting into the building and jetting down the hallway towards the main office. I fought to catch my breath before entering, only to be greeted head-on by a set of glares—identical in color and intensity.

But I returned their glare with an even uglier expression. "Don't say a word to me."

"As if anything we'd say could make you take accountability for your actions for once," Danielle retorted with a venomous bite.

But she knew her words didn't leave so much as a scratch on me anymore. I glanced past her frowning face and noticed the girl sitting in one of the office chairs. Her arms crossed over her in a hunch, but her eyes expressed concern as she returned my stare. I started towards her, but the body that suddenly blocked my path caused me to stumble, my arms now in the grasp of Allan's firm hands. "Listen to me, Brynn—"

I shook my head, pulling away from him, feeling weighed down by his closeness. "No—"

"You need to stop this," he hissed at me. "You've got to stop doing this!"

"Let go of me!"

"Excuse me," Miss Jenkins, who sat at the front desk, cut in. "Keep your voices down, please."

"Allan," Danielle came up to her brother's side, placing her hand on his forearm, "the bell is about to ring. You're going to be late for homeroom."

I pulled back hard, and he released me, though I could feel his eyes still burning into my back as I walked over to Elonie, who still sat frozen, fixated on the three of us now. I placed myself in the seat next to her.

"Elonie," Danielle spoke up, easily gripping the girl's undivided attention. "This is Brynn Walsh. She's acquaintances with that wild animal who attacked you this morning. I wouldn't trust a single word she says."

"You're one to talk," I scoffed bitterly.

"Sorry, I was speaking to my friend. Not you."

"Your little warning is pointless. We've already met."

Danielle appeared taken aback. "How is that even possible? You were absent last week."

"I had in-school suspension." I then looked at Allan, "Surprised your twin didn't mention it seeing as you both love to relish in my suffering."

My comment stabbed Allan, and he wore his anger plain on his face. "How dare you even say that?"

"Speaking of wild animals, did you tell her how you shoved me into your car against my will?"

"This is not the same—"

"Miss Davis," Principal Singh's authoritative tone shattered the walls of our conversation, bringing everyone's attention back to the current situation at hand. "It's your turn now."

I looked over at Elonie, the girl having appeared daunted and confused by the debacle between me and the Turner siblings, but now I could feel the nerves oozing from her as she stood up from her seat. Those nerves blended with mine as I acknowledged the missed opportunity. I had no idea what had happened or what she would tell Principal Singh. I just knew I'd kill myself if Jean got expelled.

Speaking of him, I pushed up from my seat and watched as he walked past Elonie, their eyes briefly meeting before the girl disappeared into the depths of Principal Singh's office.

"Those of you who are not in need of a late slip must head to their home room class," Singh iterated, specifically eyeing me and Allan. "If either one of you is still in this office by the time the bell rings you will be assigned a detention. Do I make myself clear?"

A frown weighed down my lips, but I nodded, and once she'd gotten both of our compliance, she closed the door to her office. Only then did I rush towards Jean and throw my arms around him, kissing him as if he'd returned from the dead.

"Excuse me," Miss Jenkins spoke up again, and I quickly pulled away from him, suddenly remembering where we were. "You need to go to class."

I glanced back up at Jean. "Will you tell me what happened?"

"Everything's fine." He molded his hands on my face, giving me a smile before throwing his arm around my neck. "I'll catch up to you."

We faced Allan, who stood with the door wide open already, and Danielle, who stood close by, hands tucked in her camel-toned lapel coat as she flippantly rolled her eyes.

"I still can't believe how low you stooped, Brynn. It's truly pathetic," she said. "Not to mention so disrespectful to Ethan."

Don't.

I swallowed the burn in my throat and continued walking forth, ignoring eye contact with her as we passed.

"I'll walk you to your class," Allan offered once we'd stepped into the hallway, though it'd slipped off his tongue, sounding more like a demand.

I shot him daggers. "I'll walk myself."

"Why don't you just leave her alone? She's got two functioning legs," Jean spoke up in my defense.

"Is that why you forced her to walk to school in the pouring rain?" Allan shot back.

"I wanted to walk," I argued, panic settling in.

Jean chuckled. "Is that what she told you?"

"She didn't have to tell me anything. I know you did." Allan dropped his glare to me. "And you let him."

I looked up at Jean. "I can't listen to this anymore."

"Just don't forget who started it," he replied to me.

His words unnerved me, forcing the conversation from this morning to resurface, remembering how his bass had filled the interior of the truck. Spitting fire across the seat at me. Sinking me further with his words until I'd been reduced to a ball of blubbering apologies. He'd ignored me with the radio until I'd stopped crying, then allowed me to apologize again while he'd kept an eye out for her car. I'd watched Elonie walk up those steps and enter into the school building. Him following not too far behind her. He'd only wanted to talk—to feel her out. That's what he'd said before leaving me... promising he'd come back.

"Interesting girl," Jean said to Allan, and I noticed an unusual smile growing on his face. "Terrible spy."

My eyebrows joined. "Spy?"

"I watched her go into the bathroom, and the other one followed right behind her," Jean informed me. "Wonder what all she learned from your little car trips to school."

"Nothing." I shook my head, still visibly shaken from what he'd said. "I told you we barely talked."

"You still trusted her."

The bell rang right then, but the sound barely phased me as I thought about that day she'd offered me a ride. I had trusted her. And I'd kept trusting her each day she arrived to pick me up and then take me back home again. Not knowing that she couldn't be trusted. Slowly, the sincerity of it all withered away and in its place, a low boil began, a boil that I knew would sooner overflow.

15

I had been given my first role to play. I don't know why I'd expected it to come easily. Nothing ever did come without a few scratches and bruises. I'd learned that lesson last year in my old school. A completely different cast with a similar enough setting. And the plot had surprisingly remained the same. I knew this role like the back of my hand. No matter how confused I still felt. No matter how shaken up he'd made me. I still would play this part to the best of my ability.

Principal Singh knew this role, too.

She'd most likely been the one forcing someone else to play it at some point in her teenage years. So, I'd have to play it right...convince her of everything I'd say.

She stared at me now from behind her desk. Fingers clasped. Fingernails a deep red that matched the shade on her unsmiling lips. The stern look made me question what exactly had he told her.

"You're in my office again, Miss Davis." Her chin turned upward as she raised a natural brow. "Care to tell me why?"

I relaxed my face, stalling by taking a deep, necessary breath. "Things just got blown way out of proportion this morning."

"By whom?" she asked.

"Our peers," I replied.

Now, she took that deep breath and leaned towards me. "Explain what exactly happened this morning, Elonie. Please don't leave anything out, and please don't take too much time doing so. I want the truth."

The truth. The events of the truth still played on a loop inside of my mind. The breaking news of the sibling I had on the way. The upchuck in the senior bathroom. The unexpected confrontation by him—the wild animal, as Danielle had put it. I couldn't tell Principal Singh any of these events.

So, I curated a truth of my own.

"The truth is he scared me," I began, staring directly at her. "Not maliciously. I was more startled than scared, actually. He sort of came out of nowhere."

She nodded. "Go on."

"I was on my way to the bathroom before it happened—"

"Miss Turner says you'd just left the bathroom."

"Yes," I corrected myself, and added, "I was heading back to the bathroom because it'd come on strong, and I've been...sort of... dealing with an infection."

"An infection?"

"Yes. A urinary tract infection."

"And you hadn't felt the need to use the bathroom while you were in there."

"I didn't have the urge then." I glanced at her clock then back to her. "But when he—bumped into me—it just happened."

"He bumped into you."

"Yes."

"And that startled you?"

I nodded. "Yes."

"Mr. Cohen didn't say anything at all to you?"

I cleared my throat, shaking my head. "I'm not sure if he did or not. I was too embarrassed to really pay attention to anything after that."

"I understand." Though the expression on Singh's face didn't quite confirm that she did. "You were then escorted to Nurse Miller by Danielle. The same person who, afterward, brought you here to my office and proceeded to tell her own version of what happened...a story identical to the stories of your peers who were also standing by watching it happen."

"Like I said," I repeated matter-of-factly, "everyone blew it out of proportion."

"So you have said."

My heart drummed as my eyes followed her posture, watching her rise from her seat and step around her desk. Finally, she rested back against the edge and brought her hands together at her front.

"My students are like bright bulbs, Elonie." The stern gaze had returned, but her stance exerted more power now that she stood in front of me. "Jean Cohen takes great pleasure in dimming that brightness until nothing but a dull glow is left..." She brought a single finger to her chin as her brows knit. "But you strike me as someone who has the potential to shine brighter than all the other bulbs at this school."

My lips parted, transfixed on her face. "I do?"

"Although your record illustrates quite the opposite, I'm not particularly fond of holding my newer student's past mistakes against them. I believe in affording everyone a fresh start when they enroll at this school." She gently pushed off the desk and slid her hands into her pantsuit. "And your father made it very clear that my academy was essentially your last resort."

I stiffened at her words, lowering my eyes to the floor. "I didn't know that."

"So, now you understand how important it is that you try your best to excel here. Which means..." She made her way around her desk and took her seat again. "This is the last time I want to see you in my office. Am I making myself perfectly clear?"

"Yes," I nodded, "I understand."

"Good. Obtain a late slip at the front desk and then head to class."

I did as she'd said. Waiting as the secretary at the front desk filled out my slip and then stepped out into the empty hallway with Danielle at my side again.

"What did Principal Singh say?" I could tell she'd been patiently waiting to question me when we finally exited the office. "Tell me she's going to suspend Jean for what he did to you."

I didn't want to talk about what we'd discussed in her office, but I knew Danielle expected to be told everything. And rightfully so. She had been the one who'd saved me from further embarrassment in that hallway, quickly transporting me to Nurse Miller's office where I'd been able to discard my soiled underclothes, freshen up, and then slip into one of the unused pairs she kept handy for menstruation mishaps. I'd been lucky I'd been standing when it'd happened; otherwise, my new skirt would have been ruined, too.

I basically owed Danielle the truth, slightly irritated that I'd been put in this predicament again. "I didn't tell her what happened," I said to her, avoiding looking her way as I spoke. "I was embarrassed."

"Are you serious?" Danielle sounded completely dumbfounded as she forced me to halt with her hand on my shoulder. "You have to go back and tell her the truth, Elonie."

I folded my arms across myself, tucking my chin. "I can't do it, Danielle."

"Why not?" Her cadence rose a bit, causing my eyes to snap back up to her face, noticing how wide her gaze had become. "Jean Cohen isn't a person who should be allowed to just get off scot-free."

"I know, he just—he really scared me, and who knows what else he might do if I actually get him suspended." I pleaded for understanding through my eyes. "Just let this go, Danielle. Do it for me."

She exhaled, and it brought forth a small chuckle, one of her charming smiles inching onto her face again. "Elonie, haven't I done so much for you already?"

My ears perked, watching as she stepped forward until she stood close enough that I could smell the sweet scent of cherry on her full lips. She tilted her head a little as she placed her hand back on my shoulder.

"There are only two sides in this school," she said, speaking very direct so that I consumed every word. "It would be such a shame if you chose poorly."

I still felt the weight of her hand on my shoulder once we'd gone our separate ways. I'd been curious to know what she'd meant, but my mind couldn't handle much more tinkering after the morning I'd had. I just wanted to sit down at my desk and peer out of the window, imagining things that I knew would never come true. But it brought me solace, and I needed that now more than ever.

I arrived at the front door of my French class, able to hear the voice of one student reciting from the textbook. I entered as quietly as I could once he'd finished. Closing the door as I tried my best to tune out the whispers that echoed behind my back.

"Mademoiselle Davis," Madame Etienne greeted me at the door, accepting my slip as I handed it to her. "Take your seat, s'il vous plaît."

I nodded. "Merci beaucoup."

"Excellent reading, Monsieur Deloach." She sauntered back towards the front of the class again, picking up a sheet of paper from her podium. "Now, I will assign partners for the in-class assignment."

I sat down beside the window and started digging for my supplies, listening out for my name, though I continued to ignore the other sounds around me. I knew what they were all saying. But I'd asked for it. The spotlight. The attention I always seemed to seek. I just hadn't expected it to come in this way. I should have been mortified to show my face again after the incident, but I'd chosen to come to class. Deep down, I wanted that attention. In any way, shape, or form… I still craved it.

"—Mademoiselle Davis paired with Monsieur Cohen."

The textbook I'd just pulled out of my knapsack wiggled in my grip before falling to the floor, breaking the otherwise hushed silence of the room as the simple mention of the name snatched the wind out of me.

"Excusez-moi?" Madame Etienne voiced.

"Pouvez-vous le répéter s'il vous plaît?" I nearly begged, though my tone felt strangled from my drying throat.

"I said you will be paired with Monsieur Cohen," she repeated as requested, then guided my attention towards my partner with her hand.

We stared at each other. Him holding my gaze for longer than I would have liked. But I couldn't look away from the boy sitting in the far back of the classroom. Cut right out of my view when I'd walked in. I wouldn't have noticed him even if I had been paying attention.

His height nearly engulfed the small desk he'd been subjected to, along with the rest of us. His limbs hung out from his body like a spider's ligaments would, though more meat sat on his bones than that of an insect. Not as fit as Liam, but not yet malnourished either. I hadn't truly looked at him until now. But, suddenly aware that I had overused that invitation, I looked away again. Staring down at the book that still lay flat on the floor.

"You may begin your assignment," Madame Etienne concluded. "Remember to turn in your papers à la fin du cours."

A barrel of water wouldn't have been able to soothe my parched throat, but I reached down into my bag for the flask anyway. Hoping it would at least buy me time before he'd make his way over to my desk and I'd be forced to engage with him again. This time with more opportunity to slip up and say the wrong thing. I took a long swig and waited. Then another. By the third swig, I wondered if he had gotten up and left the classroom just to avoid working on this assignment with me. I dared to glance over and see, only to find that my theory had been wrong. He still sat there. Staring at me from his seat.

My neck prickled with heat, and I reached back, rubbing my skin in an attempt to lessen the ache. Little things about the encounter flirted their way into my head, and I fought hard to keep them out. I didn't want to keep reliving the warmth of his breath on my ear. The way he'd gripped my jaw and held my head in place. Thinking about it only sent me back into the hallway with him. Stuck there with no way out.

I turned my head away and stared out of the window. Willing tears not to slip down my cheeks, squeezing my eyes until I'd successfully gotten rid of the painful sensation.

Then I got up from my seat, gathered my materials, and headed towards the other side of the room. I took a seat at the empty desk behind him, not waiting until he turned around to begin flipping to the page of our assignment, but when he did I slid my book back to make room for his. Though, I refrained from talking just yet and focused on writing my name on my paper instead. He seemed interested in taking that route, too—at first.

"Parlez-vous français?" he asked me, breaking the silent treatment as I read through the directions.

"Oui," I replied without looking up.

"Well?"

I nodded.

"Tu t'appelles comment?"

"Elonie."

His hand slid down the page of my book, and a set of five long fingers extended, successfully blocking my view of the assignment. My reading paused. But I didn't look up at him.

"I feel like I know you, Elonie." He softly drummed his fingers against the book. I noticed a few nicks on his knuckles and white crescents on his fingernails. I embraced these minute details. "I basically watched you all week."

My eyes fluttered as my breath escaped me. "What?"

"I watched you."

"Why?" I whispered.

He began making small circles with his fingertips, slowly sending me into a faint trance. "Because I wanted to know you," he answered. "What you looked like…where you live…basiques…"

"You f-followed—"

"Not at first, but you kept doing it." His fingers moved faster. "You kept being there. Picking her up. Dropping her off." Suddenly, he stopped. "I mean, who do you think you are, Elonie?"

Without much thought, I looked up at him. There we were. Back in the hallway. His face right in mine. His voice crawling inside of me again. And I sat frozen. Staring into the darkest waters I'd ever seen.

"I helped her."

He didn't even blink once as he showed no sign that he'd heard me.

"I only helped her," I continued. "She just wanted to avoid Allan. She didn't tell me why, but she just wanted to avoid him. So, I helped her do it."

"I know what I saw earlier, and I saw you go into the bathroom with a Turner."

I struggled to form my words. "She followed me in—"

"She must have followed you out, too."

"I-I was sick. She—"

"You're full of it."

"I lied to Danielle and Principal Singh about everything that happened in the hallway. They don't know anything. I won't speak to Brynn ever again—" I dropped my eyes and took a deep breath. "I just wanted to help her. That's all I was trying to do."

"That's all you were trying to do?"

"I promise."

He gently chortled. "So you're not friends with the twins?"

My heart skipped, thinking about what Danielle had said to me before she'd walked away. But, for the first time, I didn't want to know what she'd meant. I didn't need an explanation. I knew what my choice would be ever since that first visit to the nurse. Tears in my eyes as I begged Danielle to keep my secrets, not knowing it'd be in exchange for my loyalty to her group. Her side of the school. But I didn't want to be a part of her side. I couldn't be that girl again.

"We're not friends," I calmly insisted as I met the awaiting gaze that appeared almost enticed to know my answer.

He propped his arms on top of our books and leaned in closer. "Pourquoi?"

I blinked, taken aback by the question. "What do you mean—"

"Why are you pretending to be, then?" His cheek rested on his fist. "What's she got on you?"

I glanced past him. Observing our classmates seated in their pairs. Some talked in English. Others held conversations in French as per the instructions for the assignment. Madame Etienne sat behind her desk, undoubtedly still checking over the essays we'd turned in last week. A small wrinkle formed between her eyebrows in concentration.

No one acknowledged me or him as we sat a little too intimately for two strangers who'd just met. No one seemed to care that I'd been partnered with the same boy who'd ambushed me in the hallway. They'd done their whispering and forgotten about it. It amazed me just how fast they'd moved on to the next topic, the word 'spring fling' slipping out more times than I could count as I finished eavesdropping.

I figured it didn't matter if I showed him the reason why I'd had to pretend.

My fingers curled over the edge of my sleeve and slid it up, giving him a small peek at those secrets. His eyes seemed to absorb the marks. I watched his jaw constrict, the slight twist of his ruddy lips, his gaze more concentrated than Madame Etienne had looked. I let him touch my skin. His fingers gliding over the few cuts I'd exposed. He had no idea how hard my heart beat in my chest. Only I could hear it bursting my eardrums. Threatening to come through my throat. No one had ever touched them like he did now.

"Ils sont mignonne," he said.

My brows furrowed, and I gently pulled my wrist out of his hand. "Mignonne?"

"Yea."

"Comment?"

"They're small." He pressed his index finger to his smiling lips. "Mignonne…cute…"

"There are more." I crossed my arms. "A lot bigger."

"Don't be ashamed." He studied me again, hand wrapped over his fist underneath his chin. "You just needed to feel something."

"No."

"Non?"

I shook my head, uttering out, "I feel too much."

"Too much?"

"It's what's wrong with me."

"Says who?"

"Everyone," I tried catching my breath, but the words were toppling out. "Presley, Dr. Portis—"

His arms dropped as he scooted even closer to me, and my heart nearly stopped. "You're sensitive, aren't you?"

"I—"

"In the hallway."

"What?"

"You were overwhelmed."

His words froze me.

"Isn't that what you told Singh? I overwhelmed you."

My throat closed up again.

"Do I?" he asked, his voice lowering to an unfathomably quiet tone. "Am I right now?"

He'd brought me underwater again. Everything sounded muffled. In my peripheral, the foggy image of our peers slowly began to dissipate. Madame Etienne at her desk moved further and further away.

Only Jean remained.

The warmth of his hand, once having gripped my jaw with bitter contempt, now cupped underneath my knee. I questioned when he'd slipped it there. Had it been while he'd still been talking? How had I not noticed his arm reaching down, hidden by the desk we both shared, skillfully shifting upward the long hem of my skirt?

He'd reeled me in with his questioning. Or maybe I'd been distracted by those eyes that seemed to bind my soul. He knew what they were capable of, and he'd used them to his advantage. Keeping me enamored…engrossed…desperately curious. So curious that I hadn't even realized I'd learned absolutely nothing about him.

Except the features of his hands. The cuts I still wondered about that graced his knuckles. The same knuckles he pressed into my skin.

90

Gliding his fist up my inner thigh. Searching. I watched his face, but he seemed more interested in watching mine. That same curiosity in his own eyes. I knew the look all too well. He only saw me as a freak who'd put on a good show. He only wanted to be entertained again.

"There they are," he said, running his finger along another set of fresh cuts. Those I'd forgotten about.

"Monsieur Cohen?" Madame Etienne's voice suddenly swam to the surface followed by the remaining sounds in the classroom.

My eyes darted to the sudden movement of his body. "Mon crayon," Jean answered back, staring up at me from where he pretended to grab an imaginary pencil from the floor. "Je suis desolé, Madame."

My chest heaved as I straightened my posture, noticing her warn us with a disapproving stare. "Pardon, Madame."

Jean returned to his seat, angled sideways, legs stretched across the aisle. "Elonie—"

"Yes?" I asked right away, still mentally recovering from what had just happened, though unable to meet his gaze again as I hyper-focused on my textbook.

I felt him lean forward and caught a glance of his hands, still feeling the heat they'd left behind. "No more pretending."

16

I laid on the cot in the nurse's office, eyes closed to the fluorescent lights above, counting down the seconds it would take Nurse Miller to return. I felt the most relaxed I'd been all morning, despite the growing migraine that sparked last class and dragged me to the nurse's office. But at least I didn't have to sit and stare at the teacher, meanwhile painfully aware of my peers' whispering voices behind me.

Did they really think I had no idea how much things had changed? How much that I'd changed? I didn't need another reminder. I'd had enough of those last term. So much so that I'd isolated myself from everyone just to block out all of the extra noise.

I still fought to block out that noise.

"Up, up." Nurse Miller said as she entered her office. I rose to sit, and she held out my pills. "Here, you take these and come back if you have pain or feel sick."

I chased the medication with the cup of water she'd also handed me. I'd been put on a higher dosage after the migraines had sent me to the hospital last term, and Nurse Miller had been monitoring me ever since. I chucked the paper cup into the trash and grabbed my bag from the cot. I walked out of her office, the heavy door echoing in the quiet front lobby, soon the thud of my combat boots joining that stark silence. I'd made it halfway down the hallway before another set of shoes tapped against the wood panels. I don't know why I'd glanced over my shoulder. Probably the constant discomfort that weighed over me these days. Always feeling as if the grim reaper had finally come to collect me. It only made sense that it had all just been a huge mistake. Ethan shouldn't have been the one to die. Of course, it should have been me instead.

"Brynn?" The man whose shoes had been the culprit spoke my name, grabbing my attention before I could look away again.

I could've kicked myself for being so careless. "Mr. Scavelli…"

"I'm surprised I'm running into you like this." He then glanced down at the folder in his hand and, essentially, shrugged at it. "Do you mind popping into my office for a little chat?"

I started to shake my head. "Mr. Scavelli—"

"Just for a moment, Brynn. I'd really like to check on you and see how you've been doing."

My teeth snagged my lower lip, contemplating my options.

"It doesn't have to take long," he added. "And if it does, I'd be more than happy to write you a slip."

Mr. Scavelli opened his arms wide as if to embrace me from afar, his short height still reminding me of a cartoon character. It'd been my first impression when I'd first met him. I hadn't wanted to come to his office that day, but I'd been forced to by Singh. All thanks to Danielle Turner. That girl had the power to convince me to do anything back then—as if I'd been the only one with a problem.

I felt the muscles in my face soften as Mr. Scavelli gave me a smile and beckoned me over with his arm. I calmly acceded. Following him back to his office. My body warmed like an oven as I stood next to the leather armchair, remembering how I'd come here during lunch, yearning to talk to someone who cared more about me and less about my brother. Not that Mr. Scavelli had ever viewed it that way. He'd told me counselors were automatically obligated to prioritize their client's feelings above all others. I'd respected him for keeping that vow to me.

"That chair still doesn't bite."

I recognized the joke right away, a smile inching onto my lips as I sunk down into it, pressing up against its back. He still grinned as he took his usual position behind his desk and relaxed into the swivel chair.

"So, talk to me, Brynn," he began, short arms inviting me in before dropping over his rounded belly. "How was your winter break?"

My hand slid into the large pocket of my black trench coat, fiddling around with the lighter hidden inside. "I went to Paris to get away from here."

He whistled. "You kids and your vacations. I bet that cost a pretty penny."

"We used to spend our summer holiday there all the time." I scraped the pad of my fingers against the spark wheel. "He stopped going when he joined the varsity team, though. His coach always made him attend the summer camp trainings—"

"You're talking about Ethan," Mr. Scavelli noted.

My eyes floated towards the blinds covering the single window in his office. "Yes, Ethan."

"Do you think maybe you went to Paris because you miss him?" Scavelli questioned me. "I'm sure being there probably brought back a lot of good memories for you."

"No, it didn't. I kept busy." My eyes flickered back to him. "I made sure I wouldn't think about him while I was there."

He nodded, resting a few fingers underneath his chin. "Sounds like you had a good time with your aunt, then?"

"She was busy as well. She teaches English lit at the university."

"During Christmas break?"

Crap.

He always caught me.

I slid my tongue over my front teeth. "Advanced preparation for the next term. We barely saw each other this time."

"Alone in Paris…" He shrugged his brawny shoulders. "Still not too bad, I guess."

"I wasn't alone." I took my hand out of my pocket and rested my cheek on my fist, eyes fogged with memories. "I was with Jean."

He'd refused to stay behind after I'd told him about my father's plans to send me away while he took care of my mom, and I probably wouldn't have boarded that plane without him. I still didn't know what he'd told his parents. He'd told me not to worry about it, the fact that they'd believed him only mattered. I still remembered the look he wore on his face before he'd turned it towards the window. Watching the frothy white clouds disappear behind us as if he'd gone into a trance. And I'd rested my head on his shoulder, holding his hand, unaware that days later, the truth would pour out of him like water from a faucet. Leaving me soaked and heavy and aching for him to experience whatever love I still had left to give him. In whatever way that looked like—I'd give it to him.

"Brynn," Mr. Scavelli's voice startled me, and I shivered, fluttering my eyes back to his face. "Did you mean to say that?"

My eyebrows hitched. "Say what?"

"That you were with Jean."

"Yes. I went with him."

"Jean Cohen?"

I nodded.

Mr. Scavelli's expression took on another form now. The corners of his thin lips turned down. His thick, black eyebrows sewn together. Those dark brown eyes fixed on me in my chair. "Brynn, when did you begin associating with Jean Cohen?"

I felt his urgency exude from him, and involuntarily, I shifted to the edge of the seat. "The beginning of last term."

"Around the time you stopped coming to see me."

I could sense him connecting the dots in his mind.

"Did Jean tell you to—"

I suddenly rose up from the chair. "I'm sorry, Mr. Scavelli, I really have to get to class."

"Now, wait a minute," he attempted to placate me, but my nerves had already been triggered as I headed for the door. "At least let me write you a slip, Brynn."

My hand paused just before the handle. "Mr. Leech, calculus, room 305."

17

The rain had finally stopped, though it still felt below thirty degrees outside. Regardless, I'd made the short trip over to the field where Liam practiced his soccer kicks, two lunch containers in the crook of my arm. He noticed me as soon as I walked through the fence, giving the ball one last kick into the goal before breaking out into a sprint towards me. I slowed in my gait and watched him as he neared closer. His body seemed to glide effortlessly through the cold air. A pair of toned arms shifting back and forth to give him momentum. They were my second favorite part of his body.

I'd known athletes like Liam. I'd watched them over and over in my vast collection of movies. I'd even been lucky enough to date one last year before I'd ruined everything. But I'd never come across one like Liam. He didn't fit the usual mold, and that's what enthralled me. Everything about his appearance screamed cliché, yet he'd proven to be quite the opposite in personality.

We sat down on the wet bleachers—as we'd done for a week straight now—and ate our lunches together. I could already tell today would be different, though I tried to prolong the impending conversation for as long as I could. Focusing on anything but those endless brown orbs.

The rustle of leaves trapped below the bleachers we sat on. The smoky grey-blue of the afternoon sky. The discarded pickles he'd taken off of his sub. I took in everything but those eyes. But my efforts were wasted because, like a magnet to a field, he drew me in. Not by his gaze but his gentle touch on my hand. Stopping me from retrieving my own sandwich and shifting my focus directly to him.

"What happened this morning?" he asked me.

Neither of us was concerned any longer about our lunch. I know I had no interest in eating now as everything from this morning began rushing in like a tsunami. The lie trailed out before I could stop it.

"Jean bumped into me by accident, and I just..." My appetite had most definitely disappeared, and nausea quickly took its place. I fought to swallow it down. "Please don't make me say it."

He quickly grabbed the containers and placed them up a step, scooting closer to me. "I won't make you do anything, Elonie." His arm went around both my shoulders and I naturally nestled into his warmth. "I wouldn't have even believed it was true if you hadn't just told me."

I pinned my eyes to my lap. "You believe me?"

"I think the first half is crap." He exhaled, and his breath came out like smoke. "But I'm not going to press it. You're already fragile enough as it is."

I expressed my thanks by resting my head on his chest, suddenly aware of how perfectly I fit inside of his embrace, the earthy aroma of his natural musk clinging to my nose. It started a small fire in my belly that slipped down my core and made me feel like goo.

"But listen," Liam spoke softly, and I felt his eyes glance down at me without having to look up. "You have to stay away from Jean Cohen."

I kept quiet.

"He's worse than them."

"Worse than Danielle?" I mumbled, finally lifting my head from his chest and pulling away a bit to meet his eyes. "This morning, she told me I had to pick a side."

He winced. "She told you that?"

"She said there's two sides in this school and that I should choose wisely."

Liam shook his head, looking away with a roll of his eyes. "She's such a coward."

"You really think she had something to do with Ethan's death, don't you?"

"All I know is that she can't be trusted." He looked back at me as if remembering where the conversation had started. "None of them can, Elonie…now you've seen it for yourself."

I blinked in confusion.

"You gave Brynn Walsh a ride all last week, and the first thing Jean does when he comes back is target you." His expression implored me to connect the dots. "She used you and then threw you under the bus."

I pursed my lips, hiding my face as I looked down, not wanting to give myself away. Liam didn't strike me as someone who spooked easily, but he'd surely be shocked if he knew the even scarier truth. Thankfully, the sudden vibration of my cell phone rattling against the metal seat grasped both of our attention. I reached for the object and realized it'd been a text message from the very person we were talking about:

Parking lot

My heart started an erratic thump as I stood up from my seat. "It's Allan. He's saying I left my math book in the desk cubby."

"I'll come with you," he offered, "I already got in some extra practice earlier today."

"This is where you were during study hall?"

Liam chuckled. "My dad wrote me a slip just for today. I need all the free time I can get to prepare for the game Thursday."

"Unbelievable," I teased, as I'd grown used to doing with him, internally still amazed at how easy it felt hanging out with Liam after only a week of knowing him. "But I can handle it alone. I have to stop by Madame Etienne's class anyway."

"Are you sure?" He looked up at me, and I noticed the slight concern in his eyes, making him appear rather boyish and vulnerable as I peered down at him.

I nodded my assurance, tugging my sleeves over my hands so that they didn't reach for his face without permission. He simply nodded back. And I left him, waving one last time before going back through the gate.

The chilled breeze slipped underneath my skirt and painted my legs with goosebumps as I trekked back across the street, arms crossed over my body, curls gently blowing back in that breeze. Though the breeze only took half the blame for the shiver racking my bones.

I hadn't expected Brynn to ever speak to me again. She hadn't even looked at me when she'd walked into our math class just minutes after the bell had rang. I hadn't thought it possible for an already quiet classroom to suddenly become pin drop silent. I could tell she hated the attention, but her annoyance had quickly been replaced by something else. A look I couldn't quite understand until Allan stepped into the fish eye lens, I'd kept on her. He'd taken her late slip and walked it over to Mr. Leech. Meanwhile, Brynn took a seat at the empty desk nearest to the door. Never looking over her shoulder even once for the remainder of class.

Now, I chewed my lip raw, predicting what she'd say when I got to the parking lot. Did she plan to confront me for keeping my relationship with the Turners a secret? That entire week, she'd kept quiet about anything too personal. But she'd allowed me to know how she felt about them. It'd been the end of the week. The first time, there hadn't been a morning shower. I'd picked her up from the same spot I usually dropped her off. Same chunky boots on her feet. A different shade of blue jeans. That leather jacket. We sat, still slightly groggy, in silence. But I could feel her battling something inside. Finally, she'd made a comment about the weather, insisting she could've walked this morning. It'd been random…strange. But just as soon as she'd said it, she'd retracted the statement and mentioned he'd still probably be lurking the streets, waiting to pick her up. She'd been talking about Allan. She'd told me about what had happened that second day of school. How he'd forced her into his car. I'd expressed my support right away. She'd appreciated that. But now I couldn't help but feel like a hypocrite, knowing I'd willingly walked the hallways with them all day while she unknowingly sat in suspension.

I could also easily add this morning's events to the list of things weighing on my conscience. I didn't have to know the plain details of Jean and Brynn's relationship to know they were more than just friends. And I wondered if Jean had told her. But worse, if he hadn't, then I would eventually have to. Of course, I would have to. I couldn't go down this road again, knowing exactly how it would end. And I'd promised myself this time, things would be different. I couldn't mess up my fresh start, as Principal Singh had put it.

A blaring honk split my eardrum, causing me to halt in my fast-paced steps, eyes searching the sea of shiny cars until a pair of blinking headlights flashed amongst the flock. I stared at the slate gray truck while my brogues stepped off the curb of the sidewalk, seemingly gravitating towards it. I could only faintly make out the two of them. Brynn sat in the passenger side. Jean, at the wheel. Both watching me as I cut between two cars to reach theirs. He rolled down his window just as I'd reached his side, and a wave of smoke kissed my face.

"Want to hang out?" Jean asked.

I glanced past him and noticed Brynn rest her head on her hand, taking a drag from her cigarette, seemingly apathetic to my existence. I figured it would be hard to look at someone who'd betrayed her trust like I had. I'm not sure why I still climbed in that hazy back seat. My hands balled into fists in the center of my lap. Attention fixed on Jean's eyes that reached back through the rear view mirror.

"Do you smoke?"

The question seemed like an obvious one, but I struggled to produce my voice.

"Do you want a cigarette?"

"No," I blurted, instantly regretting it and racing to perform damage control. "I mean, I don't smoke."

"That's alright. I don't smoke much either."

I looked over, prepared to simply get all of my words out now that I'd found the nerve. "Brynn, I'm sorry I didn't tell you about Danielle. I just want you to know that we aren't—"

"Jean already explained everything," she spoke languidly, then looked over at him as if he'd been speaking to her instead of me. "I don't feel like talking about this right now."

I watched him reach out and gently massage the back of her neck. "Relax, Brynn."

I leaned forward—desperate. "But are you mad at me?"

"Relax," Jean repeated, glancing over his shoulder at me now. "Alright?"

I nodded, resting back again. "Alright."

"We just don't know you yet," he continued, slipping his cigarette between his lips and pulling a drag from it. "That's why I wanted you here."

"You wanted me here?"

"To get to know you a little."

I turned my head away from the smoke that drifted to the back. "What do you want to know?"

"Where's that accent from?" He looked at me through the rear view mirror again.

I shook my head. "I was born in the city. I just don't sound like it because I watched too many movies growing up."

He smirked a little. "Only child?"

"Yes," I answered, though painfully reminded of how that would no longer be the case. "Are you?"

He gave a chin nod. "It's why I can always spot another."

I smiled at that, then my eyes shifted to Brynn, whose fingers were too busy tugging at her roots. The joke didn't seem so funny anymore as I suddenly remembered her predicament.

I blinked, reaching for the door handle. "I'm sorry, I should go."

Jean suddenly shifted around. "Why should you?"

My breath hitched as I froze. His arm protruding through the crack between the door and car. My eyes flickered down to the fingers that had wrapped around my wrist—those same fingers. My chest began to heave at the still fresh memory. But he'd already pulled his hand away, using it to lodge his cigarette back between parted lips. I slowly slid back down onto the seat, watching the back of Brynn's head turn as she looked over at Jean. But his eyes were still on me, pinning me, convincing me to stay put.

"Were you homeschooled?" he asked, both long arms draped over the shoulders of his seat.

"Yes," I replied.

"How long?"

"All my life except…" I curled my fingers into my palms. "Last year was my first time attending an actual school."

"Private school, huh?"

I nodded. "I didn't like it."

"Not as fun." He took a quick drag and exhaled before leaning forward. "But then again, I've never been to one in the city."

"Why did you move here?" Brynn asked, catching me off guard but grabbing my attention completely. "Nobody ever moves here."

I swallowed tightly as her doe eyes devoured me. Somewhere off in the distance, the school bell rang, but that sound proved to be no competition for the loud pounding of my heart.

"I—I—"

"Shhhh," Jean gently shook his head, seemingly put off by the tears already rimming my eyes. "You don't have to tell us right now."

"I'm going to class," Brynn said, a repetitive beep sounding off as she got out.

Jean shifted his body back around. "I'll walk you."

My limbs seemed to activate once they began exiting the truck, imitating their behavior, though I still sniffled back more of my tears. Hating more than ever before that I'd ended up crying in front of him again. Still, Jean had reacted differently this time. Nothing like this morning in the hallway when his eyes had lingered on me with a sort of blank look…almost detached. Much different than the wildly focused stare he'd observed me with in French class. This look could only be described in one way: concern. He'd looked concerned for me. Like the sight of my tears hurt him somehow. I'd caught him glance at me again as I walked alongside him up those steps…and one last time before we crossed the threshold.

I'd been too busy wondering what he'd been thinking about that I hadn't even realized the obvious offense I'd committed until much too late. The unmistakable rasp of Danielle's voice embodied me. Reeling me back out of the trance I'd been put in. I swiftly turned on my heel and nearly crumbled under the sharp glare she gave me.

"What do you think you're doing?"

She stood there with Sophie at one side Taylor on the other, those girls also looking beyond surprised by my choice company. My lips parted, but only a fickle sound came out, adding to my humiliation.

"Elonie," Jean towered me, his voice intimately low, as if we were the only two people in the lobby, "n'oublie pas ce que je vous ai dit."

My eyes fluttered, and I faintly nodded. "D'accord."

"Run along, Cohen," Danielle cut in, already taking steps towards me. "I'm sure you can't afford to be late, given your abysmal attendance record."

Jean didn't bother replying to Danielle as he sought out Brynn's side again, both their hands interlocking before they walked away from me. Leaving me stranded on this island alone. But the words Jean had just spoken reiterated in my mind. *Remember what I told you.* I nodded reassuringly to myself, finally meeting my challenger head-on. "Danielle, please understand that I never meant to disrespect the kindness you've shown me since I arrived here, but I won't be choosing a side."

"Is this a joke?" Sophie voiced with an airy laugh. "You've been gallivanting around with us all week."

"Sophie," Danielle shook her head, "is it really that difficult to see that it isn't really her fault?"

"Danielle's right," Taylor seconded in her pip squeak of a voice.

My brows furrowed. "What do you mean?"

"I mean that it's so obvious you're falling for Cohen's trap," Danielle continued, 'tsking' her tongue at me. "The very same mistake Brynn made last term."

"Jean's been—"

"He's been what?" Her sudden laugh brought chills down my spine. "The guy made you pee your pants in front of the entire school. I wouldn't say he's been anything but the absolute worst, wouldn't you?"

My cheeks ignited with a warmth hotter than when it'd actually happened as my eyes shifted around us, spotting those that had actually stopped to listen to our altercation. I closed my eyes briefly, only to gather back my courage. But Danielle's presence proved stronger as she positioned herself right in my face.

"Choose a side," her tone melted my skin like hot lava, both eyes digging into mine, successfully putting me back into my place, "or I'll choose one for you."

18

My mom had never been much of a television watcher before Ethan died. It seemed almost foreign to see her stare at the plasma screen now. The remote control comfortably nested in her lap. It amazed me that this same woman had once been so involved in our lives. She'd been the one who'd attended the spelling bee competitions and parent-teacher conferences. She'd been the one who'd donated our outgrown things to the charity drive each year and baked brownies for our scout's meetings. She'd been the one who'd checked our homework and made sure our family looked presentable in front of the congregation. She'd always been at the center of our family, allowing my father to wear the pants and call the shots while running things from the inside. I couldn't understand how this woman, still clad in silk pajamas underneath her duvet, watching her fifth soap opera of the afternoon, could be that same person. But I guess I didn't understand it because deep down I knew that person had disappeared a long time ago. She'd disappeared right along with her son. This shell of a body was the only thing she'd left behind.

She'd had an anxiety attack the morning my father took her to see our family therapist. I'd heard her sobbing from their bedroom, and I could do nothing but sit in my shower and attempt to tune her out. My father had told me she hadn't recognized herself. She'd been embarrassed at the weight she'd lost and the state of her hair. He'd described her reaction as someone who'd seen a ghost. I thought it'd been the perfect description of what my mother had become in the past several months.

A ghost.

Almost as if she'd never even been among the living. Almost as if she'd been waiting for it to just happen. Had she wanted to die? Maybe Jean had sensed it. Maybe he'd known that's what she'd wanted.

How dare you? How dare you defend his actions!

I felt my hands shake and quickly looked away from her, lowering my eyes to the wood tray I held in my grip. "Here you go, mom."

"Just set it down right there, honey." Her voice sounded smaller today as she didn't bother to even look over at the meal, keeping a steady gaze on the actors engaged in a dramatic quarrel. I did as told, though I lingered for a few moments to see if she'd acknowledge the food.

"Dr. Patel says you should at least try to finish three small meals a day."

"I will, honey, sit," She invited me into her bubble, gently patting the blanket beside her. "I've missed you."

My eyes fluttered, misunderstanding the words that had come out of her mouth. It'd been like hearing a foreign language. She glanced at me with her big eyes—insistently. "Okay," I replied, resting my bottom on the edge of the bed, careful of the tray in front of me.

"The brunette is named Julia," my mom spoke, using an acrylic nail to point at the screen. My father had taken her to her favorite spot in the city as a treat after an emotionally overwhelming session she'd had with Dr. Patel. "She's having an affair with her gym instructor. Her husband just found out."

I stared at the two characters and screwed my eyebrows together as the shouting increased, watching the man take hold of his wife's arms and profusely shake her. Moments later, the woman landed a slap to his face and fled to the sound of a dramatic percussion tune.

"That's just horrible," my mom commented, looking to me for confirmation. "Isn't that just terrible?"

"It's pretty bad mom." I stood up from the bed and simultaneously, my denims vibrated with my ringtone. "I'm going to go eat lunch with my friend now."

My mom's lips turned down. "Do you have to?"

I squeezed my phone in my hand, observing my mom's pathetic state. It truly tugged at my heart to see her completely without purpose anymore. Did she honestly want to sit here and watch trash all day? Had I really taken everything from her? I didn't need an answer to my question. I knew I had. She would never be the same, and I hated myself for turning her into this person. My throat throbbed with pain as I looked down at my phone and quickly answered it. Jean's voice relaxed my tense muscles, and I only focused on his words as I stood next to her bed.

"I'm coming out now," I said to him, trying my hardest to hide the tremble threatening my tone.

"Is it him on the phone?" my mom asked. "Is it the boy who helped me?"

My guilt returned full swing, and I shook my head, turning my back to her, though what Jean had just told me didn't help the situation. "It's not a good idea…"

"Tell him to come inside, Brynn. I want to thank him."

"Jean, please don't—" I peeled the phone from my ear and noticed the call had ended.

"Is he going to come inside?"

I closed my eyes briefly before facing her again. A deep frown weighed down my face. "I didn't want him to come in. Why did you say that?"

Don't get mad at her.

"Why couldn't you just stay out of it?"

She's not the one you're mad at! Don't yell at her!

Our house seemed to shake as the doorbell rang throughout it. My gaze looked away from the deer-in-headlights expression on my mom's face, already drifting down the hallway as I raced to answer the front door for Jean. I pictured him standing outside…felt his arms embrace me…all before I'd even opened the door. But when I did, he rushed in, slamming it shut behind him.

My breath caught as he yanked me towards his chest and held me there. "What's this look you're giving me now?"

My eyes had to have glazed over because he'd instantly turned into a water painting. Dark olive skin blended with cedar brown locks, his facial features unrecognizable in the flood. He pressed his forehead to mine and exhaled.

"It really hurts when you do stuff like that." He began a gentle massage on my shoulders. "Why do you want to hide me from your family?"

My voice cracked as it left me. "Last time—"

"So now you think I'm dangerous."

"Please, Jean, that's not what I'm trying to say."

"Then what are you trying to say, Brynn?" His words cut even though he hadn't raised his voice at me. "Wasn't it what you wanted?"

No!

"I-I-"

"You remember what you said before we left France? You wanted them both dead, right?"

I nodded, closing my eyes as tears streamed down my face. "I'm sorry I couldn't do it."

"Say it. Say it was your idea."

"It was my idea."

"You made me do that, and now you're blaming me." He tilted his head. "Now you're mad at me."

"No—" I shook my head, doing my best to convince him. "I'm not mad at you."

"I don't think I believe you," he muttered, slipping those hands down my arms and pulling me against him. "You're just lying to me now."

"I would never lie to you, Jean."

"Honey?" I heard my mom call to me from down the hall. "Is your friend here?"

108

Jean pointed with his chin. "Prove it. Let me see her."

Don't you dare let him near her again!

I nodded, pressing my cheek to his chest. "Jean, promise you won't hurt her."

He slid his arm around my waist and took my face in his palm, trailing the pad of his thumb across my bottom lip. "I'm just going to give her a little kiss," he whispered to me. "That's alright, isn't it?"

"Yes," I pressed my lips together and tasted leftover salt on them, "that's okay."

"My sweet girl." His lips neared mine, and my eyes narrowed. "Take me to your mom."

I released a shallow breath. Closing my eyes when he took me by the hand below. I stood at his side as we walked down the hallway to her. But I stayed behind him once we stood in the room, though he'd quickly released me, leaving me at the doorway. I grasped the nape of my neck as I watched him hug my mother. My nails further deepened when his lips brushed her cheek, placing a soft kiss there, earning a startled smile from her. I couldn't hear a word they said. My ears blocked out all of it. Nothing but white noise filled my ears. But I could feel the blood underneath my fingertips. It'd been the only thing that had brought me back to the surface.

I locked myself in the bathroom of my bedroom. Running cold water and fiercely scrubbing at my nails, watching the bits of red fall into the sink. I barely felt the stinging of my neck as air seeped into the shallow cut. Anger had almost completely overwhelmed me. It'd been so long since I'd drawn blood.

The doorknob jiggled, followed by a hard knock.

I shut off the water and released the tie from my hair, spreading my dense curls out across my shoulders. "I'm just freshening up." I rolled my eyes at how stupid the excuse had sounded and turned away from my reflection in the mirror.

Jean sat on the edge of my bed, only rising when I finally walked out. "What happened to you?"

"Nothing—"

"Nothing?" He reached for my elbow as if it'd break, a stark difference from when he'd grabbed me at the door and visibly looked me over. "You let your hair down."

I eyed him closely. "Is that okay?"

He smiled. "Ask me that again."

I rested my head on his chest as he pulled me closer. Again, different than how he'd held me before. Both arms circled around my shoulders, firm as if I'd sink into the floor if he dared let go.

"Is it okay if I wear my hair like this?" I asked.

He rested his nose in my curls. "Your brother's probably turning in his grave right now." He then loosened his grip and pulled back from me. "Hearing you talk like that in his parent's house."

"Why didn't he like you?"

"I never cared about being liked," he said, backing away from me, a hand disappearing inside of his jacket pocket. "That's why."

"It's still strange," I still mused over it. "Ethan was even cordial with freshmen nerds in the chess club."

"Let's get out of here." I watched him pull out his pack of cigarettes. "I need a smoke."

We drove the slick road to the French café we frequented not far from the apartment building. Sitting at our usual outdoor table and ordering coffees with espresso shots and pastries that we only picked at, as the cigarettes had completely depleted our appetite.

I sat with my chin propped, picking the chocolate chips out of my muffin, thoughts rewinding back to the comment he'd made about Ethan, still in a perpetual loop of confusion. But it'd been nothing new. I had been left with this feeling countless times before. Each time after, Jean would mention Ethan. And he did so often. As if Ethan were somehow always on his mind, too. Almost as much as he'd been on mine since his death. But Jean never revealed much, and I'd learned not to push him. Still, it bothered me not knowing what their relationship had been like. Had I paid more attention, I would have noticed it back then. I would have easily gotten the information I'd needed out of Ethan. We used to tell each other everything.

I frowned.

No, not everything.

"Brynn," the echo of Jean's voice returned, and my eyes snapped up. "Are you listening?"

"I'm sorry." I crossed my arms on the table and leaned in. "What did you say?"

He leaned in as well. "What's on your mind now?"

"Paris," I fibbed, and then, in my best accent, I added, "l'hôtel romantique."

"You're getting good at that."

"Thanks to you."

He retrieved his small mug like the long claw in a toy machine. "You're getting that A this term. Make your dad think twice about grounding you again."

"Doesn't matter," I mumbled, slipping my finger in my mouth and sucking the chocolate from it. "None of it matters to me anymore. I just can't wait to leave this place."

A silent moment passed between us as he sipped from his coffee, deep eyes fixed on me. Instantly, making me question if I'd said the wrong thing. He set the empty cup down on its saucer, cleaning his top lip with one smooth swipe of his palm before leaning forward on his arms again. So close I could see the freckle of raindrops scattered across the defined cut of his cheekbones.

"Not having fun with me anymore?" he questioned me in that tone that made my stomach slightly twist with fond memories.

"I am," I insisted with a gentle nod. "I just can't take being here anymore…" I dropped my eyes into my own mug. "No matter how hard I try, I can't get rid of that night."

"It's because you haven't accepted it yet," he explained to me. "You keep trying to change what brought you here to me."

He'd told me this before and I know he hated when he'd have to remind me. "I just wish I could stop thinking about it. I still hear his voice—"

Jean pushed back from the table. "I'm bored of this already."

I looked up at him, the gray sky looming in the background. "Let's go to your place."

"No," He shoved his fists in his pocket, "call her up."

"Who?"

"Our new girl."

I'd caught on right away, though the mention of her quickly soured my mood. "The dance is tonight."

He shrugged. "So what?"

"Danielle is going to make her go, and she's not going to turn her down because she has no spine."

"So, we'll bail her out. Win-win."

More like a win-lose. "Jean, she's not—"

"Just call her."

19

Why had I agreed to this?

I'd asked myself this question as I'd stood underneath the hot shower, rinsing away the lethargy that had settled over my limbs, forcing me to stay inside all day.

I'd asked it again as I stood at the end of my driveway—adorned in a peasant smock I'd kept of hers—watching the sleek silver vehicle pull up to me. The make and model being identical to the one I'd torched last year.

Why?

Why had I agreed to this dance?

Why couldn't I ever stand up for myself?

Danielle had put me in the back seat with Taylor. Sophie rode shotgun. All three looked elegant. I'd gotten the chance to really admire their outfits once we'd arrived at the school. Taylor wore a blush pink tulle dress with a sweetheart neckline (slightly ill-fitting due to her lack of breast). Sophie settled on a deep ruby crushed velvet dress, a hurricane of more freckles dusted across her exposed shoulders.

And, Danielle…

I stared at her now. She'd left us at the punch table while she went to tend to yet another task, the successful flow of the dance being her first priority, after all. Jade green had been her choice. The color doing wonders at making her eyes pop. The dress looked specialty made with a long-sleeved lace top and a satin a-line skirt. She looked like the daughter of an evil queen from one of those princess movies. She looked to die. Normally, I would have played that part. The 'fawning over the popular girl' role. I'd been so good at that before. But I didn't want to be that person. I didn't want to go through it all over again. But she'd made it clear that this would be my role.

I looked back down. Peering into my plastic cup of red liquid. I thought about what would happen if I splashed the juice all over the white cotton of my dress? What would they do? Would the music come to an abrupt halt? Would they all stop and stare at me with wild horror in their eyes? Would Danielle finally label me the freak that I am and refuse that anyone associate with me any longer? Would I be free? Free to choose again.

My mouth twisted, imagining the scene I'd make, knowing I could never muster up the courage to do it. Not with everything that happened the last time I lost control. But, still, I wondered...

"Don't worry," Sophie suddenly spoke to me, coming up alongside where I stood at the far end of the snack table. "It's not spiked. Danielle made sure we had dispensers specifically for that reason."

I glanced up at her. "I thought that only happened in movies."

She chuckled, shaking her auburn curls. "Are homeschoolers always this naive?"

I didn't attempt to answer the rhetorical question. I had gotten used to Sophie's blunt speech over the past few weeks. It didn't surprise me anymore. I knew she didn't like me. I confused her. But, even more so, my hold on Danielle's interest confused her. I guess that part I agreed on.

I didn't understand Danielle's fixation. She liked to pick me apart. And I always humored her with my lies. Every day since the day she'd forced me to make a decision. I'd sat in the cafeteria booth and lied to her face about everything. My background, my family, my interests, and hobbies. The only thing that had been true French. She loved that I spoke the language fluently. She'd chosen Spanish instead but had shared that she wished her parents would have taught her the most romantic of all the romance languages. I'd been made to perform in front of her and her friends, speaking words here and there, amusing her with my talent and skill—but all the while insulting them all in secret.

I resented them.

But most of all, her.

I didn't want to be her circus clown. I wanted real friends. I wanted something new, something different. She wouldn't let me, though. She stayed lurking the hallways that belonged to her. Entering into bathrooms, exiting classrooms, meeting up, always there…always watching me as if at any moment I'd make another wrong move.

"Do you girls like how it all turned out?" Danielle's presence crept up behind me and I turned to face her, Taylor quickly joining all of us now.

The dance's theme had been an enchanted forest. We'd entered through a tall hedge maze made of authentic leaves and vines, leading out towards the center of the gym where an intimate botanical setting had been created, complete with a variety of different colored flowers, a makeshift water fountain, and bright fairy lights that hung from the ceiling. It looked magical. Exactly as she'd described it for weeks on end.

"It's beautiful," I complimented her, and sure enough, those pearly teeth of hers gleamed.

"It's perfect." Sophie beamed at her. "I doubt anyone has come close to doing spring fling this good."

"They haven't," Danielle replied in a matter-of-fact way. "I checked every yearbook available in the library just to be sure."

Taylor giggled. "You truly outdid yourself, Danielle."

"Thanks, girls." Danielle pressed a dark green manicured hand to her chest. "Your praises really mean everything."

The hand that didn't hold my cup of punch in a vice grip buzzed, and my attention left her syrupy nude smile abruptly, thankful for the sudden intrusion.

Come outside

I read the text message from Brynn, confused at the demand but quickly realizing it couldn't have come from her.

Brynn hadn't spoken to me in weeks. I'd sat in the back of our math class, day after day, glancing over at her every so often—especially when she'd be called on to answer a question. But we never talked. She'd always rush out of the classroom to avoid speaking with Allan and, I assumed, me. On the rare days, we'd have a partnered assignment, I often fantasized about her walking past the desk she'd assigned herself to on that first day—the one nearest to the door—and joining me in the back of the room. She'd sit down next to me and scoot our desks close together. We'd talk in hushed tones as we'd breeze through each stats equation. Gossiping and laughing as if we'd always been the best of friends. She'd share the reason why she quickly looked away every time Allan managed to catch her eye from across the classroom. She'd explain why our classmates stared at her like they would a foreign exchange student every time she rushed in by the skin of her teeth. She'd tell me all of her secrets. Why she never talked in class? Why she sat so stiffly in her seat? Why she always inched that hand up her neck to scratch that same spot beneath her poof of curls?

I'd thought nothing of it when I'd noticed her do it the first time sitting in that truck, but I immediately connected the dots when I'd seen it happen a second time…then a third…and a fourth…

Danielle had been talking about her.

Brynn had been the friend. The girl who scratched. Almost like a nervous tick. I could tell she hated being in that room with us. Allan and I. We made her nervous—well, him more than me. But still, I felt sorry for her. I didn't mean to make her uncomfortable. I didn't mean to trigger her itch.

Allan, on the other hand, seemed to care less. I watched him attempt to talk to her countless times before she finally began packing her things away early, seated on the edge of her chair, watching the clock, and waiting for the bell to ring so she could make a mad dash out of there. I didn't understand why it annoyed me that he continued to bother her. I'd known people like Allan and Danielle Turner. They were the kind of people who tended to get things their way. No, they expected to get things their way. Their kind always got what they wanted by any means necessary.

"Come on," Sophie's mellow pitch gained my attention. "They're about to announce king and queen. Danielle wants us to move closer to the stage for when her name is called."

Of course, her name would be called. "I…" My eyes dropped to the text message, then fluttered up back to Sophie's already judging irises.

"Whatever it is, it can wait," she concluded before walking off towards the stage herself.

I stayed put. Not by sheer defiance but because I honestly had no idea what I would do. My dilemma consisted of ignoring *his* text (because I knew instantly it'd been Jean who'd sent the demand) and heading towards the stage with the other girls. I'd stand next to them with a fake grin glued to my face as Miss Ingram announced her name over the microphone. We'd throw our arms around her after she'd successfully been crowned and completed her dreadful speech. She'd, once again, be so grateful for our praises.

Or…

I could burst right out of this school building to freedom.

I watched the other girls from my contemplating stance at the punch table. Several other students surrounded them, though most of the attendees lingered in the black shadows of the corners or lined up against the wall. Their faces were less than thrilled, which only told me that spring fling dances were just another thing to add to the list of unamusing events that happened at this school. Number one being the arrival of any new student.

"Well, the time has arrived to crown this year's spring fling king and queen," Miss Ingram announced, draped in a black sparkly garment on stage. "Everyone gather around."

My palms grew sweaty as I stepped forward in the pair of strapless heels I'd found at the back of my closet. But then, just as suddenly, I paused again. My phone had buzzed a second time and I glanced down at the new text.

I have a surprise for you.

My neck prickled with heat underneath the waterfall of my styled curls. At this point, unable to fight that unsteady sensation that made my head light and my stomach twist.

Jean Cohen had entered my dreams every night since our first meeting. Dreams that I couldn't quite understand, but I wanted to. I looked forward to seeing him every night. Staring at me with those river-blue eyes. Always from afar. Just as he did in French class. Not all the time, but I felt them when his attention found me from across the room. Dark and pulling—until I'd look and it'd end. The moment never lasted long. The dreams never lasted long, either. I'd woken up in a sweat the first time, racing over to the nook and bathing in the cool night air that drifted in from the window. My fingers had grazed my warm skin in the same way he had weeks ago. Touching the scabs of the old cuts. Remembering the way he'd assumed my need to feel, then proceeded to describe me as if he already knew me inside and out.

Did he overwhelm me?

The question he'd asked that day had become more and more obvious as those weeks passed and the dreams persisted. I found myself losing focus in class, thinking about what he thought about me now. I'd failed to stand up to a Turner. I'd failed to do what he'd said. I knew he saw me as weak. No longer worthy of being on his side. We hadn't been partnered together again, so my curiosity to know had only spiraled out of control. I'd often catch glances at him as he'd crouch in his usual fashion, conversing in French with the luckier candidate, though every chosen classmate never appeared particularly overjoyed with the experience. Another tidbit I'd learned: no one in our class liked him.

But he never seemed even the least bit phased by it. He spoke the language better than everyone, including me. The words slipped off his tongue fluidly—almost as if he were a native—and Madam Etienne never failed to bask him with her praises. But there were the days when he'd come in and slouch. Speaking the language so terribly…in a way that could only be described as forced. He'd do it on purpose, and even Madam knew. The solemn expressions she'd give him made it clear that his behavior had been a known routine. Her tolerance of him still continued to amaze me. But I sat at my little desk, wondering why he did it.

Why had he broken his own rule? What made him need to pretend?

My curiosity had done it again. My need to know consumed me and caused me to head toward those vine-covered gym doors. Stealing one last glance over my shoulder, looking towards the stage, watching as that evil green gaze devoured me once more.

The dark sky looked down on me in judgment as I stood pressed against the double doors. The hard metal freezing cold against my arms. My heart palpitated at a bizarre pace that only made the dry heave worse. I could scream at myself for how afraid I felt. But instead, I ran. I ran across the grass to the sidewalk, halting only when I saw the headlights of a familiar truck suddenly turn on.

I pulled my jacket sleeve up to my shoulder as I shifted closer to the edge of the pavement, watching the truck creep to a stop in front of me. The window slipped down, and Jean leaned on the door.

"Let's hang out," he uttered.

The three words were only three words. Simple. But, oddly, they meant so much after being silently shunned for so long. I crossed my arms and glanced past him. Brynn sat staring at me with a new intensity in her eyes. I'd never seen a more Turner-like expression on her face. Again, I felt fear.

"I just wanted to—to say—" My chest started its heaving again. "I'm sorry for—for not standing up to her. I should've—should've—"

Jean dropped his arm down, a hand pressed against the truck. "Will you just get in, girl?"

I gave a broken nod before pulling open the door and climbing into the back seat. The same smoky scent greeted me, along with that black leather feel sticking to the backs of my thighs.

"You just walked out on a Turner-led affair." Jean looked back at me through the rear view mirror, a sly smirk on his face. "I'd say all is forgiven."

I blinked, surprised at how quickly I'd forgotten what I'd just done. I knew there would be consequences. Danielle's daggered glare said just as much. But there would be no going back now. I had chosen my side. I had finally chosen freedom.

"You mentioned a surprise," I reminded him, albeit softly.

"We're heading there now." Jean glanced over at Brynn. "It's our secret spot."

I rested back and began working on calming my nerves. Something that I had never been too good at. But I didn't want to be the freak in the back seat who couldn't stop hyperventilating. I wanted to make a better impression this time. I focused on the looming trees as we sped down the dark road that my driver had taken for a week straight, picking Brynn up and dropping her off again. That week seemed like such a long time ago now. I found it surprising that Jean still had an interest in me despite the chaos of that day in the hall, but Brynn had yet to be convinced. I had lost her trust, but I would do everything to gain it back again.

I glanced at her a second time. Noticing her posture had shifted to a slump soon after Jean had mentioned their spot. It seemed more than obvious that she hadn't liked his plans. She sat with her knees hugged to her chest, one elbow on the arm of her door, fingernails subject to the ruthless bite of her teeth. I wanted to reach out and touch her. Drown her in more apologies and beg for her forgiveness. But my hands stayed wrapped in a ball at the center of my lap.

Instead of continuing down the winding road, we turned down a narrower lane off the side of it, and a sparse arrangement of trees lit up in front of the bright headlights. I could already see the glistening water through the fairly blossoming limbs until, finally, a vast pond came into view in the midst of the clearing.

"Surprise," Jean said, placing the vehicle in park alongside the grass.

I unbuckled and shifted towards the door closest to the pond, getting a closer look at the body of water tucked in this secret pocket of the woods. Their secret spot. Did this make it my secret spot now, too? Had I been inducted into their friend group by this notion alone? Did they somehow trust me with this special knowledge? My insides warmed just thinking about it.

"Très beau, non?"

I nodded, slipping my fingers behind the door latch, though I suddenly hesitated as I acknowledged the colonial-styled home overlooking the pond on the opposite side. "Are we…trespassing?"

Jean chuckled to himself, finally flicking off the high beams. "Not at all. Brynn knows the owners well."

Nothing about his answer set me at ease, and I looked at Brynn for clarity, though she seemed more interested in lighting the cigarette she'd just slipped in her mouth. I knew I wouldn't get a straight answer from either one of them. But Jean had already gotten out of the truck and ambled over to my side, seemingly making up my mind for me. I slipped out of the vehicle once he opened my door, and down my heels sunk into the moist earth.

"Is that your party dress?" he asked me, and I looked up at him, realizing the moon had settled above us, exposing his face in its cold glow.

I noticed the way he looked amused with me. The slight grin on his face looking quite out of place, given the empty stares he'd subjected me to for weeks.

"It's nothing—" I wrapped my coat further around my shivering stature, avoiding eye contact with him. "I don't even know why I—"

"Let me see it."

My eyes drifted back up to his, feeling as if I were right under a radar. "I don't think I should."

He screwed his face as if contemplating it, then gave me a nod. "No, I guess not." He let his gaze drop to my bordered-up arms. "You look cold enough as it is."

The passenger door opened, and my shoulders jumped, both of us breaking our focus on each other to watch Brynn crawl out of the truck with a waft of smoke trailing behind her.

"You ready?" He left me and walked over to her, wrapping his arms around her form, enveloping her like a blanket. "Are you feeling better?"

Brynn rested her cheek on his chest. "My mom stopped calling. Do you think she's hurt? Or maybe she's—"

"Brynn," he said her name like a hush, bringing his palms into her hair and gently forcing her head to tilt back. "Why are you worried about her right now? You're with me, right?"

She nodded. Giving him her undivided attention. Both eyes fluttering underneath his heavy gaze.

"Then be with me."

I wanted to look away. I knew I should have. But it almost seemed to creep up on me. The curiosity. The interest. It felt like watching a movie. Wrapped up in warm blankets from the dryer, isolated in my old bedroom in my old home. It felt like my childhood. I watched their movie—him kissing her. Craving to be in that scene like every romance flick I'd ever seen. Not as the main character. More like the fly on the wall. The bystander in the background. The outsider looking in. My heart drummed in my stomach as they finally pulled away from each other and remembered me. Standing there, still staring at them.

Idiot.

"S-sorry," I stuttered, dropping my eyes away again.

"Come on." Jean threw his arm around Brynn's shoulder and beckoned for me to join. "Let's show Elonie our little pond."

20

Who is she?

How in the world should I know?

I pulled another clump of grass into the palm of my hand and dispersed it, watching the shreds fall past my arched knees. Above me, the black blanket stretched out like the pond I lay near—a splatter of murky gray clouds painted across it and a mere handful of stars twinkling dimly in its threading. Beside me, Jean lay in the middle, two spider-long limbs sprawled and both arms tucked underneath his head. Elonie lay on the other side of him.

Elonie.

I looked over at her. She'd curled up on her side, two balled fists acting as her head rest, staring up at the same sky, the same moon and stars, the same boy...

Our eyes locked, and just as quickly, we both looked away from each other. Away from Jean. The only common denominator between us now. Still, I had no idea who Elonie could be. I knew that she'd practically swooped in and saved me from the trap that is Allan. I knew that she almost made me open up to her about everything during those car rides home. And I knew that she liked him. She liked Jean. But I loved Jean, and she had no idea how much he meant to me. What I would do for him.

"Can we at least talk?"

Jean's voice swam over to me and captured my attention. I rolled over onto my stomach and propped my chin up, but then so did she. Well, not quite. She lifted from the grass to a sitting posture, legs tucked underneath her bottom, hands in her lap. She looked ridiculously cold in her wrinkled dress and open heels, and the heavy brown plaid only made her look swallowed up and frumpy (not that anything about her style had ever seemed un-frumpy).

You're judging her.

So what?

It's not fair.

Life isn't fair.

I'd learned that the hard way, didn't I? Why shouldn't she? Homeschool couldn't have prepared her for this brave new world. My eyes sank into her, dissecting things that I hadn't before, noticing details that only confirmed my theory. Her eyes held a child-like innocence hidden behind their hooded shape. The unruly state of her curls only added to that naivety. I watched her look at Jean and try to hide her smile from him but to no avail. He bought it because he'd seen it for himself.

Her hurt. Her pain.

But I didn't believe her. What problems could she possibly have with her round apple cheeks and private school posture? I bet she went to church every Sunday. Baptized…the whole shebang. I knew where she belonged. She knew it, too. Not with us. Not here laying with us at our secret pond. She belonged with them at their spring fling dance.

"What a fake," I muttered under my breath.

Both of them looked at me, but Jean's expression turned slant with disapproval. "Brynn—"

"I hate her."

"Shut up, Brynn."

I blinked, startled at his words. "I'm sorry. Can we please just go?"

"Don't apologize to me. Say it to her."

But Elonie had already begun rising. "I'll just go sit in the—"

"Don't move!"

My body flinched and shifted upward. Hearing him yell never failed to shake me. He did it so rarely it almost felt like another person would suddenly take over him. I swallowed the knob in my throat, realizing that he had to be pretty thwarted by my sudden attitude as well, allowing that to justify his actions for me. Elonie had lowered down to her knees with both her arms clutching her stomach as her eyes stayed pinned to the ground. I knew how she felt. I'd felt the same way the first time he'd ever shouted at me. She wanted him to like her, as I had wanted. I still wanted that. Sometimes, I got too complacent too sure of our relationship, and moments like this only acted as a reminder that I truly had no control over it. Whether he liked me one day or hated me the next. Whether he even loved me back. He held the power to call this thing—whatever we had—quits. He possessed all of the control.

Jean lifted up from the grass and brought his knees up, wrapping his arms around them. "Elle est jalouse."

I watched his grin return before I glanced at Elonie. She drew in a breath and avoided my burning glare.

He chuckled. "Look what you did, Brynn. You scared her."

I dropped my eyes, nervously seeking out grass with my fingers and pulling it up from the earth.

"Est-ce parce qu'elle est mignonne?"

"Please stop," Elonie attempted to put an end to my public shaming.

He curled his palm around his ear. "En français."

"S-s'il vous plaît, arrêtez," she stuttered.

My eye twitched at her milky tone, the language pouring out of her smoothly and eloquently.

"Est-ce parce que…" Jean continued his playful tease, "elle est jolie?"

I absently scattered more broken grass, noting certain words. He used beginner's French. I understood enough to feel the shallow cuts they left behind. Like little nicks upon my goose-bumped skin.

"Elle est sexy?"

"Please, Jean," Elonie begged.

"D'accord, d'accord." Jean raised both palms in surrender, releasing another stark chuckle, though I felt his eyes find me in the dim light. "Brynn."

I looked up.

"Apologize to her."

My chest tightened, and I let my gaze drift back to her. "I'm—"

"En français."

She stared at me. Wearing her own look of remorse on her face. I scraped my mind for the words I suddenly couldn't remember, and the more I searched, the more the words escaped me.

"Je...suis..."

"Good..." Jean encouraged.

My eyes skittered across their faces. It didn't make sense. I'd learned the phrase in my freshmen course. I'd repeatedly written it on essays and exams. Why in the world couldn't I remember it now? Maybe it's because I didn't really want to. I wouldn't really mean it when I finally got it out of my mouth. She'd receive the apology with honey on her tongue, and Jean would simply throw his head back down into the grass, arms tucked—content again.

Désolé.

I took a deep breath and prepared the lie on my lips.

"Please don't apologize to me," Elonie spoke up before I could fib. "I should be apologizing for what I did. You trusted me. You were vulnerable with me about Allan, and I betrayed you. I just want you to know I never told them anything you told me."

"What exactly did I tell you?" I scoffed.

My words visibly silenced her.

"And if you think because I accepted car rides from you that meant I trusted you, then you're delusional," I continued, though I tried to maintain my tone for Jean's sake. "Why would I ever trust someone I don't even know?"

Elonie simply nodded. I could spot the glint of tears rimming her eyelids from where I sat, cross-legged now, openly challenging her forward remarks. Jean couldn't scold me for my choice of words. He'd asked me the same thing in the parking lot before going to confront Elonie that day. I had tried to convince him back then, but he'd seen right through my lying eyes. I guess I saw this as none other than an opportunity to show him—to prove to him—that I no longer trusted her, and I never truly did. I glanced at him, just to be sure he approved, only to realize that he'd already stood to his feet. Immediately, I regretted my actions.

"This was a mistake," he said directly to me before turning away. "Come on, let's go."

I pushed up from the grass, completely aware of the frown engraven on my face, and followed him towards the truck.

"Jean—"

"Just get in." He swung the door, and I stopped short of its edge, shoulders jumping at the hard slam.

We drove down the long road in silence. I sat stiffly in the passenger seat, scratching at my dry palms, longing for an opportunity to right my wrong. But my pride festered. Elonie had ignited something inside of me that I abhorred. The same kind of feeling I got when I came face to face with Allan in his car. This sinking gut feeling that had lassoed itself around me and tried its hardest to pull me back into the crashing waves of the past. Sitting there in the grass with her, I knew exactly who she'd reminded me of. I knew that girl. I used to be that girl. The party dresses and school night dances. The A plus papers, the perfect physique, the feminine posture, and Sunday morning church. Madness. Mayhem. It had consumed me, and I'd lost my way. I had been naive. Started to change, too. Elonie, in her baggy sweatshirt and long skirts, turns into Elonie in her little white dress and dumb heels. Running up that long sidewalk in front of her house to escape the frost of my eyes. Elonie evolving. Slowly getting lost. Never to be found. Ever again.

I hated her because I hated me.

And everything I used to be.

But I loved Jean. And, though he did not love her, I could tell… I could see it in his face; he would not let me ruin this for him. He stared at the door of her house long after she'd walked through it. I knew that look. Intrigue. Enamor. Obsession. I saw myself losing him, though he sat right beside me, only inches from my body. I dared to reach out and gently touch his hand as it still clutched the gear. Only then did he remember me. Taking in the details of my face that had changed so quickly before him.

"Please don't be mad at me," I squeezed out the words in barely a whisper.

He visibly relaxed, eyes becoming lidded. "Why do you play games with my head, girl?"

I sniffled, quickly brushing away droplets as they came, attempting to save face.

"Don't get rid of them now." He gently swatted my hand away. "Not after all the hard work you spent conjuring them up."

"Jean, I'm not trying to gain your sympathy, I just—"

"You're not?" He seemed taken aback as he shifted towards me in his seat, an arm hung over the steering wheel. "So, the stunt you pulled back there was genuine? Even the part where you used my own words against me?"

"I just wanted to prove it to you."

"Prove what? That you know how to mock me?"

"No, I was trying to show you that I don't trust anyone but you, Jean." I tightened my grip on his hand but he quickly pulled it away, and I trembled as I returned my hand to my side. "I don't care what she says to me. I don't want to make that same mistake of trusting anyone else again."

He slowly leaned back against his door. "You trust me?"

"Yes," I breathed a reply.

"Then trust me," I watched his eyes leave mine, settling on the white knuckles that gripped his steering wheel, "and remember how much I love you."

My throat grew thick as my lips peeled back from my teeth. "But she's just like them, not like us."

"What do you know?"

I swallowed.

"Look at you," he went on, lifting his posture, his glare slowly ripping into me, "judging her like the mean girl you are."

"I'm not—"

"You are. You are still like them."

My brows laced together. "Jean—"

"Do you even hear yourself? There are no try outs, Brynn. No tiny little boxes for you to check off. This isn't some stupid clique. When are you going to get that through your head?"

I briefly shut my eyes to his sudden touch, feeling his fingers grip the back of my neck and quickly pull me in. "There is no us."

I nodded again as more tears trickled down. The product of facing reality.

"You belong to me," his voice lowered next to my ear. "And she will, too. Okay?"

I sniffled, giving him another nod.

"Okay?"

"Okay."

He pressed his lips to my forehead. "Okay."

21

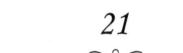

I should have known. Every movie I'd ever watched had spelled it out for me. Why hadn't I known this would be my fate? Danielle Turner wanted blood.

My blood.

How dare I, right?

I felt it when I woke up this morning. A brand new day in this bittersweet town. Bittersweet because, on one hand, I felt tortured by it. Though the rain had let up today, a nippy frost had taken its place. I should have been used to the unpredictability, but I hadn't gotten out much when I lived in the city. Our old home had been warm and cozy no matter what season. Katerina had always made sure the fireplace stayed burning during the cold winter months all the way through springtime and beyond. I'd almost never left the comfort of my bed. Presley's work hours skyrocketed after mom went away… then along came the extra help.

Oh, mom.

He knew he couldn't do it alone.

But this new house didn't feel like a home. It felt like a wooden cell. Nights were sleepless. I'd sit at the window, listening to the wind howl outside, sipping hot tea I'd made myself. Katerina hadn't followed us out here. She'd stayed in the city and probably burned some other little girl's fireplace now.

I envied her a little. But then I thought about the sweet side. Reminding myself of what I'd escaped in the city. And what I'd found here.

Until today.

Today, I felt strange. Unreal. I drifted down that carpeted staircase, deaf to whatever Presley had said to me as we headed to school then floated around my peers as light as a feather.

For the first time since arriving at the school, I felt free. Too free. I didn't meet with the girls in the senior bathroom. I didn't follow them to that same cafeteria booth. Nibbling at my breakfast muffin. Always longing to be elsewhere. I roamed the hallways freely. In and out of my classes—unbothered.

"Good afternoon," Allan Turner had popped his head into my final class of the day, that serious tone able to attract everyone's attention, including mine. "Principal Singh needs to see Elonie Davis in her office."

I'd struggled to get up from my desk, though eventually forced myself out of the classroom, clutching the straps of my knapsack as I silently walked alongside Allan. I'd had no clue of what I'd done wrong, but hearing Singh's parting words on replay in my head caused my throat to tighten almost entirely as we'd finally approached her door.

I'd made one last attempt. "Why am I—"

"My sister," Allan had only replied, the slight shake of his head expressing that he hadn't condoned whatever she'd done.

However, what did it truly matter if she'd gotten her brother's consent? Danielle had made it clear she answered to no one. I stepped into the office alone, and there she sat. One knee over the other. Both hands donning a fresh red manicure as they sat neatly folded in the lap of her skirt. But on her face is where the truth of her intentions lay. The same look she'd given me before I'd walked out of those gym doors adorned her features now. She wanted me to pay. She'd waited for the right time. The opportune moment. She'd allowed me to enjoy a small taste of freedom—a short glimpse of happiness—before completely ripping it away again.

"Please sit down, Elonie." Principal Singh stood behind her desk, only seating herself after I had. My attention shifted from her to the other person in attendance to this apparent meeting.

A stocky man with peppered facial hair dressed in khaki slacks and a maroon argyle sweater stood nearby her desk. His dark eyes seemed to dissect me, though he warmed up his keen focus by shooting me a smile. I didn't even think to return it. I only wanted to know what vile concoction Danielle had cooked up for them and had they completely had their fill of it?

"I apologize for removing you from your class on such short notice," Singh began, clasping her fingers atop her desk in usual fashion, "but you will soon understand why the matter could not wait."

I sunk down in the leather seat, not even daring to glance in Danielle's direction. "Whatever I did—"

"You're not in trouble, Elonie." Though her stern expression hadn't changed. "We're just concerned about your mental health."

"We?"

Singh allowed her eyes to shift in that man's direction, and so did I. "This is Mr. Scavelli, one of our school psychologists. He mainly works with upperclassmen and students who are high risk."

I swallowed, already feeling my tear ducts swell.

"Elonie," Singh spoke my name as if attempting to let me down gently, but that only managed to make me more nervous, "we've been informed that you have been self-harming."

My first instinct slipped out before I could stop myself. "No. That's not true."

"She's lying," Danielle easily counteracted me. "I saw the cuts on her wrist. She made me promise not to tell, but I just couldn't keep something like this to myself, Principal Singh."

And just like that, the dam of my eyes broke once again. Tears pouring down my face. Reminding me that I had been made for one thing and one thing only: misery. No matter how many attempts I made at changing or how many times I got my hopes up, I would always be reminded of what she used to say about people like us.

We could never be truly happy. So why even bother?

Mom had been right, after all. If she could see me now. Sitting there in that frigid office, clinging to the leather chair, blubbering as she, herself, had done countless times when alive. She'd smile at me and say, for the first time, I looked just like her. She'd put her arms around me and take me away from this place. This town. These people. She'd take me back home to the city and fix me tea and play with my hair as I drifted off to sleep.

I closed my eyes. Wanting to be with her. Desperate to see her face. I ignored the hands rested on my shoulder, inching away from the deep but inviting voice of the counselor.

"N-no," I stuttered through my cries, beginning to rock myself as mom would have. "Just leave me alone—leave me alone—leave me alone—"

"Elonie, it's going to be okay," his voice only moved closer, taking on a soothing tone. "No one is going to hurt you here. It'll be okay. I promise."

I felt those hands slide across my shoulders, and big arms enveloped me whole. I could feel how bad my rocking had become. But I couldn't stop. I couldn't focus on what Principal Singh had started saying or even think about what Danielle's face must have looked like by now. I had entered into a full-blown episode that so few had ever had the opportunity of witnessing.

I had become completely inconsolable.

When I'd peeled my eyes back open, I knew some time had passed. I still sat in that chair, knees pulled into my chest, cheeks as tight as leather from all of my tears. Danielle no longer sat next to me. I noticed they'd called Nurse Miller in. Mr. Scavelli had taken a seat directly in front of me, his eyes staring as his voice coaxed my head up even further. Principal Singh still stood behind her desk. Wearing an expression of pity but mostly confusion.

My heart pumped something fierce with embarrassment. "I'm sorry—I'm so sorry I—"

"It's alright, Elonie," Mr. Scavelli spoke to me, attempting to get me to remain focused on only him. "You just had a panic attack. Nurse Miller is going to assess you then bring you down to my office, okay?"

"No, please, I just want to go," I begged right away.

"Perhaps we should wait, Mr. Scavelli," Singh intruded, breaking our eye contact. "I'll need to obtain parental consent from her father."

"No, you can't tell him about this." I shot up from my seat, a sudden growl in my tone. "Danielle Turner knows nothing about me. She lied to all of you."

Principal Singh's eyes fluttered at my sudden boldness. "Nurse Miller also confirmed the cuts on your arm, Elonie."

I glanced at the woman who shamelessly brought forth her stethoscope. I backed away and brought my glare back to Singh. "There's this tree I climb to read…it's right outside my bedroom window…"

I then looked down at Mr. Scavelli. "If you've read my file, then you know that I already see a therapist in the city. I don't need anyone else picking at me or trying to—"

"Elonie, Elonie," he said, nearly matching me in height. "Calm down now. No one is going to force you to do anything. If you say the cuts were an accident, then I believe you."

I sniffled, nodding fiercely. "They were an accident."

"I believe you," he nearly cooed, placing those thick hands of his on my arms again. "Nothing but a big misunderstanding, alright?"

I nodded still.

"Well," Singh continued, "I'll still need to notify your father of your panic attack. That's non-negotiable."

I tucked my chin and slid my hand across my forehead, all of a sudden becoming extremely weary.

"Come with me," Nurse Miller brought her arm around me. "We'll do the assessment in my office."

"I just want to go."

"You'll be all finished right before the ring. Come, come."

I went with Nurse Miller, leaving them both to discuss me behind my back and think up ways they could make me confess what they clearly already knew to be true.

I sat stiffly on the cot as she prodded my throat with her fingers and lay that cold, flat end of the stethoscope to my bare chest. Swallowing the lump still encased in my throat. Contemplating returning to the city. But, then again, no. There would be nothing good waiting for me there. Nothing but more hate…more contempt… No one liked me there, and no one liked me here. Danielle would make sure of that. I'd crossed her in the most unforgiving way. She'd make sure the whole school hated me until my graduation.

The bell's ring startled me, and involuntarily, I jumped, coming out of my cyclic thoughts.

"Button up," Nurse Miller called over her shoulder, meanwhile penciling in things on my open file. "All done."

I glanced down at my tank top and began buttoning the brown cardigan jumper that I wore atop it. Outside of her office, I could already hear my peers, their voices filling the once quiet hallways and their shoes shuffling towards the exit. Suddenly, I wanted to hide. I knew word had traveled by now. Danielle probably couldn't wait to run and tell everyone the nightmare she'd witnessed in Principal Singh's office. Subjecting everyone to the horrific details and tarnishing my name once and for all.

I'd been here before. I knew the drill.

"Can I wait here until the halls are empty?"

Nurse Miller looked over her shoulder again, turned down her mouth, and shrugged. "Mm."

I took her expression as approval and lowered down onto my side on the cot, closing my eyes to the fluorescent lights. I tried not to think of the reaction I'd had, but my thoughts just kept returning to that office. Their faces. Danielle's convicted words. My sudden inability to breathe.

Panic attack.

That's what that man had called it. Dr. Portis, Ph.D. had once labeled it the same. I'd always had them. Ever since I'd been a little girl. My mom had them, too. Of course, hers were always featured with bouts of paranoia and erratic behavior. I'd overhear the doctors as I sat on the stair landing, hidden from plain sight, eavesdropping as they talked about me and mom. Some told Presley how I did it to mimic her. Others were prepared to run tests. And still, others only wanted to put me on the same sedative they'd put her on. The same one that eventually took her life.

Presley had no idea then that the worst of his troubles had only just begun. I knew I disappointed him. I couldn't stop disappointing him. We weren't made of the same stuff. He'd picked himself up by the bootstraps as a neglected child and became a success in his adulthood. Not one celebrity on this side of the country didn't know my father's name. He'd made himself a hot commodity in the professional and entertainment world. But me... I had mom in me. One tiny body filled to the brim with emotions. Too many to conceal. So much so that I often found myself ripping at the seams from simply being handled too roughly. Mom had been the same way. Too sensitive for this world, so she had to escape.

Only she forgot to take me with her when she left.

The moment the halls silenced, I left Nurse Miller's office. The suv still waited for me in front of the school. Once inside, my driver greeted me, and I curled up in the back seat, resting my throbbing head as he drove me back home. Then he left, and I teleported upstairs, locking the bedroom door, cup of tea in hand. Alone again. I stayed that way, wrapped in my blankets, until the next morning. And even then, I still didn't move. I didn't go to school that day. My driver came and left. My phone lay ringing on my bedside table. Untouched. Presley, no doubt, calling to feign concern. If he'd truly been concerned, he would have come back from the city that first day. He would have left his makeshift of a family and came to rescue me.

Mom would have.

But more likely, he'd been calling to reprimand me. Principal Singh would have contacted him about my truancy by now. Today made the third day that I hadn't been back. How could I go back after all of that? Danielle had won. She'd put me in my place. Everyone knew she would have. I should have known. I had known. I knew she'd use my pain against me. I could tell from that first day she'd seen the marks on my wrist. But I still tested her. I chose to walk away from that dance. I chose the other side. But for what? What had I gained? Brynn hated me. She'd said it herself. And Jean—he only wanted to use me for his

136

entertainment. I could tell by the way he looked at me. Watching me. Like his favorite TV show. His favorite pastime. I didn't want to be his toy. I wanted to be a human being. But I felt like a corpse, completely drained, blankly staring at the wooden beams on the ceiling.

Then, sometime around noon (or at least I guessed), the doorbell rang.

It seemed unreal at first. I paid it no mind. Possibly, the mail man making his usual route. Is that the norm in small towns like this? I wouldn't know. But then the high ding sounded again, and the mailman theory dissipated with the emergence of my triggered nerves. I lifted to my elbows. My focus was glued to the window directly across from me. The house remained as still as my body felt.

Had I just imagined it?

I watched the branches of the trees having a fit in the wind. The more I stared, the more I began to doubt what I'd heard. Allowing my body to slightly lower back down to its indent in the mattress.

Then, to my right.

My peripheral caught it.

That black shadow.

I confirmed it with my eyes, and there he stood, right outside of my nook window, underneath the swaying branches and rustling leaves of the big oak tree. I yelped and threw my shoulders against the headboard. A wave of pain breaking out across my bones. But I'd barely registered it as we stared each other down.

Those murky blues quickly defeated my softer browns, causing my eyes to flutter relentlessly. He made his way closer to my window, and I just watched as he pulled out a cigarette pack from his jacket pocket, suddenly shaking it like a dog's chew toy. My face fell in confusion as I climbed out of my bed and slowly stepped over to the nook. With one flip of the latch, I pushed open the windows, letting a chill breeze roam past me.

Jean held the pack out towards me now. "Have a smoke with me."

My cracked voice trickled out. "What?"

He pulled out a lighter as well. "A cigarette."

My eyes dropped to his offer. "What are you—what are you doing here?" I looked back up. "You shouldn't—"

"You're big on shoulds and shouldn'ts." He retracted his arm and lit the cigarette for himself, blowing smoke towards the sky. "Enlighten me. Why shouldn't I be here?"

I didn't have an answer. Or rather, I did but everything sounded so mediocre in my mind. I knew he'd rebuttal any reason I gave. So I gave the only one I knew he'd most likely accept.

"Brynn," I said.

His eyes slightly narrowed. "What about Brynn?"

"She...she wouldn't like it."

"Hm."

I zoomed in on him, watching the second wave of smoke float around him, his eyes abruptly leaving mine. I'd annoyed him, I could tell. He lowered to a squat underneath the tree, and I brought my knees onto the bench, still watching his every move. He'd rested his head against the thick tree stump, pulling his cigarette away from his mouth once again. I could see him struggling with the words on his tongue. The same tongue pressed against his inner cheek now.

Instantly, I regretted my own words, fixing my lips to take them back.

"I like you, Elonie." His long arms dangled over his knees, the cigarette held snug between two of his fingers. But those eyes looked up at me again, finding me sitting back on my ankles, fingers nervously clutching my arms. "Does that matter to you?"

I swallowed, stunned by what he'd said. A breeze came by and rustled the leaves, sweeping across my skin leaving me shivering. Or maybe my shivers were a part of the effect he had on me. My thoughts were racing. He had no idea what he'd just done. Of course, it mattered that he liked me. I couldn't think of anything that mattered more to me than to be liked. But being liked by him didn't erase the fact that Brynn still hated me. And she would continue to hate me if she knew how much I liked Jean, too.

"No," I replied back, forcing my arms to grab the window. "Please just go, Jean. I don't want to hurt anyone."

"The only person you're hurting is me." He pushed up from the tree stump and extended his arms out from his body. "Elonie!"

I froze in place, my hand suddenly dropping from the latch.

His chest heaved with growing anger. "I came here to see you. Danielle's dragging you through the mud. She's telling everyone that you hallucinated in Singh's office. She's got everyone thinking you're some sort of schizophrenic."

My face heated as I looked away from him, pushing my tongue against the roof of my mouth. "They can think what they want. I'm never going back anyway."

"Because of them?"

"Everyone thinks I'm a freak."

"So? Why should you care?"

"No one likes me here—"

"Didn't you just hear what I said?" His tone gripped me and brought fresh tears to my eyes. "I like you, Elonie."

I watched through blurry eyes as he attempted to come close, though visibly vexed at the forced distance between us. Still, he stared at me as strongly as if he were standing right in front of me. In this bedroom. As he'd done many times in my dreams.

"You don't need anyone else to like you," he spoke again with that same authority. "I'm the only one who gets you. I've been where you are. But I chose to rebel. I chose to live by my own rules, and you will too."

I shook my head. "How do you know that?"

"Stick with me." He pressed a fist to his chest, his tone softening, his eyes pleading. "Just stay with me, Elonie."

"I can't."

"Why can't you?"

I reached for the window latch again.

"Look!"

I paused, waiting, sniffling as his gaze hardened. But then, suddenly, he began peeling out of his jacket. Tossing the worn leather on the ground. Next came his shirt, which he threw down, too. I leaned against the window, seemingly drawn in, eyebrows joined at the center. His chest still rose and fell with the frustration I had caused him. But on his skin, I noticed every cut and abrasion. Every scar stood out to me. Holding me victim in its snare.

He'd been right.

We were exactly the same.

22

"I don't understand why we can't all go…I don't care about that, Dwight, I just want it like before…"

The scratchy tone of my mother's morning voice became distant as I rushed down to the end of the hall and cut the corner quickly, avoiding being swept into the drama erupting inside of my parent's bedroom. I'd begun to think I'd liked it better when she'd been in a complete daze all of those months.

You don't mean that.

My eyes rolled at the small but distinct voice in my head. In the kitchen, the hired chef stood over the large brass cooktop, whipping up the breakfast spread that my father insisted upon every Sunday since my mother's return to reality. Dr. Patel had suggested he try introducing some normalcy back into our family routine. I bet he regretted taking up that premature notion now.

"Good morning," the full-figured woman turned and faced me as I'd attempted to creep past her, a stack of white plates in her grip. "You eating breakfast today?"

My stomach growled at the mere mention of the word while my nostrils widened at the mixture of scents coming it's way like torpedoes. But I defied my carnal instinct and shook my head at her, a frown settling on my face.

"I told you I hate breakfast."

The raven-haired woman nodded her awareness, setting our China on the large island block before her. "I just thought maybe you'd changed your mind."

"Well, I haven't," I crossed my arms, watching her begin plating the food, "and it's rude of you to keep asking over and—"

"You mind putting this orange juice on the table?"

My jaw shook, and I watched her lift the glass pitcher, extending it towards me.

"You must be joking," I uttered.

She gave me a sigh before setting the drink back down. "Oof."

I watched her resume preparing my parent's feast, letting my eyes drift over each food item cluttering the vast counter top. It had looked and smelled the exact same way every Sunday morning for the past few weeks. She prepared everything from benedict to French toast to smoked salmon served on fresh bagels. An endless array of options. Still, my mother barely ate a thing.

"This is so pointless."

A bemused smirk situated itself on her plump lips. "Breakfast?"

"You make her this grand buffet every time, and she never eats anything."

"Not true. Your mom always enjoys a little banana nut muffin with her coffee."

"You just don't get it. You're only wasting your time." My eyes slowly dropped to her busy hands. "You're not going to fix her, you know?"

"I'm not trying to fix your mother, sweetheart." She glanced up at me with raised eyebrows. "She's a human being. Not a wall clock."

"Then why keep coming back here?"

"Look, I get you don't like me being here." The woman picked up both prepared plates, giving her shoulders a shrug. "But your dad hired me to do a job, so I'm doing it."

My brows furrowed, watching her leave the kitchen to go set the table. I chose not to stick around any longer, venturing outside on the terrace, sucking in the sharp morning chill to relax my nerves.

The ridiculously petty conversation still spun around my head, causing me to become furious all of a sudden, furious enough that I couldn't help but break out into dry laughter. How comical that a mere boardwalk diner cook thinks she can just waltz into our kitchen waving her magic little spatula—as if that could mend our broken family portrait.

You're doing it again.

"So what?" I clutched the edge of the stone wall and narrowed my eyes. "She's nobody special."

And you are?

My chest started heaving, and I bit my frustration out loud, "Just get out of my head already."

The French doors opened behind me, and I swiftly turned, staring as my father walked out to join me on the terrace. His forehead held a crease, and instantly, I knew something horrible came my way.

"I want you to get dressed—"

My throat threatened to close up as soon as the words began leaving his mouth. "Dad—"

"Brynn, don't debate with me. I'm through discussing the issue." I watched him bring his hand to his face and squeeze his tired eyes in a troubled manner. "It's what your mother wants, and I can't give her anything else right now."

"They'll just stare at us like we're—like we're pathetic," I still attempted to change his mind as a million horrible scenarios filled my head. "Dad, please don't make—"

"That's enough, Brynn," his voice rose an octave, more than enough to shut me up. "I said I will not discuss this anymore. You will get dressed, and you will come with us to church. It's final."

I flinched from the robustness of his tone, slowly becoming a small child again. He said nothing else before returning inside. I stayed.

Sinking onto the patio furniture, a wave of nausea hitting me faster than I'd been prepared for. I had made up my mind. I definitely had liked it better when my mom had been in a daze. At least she'd been silent. Her emotions all shut up, and her tear ducts bone dry. Not quite sure how to swallow the news of her son's sudden death. Even after the final piece of glass had been picked up from the asphalt and the last of the hideous floral arrangements had been thrown out, she'd still not been able to digest it. And my father knew she never would. He used to have no trouble telling her no. But, of course, he'd felt obligated on this particular soft spot. He couldn't deny a mother a few more memories with her only son. No matter what shape or form they came in.

But I couldn't bring myself to empathize at the moment. I couldn't stand in my closet, staring at the rows of church dresses I hadn't worn in forever, without thinking of that last day with him. All of a sudden, I'd returned to that cool summer night. The breeze ruffled my straightened hair, as I'd often worn it back then, and I watched myself rush out of that overflowing house. Burning tears streaming down my face. For the first time, I'd wanted to escape. I'd needed to get out of there. But so had he. Ethan had needed me, but I couldn't see it then. I'd been too wrapped up in that same chaos. The chaos that had finally decided to fully bare its fangs and devour me whole that day.

I brought the puffed sleeve of a burnt sienna dress up my shoulder, the discomfort I'd felt outside returning with a vengeance, threatening its way up my throat again. I couldn't fight the suffocation gripping me like the linen threads of the dress. Reminding me of what I'd done. Reminding me that it should have been me. I'd been so sure my life had been over that night, but instead—

Stop! Stop blaming yourself!

But how could I not blame myself? My fingers trembled as I yanked the zipper up my side, but guilt hit me like a punch to the stomach and caused me to double over, both my knees dropping to the closet floor. I hated thinking about that night because it always brought me here. Curled up on my closet floor again. Helpless to the memories that haunted me.

"I'm sorry," I whispered aloud, attempting to catch my breath. "I didn't mean for this to happen, Ethan. I never meant for any of this to happen."

Stop it, Brynn!

"Brynn!"

I flinched, swiftly sitting up as knocks erupted on the other side of my bedroom door. "Y-yes?" I called out as I frantically dried my eyes.

"Your mother and I won't wait much longer. I suggest you hurry up with whatever it is you're doing."

I quickly pulled my hair into a low ponytail, though it'd taken longer for me to remember where I'd put my Bible. I'd once kept it on my bedside table, but after Ethan died, I'd stowed it away, along with all of my hymns, underneath my bed. I'd no longer had a need for them, knowing that scriptures and songs wouldn't bring my brother back.

By the time I slid into the SUV, I knew we were considered late in pastoral time. My father hated showing up after his church committee had already arrived. He deemed it unprofessional. I could already feel the thick tension oozing from his spot in the front row. My mom sat next to him, wearing one of her favorite numbers, a floral accented dress in a soft champagne shade, and her long hair fastened into a tight bun. I couldn't tear my eyes away from the back of their heads as I sat alone in the back seat. Odd didn't even come close to describing us. And if I could see it, I knew everyone else would.

"Take the car around," my father said to our driver once we'd arrived on church grounds. "We'll go in through the back door."

"Maybe we should go in through the front." My mom turned her head, tilting it to sway him. "We want to look normal—"

"There's no one in the church yet, Sierra, only the members of the committee and the worship choir."

I swallowed down what felt like needles in my throat. "The entire worship choir?"

"Yes. You know the choir always performs for Sunday worship, Brynn. Nothing has changed."

"Mom," I gripped the seat and slid forward, "let's just do what dad says and go in through the—"

"Don't patronize me, young lady," he snapped, though just as quickly recovered from his anger, regardless of the damage that had already been done to my nerves. "Your mother is concerned with being treated differently in front of the congregation, and your only concern is your own humiliation."

"I-I'm sorry I—"

"Don't think you haven't done a good enough job of humiliating yourself and this family already."

"Please, Dwight," My mom gingerly placed her hand on her husband's shoulder, "not here."

I felt our vehicle come to a halt in front of the church, but I had become glued to the seat, both palms moist against the leather. A stark silence hung between us. The random outburst and clear implications behind his words had, once again, opened unhealed wounds.

"I'm taking your mother inside," my dad finally spoke again. "You can join us when you are ready."

"No," my mom's voice cracked. "No, this isn't what he would want."

My father placed an awkward arm around my mom's shoulder. "Sierra, please don't get upset."

"Ethan would have wanted us together." She dropped her forehead to his shoulder. "He would have wanted us to go in as a family."

My heart stomped around in my chest, watching my mom shed tears on his clean suit, knowing that wouldn't have been tolerated in the past. Nor would my mom have ever dared to make a scene at a time like this. Everything about this felt too soon. We shouldn't be here. But since we were already here, I would allow nobody to see us like this.

"I'm ready," I nearly blurted, although everything inside of me screamed just the opposite. "I'll go in with you, mom."

I watched her lift her head and brush tears from her eyes. "Oh, thank you, honey. Thank you so much. Mommy loves you so much."

Her words barely transpired as my eyes switched back to my father, desperate to know if he approved, but he only had eyes for his wife. He took her hand in his large palm and gently kissed the top of it, comforting her in the familiar way he used to.

My father had never been the most affectionate. A short but sweet hug or the intimate kiss on her hand were the only gestures I'd grown up seeing between the two of them. But I knew my mom would have completely fallen apart if she hadn't had him. Even though the time he'd spent at home had become shorter and the united marriage front had been completely placed on hold, he'd still taken care of her all of those months she lay in bed completely mute and detached from us. And she still depended on him to take care of her. She still needed him.

And he needed her.

But no one needed me.

The only person who had ever needed me, I'd let down in the worst way. In the most irreversible way. Of course, my father didn't trust me. I couldn't trust myself. I knew everything that I'd done. Everything that I'd been capable of, and so did he. He held onto what I'd told him about that night. Both of us had kept it a secret from my mom. If she knew what I'd done, it'd kill her. His job ever since that night had been protecting his wife—even from her own daughter.

You're not the monster.

I ignored that nagging little voice inside of my head as I followed behind my parents past those mahogany wood doors and into the church. My head instantly spun at the familiar aroma drifting throughout the building. The smell had successfully brought me back to an image of my childhood. A little girl in a pastel yellow dress and her slightly older brother sporting a nice clean suit. Both watching as the other kids ran up and down the long aisles.

The little girl sat green with envy.

It had always looked so nice from afar. To be that carefree.

That memory faded out as a few notes of the organ filled the sanctuary. In came another picturesque moment in my mind. Vivid. Like it'd happened yesterday. That same girl, no longer green, waving her arms as she swayed to the rhythm of the band. A big voice belted out of her in perfect unison with the identically clad people surrounding her. She wore a bright smile on her face. She looked truly content.

Now, that same girl took a seat in our designated pew in front. One knee over the other, clutching the Bible in my lap, though my nerves still subtly kneaded my core. The room still lacked congregation members, but my heart anticipated what I could not yet see, causing the rest of my body to suffer in suspense. Mom came to sit next to me, her make-up all touched up, but I saw right through her mask. She felt nervous, too. My father had left us to tend to his pastoral duties, though he'd promised her he'd return before service began. For now, I slipped my hand down into hers and squeezed it, reminding her of my presence.

"Oh God, I feel so silly," she stated with exasperation, holding her free hand over her trembling lips. "I thought I'd be able to feel him here of all places."

I lowered my chin, having no clue what I should say, so I said nothing. I just continued holding her hand. And I didn't let go. Not even when church members began filling the place and the dreaded murmuring finally commenced. Not even when the choir made their appearance on stage and Danielle Turner's sharp eyes locked on mine. Not even when my father returned with Dr. Turner at his side, coming to pay his condolences along with his wife and son.

Not even then.

I clung to my mom's hand like a child as I respectfully greeted all of them. Only temporarily letting my eyes meet Allan's gaze as he stood, looking down on me, no doubt wishing he could hear the thoughts whirling around inside of my mind. And maybe that's how it would have been before. I wouldn't have hesitated to tell him anything back then. It's exactly why he couldn't bear being shut out now.

"Do you mind if I sit here with you?" he asked the question I'd been terrified of hearing.

Before I could answer, my father granted him the permission he'd asked for. "Yes, keep them company while I deliver the sermon."

I tensed up as he took Ethan's spot next to me. A low simmer igniting in my veins. But I wouldn't cause a scene. No way. I knew better than that. We were raised never to act up in church. We were to be the spitting image of what my father had been preaching for fifteen years. We were to carry ourselves like the preacher and first lady's picture perfect children.

Allan would stay.

And apparently, so would his mother, who also took a seat next to mine, no doubt earning several envious glances from the ones seated behind us. The opportunity to sit in our pew had always been an honor among the congregation, but so few got that privilege, as my mom had always been selective about who she chose to surround herself with for the sake of my father's reputation. She would tell us the world is full of sinners, but the church is where all the sinners gathered together.

I remembered that now as I stared at Danielle standing in the pulpit with the other members of the choir. Her father had taken his position in front, already leading the choir in a soft hymn that I knew all too well. The people who'd continued to pour in through the entrance and the smooth feel of Allan's suit jacket brushing against my arm couldn't bring me out of the trance I had entered.

The music surrounded me. Gripped me. Forced me back into that pulpit next to Danielle, singing my heart out. I remembered how Ethan would sometimes make the goofiest faces (when our parents weren't looking) just to make me laugh.

No, no, no!

I fought the tears burning behind my eyelids as I adjusted on the hard bench. Watching my father finally take his place at the center of the altar. The hymn slowly grew less and less until only the band performed the familiar notes. Then Pastor Dwight spoke. He always became Pastor to me when the sermon started.

"Good morning," he said and a wave of greetings across the congregation sounded throughout the building. "Yes, it is a good morning, isn't it?"

Affirmations rang freely, and I glanced over at my mom, noticing her eyes were transfixed on her husband. I followed her gaze back over to him. Pastor Dwight gave her a small smile before shaking his head with his head hung low.

"God is good," he said, earning a few notes from the organist and a lot more amens from the crowd. "My wife woke up this morning and told me she needed to be here today…and, by God, she is here."

The congregation applauded. The band played louder. But I only wanted to sink into the floor. Those claps weren't for me. I hadn't even wanted to be here. I'd wanted to run. Even now, sitting here wedged between mom and Allan, I wanted to run.

Don't go.

"We want to thank every last one of you for the overwhelming support…"

I swallowed down, though my heart began a vile thump in my throat, I swallowed and swallowed it down. The lights were too bright and began to hurt my eyes. But I couldn't let them see me fall apart. I let go of my mom's hand, reaching for my neck pulling at the hair at my nape. Trying to release some of that feeling.

"Our son meant the world to us, and though he was taken away much too soon…"

My heart felt as if it were in someone's tight grasp, and their hands were only squeezing harder. My fingernails dug deeper into my skin, and I adjusted in my seat again. Too much this time. I suddenly felt the weight of Allan's eyes drop onto my shoulders. Before I knew it, the warmth of his arm surrounded me. Embracing me. Like a snake.

Don't!

That voice did nothing to stop me this time. I dove up from my seat, out of his arms, running down that aisle. The same aisle I used to dream of running down as a child. But I hadn't imagined it like this. I hadn't imagined a thousand pairs of eyes staring at me. So keen. So judgmental. But they didn't get it. They couldn't possibly understand.

No one could.

I escaped into the bathroom. Grabbing for the first thing to help me remain upright. The sink edge felt cold in my grip as I hung my head over it, gasping for air, tears flowing freely from my eyes now. But I didn't dare look up at my reflection, too afraid of what I might see. I knew my father would be upset at my dramatic display, and I hadn't expected my mother to come racing in to comfort me. I didn't know how I would explain it to them once we returned home. I couldn't put into words the intense feeling that my father's words had conjured up within me. I couldn't describe the disgust in the pit of my stomach when Allan's arm came around me. I didn't need his pity, nor could I sit through another bout of guilt for what had happened that night.

I knew what I had done. Why did my father feel the need to constantly slap me in the face with it?

A coughing fit overcame me and forced me to sit down, pushing myself against the wall. It hadn't been too long. I could go back. Or I could just slip out of the back door without anyone knowing. I could call Jean. He wouldn't want me to go through another minute of this torment. He would come get me. Give me a cigarette. Let me rest my head on his shoulder as he drove us to the pond. I'd let go of my worries there, at least until the moon came out, forcing me back home to lay in the bed that I had made.

The sound of the bathroom door interrupted my plans and caused my eyes to shift to it as I quickly pushed myself up from the wood floor, going to stand in front of the sink again. My hands flipped on both faucet knobs, but my eyes were fixed on the mirror, noticing the curly-haired girl standing in the doorway.

Leave.

My breath caught. The voice had been so prominent. I swore someone stood right next to me. But only Danielle and I stood in the bathroom now, the door closing with a hard thud behind her.

"Are you okay?" she asked me.

I shut the water off and turned around, pressing my back against the sink. "Just leave me alone, Danielle. I don't need your fake pity or concern."

Her high heels clicked towards me, and I watched as she took her stance in front of the mirror, both hands straightening her jeweled headband. "When have I ever offered you fake pity or concern?"

Don't reply. Just leave.

I walked over to the napkin dispenser, cut a piece, and began drying my hands.

"My brother is the one who asked me to come check on you," Danielle continued talking. "Even though I told him you wouldn't appreciate the gesture."

I ignored her words, tossing the paper into the trash bin before heading for the door.

"You were always the ungrateful one, after all."

My hand froze just before the handle, and a fire-red heat blanketed my skin.

She only wants a reaction.

I knew that. But I didn't care. She'd gone too far. I turned around and faced her. "Why can't you ever just shut your stupid little mouth?"

"Still a drama queen, I see."

"Shut up, or I'll—"

"You'll what?" Danielle chuckled as she crossed her arms over the long white robe she wore. "You'll lose your temper and try to hit me again?"

My stomach turned at the memory, but I stood my ground. "As if you didn't deserve it."

"No one deserves to be hit, Brynn. Are those the types of things creepy Cohen has been teaching you?"

"No, those are the types of things you taught me." I stiffened my lips, gritting my teeth. "Hit below the belt, right? Where it hurts the most."

"You were always taking my words so literally." I shook my head, watching her face the mirror again, her fingers plucking her voluminous curls with no clear consideration for my feelings. "And to think Principal Singh would ever believe you and your silly accusations."

"You lied to her just like you lied to me and your brother and clearly everyone who's ever had the displeasure of knowing you."

She cracked a wry smile, slightly turning her head and piercing me with her eyes. "What about your lies?"

"I've never—"

"You asked me to keep secrets, Brynn..." She slowly stepped towards me. "Secrets from my own brother..."

I turned to leave, but she grabbed my wrist, forcing me to a halt. My eyes dropped to her grip and then back up to her face. "Let go of me, Danielle."

She released my arm. "We used to be best friends, Brynn, and, believe it or not, I still care about you. I just don't understand why you chose to walk away from the only people who supported you through everything."

I narrowed my glare. "Stay away from me."

Danielle licked her lips and nodded, taking another deep breath. "It really is nice to see you and your mother back in church." She walked past me towards the door, though she lingered a bit once she'd reached it. "Give her my deepest condolences, will you?"

My eyes pricked as I forced tears not to shed, pressing my tongue against the roof of my mouth, holding myself together long enough to watch her walk out of the bathroom. Then, like a tsunami, they hit me—all at once—leaving me alone with my shame once again.

23

I couldn't sleep last night. Even though I'd tried my hardest, I just couldn't get my eyes to shut. I'd sat next to the window and read a book in the moonlight pouring in. I'd gone downstairs and whipped up my mom's favorite: ginger tea with honey. I'd even stood outside of Presley's study, staring at the sliver of light below the door, contemplating on knocking on it but quickly changing my mind. Finally, I'd curled up on the leather couch in the den that I hadn't gone in since we'd moved into this house. Mindlessly flipping through channels. Staring through the bright white light. Completely imagining myself in another realm.

A realm where the weather felt warmer. Not too hot. Just warm enough for shorts. I could wear them because I wouldn't have ugly scars on my thighs. My legs would be smooth and soft, my skin would glow underneath the sun's rays—unblemished and perfect. In that realm, mom would live with me. She'd be alive and well. Never sad. Not even a little. I'd make her happy like before. Presley would live in the city and never visit us. Jean would live next door and always visit. And Brynn… we'd be the best of friends.

A movie that my ears recognized brought me out of that realm and into reality. It'd been an old black-and-white drama. I closed my eyes to the sound of the actor confessing his unrequited love for his female counterpart. I'd already known how it would end, so I'd dozed off to sleep only to be awakened by Presley's voice saying my name.

"Wake up, Elonie," he said to me as my eyes fluttered open and peered up at him. "You have school."

School. Of course.

"Why are you down here?"

I slowly lifted from the couch, stretching my limbs as I became possessed by a yawn. "I couldn't sleep last night," I replied after.

He seemed to accept that answer, allowing me to go upstairs and get dressed without another word. I ambled around my bedroom after I'd gotten out of the tub, going back and forth in my head about what I should wear, but the single vibration of my phone quickly drew my attention. I stared at it from where I stood in front of my closet as if it'd just talked to me, before hurrying over to the desk where it lay silent now.

Come ride with us

My jaw slightly dropped at the message from Jean. It had been his name that appeared this time. I'd figured it would come soon—he'd officially asked for my number before leaving that day—but not this soon. I stood frozen with the phone still in my grip, not sure exactly how to respond…or if I should at all.

I finally walked out into the hall and stood at the banister, staring down at Presley as he walked out of the kitchen with a coffee mug cupped in one hand and a stapled document in the other. I'd waited until he'd rounded the staircase and finally noticed me.

"Why aren't you getting dressed?" He asked me as he slowly took the steps up. "We're leaving soon."

"I meant to tell you that I…" I attempted to think quickly on my feet. "I'm supposed to be getting a ride from someone else."

Presley continued up the stairs. "I don't have any time to waste this morning, Elonie."

"I'm serious," I insisted, turning to face him as he reached the top. "You can go on without me."

"Elonie," he spoke my name sternly, and I began nibbling at my lip. "You've already caused enough commotion, haven't you? It's bad enough you decided to skip school for nearly a week."

"I told you why—"

"And what did I tell you?"

I nodded, though my irritation with him had begun to show. "It wasn't my fault this time."

"Nothing ever is." He brought his mug to his lips as he breezed past me. "You can't afford to miss another day."

A bulb turned on over my head right then. "That's what I've been trying to tell you. Apparently, Principal Singh has a zero-tolerance policy for truant students. I found out that she's already placed me in the mandatory buddy system."

Presley's eyebrows furrowed. "What are you talking about?"

"A cruel and unusual punishment." I avoided contact with him as I walked back over to the bedroom, shaking my head for emphasis of my feigned distress. "First, I'm practically forced to be supervised by the student body president, and now this…"

"Come now. What is this buddy system you're talking about?"

I sighed, leaning against the door post. "I'm to be picked up by the student body president of our school from now on. Apparently, it's a carpool system that Principal Singh reinforces for students with five inexcusable absences."

Presley appeared stumped, though those brows only tightened further with confusion. "She didn't mention any of this on the phone."

I swallowed. "I don't think it requires parental consent…"

"That's got to be inconvenient for—"

"He volunteers," I quickly added.

His eyelids swooped down as he studied me. "The student body president is a boy?"

"You're the reason why she's treating me this way," I unleashed on him all of a sudden. "You're the one who told her everything about me. She told me how you said her school was the last resort and how no other school would take me!"

"Stop," he bit back, single handedly bringing me down a notch, frustration in his tone. "I don't have time for this right now. Just make sure you show up for school, Elonie."

I wanted to ask, *or what?* But I knew what the answer would be even if he wouldn't admit it. Presley had never been the type to show his emotions. Not like mom had. He'd always been the extreme opposite. He bottled everything up and left you stranded, alone, in the dark corners of your mind. It'd been a feeling I'd never wished on anyone.

Not even the worst of my enemies.

I took delight in the fact that I'd gotten away with the story I'd told him. Being a lawyer, he'd always been hard to fool. Not that I thought I'd actually fooled him. No, there seemed to be another reason why he'd decided to believe me. A more dire reason. I didn't have to be a lawyer myself to know exactly who filled that blank space. But I didn't care. Let him have his little family who lived at the top of the penthouse. I'd already decided to create a family of my own.

I stood at the end of the narrow path leading up to Presley's house, slightly shivering in olive corduroy slacks and a thinly knitted brown cardigan, though that quickly subsided once I noticed his truck heading down towards me.

Little remnants from that day came back into my head like photographs. Jean, sitting underneath that tree, me rested against the window, both of us talking until the sky had turned a pretty lavender shade. Then he'd told me he'd only stay longer if I let him inside. I'd known he'd been joking, but now I'd wished I'd actually had the courage to do it.

My fingers untangled from each other as the truck reached me, and right away, his blue eyes pulled me in.

I had made a plan, as I'd gotten dressed, to remain cool this time. I would go out and wait for him to pull up to the curb. I wouldn't get flustered by his smile, nor would I freeze up from those daggers she always had in her eyes. I'd simply take a deep breath and get in.

But they couldn't make it easy for me. Not even just this once.

"Hey, girl."

Those two words comforted me more than the warmest blanket. I no longer felt the chill in the air as I'd climbed into the safe haven of the back seat. I only felt the thump of my heart loud in my ears. Only in that moment had I realized that I'd missed them. The weekend had suddenly seemed too long, and I began wondering how I would continue to withstand it. That had been until I'd noticed the scars on Brynn's neck. I could tell the fresh ones from the older ones. But still, I'd never seen so many in a spot like that before. My mind had immediately sprouted with unspoken questions.

Why had she done it this time? What had made her so uncomfortable she'd had to scratch that deep? And why had she chosen to display them for all the world to see?

I wondered. So much so that I had completely spaced out. Entering the trappings of my mind. No one talked. No one said a thing. To me or each other. We drove the streets in stark silence, each of us no doubt curious about each other's thoughts but unsure of how to proceed.

The weekend had been too long. I could tell so much had happened, but I really wanted to know.

I wanted to know them.

Jean pulled his truck into the parking lot of a café that I noticed sat in the same vicinity as Brynn's complex. More questions sat on my tongue as the sound of Presley's rigid tone echoed in my ears. But I let those questions rest there on the tip, instead following in their footsteps towards one of several bistro tables out in front of the small café.

"Sit," Jean said to me, having noticed me taking in our dilemma—a single pair of chairs situated at the wicker table. "I'll go order something."

Before I could protest, he'd taken off, leaving me in suspension with my eyes lingering on Brynn. She'd already seated herself, both her hands tucked in the pockets of her jacket and her attention focused on anything but me. I felt my eyes flutter a bit as I finally lowered to the other empty chair. She seemed annoyed at that as she turned her head and released a quiet sigh past her fairly chapped lips.

I forced my gaze elsewhere. Hearing the sounds of tires as cars passed behind us along the street. Then, the faint rustle of a few abandoned leaves being scattered by the wind into the dewy grass. But sure enough, my stare returned to Brynn, and mentally, I geared up the courage to say something.

Anything.

"I like your beauty mark." I raised my frail arm and gave the decently sized dot adorning her cheekbone a point. "I always thought ones like that were only used as props in movies."

Brynn only licked her lips and squinted her eyes as she continued staring off into the distance. I stabbed my tongue into my cheek, lowering my eyes to my arms folded on the table.

"I really feel bad for not trusting you about Danielle."

She finally glanced across the table at me. "You don't know me enough to trust me."

"Still," I continued. "I get it now."

"Do you?"

I would have been forever trapped in her hard glare had Jean not made his return to our stoic little table right then. Grabbing a nearby wicker chair and plopping down onto it. I tore my eyes away from Brynn and over to him, watching as he plucked the cigarette wedged behind his ear.

"So." He twisted it between his fingers, glancing in her direction first. "What did I miss, Brynn?"

"Not much," she muttered on a heavier sigh.

"Really? All that time and nothing…"

Sometimes I just couldn't control it. The word vomit just forced its way out.

"Brynn had warned me about Danielle," the words toppled out. "I was just apologizing for—"

"It wasn't a warning," Brynn lightly rebutted.

"Are you worried about her, Elonie?" Jean suddenly asked.

I felt put on the spot, quickly regretting bringing up the topic now. "No, I'm not worried."

"You still are." He rocked back on his chair, arms folded across his chest. "But you shouldn't be."

I noticed blurry movement in my peripheral, but the sight of Jean finally lighting that cigarette he'd been holding onto kept my attention. Again, I thought back to our conversation at the window. He'd definitely spent a great deal of time making me feel better about the entire situation. I could tell how it bothered him that I still lost sleep over it.

"Three cappuccinos," The barista had reached our table, placing the mugs down with a stack of white saucers. "And one warm blueberry muffin."

My eyes followed the plate with the muffin as she set it down in the center of the table. Confusion masking my face.

"Blueberry?" Brynn beat me to the punch, though her question hadn't been the one that had muddled my mind.

"It's for Elonie," he said, leaning up to the table slipping his hand around his mug. "Since she's the only one who eats."

His words further perplexed me. "What do you mean?"

"It's a joke," Brynn cut in with insistence in her tone.

Jean nodded and brought the coffee to his smirking lips. Brynn mirrored his movements. But I still sat there with a deer-in-headlights expression, no doubt. He finally reached for the plate with the muffin and slowly slid it in front of me.

"Try it," he said.

"I-I don't understand."

He dug his fingers in and broke a piece off the edge. "They make them fresh every morning."

My eyes switched between his face and his hand, unsure of what to do or what any of it meant. Why weren't they eating, too? I shook my head and gently pushed the plate away with my fingers. "I'm fine."

"Come on. You must be hungry."

I heard a spark and shifted my eyes over to Brynn, who currently lit the cigarette in between her lips. Her hand curled over the end to combat the breeze. My eyes focused on the orange ember at the end of the stick as she sucked in a breath and slowly exhaled. Suddenly, I heard my own breath loud in my ear.

"Elonie," Jean's gripping tone shattered my trance.

I quickly looked back over at him, noticing he wore somewhat of a grin on his face. The strangest thing.

"Do you want one?"

"One what?"

He chuckled and quickly reached into his jacket pocket, pulling out a pack. I watched him slip out one of the sticks and hold it out towards me.

"It'll hold you over until lunch." He slightly wiggled it between his fingers. "Go ahead. Take it."

I hadn't been able to stop my hand from reaching for it. It had happened so fast. His voice did that. Before I knew it, I'd slipped it between my lips, gazing down while Jean cupped the end for me.

The fondest memory hit me as soon as the smoke reached my throat. I immediately choked and found myself coughing belligerently. The same thing had happened that time, too. I could see my mom's face behind my closed eyes…felt her hand rubbing my back…heard her bright, airy laugh…

"Relax," Jean said, though he sounded a lot like mom now. "It'll pass…"

I nodded, opening my eyes bringing it up for a second go. This time, it went down easier, and I exhaled it smoothly past my lips.

"Good," Jean said as he shoved the box back into his pocket and took a quick drag himself. "You're a natural…like Brynn."

I could feel the corners of my mouth tug as I looked over at the girl who sat with her chin propped on her palm, smoke trailing from her still-burning cigarette. She wore just the opposite of a smile on her face, and I looked away again.

"Are we going to school?" I asked Jean.

He laughed a bit. "You sure you're ready to go back there?"

I shrugged and let out a sigh. "It's now or never."

He seemed to understand what I meant without me needing to say more. We soon finished our coffees and piled back into his truck, heading to that place we all despised. But I could tolerate it better knowing that I could walk in with Jean and Brynn without getting harassed this time. I had managed to fully sever whatever I'd had with Danielle. But I still had to face the consequences of my actions. I'd attempted to run from them by staying away, only realizing I'd only managed to prolong the inevitable. And now I would have to face it head-on.

"Hi," I greeted the woman behind the desk once all three of us had walked into the front office. "I'm supposed to meet with Principal Singh about my absences."

The woman wore the type of reading glasses with a crystal beaded chain, and they dangled as she lowered them down her nose. "What is your name?"

"Elonie Davis," I replied.

"Take a seat, Elonie. I'll let her know that you're here." Then her nut-brown eyes traveled past me and pinned themselves on Jean, who stood slightly off to the side alongside Brynn. "Is there anything I can help you two with?"

I felt Jean's presence before he came up behind me, dropping his hand on my shoulder, his fingers gently pressing into my skin, and the faint leftover scent of his cigarette enveloped me. "Just here to support our new girl, Miss Jenkins."

"Is that really necessary, Mr. Cohen?"

"No," Principal Singh's voice caused my neck to jerk as I looked over, watching as she crossed into the premises of Miss Jenkin's desk area. "It's not at all necessary." I noticed the tension in her posture and the frown settling on her firm features. "Mr. Cohen, remove your hand from this student's shoulder and head to the cafeteria, library, or any other available facility that isn't my front office."

Jean's body straightened, and I felt his hand slip away, leaving a tingly sensation behind. I didn't look back over my shoulder, but I could still feel his heavy gaze as he backed away. Principal Singh didn't move an inch until the front door had closed, the loud sound causing my shoulders to jump, only then did she motion me into her office.

"Please remain standing, Miss Davis. This won't take long," Singh said as she took a seat behind her desk and slipped out a few documents from an ash-gray folder. I watched her pick up a nearby pen and extend it towards me. "I'll need you to sign."

"What am I signing?" I asked right away.

"These are the documents that show your acknowledgement of your mandatory counseling sessions with Mr. Scavelli," she explained as she placed the pen on top of the papers. "Scheduled to begin this afternoon."

I hugged myself, becoming more uncomfortable as I stood there listening to her. "Mandatory counseling? Isn't that unethical?"

"I'm afraid it's either this or a two-week in-school suspension," Singh continued, fingers entwined on her desk. "Truancy is simply impermissible at my school, Elonie."

My throat dried upon hearing the alternative option. Two weeks without ever seeing Jean? I shivered at the thought. "How long would I have to go?"

"Mr. Scavelli has recommended you see him three times a week to start. You can do this during your leisure period."

"Three times a week?"

"For the remainder of the school term."

My head shook without my say. Overwhelming emotions toppling one after another. Threatening to consume me.

"You seem disturbed to hear this," Singh said as she slowly rose from her seat. "But it's no different than the therapy you receive in the city, isn't it?"

And there she appeared.

The mean-girl-turned-woman in the flesh.

Now she knew everything about me, and she had all she needed to use against me. But I noticed something settled onto her face. Something vague. I couldn't quite place it yet.

Still, I raised my chest and forced my chin up in protest. "I'll need to talk it over with my father."

I could tell she disliked my sudden audacity to undermine her, and I watched as she finally stood to her full height. "I've failed to mention the amount of zeroes you seemed to have accumulated during your days of absence." She then leaned over her desk and pushed the paper towards me with her finger. "Which will all remain unexcused unless you take the route I'm offering you."

That vagueness had become not so vague anymore. Her determination had become more evident. She craved my obedience. She needed this to go her way. But why? What did it mean to her if I attended counseling or not? Or maybe none of this had been about me at all. Maybe I hadn't looked at the bigger, more obvious picture.

Regardless, I had nothing else left to plead my case. Presley would be livid if I jeopardized this fresh start. I knew I couldn't afford any failing grades. So, I signed away. Feeling as though I'd sold my soul for the second time.

I watched as she plucked the paper up and slipped it back into my file, a cold sweat breaking across my neck. "Am I free to go?"

"You may."

I swiftly turned and headed for the door, but as soon as my fingertips grazed the handle, she spoke my name. I slightly turned towards her again.

"You remember what I told you about Jean Cohen, correct?"

I nodded yes.

"Good. Do your best not to forget."

It felt like dejavu as I walked away from her front office and made my way down the hallway. Except this time, I walked alone... without Danielle... but still harboring that same unsettling feeling inside. I couldn't face Jean. Not right now. I knew he must have messaged me. I could feel the weight of the text in my cardigan pocket. But I couldn't meet up with them without being reminded of how I'd failed again. I hid out in the library as I'd done before. But nothing could distract me from what I knew I would inevitably have to face. And soon enough, the bell rang, alerting me that the time had come.

I arrived to French class before anyone else had. Taking my seat after greeting Madame Etienne, busying myself with removing my supplies from my knapsack so I wouldn't have to watch my classmates come pouring in. But my hyper-focused nosedive into my textbook did nothing to repel Jean from walking over and lowering to a squat below my desk.

"Singh had enough of your face yet?" he teased, gripping the edge of the desk as he glanced up at me. "How pissed off was she?"

"Extremely," I replied.

"Don't let her scare you."

I swallowed, refusing to make eye contact with him.

"Hey," He brought his arm across the book, blocking my view, forcing me to finally look down at him. His eyes already held so many questions, but he asked only one: "Ce qui s'est passé?"

My lips parted, but no words came out. He noticed my hesitation, but before he'd had a chance to say anything else, Madame Etienne's delicate tone entered our intimate space.

"Revenez à votre place, s'il vous plaît."

Jean slowly stood to his full height, towering over me now. "D'accord, Madame."

My heart began a wild patter in my chest. My eyes attempted to refocus on the words in my textbook, but everything suddenly looked dizzy. Madame Etienne's continued greetings were foggy—in and out.

Why had I signed that stupid paper?

Presley.

I could see him now, staring at me with disappointment, just like the day he'd found out everything I'd done. I shut my eyes, but he still appeared.

Why, Elonie?

Why do you do these things?

Why do you always get yourself into trouble?

I knew how much he resented me. She and I… we were too much alike. And every time I screwed up, I reminded him of her. Every time, I just couldn't seem to do right. I didn't blame him for seeing her when he looked at me. I felt I had already become her in so many ways…

"Prenez vos places," Madame Etienne's voice slowly seeped back in. "Hurry everyone, take your seats."

I rested my head on my palm, forcing my eyes to remain fixed on my teacher's face. Except I didn't really feel that weighted sensation piercing my skull like I had before. It made me wonder… My eyes shifted to the floor then, cautiously, I glanced across the classroom. I'd been right. Madame Etienne held Jean's attention. Not me. My eyes quickly shot back over to her just in time to hear today's assignment slipping past her stained red lips.

"I'll begin the pairing…"

Of course. How could I have forgotten? Our weekly conversation assignment. I looked around the classroom as she began calling out names, watching each of my classmates rise from their seats with the eagerness of a sloth, but that gripping pull—it had returned. Jean and I locked eyes just as she spoke our last names. We were partnered again. It'd been so long since that first and only time. I had begun to think he'd planned it as he made his way over to me. That long gait in more of a rush than our classmates.

"Remember to ask the questions from the given scenario in your textbook," Madame Etienne reminded us, "but you are also free to create your own."

Her voice had slowly begun fading away again as I watched Jean grab the abandoned desk across from me and push it right next to mine. I noticed his attempt to sit closer to me this time. I liked that he wanted to be closer to me. He seemed comfortable around me. Although, I couldn't know this for sure.

Jean had proven to be more difficult to read than anyone else. Normally, I could make out the emotions behind an odd facial expression or spot the underlying meaning of a tone. But Jean perplexed me. He only showed what he wanted to show. But, even then, nothing proved reliable.

Like now.

I thought for sure he'd immediately begin interrogating me with questions. One after the other. Pulling out the truth like a rainbow streamer being pulled out of a magician's hat. But he only sat there, scanning my face as if the answer itself would appear on my forehead. Or maybe I'd been wrong. He lowered his gaze and my eyes followed, watching him take my hand, feeling those tingles spread across my palm as he grazed my skin with the tips of his fingers.

He seemed to have remembered something and chuckled to himself. "Mon mignonne…"

My heart fluttered. I had been wrong. He didn't want an answer. He just wanted my trust. Above everything, he needed me to know that he cared about me—and that I could trust him.

"Jean," His name barely escaped my lips, but I'd gained his attention, "please don't be mad at me."

He fastened his eyebrows tightly. "Mad at you?"

"Remember what you said about rebelling…" I began telling him about the conversation with Principal Singh. His expression remained rested until I mentioned the ultimatum she'd given me. "I want to rebel, but I just can't do it. She's threatening my grades, and I—I just can't risk messing things up again."

Jean glanced towards the front of the room and heavily sighed, breaking our hand hold in order to sift through the textbook. I slowly followed suit. Gripping my pen as I wrote my name in my notebook. I felt him shift again as he cleared his throat. I tried to remain calm as I awaited his response, but my thoughts roamed free in my mind. Torturing me with an endless list of assumptions.

You're a coward.

He's never going to accept you now. You always ruin everything.

"Voulez-vous commencer?"

His low tenor swept the ugly thoughts in my mind away, though the harsh remarks had already trickled out of the corner of my eyes. Hidden behind the hand, I'd quickly brought against my cheek.

"Bonjour," I uttered with a light sniffle. "Comment allez-vous?"

"Pas bon." I felt his gaze return to me. "I don't feel so good."

I watched a teardrop fall onto the page and every word became blurred in my vision. "Pourquoi?"

"Elonie," He quickly filled that small gap between us, though he did not touch me or attempt to soothe me in any way, but I could clearly feel the angst bursting within him. "I really like seeing you."

I looked up, exposing my wet eyes, but too consumed by the words he'd spoken to care. "I like seeing you too."

He reached for my face and quickly brushed a few tears away from my cheek. "Stop crying, alright?"

I nodded. "What am I going to do now, Jean?"

"Go back after class and tell her you want to take the two week in-school and make up the zeroes that way."

I knew I must have appeared floored because he put his hand on my shoulder and said, "trust me," and I did. For some strange reason, I completely trusted him.

24

If I could reverse time, I would relive Paris. Getting rained on while walking back to that little hotel on the corner with the single bed and draped view of the cobblestoned city. Intimate conversations. Him and I. Feeling like we were the only two people in the world…

I'd go back to studying for math tests on my brother's bedroom floor. He would lay sprawled in bed with his own textbook draped across his stomach. Both of us teasing each other relentlessly about frivolous things. Of course, I'd ultimately lose the battle, Ethan always needing to have the last word. On the rare occasions that we did argue, we would go for hours, sometimes days, but we could never stay mad at one another for too long. He'd cave. We'd walk to the parlor down the street and he'd buy me mint chip as an apology. (Sometimes, I'd even cave first and treat him to a movie in town with money from our allowance). We were always taught to fight fair and never to hold a grudge. God can't forgive those who can't forgive, our mother would always say.

If only I could…I would go way back.

Back to the beginning of sophomore year. Back to my innocence. Back to that night so that I could make it all better. Ethan would be here…teasing and laughing…still having the last word.

I stood in front of the picture window of the hotel room. Gazing out at the dark city with all of its different lights. Remembering how much I'd enjoyed coming here with Ethan. Usually, on days when mom would need her nails done or jet out for a day of retail therapy. Everyone knew the shops were way better in the city. But Ethan and I would escape from the monotonous routine of shuffling in and out of boutiques and jump in a cab towards the nearest record store or art gallery. We'd stay gone for hours. And mom never seemed to mind. Secretly, she'd needed it, too. Space. A little time to herself. A breather from us kids.

But all of that had changed.

My mom could no longer do anything alone. She had become fully dependent on whoever happened to be nearby. I knew I didn't deserve to be irritated by it. Again, I'd caused all of this. But I couldn't understand why she'd wanted to come here—of all places. And, moreover, why she'd felt the need to bring her.

I turned away from the window and walked back over to the queen bed my mother and I were now meant to share. But my glare remained fixed on that woman. The woman who'd felt it appropriate to accept an invitation to a family affair. The woman who donned the ugliest flannel pajamas and had already made herself quite comfortable underneath the heap of white bedding next to us. That woman who my mom had, for no apparent reason, grown very fond of in only a short time.

I didn't understand it. This sort of thing would have never happened before. She barely knew this lady, yet she said her name as if they'd always been the best of friends.

"Angela," my mom spoke again as she stepped out in a frost-white robe that hung to the floor. "Are you sure you won't join us at the spa?"

I crossed my arms over my identical robe and challenged her with my expression, noticing how she attempted to avoid my eyes.

"I'm sure, Sierra." Angela's smile grew despite the tension I knew she felt from me. "Today has left me completely pooped—in a good way." She laughed, and my mom grinned. "I don't think I've ever explored the city like that in the fifteen years I've lived here."

"It still amazes me how you moved here on your own at seventeen." My mom shook her head as she took off the diamond studs tucked in her ear lobes. "We would have had a fit if either one of the kids…"

I quickly pushed up from the bed and headed to the spot where I'd left my slippers, quickly shuffling into them before grabbing my cell phone on the nightstand. The whole point of this impromptu stay in the city had been to help take her mind off of Ethan, and here, this woman had her bringing him up again. My father had basically forced me to come here with her after the fiasco at church. He felt it would do me some good as well. But so far, this entire visit only managed to make me feel worse. It'd been the first time that I stayed with her as she did her usual shopping. No Ethan here to whisk me away and all.

I got the matching French tips and entertained a couple of spring dresses she'd picked out for me from the racks, but, all the while, I missed him. I didn't belong there. Shopping with my mom. I belonged in some grunge record shop with a marijuana stench, sifting through old blues and soul albums stuffed in milk crates. I belonged in a bright white studio, giggling while Ethan pretended to critique people's so-called masterpieces, only to always find myself later gripped by one special piece out of all the rest. One that truly spoke to me.

"I'm ready," I announced at my position in front of the door. "Let's go down before it gets too late."

"I'm coming, I'm coming." My mother gently laughed but it only made me more annoyed as she continued moving at a snail's pace. "I just wish Angela could join us, that's all. You've been in a little mood all day. Don't think I haven't noticed."

A heat wave flushed my skin, and I grew hot underneath the thick terry cloth. I didn't respond to her. What could I say? She hadn't been wrong. But I didn't like feeling embarrassed in front of Angela, of all people. My eyes glanced over to the woman now, but she had completely checked out. Something else holding her attention now and that something instantly made me cringe.

"I'll go wait in the lobby," I said before yanking the door handle and leaving out.

I took the elevator, attempting to calm down, though the tugging sensations at my heart wouldn't let up. I finally made it into the hotel's lobby and took a seat, suddenly very unaware of my current state of dress and more consumed with that last image in my mind. Angela sat up against her pillow, wearing a pair of glasses that I hadn't even seen her put on and reading from a leather bound Bible spread across her lap.

My fingernails dug into my wrist.

My throat bone-dry.

Suddenly. Another image. Ethan, sitting up in bed, nothing but the desk lamp on. Every night before we went to sleep, he'd read aloud, and I'd sit there on his floor and listen. Every single night since we were little.

He would read it out loud.

"Brynn," my mother's voice dissolved the glue that had me stuck in place and I immediately stood to my feet again, noticing the expression she wore appeared less than pleased. "Brynn Clarise Walsh, that was incredibly rude of you. You should be ashamed of leaving your mother like that."

"Me?" I argued my defense. "You embarrassed me in front of that woman—"

"That woman? God, where has my daughter's manners gone?" My mother glanced around the lobby as she fussed with the strap of her robe, eyebrows strewn together tightly. "Well, there's no use causing a scene about it."

She began walking towards the direction of the salon, and I dragged my feet as I followed behind, knowing it meant the conversation would not be revisited tonight.

Unfair.

All of this.

I hadn't even wanted to come to the city. I would have much preferred to be doing anything else but gallivanting around, pretending everything in our lives had suddenly gone back to normal. I know it's what her therapist wanted. I know it's what they both desperately wanted. But it would never happen. My mom would never be able to fully heal until she knew the truth, and my dad would never be able to comfort her like he wanted to until he told her the secret we'd been keeping from her. And none of that could happen until I disappeared. Forever. Just like Jean had promised we would.

As soon as I closed my eyes—forcing myself to relax as the masseuse kneaded her fingers into my deeply knotted skin—I saw his face. His dark blue eyes were lidded sleepy-looking, similar to how he'd looked in Paris. I could feel his fingers in my hair, massaging my scalp, comforting me as he often did. I could hear him asking me again. That four-word question.

What do you want?

And I remembered what I'd told him. First them, then me.

It hurt to think about how convinced I'd been. After hearing about his fantasies…hearing about his plans to do the same… I'd been so sure that had been what I'd wanted, too. And he'd supported my decision. But I didn't want to do that anymore. I didn't want to hurt my parents. Maybe Jean's parents deserved to die, but mine did not. I now knew what would fix everything. But each day that dragged on only reminded me that I couldn't. At least, not yet. Jean wanted me to wait until he could be sure I would not change my mind. It's what he'd told me on the plane ride home. Squeezing my hand and making me promise I wouldn't try anything when we got back. And I hadn't. I'd kept that promise. No matter how strong those urges had hit me in those first couple of weeks of school, I'd resisted. I'd smoked my cigarettes and kept to myself and resisted those awful feelings I woke up with every morning and went to sleep with every night.

But I couldn't last for much longer. Jean knew this. I'd brought it up to him again before I left for the city, though that had proved to be a huge mistake. Jean had a fragile heart, and it had taken a little while for me to understand just how fragile. It hadn't been until he'd told me about his childhood that I fully comprehended how deeply scarred he'd become from the constant pain he'd suffered by their hands. And he'd showed me those scars. His hurt. Something he'd never shown to anyone else. He'd trusted me with that, but sometimes, I made mistakes. Sometimes, I became selfish and overwhelmed by my own hurt. My own pain. I threw it on him, expecting him to make it go away, not realizing that he still had his own demons. And I saw those demons every time he got angry with me. I saw them in his eyes. Heard them in his voice. Felt them in his touch. He became a different person. A person who wanted to hurt me as much as I'd hurt him. A person who wanted me to feel his pain, too. He used to get mad when I wouldn't fight back. I'd never wanted to hurt Jean. But he needed that reciprocation. He used to beg for it. Telling me how it made him feel—like I actually cared about him—and I'd wanted him to know how badly I did. It no longer confused me to see those marks on him afterwards. I knew what they meant to him. I knew how comforting and familiar they were. But it still saddened me to do it. It hurt me to hurt him in any way.

YOU DID NOTHING TO DESERVE WHAT HE DID TO YOU!

I flinched away from the booming voice in my head and let out the loudest yelp, instantly feeling the kneading hands leave my body. A concerned tone filled the once-relaxed atmosphere.

"Brynn—"

I rushed off of the platform and grabbed my robe from the hook, ignoring my mother's frantic calls. I ran out of the room and into the hall, where a gust of air slapped me, and I stumbled against the wall with closed eyes. No longer able to fight the voice that continued to scream at me. The voice that undoubtedly belonged to Ethan.

"Sweetie," my mother's voice floated down to me. "What's wrong? Tell me what happened—"

I only sobbed.

More feet shuffled around me. More voices that I didn't recognize.

TELL HER, BRYNN, TELL HER WHAT HE DOES TO YOU!

"No!" I screamed back, tears streaming down my face. "No, I can't, I can't." I curled away from my mother's hands as she attempted to console me. "She wouldn't understand."

"Sweetie, who?" My mother nearly sounded as if she were crying now. "Who wouldn't understand?"

I shook my head and pressed my forehead to the cold floor. "He talks to me..." My voice trickled out in a whisper. "He..."

"Please, honey, let's get you up." She began pleading with me as she wrapped her arm around my shoulders. "Let's get you back to the room. How does that sound?"

"How does that sound?" I laughed aloud at the irony as I pulled away from her. "God, mom, now you're embarrassed of me?"

"No, sweetie, no, I'm not. I'm just trying to help."

I rolled my eyes behind my closed eyelids, sniffling back tears, memories of my mom getting into that tub surfacing. I felt the pit of my stomach churn.

BRYNN!

I shook my head and began pushing myself up from the floor. "Leave me alone, Ethan."

I refused to be escorted into the elevator. I walked across the lobby and entered alongside my mom. Vowing to remain silent. No matter how many questions she asked on the way up. But she didn't ask anything. She only held me as I leaned against the metal walls, hobbled down the hallway, and into our hotel room. She finally let me go and I shut them out, sitting on the other side of the bathroom door with the shower water running. Wondering what my mother would tell him when we returned home, eventually feeling too exhausted to care, not realizing that I had nodded off on the cold tile until a hard knock from the other side stirred me.

"Jean," I gasped, only to quickly realize my surroundings and become disappointed all over again.

"Brynn?"

That voice. It didn't belong to my mother. It belonged to her. Angela.

"What?" I muttered.

"You plan on coming out anytime soon?"

"No," I huffed.

"Your mother cried herself to sleep hours ago. You're basically in the clear."

"What makes you think I'm only avoiding her?"

"You're not fooling me. I know you could care less about what I think."

I sighed and pushed up from the floor, walking over to the shower and finally cutting the water off. Then I turned and faced the door. "I'm avoiding this. The heart-to-heart you're attempting to have with me. Except I never asked for your opinion."

"I'm not trying to give it."

"Really?" I chuckled mirthlessly. "It sure seems like it to me."

"I care about your mother—"

"You don't even know my mother," I actually laughed with disbelief this time. "You only know the reincarnated version of her."

"You didn't let me finish—"

"Because I don't want you to finish. I don't want to hear anything else from you. I don't want to hear anything else from anyone!" I gripped my hair and closed my eyes. "I just want to be left alone."

A long, silent pause passed between us. I had begun to think I'd successfully scared her off until she spoke up again.

"He heals the brokenhearted and binds up their wounds," Angela said, her voice as gentle as a kiss and as soft as a dove. "Psalm one forty-seven, verse three."

My insides began that slow churn again, but in a different way, and I slowly lowered down to a curled squat. "No, not for me. Not this time…"

I had hoped she hadn't heard me, and maybe she had or maybe she hadn't, but she didn't say another word except goodnight, and I listened to her footsteps as she walked away.

25

I had done it again.

Or, rather, I could feel myself doing it again.

Reverting.

Becoming bad.

Going against better judgment and acting only on selfish desire.

I wanted Jean.

I wanted Jean like I'd wanted Cole. Maybe even more than I'd wanted Cole. A lot more than I'd wanted Cole.

I remembered how easy it'd been to learn Cole. His likes. His dislikes. Interests, hobbies, favorite places to go in the city. Slowly, I became those things. I liked the things he liked. I disliked the things he disliked. I became interested in his interests and took on some of his hobbies—even popped up at the places he frequented in the city.

And he hadn't noticed at all.

Too preoccupied with the sugar-sweet smile I'd often given him. Cole had fallen for those types of things. And I had even begun to notice that Liam had, too.

Liam had fallen for me.

It's not something he'd admitted aloud. But he hadn't needed to. He'd told me with those brown eyes. Those eyes that normally looked at me with warmth and intrigue. Until yesterday. Our first fight. Not sure if I could even call it a fight. But we'd spent the remainder of study hall in stark silence. I had continued to feel his glances, but he never bit the bullet. Not once did he give in. It frustrated me to know that I'd made him that upset. Even now as I thought back to that short but intense conversation between us, I regretted some things I'd said. But I didn't regret defending Jean. It'd felt like it'd been my duty to stick up for him. Especially given all he'd done for me.

Jean's advice had worked.

I'm not sure why, but it had. It turned out Principal Singh had been bluffing. She'd visibly appeared taken aback when I'd returned to her office and voiced my demand. Jean had said to do it with as much confidence as I could muster in my tone. Don't back down, he'd said. And I hadn't. For the first time, I'd approached someone with complete confidence and a cool head. She'd attempted to coerce me into choosing therapy like Jean said she would, but I remained insistent. I told her that she couldn't make me attend and when she found no loophole with that, I went on to mention the agreement she'd made with Presley.

"Two weeks of in-school suspension would definitely make him doubt your history with rehabilitating difficult pupils," I'd iterated, remembering how Danielle had sat with knees crossed and proceeded to mimic that posture. "I mean, the way he speaks so highly of your reputation…it'd be a shame if he lost trust in your capabilities."

Singh hadn't liked my threat. I could tell by the way her black eyes pierced me, and, for a second, I had almost taken back everything I'd said. But then she'd let me go. Without another word. I didn't know what it meant exactly. Why hadn't she felt the need to respond? I tried not to dwell too much on it. I'd tried to be grateful that I'd gotten out of my consequences. But that final expression on her face spelled bad news. I'd challenged a woman who clearly didn't like to be challenged. I'd still been worried about it as I'd sat in study hall much later, unaware that Liam had entered the room and spoken my name twice. I should've known our conversation wouldn't have gone well. My mind had been preoccupied. I hadn't been interested in anything but seeing Jean and telling him how everything had gone.

But Liam wanted my attention, too.

He'd grown almost dependent on our talks and our lunch meetups. But I couldn't waste any more time with him. I knew what I wanted. By the end of the argument, he did too. And it'd upset him. I think I'd betrayed him, but I didn't know exactly how. Liam had told me to stay away from the Turners, and I'd listened to what he'd said. I'd stayed away. But I didn't understand his problem with Jean. And even when I finally asked him about it, still buzzing with the courage from earlier, he'd offered me the only explanation he had:

"Ethan never liked him."

But I didn't know Ethan. And the fact that his sister despised me didn't exactly make me feel as if he would have liked me either. But, overall, I didn't want to hear no this time. Not from him or anyone.

I wanted what I wanted.

Not Liam.

Jean.

So why couldn't I get those brown eyes out of my head? Why did I want to message him right now and apologize for the things I'd said in anger? Why did I still need his forgiveness?

These questions went unanswered as I sat at the large oak table in the kitchen. Head bent over a fresh novel. Waiting for the doorbell to break the overwhelming silence and tame the chaos in my mind. Presley had stayed in the city again. This made two weekends in a row that he'd decided to spend time there. Probably keeping himself busy to avoid me. Or possibly attending doctor checkups with the mom-to-be. I still hadn't met her. But I had looked her up for the first time last night.

Curiosity.

I scrolled through pages of images, seated at Presley's desk, the bright white of the computer glowing against my face.

She looked nothing like mom.

Her curls stopped just before her chin, and her dark eyes were way too far apart. She stood much taller than mom had. Much skinnier, too. Hiding that baby bump from paparazzi would definitely be a task. She didn't seem to be anyone special. Not an actress or a singer. Her parents were socialites, and she grew up filthy rich.

Again, nothing like my mother.

I'd stopped scrolling when I found a picture of Presley rushing down the courthouse steps with her in tow. Both donning the darkest pair of shades. I stared at that picture, taken only a couple months ago, until my eyes began to droop and my head grew heavy.

It hadn't been a pretty sight to wake up to, that's for sure.

My cell phone finally vibrated next to my book, and I quickly snatched it up.

Come outside

My heart fluttered as I shoved my book away, standing to my feet and grabbing up the sweater hanging off the back of the chair. But I calmed down once I got outside. Taking the stairs with poise and walking the pathway carefully to avoid tripping and making a fool of myself. I didn't even look up until I had nearly reached the end. And when I did, Jean stood there, leaned against the door of his truck.

Laughing. Why in the world was he laughing?

"Do you always stare at your feet like that when you walk?" he said to me.

Shoot. He'd seen that?

Of course, he had.

I shrugged to avoid stuttering over my words and walked past him, rounding the front of the truck and getting in on the other side. I secretly rolled my eyes at myself as I strapped in, feeling the vehicle shake as he followed suit. It felt odd sitting up front like this. Knowing that—

"There's no reason to be nervous."

He faced me, and I couldn't keep myself from meeting his gaze. "Why not?"

"Because we're not doing anything wrong." He cocked his head slightly. "Are we?"

I thought about it. Staring at the question lingering in his eyes. Feeling an ache in the pit of my stomach that didn't quite agree with his words. But I knew I couldn't tell him how I really felt. "I guess not."

He tugged in his bottom lip as he smiled, facing forward again. "Where should we go first?"

"How should I know?"

"You liked the pond, didn't you?"

I nodded with certainty.

"We can go back if you want."

I glanced out of the window. "Can you show me around first?"

I forgot about the stakes as we drove through town. Rolling the window down and letting the breeze tousle my curls. A certain warmth replaced that unsettling feeling from before, and I finally allowed myself to relax. Breathing in the afternoon air that smelled of pine trees and the aftermath of a rain shower. I could have gotten out and walked if Jean hadn't been speeding down the wet gravel so fast. But the way he drove excited me. It made me feel wild and free.

We passed by the fire station, the local library, and a few churches scattered throughout the town. Jean would sometimes say things, other times, he remained silent. But it all felt good to me. I felt comfortable being with him. Exploring his little town.

Our little town.

For the first time, I felt like I could belong here. As long as I stuck with Jean, I could figure out how to rebel and throw away my cares like he had. I could survive here. I just needed to believe that I could.

We arrived at the pond as the sky began darkening in shade and evening settled in. But Jean didn't immediately get out of the truck, though he cut the engine and the headlights, enveloping us in the burnt orange tint of the setting sun.

"The grass is wet from the rain," he said as he draped his arms over the steering wheel and leaned up. "You still want to sit out there?"

I looked back at the pond. "I don't mind."

"Are you still nervous?" The question caught me off guard. I honestly hadn't thought about Brynn again—at least not until just now. "What if I told you that she knows we're here?"

"It's fine." I searched his eyes. "We're not doing anything wrong."

"C'est mignonne," he said with a chuckle, resting his forehead on the wheel. I glanced back out of the window. "Maybe we should leave then."

"Don't leave, Elonie." He sighed and slowly lifted his head, setting his lazy gaze on me. "I don't want you to leave."

I swallowed.

"I just think it's funny how weird girls are." He rested back against the seat and arched his leg up, throwing his long arm over his hoisted knee. "She's intimidated by you, too."

His words gripped my attention, and I shifted to face him, sinking my shoulder into the seat. "Why would she be intimidated by me?"

"Because she's jealous. She knows that I'm into you."

My eyes lowered to my palms.

"I really like you, Elonie," he added, and it sounded even better, leaving his mouth a second time. "What can I do?"

I rested my head, silently pondering, convinced that anything I could say wouldn't help the situation. But I couldn't keep my feelings at bay this time. No matter how hard I tried. I had to tell him.

"But I like Brynn, too," he continued, causing me to swallow the words back down my throat. "She can be sweet when she wants to be…"

I stared at him as he glanced up, grabbing hold of the coat hanger. The sun had nearly set and we sat in an even darker shade now. Almost completely masked.

"We're missing it," he muttered as if he'd just read my mind.

I fought to tear my eyes away from him only to look forward again, gazing out at the pond that had a sparkly surface now. I unbuckled my seat belt and pushed open the door. I walked towards the water. I sat down. Moments later, he joined me, and we sat there in the wet grass together. Watching the dark orange orb disappear only to be replaced by the glowing white one soon after. By then, he'd completely laid out. Smoking from a cigarette. The smoke floating up towards the scattered stars. I joined him when he tugged my sweater sleeve and pulled me down, handing off the burning stick to me. As I took a few drags, I couldn't help but think that so had Brynn, in this way, exactly like this. But, in so many words, he'd asked me not to care about that. And so I didn't.

"I saw you walk over to the bleachers that day," he said after blowing the last bit of smoke from the cigarette. "You know, the day I text you from Brynn's phone. You had on that brown skirt that rose, kind of, up to your knees."

I knew the exact day he described. How could I forget it?

"Who were you meeting out there?"

I turned from my side onto my back again, staring up at the night sky. "Liam."

"Ackert?"

"We normally—" I suddenly thought about how that tradition might no longer be a thing we did anymore. "I mean, we used to meet up for lunch there."

Jean became silent again. I took a glance at him and noticed nothing, as it had become too dark to pick up on any signs. Not that it made a difference. I couldn't tell what he'd been thinking regardless.

Jean finally chuckled to himself. "I bet he's told you to stay away from me."

"He may have mentioned it," I admitted.

"Well, you clearly don't care about his opinion." He turned on his side now and rested his head on his palm. "What else did he tell you about me?"

I faced him again, too. "Nothing except…"

"Except?"

"Brynn's…" I struggled with how to formulate my next words. "Brynn's brother Ethan didn't really like you."

"That's all he said?" He laughed. "And here I thought it was something bad."

"Why didn't he?" I saw his arm move and assumed he'd started picking at the grass. Immediately, I felt the question had been way too forward. "Never mind, you don't—"

"Ethan Walsh didn't like me because he was intimidated by me," Jean suddenly replied. "Of course, like his sister, he wouldn't dare admit that."

"Why was he intimidated by you?"

"All of those Bible-thumpers are." Jean exhaled and rose up from the grass, sitting with his arms dangling over his knees now. "So self-righteous, yet so in fear of what they don't understand...what their perfection won't allow them to understand."

"Was Ethan..." I joined him in an upright position, tucking my legs beneath me and resting back on one arm. "Was he like the Turners?"

"They're all the same to me."

I wondered what he meant by that. "What don't they understand?" I asked instead.

He seemed to look over his shoulder at me, and I stared at him through the black-blue tint. My chest slowly knotted, and my palms broke out in a sweat—as if my body suddenly knew something that I didn't.

"You know why I like you, Elonie?" his voice held a softer edge as he leaned back on his arms, putting us in such close proximity that I could smell the well-worn scent of his leather jacket. "You let me see your scars. Everyone else here spends all their time pretending they don't have any but me and you. We can't help but feel ours everyday." He then brought his face even closer to mine. "We don't play pretend."

The words sat there on the tip of my tongue. But I didn't dare speak them aloud. Why ruin this moment? He didn't need to know that ever since I could remember, I'd been playing pretend. I used to recite romantic lines from my favorite books or act out dramatic movie scenes in my bedroom. It had been all I could do to feel somewhat normal after mom died. She'd loved the arts, and she'd doused me in everything she'd ever watched or read from an early age. Nothing had been off limits for my little innocent eyes. Presley hadn't liked it, of course. He'd warn her that watching filth would make me grow up too fast. And she would always tell him to relax… I still haven't grown up yet, she'd say.

"What's on your mind?"

Jean pulled me in with his tone, and my eyes fluttered in the dark. "I was just wondering the same thing as you."

"Really?" He chuckled.

"I can never tell."

He sucked in a breath and gently exhaled, warming my cheeks with his breath. "Just thinking of how good you always smell."

I began leaning away but froze at the touch of his skin on mine, his fingers wrapped around my wrist, slowly bringing my arm upward. I could barely see it happening, but I didn't need to. I felt everything. Every goosebump raised. Every hair stood up. He tugged my sleeve up and lowered his nose to the center of my wrist. Inhaling deeply. I couldn't stop the shiver wracking my body.

"Also sweet…"

I pulled away as soon as his lips grazed my skin, clutching my wrist with my other hand.   "Before," I explained, "you said there was nothing to be nervous about because we weren't doing anything wrong, but maybe this is something wrong."

"I don't think it's wrong," he mumbled, though he fell back onto the grass anyway.

I stared out at the pond. Watching it glisten under the moon. Listening closely. The cicadas were out and only growing louder. Like the chaos that, once again, made its home inside of my head.

"We decide what's right or what's wrong, don't we?"

I drew my knees up to my chest, grinding my teeth into my lip as I struggled with an answer. My silence didn't stop him from continuing on as he raised up from the grass again, inching dangerously close to me.

"Elonie," He spoke my name like a warm blanket fresh out of the dryer. His voice brought me comfort, and I turned my head towards it, hanging on by a thread, "do you believe in God?"

My eyes, that had slowly begun to close, quickly widened with surprise. "What?"

"I just want to know what's stopping you from doing what you clearly want to do."

"Brynn—"

"Why do you care so much about what Brynn Walsh thinks?" he cut me off, a slight irk in his tone.

"It's not that—I just—" Panic settled in as memories came back like pictures in a vintage stereoscope.

"She doesn't care about you."

"I know that."

"She only cares about herself. They all do. You don't want that, Elonie, I know you don't. You don't want to be just like the rest of them—all high and mighty and above it."

I stayed silent, but apparently, that hadn't sat well with him as I felt him suddenly shift back. "Or is that what you want? To be a Bible-worshipping freak like them?"

"N-no—"

"Only doing what your God tells you to do. Only believing what He thinks is wrong and right. Never thinking for yourself—"

"No!" I pushed up from the grass and stood to my feet. "You don't understand. My mom got away—she—she wanted to leave all of that behind. She knew they'd be ashamed of her if—"

I only saw the blackness behind my eyelids as I held myself tightly with my own arms. So tight that I didn't even notice when a firmer pair wrapped around me. Pulling me towards a warm body that had the power to calm my shaking core. With just a touch, I completely fell apart and succumbed to Jean's embrace.

"Come on," he muttered into my hair, gripping me tighter with those hands. "I'll take you home."

I sat in the passenger seat again. Although, this time, the excitement I'd felt earlier had completely vanished, and, in its place, a solemn heaviness settled throughout the truck.

The word vomit…it'd completely taken over this time. I hadn't meant to tell him those things. I don't know why I'd said all of that. I hid my face, sickened by my behavior and wayward emotions. I hadn't wanted Jean to see me like this again. Reactive. Unable to control what came out of me. I knew he'd silently made his judgment this time. He no longer wanted anything to do with me. He wanted me gone. Out of his sight. I should have known it would come sooner or later. I had always been too much for people. And no matter how much I attempted to hide it, I always ended up showing the worst parts of myself. Scaring away anyone who ever dared to get close to me.

Exactly like mom.

But now I wished, for the first time in my life, that I could be nothing like her.

"Elonie—"

"I'm sorry, Jean," I spoke softly.

We sat in front of my house, and I continued staring out of the window, watching that huge tree outside of my bedroom, yearning to escape into its ominous limbs. The heat from his palm caused me to blink away from the dark scenery, and involuntarily, my head turned towards him. My heart galloped beneath my chest as that palm of his gently tightened on the back of my neck. The tips of his fingers became tangled in the curls that lined my nape, refusing to let go.

"Tu veux toujours m'embrasser?" he asked.

The question floated through the air between us. Breaking through that tension. Shattering it. But I hesitated. Reading the features that seemed almost amplified against the dark backdrop but revealed again in the dim orange tint of the overhead light. What did I read? Will. I saw it in his clenched jaw and unfaltering stare. I felt it in his persuasive touch. That overwhelming will drew me in more than ever before. The last ounce of self-control I still had suddenly fled from me.

And then I did it.

I kissed Jean Cohen.

26

It'd been weeks since I last heard Ethan's voice. I thought it would be nice to finally have him gone, but for some reason, I couldn't sleep again. Not that I'd really been able to before. But this felt more agonizing. I didn't understand what had happened.

Had I officially gone crazy?

I felt crazy. But maybe this all came with the territory. Dr. Patel had warned about this sort of thing happening. That had been the first and last session I'd gone to after Ethan passed away. I couldn't stand talking about him out loud as if he weren't still here. Haunting me. Not yet with his voice, but with the last words that we'd spoken to each other. The short-lived argument that I prayed every night about while he lay hooked up to monitors. I'd asked so many times for forgiveness and vowed never to fight with him again if only He'd wake my brother up.

But it never happened.

I should have known it wouldn't have been that easy. No amount of prayer could have reversed what I'd done to Ethan. I'd had to find another way to make things right. And no one could change my mind about it. Especially not Angela Pacino.

"Try a bit," she said, sliding a plate towards me from her position behind the island. "You know you want to."

I had been on my way outside to sit on the terrace and wait for Jean to show. He'd been late picking me up for the past several weeks. I knew why but chose to keep my comments to myself when I'd noticed Elonie sitting comfortably in the back seat that first day. I didn't need an explanation, after all. It had become obvious she wouldn't be going anywhere anytime soon. And I'd been left with the difficult task of getting over it. But I had only realized how difficult that would be once the lateness began. Then the lunch hangs. Then, the long drives home.

"That looks disgusting," I replied, staring down at an English muffin coated in hollandaise sauce.

"Your mom loves it," Angela leaned on the counter edge and flashed that amused grin I'd grown to abhor. "It's one of her favorites."

I returned a sarcastic smile, continuing my journey past the kitchen, only to be halted once again by her nail-scratching voice.

"Did she tell you about the Bible study?"

I rolled my eyes. Unable to help it. She honestly irked me that much. "No, she didn't."

"We're having one this evening. Nothing fancy, just the two of us. But we were hoping you'd join in."

"Even if I wanted to join in, which I don't, you can stop pretending like she actually wants me there when I know she doesn't." I crossed my arms. "Especially not after what happened in the city."

"But she does want you there," Angela moved out from behind the counter and stood at the end with one palm holding her weight on the surface. "I would never side step your mom. We were discussing John at our last one, and she told me about a scripture you used to like—"

"Shut up," I snapped, and her dark eyes widened, making my face hot with embarrassment. "She-she shouldn't be telling you anything."

"Brynn—"

My phone began to vibrate.

"I have to go," was all I said before racing out into the comfort of the elevator, wanting to erase that upset look on her face from my mind.

Jean waited in the driveway outside, and I couldn't have been happier to see him—though the emotion quickly subsided once I realized Elonie. She sat in the passenger seat. My seat. Immediately, the anger from moments ago began to simmer within me again. I yanked the truck door and threw myself into the back seat, all the while keeping a sharp glare on the back of their heads.

"Relax," Jean said to me.

But I couldn't possibly relax. Not when I felt as though I could literally burst into a million pieces, and nobody would even bat an eye. I had a lump as big as a boulder in my throat, and I knew if I let even a single tear drip down my cheek, there'd be hell to pay. So I focused on anything but the hushed tone she spoke to him in... the occasional laugh that drifted into the backseat...the fact that my presence suddenly didn't matter to him at all...

He only saw Elonie.

Cupping her mouth as, she laughed a little too hard at something he'd said. Half of her face hidden by her rambunctious hair, but I could see just enough to tell that she looked happy. Happier than she'd looked since arriving at our depressing little town. But she didn't get to just trample in and steal it all for herself. No, I wouldn't let her have him all to herself.

"Does she know?" suddenly, I asked.

The question had been a success. I'd completely grabbed their attention. I stood front and center now.

Jean looked back through the rear view mirror, a slight twitch jumping in his cheekbone. "Does she know what?"

"Our plans," I replied, holding those blue eyes captive. "Just thinking maybe she shouldn't get too comfortable."

"Hey," Jean's voice rose an octave. "What's your problem? Didn't I say relax?"

I nodded, becoming squeamish all of a sudden. His voice did that to me. It'd been happening a lot more lately. I hadn't fully gotten used to its biting tone. I decided I'd let it go for now. Avoiding his gaze the rest of the way to school. But at least I hadn't been victimized by any more of those bubbly laughs.

I escaped the claustrophobic confinement of his truck as soon as we got parked and hung back as we walked towards the school building. Finally, I excused myself as soon as we entered the lobby, making a dash for the nearest bathroom, desperate for a quick breather. I felt drained. Depleted of all energy…like someone who only crept closer and closer towards their demise.

It didn't scare me anymore to think about that final day. We'd dwelled on it together in Paris. Jean had a plan already mapped out. He'd said he'd had it for a while, adding to it here and there, changing small details when necessary. I remembered shuddering while listening to him describe what he wanted to do and how he wanted to do it. He'd made it seem like an art form the way he'd explained it. I'd begun to picture it so vividly in my mind that I'd begged him to stop. I couldn't bear the image any longer. But he'd made it clear that, eventually, I would be able to see the beauty of it all. Eventually…

I stared at my drenched face in the mirror after having splashed it with water from the sink I stood over. Breathe. I repeated the word in my head as I inhaled and exhaled my deep frustrations. Screaming at my reflection would have probably been most ideal. Instead, I could only cringe as I looked away. It had become difficult to see myself after that night. Too many images tended to surface, and they were all ugly. The hidden scars of my pain always attempted to expose me. I knew I would no longer be viewed as perfect in the eyes of my peers anymore. The days of admiration and reverence were long gone. Not that I'd ever truly earned them in the first place. My popularity had been solely based on the family I belonged to.

My father. The town pastor.

My mother. The soft-spoken, well-mannered, southern belle who'd captured not only my father's heart all those years ago but apparently everyone she seemed to come across in life.

And Ethan. My handsome, intelligent, athletic older brother who'd had my mother's kind nature and my father's tenacious spirit. Also, the most grounded teenager anyone had ever met. My brother had been perfect in my eyes. He could do no wrong. He'd honored our mother and respected our father. He'd never cut class, rarely told a lie, and always tried to do the right thing. Everyone had loved him. But I'd loved him more. And I missed him every day.

The sound of a toilet flushing startled me, igniting my frustration again as mental images of my brother's face dissipated, and I looked over my shoulder, cutting my eyes at the person walking out of the big stall at the end. Sophie James staggered in her footsteps upon noticing me. Both green eyes wide as if I were a car with bright headlights and she, the unlucky deer.

My eyes dropped to her hand that she so conveniently pinned behind her back. But it'd been too late. I'd seen the mini bottle filled with that familiar green shade of liquid, and immediately, I'd recognized what she'd been doing all this time behind that bathroom door.

I shook my head and turned to leave.

"W-wait," Sophie said with a hard sniffle. "Um...do you still have...um..."

"I only have ibuprofen from Nurse Miller," I quickly interrupted her, annoyed that we were even having this discussion. "Aren't you better off going to your best friend, the pharmacist? I'm sure she'd have whatever it is you need."

Sophie rotated her jaw, and I watched as crinkles formed on her freckled chin. "She isn't...we aren't friends anymore."

I knew my expression looked surprised because Sophie's face only became more crumbled until she had completely fallen apart, leaking out like a faucet on steroids. I could only stand there and watch as she sobbed into a bundle of paper napkins she'd torn from the dispenser.

Not friends anymore?

Surely, she had to be joking. Sophie and Danielle had been friends before I had even stepped a foot into this high school. Everyone knew they'd been stuck like glue since their freshmen year. Wherever Danielle went, there Sophie was, always right beside her. Like a designer handbag in the crooked arm of a socialite.

"What?" I questioned to gain clarity.

Sophie continued blowing her nose. "She stabbed me in the back."

"Why?"

It's not like I didn't believe her. I knew what Danielle was capable of doing to those who got in her way. But Sophie had never dared to do that. She'd never wanted to risk losing their friendship. But something had clearly happened, judging by how completely torn up the girl who stood in front of me appeared. Her face and neck had reddened even more than when she'd walked out of the stall, and she walked with a slouch as she clomped towards the trash bin in her heels.

"I got nominated for prom queen," Sophie finally answered, turning to face me with her arms crossed on her stomach. "She wanted me to drop out, and I told her I would, but I guess she—she didn't believe me after what happened yesterday."

I tried not to be too eager but I couldn't help asking, "What happened?"

"Somebody posted the announcements online, and my picture got a ton of likes." Sophie took a deep breath and rolled her eyes as more tears shed. "I guess she felt threatened, which I don't understand because her picture had way more likes than mine—"

"What did she do, Sophie?"

The girl had fully broken out into another spell, and I watched her slide down the wall, pressing her chest into her knees. I rubbed my hands at my sides as I stared down at her. Then I rushed over to the bathroom door and locked it. The last thing she needed was some random freshmen barging in. It had just dawned on me what bathroom we were in. I shook my head at the memory of the silly rules we'd been so hellbent on enforcing. Funny how none of it mattered to me now.

"She's honestly the most evil person I've ever met in my entire life," Sophie sobbed on the floor.

I could have told her that. Well, I did tell her that but that had been so long ago. If only she'd listened, then we wouldn't be having this conversation right now. Sophie would be running for prom queen without the looming threats from Danielle stressing her out from behind the scenes. She wouldn't be puking up her breakfast or ruining her make-up from all the tears she'd already cried. But Sophie hadn't listened to me. She'd stuck up for her oldest friend. The way I'd known she would.

"What did she do, Soph?" I asked again, albeit gentler.

Sophie sniffled, using the back of her hand as a wipe this time. "You-you know Kyle Baker? He has second-period trigonometry with Allan?"

I tried my hardest to avoid looking too irritated by her question. It's not Sophie's fault she'd become so undeniably involved in the lifestyles of other people that she couldn't recognize when someone was so plainly not. Her mother had a reputation of being the town gossip—in and out of church.

"Doesn't ring any bells," I uttered instead.

"I think he might've been at the party last—oh." Sophie paused mid-sentence and quickly looked away from me. "I'm so sorry, it just slipped…"

"Forget it. Just tell me what happened."

She curled her fingers under the brim of her skirt, seemingly hiding her eyes from me now. "Well…we kind of started dating after the spring fling."

"Kind of?"

"Well, nobody knew about it except Taylor…and then Danielle found out."

Emotions that I'd thought I'd buried began bubbling up to the surface, and I had to close my eyes to contain the aggression that still festered inside of me. "She told everyone."

Sophie sniffled again and tucked her chin. There had been no mistaking it this time. If she could crawl into a hole right, then she would have. My eyebrows joined at the center as I waited for her to come clean.

"A couple weeks ago, I stayed over at her house. Taylor was there, too. Things were fine, but Danielle got bored, so we started a game of truth or dare. As soon as I picked dare, Danielle told me to call Kyle." Again, she sniffled and kept her head low. "He didn't answer, so she said the dare didn't count. So that's when she dared me to send him a picture."

My heart sank. "God, Soph, you didn't."

"Taylor kept egging me on," Sophie continued explaining, "saying she'd done it before and it was no big deal. So I did it…but I never thought she'd…"

"How did she get a hold of the photo?" I immediately asked.

"She'd asked to borrow my phone for something." Sophie shook her head. "I can't even remember what for but that had to be when she sent it to herself. She was just waiting for me to betray her."

I felt numb by her words. Suddenly reminded of all the horrible things I'd helped Danielle do in the past. Only to have her turn around and do those same things to me. "Does Principal—"

"She believed her," Sophie said. "Danielle told her I'd sent the picture to Kyle, so I was probably just doing the same thing to get attention from other boys."

I should have known. Now, even as I thought about the question I'd almost asked, I felt stupid for even attempting to ask it. Of course, Singh would believe one of her star pupils against the accusation of a mere copy-and-paste version. Experience led me to this conclusion.

"I don't know what to say," I spoke, clutching my elbow. "I'm sorry you had to go through that, Sophie."

Sophie gripped the ends of her skirt now. "I just don't get it. She's supposed to be my best friend."

I glanced to my side, recognizing her words verbatim.

"I should have listened to you, Brynn."

Her words brought my attention back to where she now sat with her legs stretched out across the tile.

"You warned me and I just laughed in your face." She still held traces of tears in her reddened eyes. "I guess I just never thought that it would happen to me, you know?"

I nodded. "I know."

"I never thought she'd turn on me."

"What are you going to do now?" I asked, genuinely curious.

"I don't know." Sophie rested the ball of her head against the wall and stared up at the ceiling. "I'm disqualified from the race and my dad is already threatening to send me to an all-girls school to finish out the school year."

"That's pointless." The words blurted out from me. "You'll be graduating in only a couple of months."

"You know my dad's extremely religious," Sophie said, and then surprisingly laughed, "He called this school a bad advertisement over the phone. You should have seen Singh's face."

I could picture it now. All screwed up and intolerant. "Well maybe it's what's best. If I could leave this place, I know I would."

"I'm surprised you even came back from France."

"How did you know I was in France?"

"Well, a lot of people at church were concerned about how you and your mother were doing. It's not like you ever came back to sing in the choir or anything."

"Why would I?" I became tense all over again and brought my arms across me as a defense. "Tell me exactly how that would have helped fix anything?"

Sophie now wore the expression that Angela had donned this morning. I knew I'd overreacted but I didn't feel bad for doing so. I had become fed up with defending my actions. I didn't need to give anyone an explanation for anything. No one understood what it felt like to lose my brother and still be expected to put on a nice dress and a big smile for church as if nothing ever happened. As if I would get there and, suddenly, Ethan would be sitting in the pew or reading near the altar. As if any of those songs meant anything to me anymore.

I'd had the same argument with my father before he'd decided to send me to France. He couldn't understand it. My defiance. My unwillingness to play happy little church home any longer. My brother had just died. So I had decided right then and there that I had officially had enough of pretending like everything was good. For once in my life, I refused to play pretend.

"I'm sorry, Brynn, that was forward of me," Sophie immediately apologized.

"Well, you always were forward, Sophie." I rolled my eyes and sought out the door lock with my hand. "Anyway, I hope everything works out for the best."

"Wait—"

I sighed and glanced back down at her. "What now?"

"Thank you." Sophie pushed up from the floor and brushed off her skirt. "For listening to all of that. You really didn't have to, but you did. That means a lot—especially after how I treated you back then."

I nodded. "Bell's about to ring, so I should go."

"Um, one other thing—" Sophie's jade eyes skittered away from me, intentionally avoiding eye contact again. "I should have told you this before, and I know you'll hate me for it, but that's okay. I know I deserve it."

My palms grew cold as my hand lowered from the door lock, and I had a gut-wrenching feeling all of a sudden. The kind of feeling that I had before I found out about Ethan's car accident. As if some deadly tornado had entered my path, heading directly toward me, and I had no shelter to protect myself from it.

No. I didn't want to hear what she thought I needed to know. But I couldn't move. I couldn't breathe. I just stood there with open ears, forced to listen to the words spilling out of her mouth.

"—and he was acting really strange like he couldn't stand up, so we both put him on the bed—"

My heart throbbed against my chest, and I heard it in my ears. It's sound competed with Sophie's voice.

"—That's when Liam barged in and—"

Breathe. Breathe. Breathe.

I repeated it over and over again. But this time, it didn't work. The fluorescent lights became blacker as my head grew light. Parts of me were going numb. I could barely move.

Help me!

Couldn't she see that I needed her help? Couldn't she hear me screaming?

Help!

But my mouth did not move. My lips could not part. The words escaped me, and my limbs became frail.

Black spots. Everywhere.

That had been the last thing I saw before succumbing to the darkness again.

And when I awoke, the brightest light shone down over me. It hurt to open my eyes, but I slowly peeled them apart. Accepting more, little by little, until the face hovering over me came into full view.

"Allan," I uttered, flinching at the sound of my cracked voice.

"Hey." The boy sat crouched down next to me, gripping my hand in his larger one, a relieved smile on his face. "Don't try to sit up."

I lowered my head back down, partly due to the tension building in my neck. "What…what h-happened—"

"You fainted," he said. "Sophie came and got me as soon as it happened."

"I fainted?" I asked him in disbelief.

"Yes," Nurse Miller spoke up from somewhere behind him. "Your blood pressure was very low. Have you eaten breakfast today, Brynn?"

I avoided the question by closing my eyes again, though I'd forgotten who still sat next to me.

"Brynn," Allan said my name with slight urgency in his tone. "Have you eaten anything at all?"

"I was…I was on my way to the cafeteria…"

"Get her something from the fridge in the back," Nurse Miller ordered Allan as I heard her footsteps descend away from us. "And make sure she eats it."

I rolled my head away as Allan stood up and left the side of the cot I lay on. I watched the million little sparkling bursts of light behind my eyelids, dreading opening them back up and being flooded by the light once again. Allan soon returned bearing not so desirable gifts. In one hand, he held a breakfast muffin and, in the other, an energy drink.

"For the electrolytes," Allan said when he'd noticed my confused expression towards the bottled drink.

"I'm really not hungry."

"Well, that's too bad because you're going to eat."

My eyebrows bunched. "You're not going to feed me like a dog."

"I didn't intend to feed you like a dog. I intended to feed you like a human girl who's just fainted and can't do it herself."

Already, I had become bothered by his presence and familiar banter, but I didn't have the strength to argue with him. I watched him peel the paper from the muffin and break off a small piece with chocolate chips embedded in it. My fingers gripped my jeans as he brought it near my mouth, beckoning me to part my lips, slipping it in when I did. The chocolate chips were cold, compliments of the refrigerator the muffin had been sitting in. I don't think I'd ever tasted anything more unappetizing. I only let him feed me two more big pieces before I quit. He seemed to be pleased enough and handed over the drink for me to sip on.

I tried to relax as I lay there, but Allan's gaze pulled my attention back to him, his face still basically hovering over mine.

"What did Sophie say to you?" Allan asked the question I should have known he'd been dying to ask.

I would have completely forgotten about the last part of our conversation had he not brought it up again. Had he just let it float into the realm of lost information that I had probably also forgotten about. Had he just left it alone instead of picking at that bandaged wound again? The wound that I had been trying desperately to keep patched up. If only he'd just let it be, then I wouldn't have felt everything suddenly rushing back to me at warp speed. Causing me to choke on the liquid I sipped at with ease only seconds ago. Causing my heart rate to shoot back up to that unbearable aching speed. Causing my eyes to mist over with more tears that had collected in parts of my body I couldn't even fathom. Places I didn't know still hurt until Sophie's words had bruised them up again.

Allan pulled me up by my arms and wrapped me in the tightest embrace. And I disappeared inside of that embrace. Curling into the smallest ball and drowning his threads in my tears. But I sobbed for Ethan. I wanted Ethan. I wanted his hug. His embrace. Knowing that it would never be possible only hurt that much more.

Tell him. He needs to know.

I gasped and clutched Allan's sweater in my grip, blinking rapidly as I looked up at him. Allan sank his eyes in mine, relaying something to me without needing to say a word, and I received it loud and clear. But it hurt, and I looked back down, burying my head in my arms.

"Brynn," Allan's voice swept over me as he pressed his hand against my back. "What's wrong?"

I wept a little softer now, though my face still leaked to no avail.

Tell him, Brynn.

I shuddered but lifted my face again, giving them what they both wanted. "Sophie...she told me she...she and Danielle were there... with Ethan...the night he..."

Allan looked troubled, possibly slightly more than he already looked before. "With Ethan, where?"

"I don't know she..." I took the deepest breath I could muster and continued talking. "She said he was upstairs with Danielle when she walked in. He was...he..."

"Take another deep breath," he instructed me, and I did.

"Sophie said he could barely walk by himself," I explained it to him as she'd told me, surprised by how much I'd remembered given my unsteady state when she'd said it. "They put him on the bed, and Liam—"

"Liam?" Allan seemed stunned.

"She said Liam barged in. He was mad because he-he saw us fighting. She said that's what he told Ethan and what made him come downstairs—"

"Brynn—"

"It's all my fault," I cried, ignoring the attempts he made to clean my face. "If I had just told you when I found out, then you wouldn't have been so mad at me, and we wouldn't have argued that night, and Ethan would still be here, and our baby—"

"No," Allan scolded me, those same hands gripping my soaked face in his hands. "I don't believe that, Brynn. You couldn't have stopped what happened that night. No matter what you did or didn't do."

I shook my head. He didn't have to believe it. I believed it. I knew things would have been different if I would have made better choices.

I knew that, and somewhere deep down, I believed he knew it, too.

27

"De quelle couleur sont mes yeux?"

"Chocolat…"

"Chocolat?"

"Mm, chocolat noir."

"Non, mes yeux sont bruns."

Soft laughter filled the quiet room.

"D'accord."

"D'accord."

"Quelle couleur sont les miennes?"

"Hm?"

"Mes yeux."

A few more chuckles.

"Facile, la mer."

"La mer?"

"Oui."

"Ou l'océan?"

"Non. La mer…la mer bleu foncé."

Claps erupted across the classroom, and I exhaled with what had to be the cheesiest grin. I couldn't help staring at all of them. All of our peers. Applauding us.

Me.

"Très bien," Madame Etienne praised from her place at the podium in front. "You both will get an A on the assignment. Très bon travail."

Those words made my heart flutter, and my eyes floated towards Jean. We had done a good job, hadn't we? I felt his hand squeeze my knee as if to quietly confirm it. My knees were angled toward him underneath the desks we'd pushed together. I had gotten used to seeing us like this ever since we'd become permanent partners. Madame Ettiene seemed to like what I'd brought out of him. Jean no longer did that thing he used to do so much. Pretending to be awful at French, pretending to hate this class…

I'd found out just the opposite had been true a couple of weeks ago at the pond. Seated on an old blanket I'd hauled along for the grass. That blanket lived in the bed of his truck now, right next to the ruined pair of brogues I kept forgetting to take home with me. I guess a part of me wanted them to stay there. Knowing something of mine had a home in his truck made me giddy. Yes, that's exactly how I would describe that feeling. It burned inside of me every time his leg brushed mine underneath our desks, or his voice lowered several octaves before spilling a secret, or those deep blue eyes gazed at me as if I were the most difficult puzzle to solve.

Giddy.

Every time I left the house to spend mornings and, afternoons, and evenings with him. Not ever feeling time pass by.

Giddy.

Every time, he called me by my nickname. Mignonne.

Sometimes, I copied it in my notebook when class got boring, and I'd find myself in a different world. No longer the new girl. Fully acknowledged. Fully known. And everyone in school would like me. But I would no longer care. As long as he still liked me.

"Who knew they'd actually get a kick out of that?" Jean cracked a smile as he slipped his pencil behind his ear. "I guess all of that hard work of mine really paid off."

I couldn't help but giggle and shake my head. In truth, he'd only spent a short time learning our skit. The day it'd been assigned, I'd gone home and worked on it, letting a romance flick play in the background. The more I sat and listened to the sultry script the more the words of our own skit came to me. I'd only revealed the finished work to Jean when I'd fully memorized each line, sitting there on the edge of the pond, acting it out with as much mystique as that classic noir film. I still remember the expression he wore on his face. Full of depth and adoration. He'd made me perform it three times for him, and by the third, he'd been able to perfectly deliver the poetic lines himself.

The classroom broke into yet another loud ovation, and it startled me, forcing my attention back towards our teacher. I couldn't ignore the nagging feeling scratching at my throat as I heard Madame Etienne give out identical praises to our classmates.

"Do you think she's going to say that to everyone?" I muttered loud enough for only Jean to hear.

He chuckled softly. "Êtes-vous jaloux?"

"Non," I denied, though my next thoughts left my mouth quickly to expose me. "Maybe she didn't really like ours."

"Se détendre…" He draped his arm across the back of my chair and pulled forward, but it'd been the shallow sigh he'd let out that unnerved me. "Etienne ate it up. We probably reminded her of a countryside beau she used to hook up with back in her youth."

Normally, I would have felt that familiar twinge of wonder at the mere mention of France, unable to resist the urge to learn more about this countryside he spoke of. Ever since he'd told me about his visit there, I'd been overwhelming him with questions, and he'd acknowledged each one with an amused sort of zeal. But something else replaced that urge to hear him reminisce aloud. An off-putting sensation that had begun its slow crawl in the pit of my stomach. I recognized it immediately. It brought back the doubt and the worry. It made me insecure all over again.

Had none of this been real?

Would I soon wake up from the fairytale dream that I'd been living for the past few weeks?

I fought the desire to pinch the hot skin that sizzled underneath the sleeve of my shirt. I didn't want to wake up. Not yet. Just a few more blissful weeks would satisfy me. Then we could go back to the days where I'd anxiously sit next to the window, waiting to spot him in the crowd of students that toppled in every morning, only to be severely gutted when he'd finally wade in, take his back seat, and not even bother to glance my way. I despised those days when the only time he'd look at me had been when he felt certain I wouldn't see him. But I always saw him. I always noticed him. Ever curious about how he saw me. If he even noticed me.

Those same questions had returned this morning when he'd finally shown up to class right before the bell rang. It'd been a long time since I'd been in the position of having to watch him take his seat. I'd gotten so used to us walking into class together. But my nervous system kicked into overdrive when he failed to make eye contact with me. It remained that way until Madame Etienne instructed everyone to pair up and begin our skits. That skit brought him back to life, and it made me temporarily forget the space he'd placed between us and the hard expression he'd previously worn on his face. But the high of staring into his eyes had come down. The warm sensation where his palm had touched my skin had grown cold. That dreaded feeling had returned, reminding me that I had no control over time and that time was slowly running out.

He would soon see right through me like everyone always did. He would get fed up. Exhausted. Bored… he would leave me or force me to leave him. But I couldn't let it happen yet. I wanted to experience more. To know more. I wanted to prove myself worthy of more time to enjoy him.

"Jean, I—"

"Let's skip," he suddenly spoke as if he'd already been pondering the thought.

I actually felt my eyebrows pull in, and my eyes widen, and I hated that. A frown had already begun to take form on his face in response to my unspoken rejection. I quickly dove in with an apology.

"I'm sorry—that caught me off guard."

"Forget about it."

"No, I want to do it, I do."

"But you're still worried about Singh." He rested back in a slight slouch. "I told you she's harmless."

"It's not her, it's my dad." I regretted the words as soon as they toppled out but I couldn't take them back now. I had to keep going. "He made me promise I wouldn't get into any more trouble."

"Your dad."

I nodded.

"He must be really strict on you."

"He is," I confirmed, a little too eager to reassure him of what I knew to be far from the truth.

Judging by the sudden look on Jean's face, he seemed to have some inclination of that, too. "You've been out with me almost every day since our night at the pond. Brynn's dad is strict, not yours."

I had no doubt that he'd seen my throat jump as I swallowed down my humiliation.

"It's all right if you're a daddy's girl," he teased, though this time, I clearly detected the passive-aggressive lilt in his tone. "Most girls are."

"I'm not," I snapped.

He crossed his arms, tucking his hands in his armpits, a new grin on his face. "You're right. You don't bring him up nearly enough—I mean, until just now."

He kept me bound in his gaze. All other voices had faded into the background, along with my petty concerns about our skit from before. The only thing that concerned me, excited me, overwhelmed me, had entered my life only a few short months ago but had quickly become the center of my world.

I didn't want to lose him.

"Okay," I agreed without a trace of hesitation this time. "I'll skip with you."

But he shook his head at me. "Just meet me in the lot after school. We'll do something else."

I attempted to hide my disappointment. "Okay." But then, because I couldn't help it, I asked, "Are you mad at me?"

I could tell he'd liked the question as he smiled. "I don't think that's possible, Elonie."

And I liked his answer.

I'd hustled in and out of my classes. Unable to empty those words he'd spoken out of my head. Maybe I'd been wrong. Reading too much into things, as usual. Maybe I had nothing to worry about. But I couldn't say the same when it came to Liam. He'd been distant in study hall, only sticking to the bare minimum during our short-lived conversations that seemed to have become more infrequent as the weeks went by. I knew exactly why, though. It had been no secret who I'd chosen as my ally. Anyone who had eyes had noticed how inseparable Jean and I had become. While some appreciated it, like Madame Ettiene, others had only grown irritated by our friendly display. Danielle fed me nasty looks whenever she got the chance. I made sure that those chances were not frequent by avoiding her as much as I could. I couldn't remember the last time I'd ventured into the cafeteria where her posse usually lurked in those tight diner booths. A sharp black coffee at the café in town usually held me over, and, of course, cigarettes helped. I still got nauseous after smoking one, but they definitely helped. That only left the hallways and the girl's bathroom as fair game. Needless to say, I hadn't been invited back into the senior bathroom since the spring fling.

Liam, on the other hand, had clearly become tortured by my new friendship. But we had no way of avoiding each other. We were confined by our assigned seating and forced to act as if things were casual as always. We knew they weren't, though. We still hadn't formally made up from our small fight. We'd only brushed it under the rug and pretended that it'd merely disappear on its own. Or, at least, I had.

I'd pulled a Presley.

Liam hadn't forced me, though. He'd remained cordial and so patient, even though we knew my way of handling this only prolonged the inevitable. Inevitably, we'd have to talk about more than his upcoming soccer games and what new book I'd checked out from the library. Neither one of us had ever minded discussing these topics before. I'd sit there explaining how a dramatic twist had just occurred in my novel, and, in turn, he'd inform me of the kicks he'd still needed to perfect (the same kicks that I always ended up watching him practice on the field). But until then, I had become content with leaving things as they were. No one could make me feel bad about the final decision I'd made.

Not Danielle.

Not Principal Singh.

Not Liam.

Not even…

"Brynn's not coming."

The sun became dulled by the looming gray clouds overhead as we stood together in the parking lot, having just escaped our prison moments ago. Jean leaned against the hood of the truck, smoking a cigarette, never fazed by who might see him.

"She never showed up to class…I thought maybe she'd left after what happened this morning…"

He shrugged and took a sharp drag. "She looked pretty fine to me."

"Was she—did she really seem okay? I-I mean—did she actually—"

"Turns out the redhead made it all up."

I blinked wildly. Made it all up? I didn't believe that for a second. I'd never seen Sophie look so concerned about anything unless it involved the current topic of gossip. But I didn't say that. Instead, I asked:

"Is it because of me?"

"What?"

"The reason why she isn't coming with us."

"No." He tossed down his cigarette and turned away from me, walking towards the driver's side. "She has other plans."

Plans. The word struck me as I followed suit, climbing into the seat and strapping myself in. Brynn had used the same word this morning right before she'd disappeared, only to be discovered passed out in the girl's bathroom by Sophie. At least, that's what Sophie had relayed to us with a reddened face and tear-stained cheeks. I'd forgotten my cardigan in my haste to flee the heavily tense truck and had decided I'd go back to retrieve it before the morning bell rang. We'd made it to the brick steps when Sophie's frazzled state stopped us dead in our tracks. She willingly poured out the details of what happened. I only stood there silently, hanging onto every word that fell out of the crying girl's mouth, then Jean left. I thought about going after him. But my feet wouldn't allow it. I chose to sit with Sophie on those steps, fishing for more details, a solid reason for it all, but Sophie only continued to lie. She fumbled over her words and avoided eye contact until the bell rang, and she scurried off to class. I had been left high and dry. Still desperate for the truth. But my eagerness had been placed on hold when I saw Jean walk into the classroom.

He hadn't looked happy.

Not even relieved.

He'd looked ill.

And, suddenly, that concern for Brynn vanished. I'd only been interested in finding out what had caused that lifeless look he wore like a mask on his face. Glancing over at him now, I knew he kept something hidden from me. He bore the secret in his deep-set eyes. And I knew it involved her. She'd hurt him in some way. No doubt to get back at him for all the time he'd been spending with me. Brynn hated this more than anyone else. She barely said a word when we were all together, pretending as if I weren't there, most likely wishing I would go away.

I understood her silent plight. I had been in this position before. But I didn't want to replace Brynn like I'd replaced Lana. I'd learned my lesson well. I wanted us to be friends.

All of us. Like a family.

But she didn't want that. She wanted Jean to herself. Becoming even more determined to shut me out. Even more than she already had. I'd sit in the back of our math class, just dying to know what went on inside of the head of the girl who scratched. Maybe I didn't care to know anymore. Maybe that's how this would end. I'd never achieve that friendship that I'd desired so strongly at the beginning of it all.

From that day I'd spotted her walking alone in the rain, I'd only wanted to someday call her best friend.

But we don't always get what we want. No matter how bad we want it.

"Are you coming in?"

I looked in the direction of his voice, realizing that we'd already stopped and were now parked in a roundabout in front of a foreign residence. I must have zoned out entirely, although it'd still felt like we'd only been driving for a little while. Nonetheless, I unbuckled and got out, heading around to his side of the truck. Stunned when he reached for my hand and laced it in his. My throat quickly dried up as I began scoping the premise.

"Don't worry." He laughed at my nervous display. "No one's home."

I relaxed a little, feeling silly for even thinking he'd want to introduce me to his parents. Nothing about our relationship had escalated in that direction. If anything, everything had completely de-escalated. It hadn't been that long ago since we'd shared a kiss in front of my house that night, but it felt like ages ago. Jean hadn't even bothered bringing it up before today. He'd treated me exactly the same as before it'd happened. I, on the other hand, hadn't been able to stop replaying it...

We walked the narrow path, in between freshly cut hedges, up to the front entry. The perfumed scent of the rose bushes lingered in the air and instantly swept me into a heady frame of mind. But as I passed the threshold into his home, that feeling dissipated, replaced by an all too familiar one. The impact forced me to a stand still, and I felt Jean's hand drop from mine as he faced me.

"What's wrong?" he asked.

"N-nothing. It's just—it feels like..."

"Like an empty vessel."

Which made no logical sense because the place had been sufficiently adorned with every necessity known to man. The living room blinded me with its gaudy and intricate patterns, and I had no doubt the rest of the rooms had no less to offer in that department. But nothing felt warm. Nothing felt like a home. Only an intelligently decorated house.

"Don't look so disappointed," he commented. "You haven't seen the best part."

I followed him past the foyer, across the way, into a dining room set up, and then through the French double doors leading back outside. He quickened his pace and I struggled to keep up as we crossed the large patio and eventually broke out into a jog onto the massive courtyard garden.

"Much better than sitting in that stuffy old living room, right?"

I giggled as he threw himself back onto the grass, propping his hands underneath his head closing his eyes to the dull glow in the sky. I took in the spacious back area for a moment longer before going to join him down in the grass.

"Is this where you come to think, too?" I teased him based on prior knowledge he'd shared with me.

He chuckled. "I hate being home, but I used to come out here a lot when I was young. Back when I didn't know how to drive." He lifted up from the sharp blades. "Now I just go to the pond."

I glanced around with a smile. "I like it."

"Knew you would."

Pretty soon, the sky took on another shade—a deep twilight blue—and we transitioned over to the white French patio seating.

"Do they come home on the weekends?" I asked, resting my chin on my knuckles, giving him my undivided attention.

"Sometimes." Jean rubbed his fingers against the table, eyes absent as he spoke. "My dad rarely does, though. He's always in the air for work."

"Presley—I-I mean, my dad—"

Jean laughed and brought his gaze up. "You call your dad by his first name?"

"No," I shook my head, then shrugged, "it's just how I, kind of, grew up knowing him."

"Care to elaborate on that one?" He leaned back and dropped his limbs on the arms of the chair. "I'd love to hear about it."

My cheeks warmed under the steadiness of his gaze. I'd managed to go this far without revealing anything about myself. Now, he'd put me on the spot, and I had no choice. Those blue magnets pulled me in. Aching to get up close and personal.

"It's silly, but my mom never referred to him as dad or daddy when I was growing up. She would just call him by his name. I guess I just got used to hearing it."

"But you don't call him Presley. Why not?"

"I used to, but he got really angry about it one day." I recalled the memory, experiencing that same hard thud in my chest as I had that day. "I didn't really understand it at the time. I just don't call him anything now."

"Interesting." He tilted his head as if to analyze me, and I gently lowered my arm, suddenly self-conscious. "Your folks are twisted too, aren't they?" I swallowed, but that tight pull in my throat didn't let up, and he leaned forward. "I notice how you avoid talking about them. I'm the same way, normally, but with you, it's different. You get where I'm coming from. You know what it's like. I think maybe I can be that person for you, too."

I stiffly nodded. "Maybe."

He smirked, taking my hands in his. "Tell me a secret, Mignonne."

Why did my eyes betray me now? They'd been dry for weeks. I'd been happier than I'd been in a long time. There hadn't been any need for tears. But the floodgates had opened up again. Blurring my vision. Turning Jean's face into a water painting. I attempted to release my hands but he only gripped tighter. My chest seemed to float on its own. My skin grew hot against his. I knew what was happening.

"Hey, look at me," his voice swept in and caught me, bringing me back, stabilizing me. "It's okay. Trust me."

I sniffled, blinking out more heavy droplets, nearly hearing them splash against the table in the heavy silence surrounding us. His thumbs massaged my hands, prompting me, leading me to speak. So I spoke. I uttered words that I hadn't said since Dr. Portis, Ph.D had invited me into his office that first day.

"My mom…she…" I sniffled again, dropping my gaze as if I were to blame for the words coming out of my mouth. As if it were somehow my fault. "She committed suicide when I was twelve."

I shut my eyes as soon as the words were fully out. Blocking the events of that day again. The lights. The sirens. Their locked bathroom door.

"Shhh, shhh, I've got you now." Jean's arms enveloped me, pulling me in tightly, just as he'd done at the pond.

His calming voice only beckoned more sobs out of me. It sounded just like Presley's had that night. His tone had been gentle, arms locking me in his embrace, having picked my rocking form up from the floor as if I were a small child again.

I could still feel the plush carpet between my toes as I'd raced to their bedroom. Presley's strangled cry had woken me up in a cold sweat. I'd never heard anything so deeply pitiful in my life. But he must have detected my feet before I'd crossed the banister because the next thing I heard had been the resounding slam of the bathroom door.

Never opening. No matter how hard I yanked and clawed at it. Eventually, the only thing I could think to do was cry. I knew mom would hear me and come quickly. She always did. But not this time. I cried myself dry, and even then, my hoarse voice echoed throughout the house in pain.

"I wasn't allowed to see her," I uttered with my head still pressed against his chest, my cheeks dampening his black tee. "Presley kept me away from all of it. I fought him so hard, but all he did was rock me back and forth until I wore out. When I woke up, I thought it'd been a dream, so I—" My voice cracked, and I sucked my tooth, hiding my face in his chest. "I ran out of my room, calling her name, but she never answered."

"And that was the last time you saw her." Jean presumed as he rubbed my shoulder. "No goodbyes or nothing."

"I was so mad at him," I took a deep breath, "but I know she wouldn't have wanted me to see her like that. She'd tucked me in that night and I still remember her hovering over me—smiling at me— telling me she loved me."

Jean's fingers slid into my hair, and I closed my eyes, wrapping my arms around him this time. Holding him as if he had suddenly become her. I didn't want to let go of his warmth. It comforted me to know that he knew this part of me now.

"I love you, Jean," the words trickled out before I could stop them, and I stiffened a bit, unsure of how to fix my careless mistake. "I'm— I'm sorry, I—"

I felt his chin rest atop my head as his fingers continued their slow caress woven in my curls. "Say it in French, Mignonne."

I hesitated at his request, but that fleeting moment of doubt quickly surpassed, and I repeated in the most assured way,

"Je t'aime, Jean."

28

I never used to sit outside on the terrace as much as I tended to now. Back then, the thought wouldn't have even crossed my mind. I'd always been way too consumed in everything else but being at home. Stopping to smell the roses had never applied to me. I'd always wanted to do this and that, go here and there—and the arguments I'd stir up when I couldn't get my way.

No one had been able to slow me down back then. No matter how much anyone had tried. I'd go searching for more thrill…more excitement…always more…

Now, I only wanted less. I wanted what I'd pushed away so many times before. Peace and quiet. But it seemed to be impossible.

Sophie's voice had followed me all the way home. Sitting with me at the dining table as I pushed food around my plate. Standing with me as I rinsed under the shower beads. Resting next to my ear as I attempted to get sleep. And again, this morning, I'd awakened from the sound of it in my head. I couldn't escape. No matter how much I tried. I couldn't escape what she'd told me.

Yet another thing I could add to the list of things I'd done wrong that night. Too consumed. Too involved. That night had been no different. I'd selfishly placed myself in the middle of it all. I'd shamelessly flaunted around as if I were invincible. I had believed that for a while, up until Danielle proved me wrong and put me in my place. Knocked me right off my high horse. Then, things had really turned for the worse. My reality had changed too quickly, and I had become angry and obsessed. But I'd still wanted freedom. I'd still wanted that rush that came with the chaos. I'd gone there to prove a point but I'd only ended up proving everyone right.

It was me.

I had been the problem. And still was the problem.

A sliver of movement caught my eye and I turned my head, noticing Angela standing at the doors. Then my eyes lowered to the silver bar cart in front of her, and my annoyance refused to stay hidden. I stood up to leave just as she'd gotten the doors open.

"Going so soon?" I hated that little teasing tone she kept up with me. Like an overtly exuberant kindergarten teacher. It pissed me off.

"Suddenly, I can't concentrate," I replied.

Angela found that funny as she chuckled, getting the cart situated. "Well, I didn't mean to disturb you. I usually come out here once or twice a week and read."

I glanced down at that same leather-bound book she toted, bringing my arm across me. "Don't let me hold you up."

"Don't let me scare you off," she playfully retorted, taking up the hot carafe and a mug. "Have a cup of coffee. It's a fresh brew."

"No thanks."

"Come on. It's Colombian."

What choice did I even have? I could either stay out here with her (making her swear to leave me alone) or go back to my bedroom, where I'd, no doubt, be bombarded by Sophie's revelation. Reminded of how I hadn't been there to help my brother when he'd needed me the most. Reminded of how everything could have gone differently if only I'd just—

"Fine." I went and plopped back down on the cushioned couch. "Just one cup."

Angela held out the mug. "Here you go."

I cocked my eyebrow. "Aren't you going to bring it to me?"

"Why would I bring it to you?"

"Because you work here."

"True," Angela placed the mug back on the glass top, "but your parents pay me, not you."

I clenched my jaw.

"But I can definitely bring it to you if you ask nicely," Angela finished.

"Has anyone ever told you how annoying you are?" I huffed, getting up to go retrieve the mug.

"Mettersi d'accordo." The Italian rolled off her tongue with ease as she laughed again. Somehow, it felt better not knowing what she'd said. "Cream and sugar?"

I waved my hand and returned to my seat, gripping the piping-hot mug. Angela took her place on the teak armchair, setting her cup of coffee on the side table before flipping open the Bible on her lap. I had noticed the gleam of the gold inscription as the sun beamed off of it and remembered how my brother's had looked almost identical. Jet black and worn. But the inscription had still been intact and shimmering. We'd gotten new ones as gifts a couple of winters ago. White leather with our initials in gold lettering. I'd toted mine around, of course, showing it off in front of Danielle and Sophie. Ethan, however, hadn't been able to let go of his old one. He'd loved that Bible so much. The appeal of fresh leather and crisp pages hadn't been enough to replace it.

I'd brought it back from the hospital the night after he'd died. I'd wanted a piece of him close to me. Thinking that I'd still be able to feel his spirit amongst the dog-eared pages. But the more days passed by, the less and less I'd been able to read. Until I'd put it, and everything else, away for good.

I glanced over at Angela as she quietly read to herself, sipping at her brew every so often, truly engrossed in the Word.

"What book are you reading?" I'd asked all of a sudden.

I had no idea why I'd done it. I didn't want to know what book she was reading. I didn't want to know anything about her. I wished I could take the words and swallow them back down into the black pit of my stomach.

"Esther," Angela answered me anyway.

I frowned as if I hadn't been the one who'd spoken first. But I wouldn't make the mistake again. I bit my tongue and took a sip of my coffee. A few moments later, a bird made its way over to the branch of one of the potted plants. I watched it hop towards a luscious green leaf and begin pecking at it. I focused on it in hopes it would keep me distracted from my thoughts about Angela and, Sophie and…Jean.

My hands tightened around the mug.

Jean.

I could see his face as if he sat right next to me. My efforts had failed. The bird faded into a blur as his grimace grew more vivid. He gifted me that look every time I caught his eye in the rearview mirror. I'd been shunned to the back seat all week. Though I hadn't questioned the punishment, I still didn't understand why he'd turned so cold towards me all of a sudden. I'd done what he'd asked. I'd ignored that itch to say something each time I noticed Elonie sitting up front—in my seat. I'd bit my tongue when she'd speak in that airy tone of hers or reply back to him in their shared second language.

I'd let it be.

I'd let her be.

So why had he still looked so disgusted with me?

I'd wanted to ask so many times, but I could tell he'd been avoiding me. Usually, we'd meet up for lunch and head to the parking lot, where we'd sneak a cigarette as we watched our peers move about like ants under a magnifying glass. Then that would get boring, and we'd end up talking about our plans for graduation night. He'd get amped up describing what he'd say in the letter to his parents or guessing how they'd react once they found out what he'd done. I enjoyed seeing him so happy, knowing that soon he would finally be rid of them for good. That's usually when he'd ask me to climb into the back seat. And I never turned him down.

That hadn't happened in a while. Jean had become preoccupied. Elonie had stolen his attention away.

Elonie—with those big, brown, adoring eyes.

Elonie—with questionable intentions and endless amounts of obscurity.

Elonie—all the way from the city—with no harsh accent, speaking fluent French, mastering calculus, and bearing tiny hidden scars.

What else could he possibly need to know?

"So, have you?"

I flinched, glancing over at Angela, my eyelashes beginning to flutter. "Have I what?"

"Have you ever read Esther?" She lifted her mug to her lips, peering at me over the brim.

I wracked my brain. Pushing aside my thoughts about Elonie as I remembered what we'd been talking about. The book, still laying wide open in her lap, helped jog my memory.

"I don't think so," I replied, though vaguely unsure. "It's been a while since I've read, though."

"Esther is one of my favorite books," Angela said, a sort of glint in her nut-brown orbs as she reflected. "It's always like I'm reading it for the first time."

I leaned back, resting my coffee in my lap, forcing my gaze back over to that potted tree. I frowned as I noticed the bird no longer munched on its leaves. No longer providing me with a distraction.

"The king's arrogance always irritates me," Angela continued on. "The nerve he had to just replace his wife like that—at least she had some dignity, you know?"

"I told you I haven't read it," I reminded her with a bitter edge in my tone.

"Oh, right, sorry. I just can't stand it."

Seriously, Angela?

I know what you're trying to do. She wanted me to pry. She wanted to lock me in so that she could feed me another one of her helpful scriptures that would inevitably make me feel worse about myself and want to strangle her at the same time. No way. I would not fall for this trap.

"But I guess this story would've ended differently had she stayed." Angela chuckled to herself and shook her head of choppy brown locks. "Don't you wish that some characters had their own little side stories? I would've liked to have seen Queen Vashti's reaction to all the virgins he'd called in to replace her."

"What?" The question flew out before I could stop it.

She nodded. "I said the same thing when I first read it."

I brought my mug up to stop my mouth from further embarrassing me. But I thought about what she'd just told me. The story didn't sound familiar at all. Not something that my father would have chosen for Sunday morning service. I wondered about the rest of the story as I took another sip, although it pained me to be so interested.

"Wow." I looked over and noticed her checking her watch. "I better wrap this up."

My eyes followed her movements as she closed the Bible and then her eyes, slightly bowing her head in silent prayer. I wanted to look away, but I couldn't. I stared at her like she were some sort of circus clown act, immediately looking away as soon as she opened her eyes.

"Your parents will be back from the gathering soon, and I still have to pick up some things for lunch." She motioned her hand towards my mug. "Are you finished?" I nodded and handed the nearly finished coffee to her. She walked both mugs back over to the bar cart. "You can come along if you want."

"No, I'm okay."

"I forgot you'd much rather be stuck in this big old apartment all by your lonesome…" That teasing tone had returned, and I rolled my eyes. "Come on, some fresh air will do you good."

"Yea, that's why I came outside, but I should've known you'd come out here and ruin it for me."

Angela laughed.

I frowned.

"I'll be leaving in fifteen minutes."

She pushed the cart back inside before closing the doors behind her.

I sat, staring at the glass, my ankle shaking down below. I had fully decided she had to be a masochist. No question about it. No person in their right mind would still want someone who berated them every chance they got to come with them anywhere. Yet, Angela wouldn't give up. She refused to back down, and it only fueled my frustration even more.

But I had been faced with a choice between the lesser of two evils once again. I could stay out here on the terrace where I knew, eventually, Sophie's voice would manage to seep back in and continue its torment. Or I could go grocery shopping with Angela. Less than ideal company, but at least I'd be distracted and away from the silence that threatened to absorb me if I stayed here.

In truth, I knew I had no real choice. I couldn't sit through another hour thinking about the events of that party and all the mistakes I'd made that night. I refused to drown myself in further agony. I'd go with Angela. I'd listen to her insufferable accent and cringe laughter a little while longer.

Long enough to make it to the afternoon, then I'd crawl back to my room and wallow in all of my misery.

"You might want to ditch the leather," Angela suggested once I'd appeared from my bedroom.

My eyebrows hiked up. "Excuse me?"

"We're walking to the store."

"Walking?"

"It's such a beautiful day. Why waste it?"

No. Maybe I couldn't do this. "I'm not changing."

"Okay. Suit yourself."

I glanced down at my jacket, fingering the thick leather. I'd felt the temperature as we'd sat outside moments ago. Even I'd begun to sweat a little in the loose pajamas I'd had on.

I already hated this.

I hurried back into my room, peeling out of my jacket and tossing it on the bed. Then I grabbed it back and screamed into it. Long enough to release some of the tension that had quickly built up within me.

Not that Angela had caused all of it. She'd only been the icing on the cake. I'd been dying to let out my frustrations all week, but they'd been stifled by the expectations that still plagued me. The breakdown I'd suffered in Nurse Miller's office shouldn't have even happened. I never allowed myself to get that vulnerable. Not with Allan. Not anymore. But something in me still wanted to let him comfort me. I realized that I'd missed those arms around me. I'd held him back this time. Not wanting to let go just yet. But, afterwards, those warm feelings turned sour. It had been wrong to go back and relive those ugly things from our past. I wanted to forget them. I needed to forget them, and I couldn't do that with Allan. He would never let me.

"Brynn, are you almost ready?"

I snatched the leather off my face, feeling a sense of dread that hadn't been there previously but slowly crept into my stomach and severely twisted it. I had just realized what I'd agreed to. I hadn't gone out much after the car accident. His hospital room had been my safe haven. And, when Ethan finally passed, I hadn't left the house for anything. Not until I met Jean. He'd gotten me out of the dark corner of my closet. But now she expected me to just walk right into the local grocery store as if everything had gone back to normal. As if I were somehow back to normal.

"I'm not going," I shouted to make sure she heard me.

Silence followed. But in seconds, I heard her footsteps nearing my bedroom door. And then a knock sounded on the other side. "Brynn—"

"Don't come in here." I trampled forward, accidentally dropping my jacket, only to be confronted by the chaos of my bedroom floor when I'd bent down to retrieve it. "I changed my mind, okay?"

"Look, don't worry about the jacket. I just thought it'd be a good idea to—"

"No, it's not about the jacket. I just don't want to go anymore."

"Why not?"

I heard the disappointment in her tone, but it only irritated me further. "I just don't want to. Just go without me, okay?"

"Okay…as long as you're sure."

"I'm sure."

"If your parents make it back before I do, just tell them I needed to grab some things from the store."

I closed my eyes. "I'll tell them."

When I had felt sure she'd left, I slowly stood up from the floor, standing immobilized in the center of my bedroom. But I didn't feel relieved. I felt like a coward. Still, I knew I'd made the right decision. I knew I would have panicked. Something would have triggered me. Something familiar—the friendly smile Mr. Culpepper used to give us as he weighed and packaged our meat behind the counter—the spicy aroma of the apple cider our mom would buy to placate us as kids forced to tag along on a chilly afternoon grocery trip—the memories of picking up microwave popcorn and tubs of mint chip because late night movies just weren't the same without our favorite snacks.

You would somehow always manage to burn the popcorn.

A sudden laugh bubbled out of me, and I quickly slapped my hand over my mouth, my eyes expanding as I looked around my room.

You should have gone with her, Brynn.

I gasped and fell back onto my bed. "S-stop that."

Silence returned.

My hand came to my heaving chest. "Ethan?"

She only wants to help.

I continued looking around the room, though my head shook in disagreement.

Trust me, Brynn.

"No, she—she's just our chef—"

He laughed, and I sprung up from the bed.

She's more than that.

"How are you doing this?" I asked as I began pacing around my room. "How have I been hearing you? Why am I still hearing you?"

Because I'm still with you, Brynn. I've always been with you.

My eyebrows knitted, heat flushing my face. "No, you died, you left us."

I did die, but I didn't leave.

"This isn't real!" Tears pushed forth and glazed my eyes, making me even angrier. "None of this is real. It's not really you!"

But it is. You can hear me, but you're not listening. You were always bad at that...

I couldn't mask my confusion even if I tried. His voice sounded so clear in my head. "Ethan, please stop, I can't take it, please." I gripped my face in my hands and let out a heavy sob. "I can't take hearing your voice like this every day. I know it shouldn't have been you, and now it's haunting me."

Be strong, Brynn. Give Angela the chance to show you... you'll see why it had to be me...

I uncovered my face, sniffling. "Ethan..."

My eyes searched for him as if he'd suddenly appear in the flesh, right in front of me, but I knew that he wouldn't. None of it was real, and knowing that only made me yearn for it to be. I wanted to believe that miracles like that could happen. Maybe if I wiped my eyes hard enough and walked into his bedroom—the one place no one had ventured into since he'd left—he'd be laying right there. Ankles crossed. Reading out of that worn leather Bible again. I started crying, simply thinking about how he'd glance at me and smile before continuing on.

"Ethan," I called out again. "Ethan, please, don't go."

I won't leave you, Brynn. I'll never leave you.

"What am I supposed to—"

The doorbell's ring chimed throughout the house, startling me causing me to freeze in place. My ringtone followed. Both sounds pairing together. Triggering my flight or fight. Then, in an instant, everything went dead silent. That's when it hit me.

I remembered this.

"Jean," I whispered.

I didn't bother grabbing my phone this time. I sped out of my bedroom, stumbling down the slick marble hall, but having no concern

224

for the scuff marks my boots would undoubtedly leave. My dad would be angry. My mom would become stressed from his scolding and want to lie down, which would upset him more. But I couldn't let Jean wait any longer.

Letting his brain catch fire.

The thought alone sprouted an itch along my neckline, and I fought hard not to scratch. I wouldn't let my nerves overwhelm me.

Brynn...

I stilled. My palm hovering over the doorknob. "Ethan?"

Please don't do this.

In my bedroom, I could still hear my ringtone screaming at me. My hand began to tremble as I swallowed my stomach down. "I have to, I'm sorry—"

NO!

I opened the door, out of breath and confused to see no one stood there, but as soon as I stepped out into the hall, I spotted him in front of the elevator. "Jean—"

The elevator dinged as it opened up to receive him, but Jean had already turned around, filling me with the coldest chill as he returned my gaze. I started down the hall. Taking several deep breaths as I neared him. Noticing Ethan no longer spoke to me and experiencing a twinge of pain flare up at the mere thought that I could possibly never get to hear his voice again. But I couldn't focus on that now. I was too busy watching in terror as the flames danced around Jean's head.

"You're playing games with me." His voice sliced through the air like a jagged knife, his body moving towards me even quicker.

"Jean—"

"No!" His voice boomed down, splitting into my core. "Don't lie to me, Brynn."

I shook my head, opening my mouth, though no words came out.

"Tell me the truth." He trapped me against the wall. "He's here with you, isn't he?"

My ear still rang, and everything he said sounded muffled. But I felt his anger bursting from his body, burning against mine. "No, nobody's here."

"Why should I believe you? You're a liar."

He pulled away from me, and I sank to the floor. "Please, Jean, please don't—"

"I want to hear it," He grabbed my face and pressed my head against the wall. "Admit that you lied to me."

I could barely move my mouth but I managed a nod, though he could tell that I only wanted to appease him. And that just made him angrier. "Louder!"

"I lied to you!"

He released my jaw, and I attempted to straighten up, pushing myself further against the wall. My heart had detached and was throbbing somewhere next to me. I was sure of it. And with all my crying, no wonder he couldn't hear its small squeal as it passed away on the floor. I sat there as an empty shell, waiting for him to put something better into me. Like he always seemed to do. But something felt off. Something felt different this time. Jean still stood over me, breathing hard, completely engulfed by those flames now.

"So you're back with him then."

Everything suddenly clicked in my brain. "Allan?"

"Who else?"

"We're not back together, Jean. I promise you we're not."

His jaw locked and unlocked, those eyes picking me apart, waiting for a single oddity. I widened my stare and forced my face to relax. I knew it was the truth, but he would need convincing, though he began shaking his head, which let me know there was more eating away at him.

"But you will be."

"No, I don't want him."

"But he wants you." Jean crouched down, leveling with my screwed face, though his face looked unrecognizable through my tears. "And now it all makes sense."

He placed his hand on my stomach. And just like that, the rest of me unraveled. I crumbled like a rock that turned out to be made of pure dirt. And I saw myself—scattered all over the floor.

"Do you want to know how I found out?"

I didn't, but the protest itself sat lodged in my throat.

"You told me, Brynn." He grabbed me towards him, and the noise that left me sounded as wounded as I felt. "The day you chose his comfort over mine."

My eyes fluttered as he forced me to relive that moment minute by minute. I could only hang my head in shame. He let me go and stood to his feet again. I prayed that he would say something before he left me to wallow in the lake of tears I'd created. But before he could say or do anything, the elevator dinged, and those doors opened, allowing Angela to step out into the hallway.

I wanted to leave my body right then.

"Oh, my god, Brynn!" She rushed over and crouched down next to me, her hands turning my jaw. "You're hurt—"

That voice. It made me sick to my stomach. I couldn't even get my voice to say what I wanted to say. She already had her eyes on Jean.

"You did this to her," Angela accused him.

"He didn't do anything!" I used every bit of strength I still had left to stand up from the floor. "Just leave us alone, Angela."

But Angela ignored me. That curt Italian flew out of her mouth like knives, and her accent grew thick with anger.

"Don't think I won't call the police on you!"

"You wouldn't dare," I bit.

Angela shot me a look. "I most definitely would."

"Stop acting like you're my mother when you're not!"

"Bene, allora, would you prefer I get them on the phone instead, Brynn?"

The threat silenced me as a wave of nausea rushed in with the image of my father's face if he were to be brought into all of this chaos.

Jean didn't give Angela the satisfaction, however, as he turned towards the elevator. Not having said a word to either of us.

I rushed after him. "Please, Jean, how can I—"

"Stay away from me," he said, cutting his eyes down at me, and I noticed for the first time the wetness in them. "That's what you can do."

My jaw felt mechanical as I attempted to come up with something that would satiate him. But he'd rendered me speechless.

Nothing even broke inside of me as I watched him walk into the elevator and as it closed itself again.

There was simply nothing left to break.

29

I was back in the city.

Not because I'd wanted to be. This time, I'd been forced. My follow-up appointment had arrived. I was on my way to see Dr. Portis, Ph.D., for the first time in three months. It hadn't been something I was necessarily looking forward to. I would have much rather preferred to stay behind and wait for Jean to pop up at the end of my driveway.

I'd hoped to go back to his house this weekend. I'd dreamt about it last night, actually. Every detail had been so vivid. We were outside again. Under the beaming sun. I sat cross-legged in the grass, and Jean lay with his head resting on my lap. Both of us watched a ladybug crawl between his fingers as I slowly dragged mine through his slippery locks. At the table we'd sat at before were two people with blurred faces. His parents, I think. Talking amongst themselves…though, suddenly, his mother had called out my name. *Elonie!* And asked, *have you two set a date yet?*

At that moment, her face became so clear—she looked just like Madame Etienne.

That's when I woke up. Excited and confused and still foggy with sleep. But I'd fought the urge to stay in bed. I wanted to tell Jean the bizarre dream and that had been my plan until Presley had phoned, reminding me of the appointment. Erasing all of the embellished scenarios I'd created in my head of how the conversation would go.

Presley had also informed me of the additional plans he'd laid out for me, and I'd sat on the edge of the window seat, listening to the cruel agenda.

He'd gone behind my back. I should have known eventually, he would. He'd never been the confrontational one, after all. But it still frustrated me because, once again, I hadn't seen it coming. Before, I would've prepared for his usual sly tactics. I would have booked a hotel downtown or set the tone to call in sick. Or, even better, I would've contacted Dr. Portis, Ph.D without Presley's knowledge and arranged a virtual session, avoiding these circumstances altogether.

But I hadn't done any of those things and now I suffered the consequences.

I couldn't help that I'd given my entire focus to Jean. Even now, I wondered what he must be doing.

We'd talked a little over the phone before I left. I could tell he'd been upset after hearing that I'd be out of town this weekend. I'd joked about meeting up with him somewhere in the city. It'd felt good to hear his broken laugh. But I didn't bring up the dream. I wanted to tell him in person. I wanted to watch his expression as I told him, similar to the way he often watched me when he told me his dreams. Last night was like that. He'd brought me back to my dark and empty house sometime around midnight, but I had refused to go in. I'd barely wanted to leave the pond. Time slowed down there, underneath those stars, wrapped in his arms, reciting his favorite words. I never wanted to leave. I never wanted to go back home or back to school. I just wanted to stay there. Listening to Jean. Looking at Jean. Loving Jean. Why would anyone want to go back to reality? He'd given me a sleepy smile in response to my pout, pulling me close enough to kiss, which only worsened my desire to feel his lips on mine again. Then, in the drowsiest tone, he started telling me his dream.

"Elonie."

"Hm?" I lifted my gaze from the pewter gray carpet and settled it back on the crow's feet etched in the corners of Dr. Portis's eyes. "S-sorry, I was just thinking about what you'd asked."

"Which was?" He challenged me.

I frowned, straightening in the uncomfortable chair. I didn't remember it being so uncomfortable before, but maybe it was just me. Maybe I was just uncomfortable here. I used to not mind coming to these sessions. He seemed to be the only human being to understand what I'd been feeling back then. And that had been all I'd really wanted. But for some reason it didn't feel right opening up to him right now. It felt almost like a betrayal.

"I must have zoned out a little." My fingers unlocked below, and I brought one hand up, pushing my hair behind my ear.

"That's quite all right," Dr. Portis, Ph.D glanced back down at his notes, jotting something with his pen. "I understand it's been a while since our last conversation. I expected you to be a little standoffish with me."

I nodded as if to agree, but the only thing on my mind was the wall clock centered right above his desk. I took the opportunity to glance over at it again, though I regretted it as soon as I realized we weren't even close to being finished. Not that anything great waited for me at the other end of this rainbow.

"You mentioned that your experience at the new school has been good so far." He crossed his leg over his knee, exposing a pair of maroon argyle socks and slightly leaned back in his chair.

I once enjoyed critiquing his interesting sock selection as a way to lighten up the formal sessions. Now I just stared at them, listening to the tick of the clock, willing time to speed up.

"Yes," I confirmed with another nod. "I like it."

"What do you like about it?"

"Well, it's smaller."

"Do you think that makes it easier to navigate?"

"Yes."

"What about your classes? Your teachers?"

"I like my classes." I watched his foot shake. "I really like my French teacher, Madame Etienne."

"So you decided to take French, after all." He chuckled, and I looked up, reminded of my previous stance. "Well, I'm amazed, nonetheless."

I nodded quietly.

"And what about your friends?"

My eyes flickered. "Friends?"

"Yes, have you made any new friends at this new school?"

"Yes," I answered right away, Liam's bright smile shoving its way into my mind. "I-I mean, no."

"Not one new friend?"

"I mean—" I shook my head and pushed my hair back again. "I do have a new friend. One new friend."

"Very good. Do you want to tell me about this new friend?"

I locked my fingers again. Staring directly at him. "His name is Jean."

"I assume he's in your grade."

"No, he's actually graduating this year."

"A senior?"

I nodded.

"Okay. Tell me a little about him."

"Dr. Portis, I really don't—"

He chuckled again. "Dr. Portis? You'd think I'd lost my Ph.D."

I sighed, wringing my fingers. "Can we talk about something else?"

"Of course." He looked down at his notes and then closed the notepad altogether before leaning up. "Elonie, if I may be so forward, you seem to be more than just standoffish today. Is there any reason as to why?"

I shook my head.

"Are you sure there's nothing you'd like to talk about? Three months is a long time for nothing to have happened."

"A lot has happened," I started, feeling a small smile inch onto my face.

"Have things been all right with your father?"

Any trace of a smile vanished, and I closed up, lowering my gaze again. "Things are fine. He mostly stays here in the city."

"I see." He adjusted in his cushioned seat, and his legs switched over. "Does that bother you, Elonie?"

I shook my head.

"Not even a little?"

"I prefer it."

"Hm."

I looked up at the clock again. It'd looked as if it'd barely moved an inch.

"Elonie, do you mind if I…do you mind if I ask you about your mother?"

My eyes shot over to him. "Why?"

"Well, I just wanted to check and see how you're coping with your memories. Remember we talked about the methods you could use when you feel—"

"I've been using them," I assured him, then I scooted to the edge of my seat. "Maybe we should end now. I have to meet with my dad for lunch soon. "

"Elonie," he gently said my name, but I already felt the walls caving in.

"The restaurant is in midtown, and our driver—"

"Elonie, please." He stood up as I crouched down in my chair. I watched him walk over to his desk. "These appointments are not intended to ambush you. You're free to cut our sessions short at any time."

I nodded, letting out a short breath. "I'm sorry, I just—"

"No need to apologize. We'll just set up our next meeting in about a month. What do you say?"

"A month?"

He faced me, one hand holding my file, the other sifting through the pages inside of it. Dr. Portis, Ph.D hadn't lost his height with age.

He stood like a towering building in his button-up cardigan attire. I used to imagine him as my father so many times. Sometimes, it felt as though I could be his daughter. Until I found out that he already had a daughter—and a granddaughter. That news had crumbled my make-believe world into pieces. But he'd had no idea I used to think of him that way. All he'd known was what I'd shown him. What I'd allowed him to see. He wouldn't have even known about mom if Presley hadn't mentioned it. But we'd rarely talked about her. Except for those few times, I'd let my emotions get the best of me. But that couldn't happen this time. I had to control myself. I had to get out of his office.

"I would really like it if we met a little sooner this time."

I thought quickly on my feet. "Can we meet virtually?"

He raised a graying eyebrow. "Virtually?"

"I think it's best given the distance, and maybe it will help me feel more comfortable opening up if we're not so…face to face."

"I see." He returned his gaze to the documents. "I'll set it for virtually then."

I sighed again in relief and smiled to myself. "Thank you, Dr. Portis—" He looked at me, and I laughed, "Ph.D."

"You're welcome."

I grabbed my bag from the floor, bringing it over my head, then rose out of the uncomfortable chair. He gave me a smile as he followed me to the door.

"Elonie," He caught my attention as I stood outside of his office, "I want to give you two challenges for next time."

I swallowed but accepted his words with a nod. "Okay."

"The first thing I want you to do is continue using the methods I showed you to handle any upsetting memories and feelings that occur. You need to feel comfortable with accepting the negativity as it comes in order to best handle it." He raised his chin. "Remember, try not to rely on others or self-harm in order to fix the problems. Those are only avoidance mechanisms."

I bit my inner cheek as I nodded, waiting for the next instructions.

"The second thing I want you to do is more of a homework assignment," he continued with a softer expression now. "I want you to write a letter to your mother. It can be about anything you want." He then smiled again at me. "Can you do that for me?"

I closed my eyes briefly, then answered, "Yes, I can do that."

But I knew it would be hard. I thought about the letter as I climbed into the backseat of the awaiting car. Closing my eyes as I leaned against the door—sunshine on my cheeks—and imagined her.

What's this, choupette?

I smiled, staring at that perfect smile, those frizzy braids she wore down her back, those liquid eyes… like dew drops on a maple leaf.

I made you a present, mama.

For me?

Those eyes lit up as I remembered that day, watching her take the piece of paper out of my small hand. I'd been just a kid then, but I'd been so sure I'd had the cure. In that one little drawing of me and her, I knew I could fix my mother.

Thank you, chouchoutte. My pretty little girl.

My sweater pocket began to buzz, and I opened my eyes, sniffling as I reached for my phone.

305 Parker Ave

I squinted, reading the text again, before feeling my heart catapult against my chest.

"Excuse me," I called out, quickly gaining the attention of the driver. "Can you go to 305 Parker Ave instead? It's still in midtown."

He glanced at me through the rearview mirror, and I stiffened. It had been the first time I'd actually taken a good look at him since my father hired him as our driver. I immediately felt scolded by those dark irises, but he gave me a firm nod, silently agreeing to drop me off.

I took a deep breath, attempting to unravel the tension within me and focus on my excitement. Jean had actually come all the way to the city. Just to see me. I bit my lip to keep from grinning too hard. I hadn't wanted to meet with Presley anyway. I knew all he'd want to talk about was her. I guess this was payback, after all—at least, I had no doubt that's exactly how he would see it.

Nice try, Presley

305. I looked out of the window as we slowly pulled up to the curb, where the gold numbers were printed on the long hotel awning.

"What time should I return, Miss?" the driver asked.

I swallowed the nerves that had started crawling up my dry throat and met his gaze in the mirror again. "An hour, maybe?"

His eyelids swept down, expressing his displeasure with my answer.

"An hour is fine," I repeated with more assurance. He seemed to accept it. "What's your name, if you don't mind me asking?"

The question sounded absurd, leaving my mouth. It'd been months that I'd been riding in this backseat with him at the wheel, and not once had I bothered to learn his name. It hadn't been that long ago that I'd refused to accept my new circumstances altogether. Hiding out in that cold bedroom every single day. Only finding solace on that rickety window seat. I'd wanted to cut deep enough so that I could escape the gloomy prison he'd moved us into. I'd wanted to escape everything. But now I couldn't even fathom never meeting Jean. It caused a pain in my chest just thinking about it.

"Benjamin Dempsey," my driver said, seemingly caught off guard.

I smiled at him. "I'm Elonie. It's nice to meet you, Mr. Dempsey."

He returned my smile with a nice hearty laugh that shocked me but also filled me with the warmest sensation, completely erasing my nerves. "It's nice to finally meet you, too, Elonie," was all he said before seeing me off.

I watched the big black vehicle driving further and further away from me as I stood on the curb. Still beaming from ear to ear.

"Hey girl," a familiar voice called out.

I turned around so hard I nearly tripped over my heel, and there Jean stood in front of the glass entrance, giving me one of those smirks of his. I didn't know what had come over me, but I ran to him. And I didn't stop until I reached him, throwing my arms around his narrow waist, pulling him in tight. Even as I did it, I felt how completely pathetic and desperate it must have looked. But my arms wouldn't let me let him go.

"What? Did you actually doubt me?" he asked as he laughed above.

I sunk my nose in his leather, shaking my head so I wouldn't lie. "I'm just so happy to see you."

"I couldn't let you wander these mean streets alone, now could I?" He brought his fingers to the root of my hair and lifted my head to meet his gaze. "Look at this face."

"Oh, no, don't look—" I quickly covered my eyes as my cheeks became warm. "I'm a wreck."

He chuckled, taking hold of my wrists and gently guiding them down. "Did I ever tell you that I like the way you look after you cry?"

"No, that's silliest thing I've ever heard," I said.

"But it's true," he continued, resting the back of his fingers against my hot cheek, brushing his thumb along my skin. "Tu es toujours aussi belle pour moi."

I closed my eyes as he came closer. Feeling the ground disappear underneath me. My body had become as the clouds that floated far above the awning we still stood underneath, having little awareness of the passerby, simply enclosed in the bubble we'd formed around us.

His soft lips settled on my forehead, setting off tiny sparks throughout my face. It hadn't exactly been what I'd expected. I wanted what I'd seen so many times in the movies. I wanted him to kiss me right here, right now, for all the world to see.

"Where should we go first?" he muttered, his lips tickling my skin.

I hadn't opened my eyes yet. Intent on making the moment last. "I guess I'm a little hungry," I still answered.

His lips spread into a smile against my forehead. "There's a café a few blocks down the street."

I thought about Benjamin and how I'd told him to return in an hour, gearing up to relay the same thing to Jean, but as soon as I opened my eyes and saw his locking me in their grip, I just couldn't get the words to come out. "Okay."

He hailed a cab like a pro, and we slipped into the backseat of it, directing the driver where to go. He held my hand the entire ride to the small bistro on the corner, and even when we got out, he still latched onto it all the way up until we were seated by a barista. The menu made my mouth water upon viewing it, but I'd waited to see what he'd order before saying anything. He'd asked for their house blend coffee and a roasted turkey sandwich along with the soup of the day. I tried not to appear too stunned as I asked for a coffee and their soup, as well. He didn't appear as if anything were out of the ordinary as he placed his gaze on me from across the table once our barista had gone. I followed in his nonchalant mannerisms, leaning up when he did, gaining a chuckle out of him.

"Is this the first time you've been back since you moved away?" he asked.

I picked up my rolled silverware just to have something to distract myself with in case any uncomfortable questions came up. "Yes. There's nothing really to come back to." I shrugged my shoulders. "I guess I burned a lot of bridges when I lived here."

He nodded, lowering his eyes. "Maybe it was for the best."

"Yea?"

"Yea, I mean, all of those burned bridges landed you here with me."

I smiled a little. "They did, didn't they?"

Our waitress returned moments later with our meal, and I took that chance to change the subject. I wanted to remain in a good mood for as long as I could. That meant no more shedded tears or unwanted memories about the past. I would make this day a happy one. I knew I could do it if I tried.

Jean made it easy, though.

He kept me entertained with his stories. Especially the ones about the places he'd traveled to. It still amazed me how many places he'd already been in such a short span of his life.

"Are you being serious?" My eyes widened as I set my coffee back down. "Insects?"

"Mhm. Deep fried." Jean tore a strip of lettuce from his barely touched sandwich and tossed it in his mouth, grinning at my expression. "It's actually not bad."

"You tried it?"

He laughed aloud as he leaned back in his chair. "No, I'm kidding."

I frowned at his teasing, beginning to stir the remainder of my soup, which had become cold. "Remind me never to visit Japan."

Jean sighed, flagging down our barista with his hand before going into his jacket for his wallet. "Where to next?"

I pushed the saucer that my bowl sat on, slightly twisting my lips. "Actually…"

"What? You're already bored of me?"

"No—" I sat up on my toes, prepared to reassure him, although his attention had been temporarily grabbed by the barista clearing away our dishes.

"Was there anything wrong with the food?" she asked him as she set his plate on the large platter she held.

"It was delicious," he replied, plucking a cigarette out of his box.

"Oh, sorry, but you can't smoke that here."

He cocked his brow. "We're outside."

"My boss doesn't let anyone smoke on the patio." She shrugged one shoulder, and my eyes dropped to her nametag: Fatimah. "It's just the rules."

"Is that so?"

My breath caught as he inserted the cigarette between his lips anyway, and the barista's hand found her hip.

"Hey—"

"Relax," he uttered, the stick wobbling in his mouth. "I'm not going to light it." He then gave her a subtle smile. "I just don't do too well with rules."

Fatimah shook her head as she rolled her eyes away, but I noticed a hint of a smile. "I'll be right back with your check."

Something about that short moment made my insides squirm. Fatimah couldn't have been any real threat to me. Sure, she had gorgeous dark features and some sort of foreign accent, but what were the chances of them seeing each other again? My fingers drummed along the table, my fist tucked underneath my chin, so wrapped up in my thoughts that I hadn't heard him saying my name.

His hands were warm as he took mine, and I looked up, giggling at the cigarette still hanging on for dear life. "What were you thinking about?"

I couldn't tell him the truth. The truth being that I had already imagined myself getting picked up from the hotel, us saying our goodbyes, me sitting in the backseat plagued by the thought of him heading back to the café just to get her number. I couldn't tell him that.

"I was just thinking about the bookstore I used to go to," I said instead.

He smiled with all of his teeth, and I reached for the cigarette, pulling it out. He laughed and wiped away his drool.

"All right. Show me this bookstore of yours, then."

I hailed the cab this time. Suddenly very eager to be rid of this bistro, Fatimah, and all of their silly rules. But traffic had put us at a standstill. I didn't mind, though. I liked being stuck in the city with him. It still felt like a fever dream, and occasionally, I glanced over at him. Catching him taking drags from his cigarette while the wind from the open window blew a gentle breeze on him. He hung his wrist out, tapping ashes onto the street, and I found myself locked in again.

I understood more than I ever had before. Or maybe I just hadn't wanted to see it then. But it all made sense to me now. Brynn had every reason to be jealous. Fatimah had proven that point. Losing Jean's attention felt almost sinful.

Unnatural. Unforgiving.

Not because of the way his physical presence always managed to fill up space and time, not because of the chilled tone of his voice that commanded even the loudest of rooms. And, surprisingly, it had nothing to do with those sea-glass eyes of his.

Having Jean's attention made me feel alive.

I knew my blood didn't run cold because I felt its heat coursing through my veins every time he touched me. I felt my heart pump with the strength of a horse when he merely looked at me. I knew I looked the perfect image of health when my cheeks warmed underneath his heavy gaze as he spoke French to me.

Jean Cohen had given me a reason to keep living.

I led the way into the bookstore once we arrived. Absolutely nothing had changed except for the person behind the counter. But, then again, I hadn't ever come often enough to become truly accustomed to the staff. Only ever after my therapy sessions did I get the privilege of exploring the endless shelves filled with dusty books that I could add to my small collection. "So, this is where the bibliophile got her start." Jean walked up behind me, muttering close to my ear. "Please tell me I'm the only guy you've ever brought here."

I giggled. "Of course."

He nodded, both hands behind his back as he paused where he stood. "I actually believe you."

"No one knew I'd come here." I crossed my arms and squatted down in front of the poetry section. "This was sort of a thing I kept to myself."

"Why?"

I plucked an author I recognized from the stack. "I guess I didn't want anyone to ruin it."

"Am I ruining it?" He got down with me, and I looked over at his smirking face. "I can always go if you two want to be alone..."

I stifled my laugh again. "You're ridiculous."

We ventured further, and I toted the book I'd decided to get as we traveled between shelves into mysterious and foreign territory. Sections that I hadn't even bothered to check out before. Some books boggled me, and others made my face flush. Until finally, we stood, arm to arm, flipping through coffee table books with travel photography and the like. By the time we stepped back out onto the sun-beaten pavement, I knew that my time had run out, but I still didn't want to leave him.

"Any other suggestions—" He stepped forward into my shadow, and I fought the urge to wrap my arms around his neck. "Or we can just head back to the hotel?"

I knew I had to tell him about Presley's diabolical dinner plans, but just as I'd begun opening my mouth, my jaw locked in place—followed by the rest of my body. Jean's focus had shifted over my head. The tight clench of his jaw being an exact enactment of the ache that formed in the pit of my stomach after hearing my name.

"You move fast, don't you?" Danielle commented once I'd turned around and feasted my eyes on her. Taylor Wong stood right beside her. Both girls toting shopping bags on their arms. "Wasn't there a third party included in this little cult?"

"Brynn and I aren't involved anymore," Jean's voice left him in complete nonchalance.

I could barely swallow down the boulder in my throat, unsure of how to put my voice box back together to form coherent speech. But my silence had been enough for Danielle to put her own pieces of the puzzle together.

"Oh, I see." She and Taylor glanced at each other and laughed. "Well, you know what they say—once a backstabber, always a backstabber."

The word left a gash on me that stung, and impulsively, my comeback flew out. "You're the only backstabber here, Danielle."

"Aww," Danielle gave me an impish stare. "Sweetie, no. You must be faint from whatever spell you've been put under. You see, I'm not the one who betrayed the only person who had the dignity to stick up for you when you had your little accident in the middle of the hallway. Or did you forget about that?"

Taylor giggled into her cupped hand. "How could anyone forget about that?"

My eyes bulged as I lowered them to the pavement. Memories of that day crashing back in like a tsunami.

"You know what, I still can't forget," Jean spoke up again, though he barely sounded audible due to the muffled fog in my ear. "Our little meet-up in the hall that day…"

His voice went out. Leaving me underwater. I closed my eyes and tried to bring myself back to the surface.

"…I think I still know how to make you that desperate again."

My eyebrows knitted, and my eyes shot up just in time to catch the scowl on Danielle's flawless face, and for the first time, she'd properly acknowledged Jean. I imagined those green eyes held a thousand daggers, and each one was strategically slicing his body into tiny pieces of flesh.

"Come on, Taylor. My life is wasting away the more I stand here." She led the girl, who had completely gone silent after Jean had spoken, but Danielle stopped just short of passing by us, her eyes settling on me. "Don't even think about showing up to my prom, Elonie."

I didn't bother replying. I didn't even think I had any words left in me. Her presence lingered even after she'd left, causing me to feel suffocated in a way that even the fresh air surrounding me couldn't fix. The memories hadn't left with her. She'd conjured them up, and now they caused a flood in my mind. Jean must have noticed my struggle because those arms pulled me in, those fingers caressed my neck, and that voice told me to breathe.

"Just breathe, Mignonne."

I tried my hardest. But I could only manage tears at this point. Feeling as disgusted and overwhelmed with embarrassment as I felt in the hallway that day.

"Don't let her do that to you," he said, massaging my scalp as I leaked out. Ruining my chances for a scene like the one I'd imagined us having earlier. This had to be the complete opposite of romantic. "Don't let her win."

I attempted a deep breath as I finally gave a small nod. His words brought me back to the nook, and they comforted me.

He kissed the top of my head before lifting my face to look at him. "Let's go back to the hotel, okay?"

I suddenly remembered the dilemma I still faced. "I can't."

He appeared stumped. "Why not?"

"My dad wants me to have dinner with him tonight," I explained whilst taking short breaths. "He's already made reservations uptown."

"Just don't show up." He slid his hands down to my shoulders and gently gripped me. "I want you here with me, Elonie."

My lip curled in a smile. I wanted to be with him, too.

So I went back to his hotel. Knowing eventually I would get another phone call. The first one had come earlier, around the time we'd gotten seated at the café, but I'd ignored it. I hadn't wanted any distractions taking me away from the short amount of time I'd had with Jean. I had no idea what I would say anyway. Nothing else seemed more important than this. Not even the fact that I had basically betrayed Benjamin's trust.

"Do you think he'll wait out there all night?" Jean asked as he unlocked the door to his room.

I shivered from the cold air that seeped through the crocheted holes of my sweater, half listening, half absorbed by the posh apartment-style suite. "I hope not…"

My eyes wandered around the intimate space, momentarily causing me to forget how I'd practically dodged a bullet downstairs, having spotted our SUV parked curbside in front of the hotel. Benjamin still sat waiting, but I knew Presley would not make him stay there all night. It felt good to inconvenience Presley, but Benjamin didn't deserve this. I'd instantly regretted ever introducing myself as we raced into the hotel's lobby, Jean having lent me his jacket to cover my head. I held that leather jacket at my front now as I explored each area of the suite before being pulled in by the wrap-around terrace outside.

"It's beautiful," I uttered once Jean walked up beside me, staring out at the view of the city.

"Have you never been this high up?"

"Once." I glanced up at him. "But I barely remember. I was so little."

He shifted around, pressing his back against the stone railing, both arms perched on either side of him. Just like that, I forgot about the view, granting him my gaze in return.

"Isn't it funny how you can know so much about a person yet so little at the same time?" His eyelids swooped down as if he were thinking deeply about it. "That's how I feel when I'm with you."

I didn't know what to say. I just kept my eyes on him. Watching his red lips form a smile, he kept to himself.

"I guess that's how you feel, too," he assumed.

I sheepishly nodded. "I had no idea you'd—well, that you and Brynn weren't friends anymore."

"Yea…" He sniffed, scratching his jaw, then running those same fingers through his hair. "I can't really talk about her right now."

"But if it was something I caused—"

He laughed, tossing his head back. "Not even close."

The curiosity bit at me now. I desperately wanted to know the reason. But I could tell he wouldn't budge, and I was in no position to make him. After all, we were just friends, too.

It had taken me a while to believe that about him and Brynn. I remembered the day I'd finally mustered up enough courage to ask. I didn't know what I'd hoped to achieve from gaining an answer. I just hadn't expected to be told—

"We were just friends," he spoke again with a shrug of his shoulders. "Friends grow apart. It's just how it is, you know?"

No. Not really. Because Jean was the only real friend I'd ever had. "Do you miss her?"

He didn't know, but I noticed how the question made him wince as if I'd reopened a fresh wound. But the expression had been quick, and slowly, he faced me. Reaching out and tucking away a poofy strand that whipped against my cheek. I hadn't even felt it, too wrapped up, anticipating his next words.

"I've got you now," His eyes seemed to follow his fingers that remained in my hair, gently caressing the underside as if I were his pet cat, "don't I?"

I could feel my knees weakening as he continued the gentle stroke; my voice lodged somewhere in my throat, and my brain liquefied into soup. I could barely keep my eyes open, but I felt him inch closer to me, and the smaller the space got, the more oxygen left my body. Until my chest was fully heaving. That conniving little organ doing backflips inside of it.

"Mignonne…"

"Hm?"

"Tu veux toujours m'embrasser?" He whispered it.

My eyes closed at the familiar French leaving his mouth, simply nodding my head again.

His fingers grasped my jaw. "Je veux vous embrasser…"

"Embrasse-moi."

I realized my voice. Startled by how raw and breathy it sounded but excited that I had become a scene. We had become a scene. I wished that I could see it all happening. But this was better. Jean's lips brought me out of my head and back to the surface. They moved against mine like a paintbrush. Feeling even better than they had before. Everything around us grew so quiet and then, nothing but silence. And his hands, gripping me, face…neck…hair… I began to sink under his overpowering need for me. But I held onto him. Letting him lead. Following his every move.

My chest only worsened as the thump became maddening, sending all kinds of signals throughout my body but completely omitting my head. My brain sat inactive. My thoughts were placed on hold. Jean continued to lead me. Over the threshold, back into his suite, on top of that bed.

The same bed that I'd barely glanced at walking in. Having no clue of how things might end up. Only being wrapped up in the ambiance and the view and the way his leather felt on my skin.

"Wait," I pulled my bruised lip away from his, clutching his arms as I raised up to my elbows, "I left your jacket out there on the ground."

Jean's face, now flushed, appeared baffled, almost as if I'd spoken gibberish, but realization soon hit and brought forth a belly laugh out of him. I watched as he flipped over onto his back.

"You crack me up, girl."

I chewed into my lip. "Sorry, I don't know—"

"It's okay."

I sat up further, face in palm. "I'm such an idiot."

"Hey…" I dropped my hand and glanced at him, letting him take my wrist and pull me down, too. "Don't be so harsh."

He brought my wrist to his lips, pecking at it softly, and my insides crumbled and withered away. I went in for more.

Wanting to feel those lips on mine again.

Somehow, even more than before.

He wanted the same. I could tell by the way he greeted my mouth again. Cradling my head like a familiar lover. Like someone he'd been kissing forever.

"Elonie," he breathed my name just as I'd come up for air again.

His expression made me pause, a flurry of thoughts rushing back to the forefront. "Yes?"

He brought his arm across my waist and pulled me closer to him as we lay face to face. "Have you ever done this before?" I stiffened, and I must have looked guilty because he slid that hand up my back and began to rub. "It's all right. You can trust me."

Those exact words had been spoken to me before. But I refused to compare Jean with him. Still, images of Cole began to form in my mind. Images that I couldn't bear to see after everything that had happened. I didn't want to remember how he used to kiss me underneath the breezeway between classes. Or hidden in his car after swim practice.

The memories left a bad taste in my mouth now.

"I've kissed before," I confessed half-heartedly.

Jean cracked a smile. "Anything more than that?"

My eyes fluttered. Reading between the lines of those deep irises. My lips parted. The truth sat right there in its usual place. I nodded as a reply. Anything to keep me from having to lie straight to his face. But Jean saw beyond it. My eyes stung from the dissection they were getting. I had to look away.

"I only ask to know how gentle I should be with you."

My heart melted at his words, heat rising up my neck and reaching my face, fully breaking me out. I felt horrible for lying now. But I couldn't even focus because his lips found mine again. The heat transferred directly to the kiss and swiftly relieved me of that tension. My mouth had turned sore from all the pulling and stretching that. It hadn't been too long before I'd needed rest again. Jean, however, needed none. He'd naturally moved down to my neck. But my tremble forced him to stop, even though the pained expression on my face would have told him otherwise.

"So you are."

I could only utter a meek yes as we stared at each other, him looking down at me and me up at him.

"I'll be extra gentle then." He lowered again and pressed his lips to my forehead. "You can trust me, Elonie."

I closed my eyes. Holding onto him tight.

I trust you, Jean Cohen.

I think I always have.

30

"*Brynn… are you even listening to me?*"

A *sharp ringing tone cut my eardrum, and I flinched, cupping my palm over my ear. My surroundings—a claustrophobic cage on wheels—immediately reminded me of where we were headed. I sunk lower in the passenger seat as I mashed the window down.*

"I just want to sit here in peace and quiet, Allan," I uttered.

His eyes drifted back over to me. I didn't even need to look at him. I felt them, heavy and pitiful. "Brynn, just tell me what you need."

"I just told you," I snapped, feeling only slightly sorry for being so harsh. "I need peace and quiet. That's all I want right now."

He didn't say another word. I nestled my cheek onto my palm and glared at my reflection in the rear window. I didn't even recognize the girl sitting there. The disheveled curls. The reddened eyelids. The permanent frown. She definitely didn't look like me… or who I used to be.

I looked away from the image, focusing on the wind lapping against my cheeks, feeling its frost for the first time in weeks.

If it had been up to me, I would have never left that closet. I would be content if I never left the house again. But, of course, I was still a kid. Even though I no longer felt like one. Inside, I felt like I'd already lived so many lives. I felt like I'd already died so many times. But my father didn't understand. He reminded me of the responsibility I still had. He said I owed her that much. And I guess I did.

I did owe my mother.

But I knew the only way to truly repay her didn't involve being lugged back to this dull brick prison.

"Allan," Danielle called out to her brother once we'd entered the packed cafeteria, "over here."

I already felt like climbing out of my skin the moment we'd stepped foot inside of the school. All of the memories rushed forward to greet me, and I'd almost suffocated from merely the smell of these inner walls. I'd begged not to be sent back.

How could I walk through these halls without seeing him? How could I go about my day knowing he was no longer here? Nothing would be the same without him. And I didn't want to pretend.

I refused to pretend.

Allan led us over to their usual booth. Acting as a human shield. I wished he wouldn't try so much. I hated that he insisted on doing things for me. Not like it was a new trait of his. But for some reason, I could stand it even less than I could before.

He'd picked me up from my house. He'd made sure my assignments weren't missed. Always trying to come by and check on me day after day. But I despised his attempts. I despised him. And I had no idea why.

"Brynn," Danielle said my name like a sad hymn. "I've missed you so much."

I dared to meet her gaze, staring straight through her. Her words didn't matter much to me. It was that expression on her face that unnerved me. I'd seen it time and time again. Usually, in situations where she needed attention or wanted favor. I could tell she craved both. Their attention, my favor. I saw the unspoken apology in the depths of her snakeskin eyes, but I remained unmoved. Keeping my mouth shut in fear of letting something nasty slip out.

"We really have, Brynn," Sophie backed up her friend's claim, nodding her head as if that could somehow make Danielle's words genuine.

Allan glanced down at me when I still hadn't replied. "I'm going to grab breakfast. Do you want anything?"

"No," I said.

"Come on, Brynn." His tone lowered, and I felt his hand on my back. "You need to eat."

I didn't have the same self-control when it came to Allan. My eyes shot up and pierced him with daggers. "Don't touch me."

"At least sit down, Brynn," Danielle insisted, rising from her seat and presenting the empty spot next to her. "We want to tell you about the flower memorial we're planning for Ethan's locker."

Her words stilled me, and a bitter bile sensation journeyed up my throat. "I don't want to sit down, and I don't want any breakfast." I could feel my heart racing as the voices surrounding us quieted under my stern tone. "I just want you to leave me alone." I then looked back up at Allan. "Both of you."

Allan swallowed down, looking every bit like a hurt puppy. I couldn't bear to stand there and stare at the frown weighing down his face. Though I could still see it, penetrating through the blackness, as I sat in the bathroom stall moments later with my head buried in my arms. I didn't like that look he'd given me. It conjured up too much pain between us.

"Brynn?"

I gripped my arms tighter, refusing to lift my face. "Go away, Danielle."

But her little heels only tapped closer to the stall I hid in until she finally stopped right in front of the door. "We all understand what you're going through, Brynn, but don't you think that was a little uncalled for?"

A familiar flame lit inside of me, and I scrambled up to my feet, yanking the door open and giving her the hardest glare I think I'd ever given her. "What did you just say?"

"I'm saying you don't have to cause a scene in the middle of the cafeteria—"

"My brother is dead."

Danielle pressed her lips as she folded her arms across her torso. "I know. And I'm really sorry about that."

"I'm so tired of hearing that." I laughed mirthlessly as I walked towards her. "I mean, what does that even mean? Why on earth should you feel sorry? It didn't happen to you. For once, something doesn't revolve around you, Danielle."

"You really shouldn't use your brother's death as an excuse to act like a brat."

"You really shouldn't use my brother's death as some sort of sick scheme to gain more brownie points." I narrowed my eyes in bitter contempt. "As if I haven't already seen your true colors..."

Danielle huffed and turned away from me, but not before I noticed an odd, unfamiliar expression cross her otherwise normally bright features. "I'll tell my brother you just needed to calm down and freshen up and that you'll join us again in a few."

"How about you tell your brother to stop acting like things are back to normal? We're not together. He doesn't need to check up on me or take me to school anymore."

"First of all, your father is the one who spoke to mine. He suggested Allan drive you. How else would you get here? We know you haven't driven your car since the—"

"Just tell him I'll figure it out on my own!"

Danielle pulled both tan eyebrows together and gave me a sharp look. "You're lucky Allan even cares after everything you put him through."

With those final words, she left me, the bathroom door swinging shut behind her. And that heavy silence followed. But I couldn't breathe. My chest heaved, and no amount of deep breaths resolved it. I had to go. I had to leave this place and this time, never come back. I rushed out of the bathroom and headed towards the front office. Ignoring the eyes that watched me as I outwardly panicked.

"I need to speak with Principal Singh right now." The words toppled out of my mouth as I fought to catch my breath.

Miss Jenkins looked up from her computer, eyes widening with concern. "Oh, welcome back, Brynn. I'm so sorry about—"

"Miss Jenkins, please, I just need a dismissal slip."

"Dismissal?"

"I don't feel well, and I want to go home."

"Okay, dear." Miss Jenkins nodded and pointed to the chairs behind me. "Take a seat over there. I think she's finishing up a phone meeting. It shouldn't be too much longer, but I'll notify her in the meantime.'"

It wasn't exactly what I'd wanted to hear. I'd wanted to be told to go right in. I didn't want to wait. I just wanted to leave. But I figured anything was better than being around them a minute longer.

I sat down. Fixing my gaze on Singh's office door. Aware of Miss Jenkin's occasional glances, though I didn't allow it to bother me. I knew what everyone thought about when they saw me. That's why I'd chosen to stay holed up inside. I couldn't stand all the pleasantries. I hated being felt sorry for.

I chewed my lip and chipped away at my nails as I waited for that door to open up. Becoming a little too excited (to the point where I'd jumped up) when I finally heard that wonderful sound. But I was wrong. The door that had opened was not to Principal Singh's office. It had been the front door of the main office. That short-lived sensation dissipated, and I sunk back down onto the chair, becoming irritable again.

"How can I help you?" Miss Jenkin's petite voice questioned the student.

"I need to speak with Principal Singh about a test score."

"I'm sure that's probably something more suitable to talk over with your teacher."

"Hollandsworth sent me up here." A deep chuckle gained my attention, and I turned my head to the side, noticing the gangly guy folded over the counter. "He thinks I cheated since I missed a few classes this week, so he's leaving it up to Singh to decide what happens."

"Okay, well, take a seat, Mr. Cohen. She'll be with you shortly."

He leaned up from the counter, and I quickly looked away, forcing my attention to my bitten nails again. I listened as he moved across the hardwood floor, choosing that empty seat directly across from mine, that dingy leather jacket creaking as his hands settled into its pockets.

But I didn't dare look up. I ignored him, as I often had before, minding my brother's only demand. It amazed me, even now, that I'd actually listened to him. I didn't necessarily have a rap sheet for listening to anyone. But I had stayed away from Jean Cohen. It'd been something I hadn't found hard to do. He'd never struck me as someone worth getting to know.

"Hey, girl."

I lifted my gaze. My irritability trumping my willpower. Those deep eyes of his were droopy as he sat slouched, curling his lip at me.

"My name isn't girl," I said with a small bite in my tone.

"Yea, I know your name. It's Walsh."

I rolled my eyes away, checking Principal Singh's door, only to be let down again.

"What are you here for?"

My eyebrow cocked at him. "Excuse me?"

"Are you in trouble with Singh, too?"

My face rested again, realizing he hadn't meant any harm by the question. "I'm going home."

Another deep chuckle slipped out of him. "Didn't you just get back?"

I swallowed and lowered my eyes to my lap. "I don't want to be here." I picked at the old skirt I wore, fingering a loose thread to distract myself. "What does it matter to you anyway?"

"It doesn't." He finally raised up and leaned forward, resting his dangling arms on his legs. "I guess I'm just captivated that a Walsh is still even talking to me."

"It's Brynn," I shot back, hardening my gaze. "And I'm actually done talking to you."

A silent pause hung in the air between us. I had already looked away again, but I still felt those blue eyes watching me. Reminding me of the few occasions when I'd used to see him in the hallway. I'd always had Allan or Ethan to protect me from getting pulled into an unwanted conversation.

Neither one of them seemed to like Jean. But it saddened me knowing that even that had changed. I was now left alone with the beast that roamed the halls of this school, and I only had myself to fend for.

"Don't leave."

His voice startled me, and I glanced back at him, noticing he held out his keys towards me. "What?"

"I'm parked in the lot," he explained. "You can hide out in my truck until the bell rings."

"I'm not—"

"Come on. Don't be proud."

My lips parted. But the sound of a door opening caught both of our attention before I could retort.

"Miss Walsh." Principal Singh's solid tone parted through the hushed silence of the office.

I looked at her expectant face and then back at Jean. He suddenly tossed me his keys, and impulsively, I caught them.

Shocking myself.

"Mr. Cohen, what is the meaning—"

"I changed my mind." The words seemed to be someone else's, but they succeeded in cutting Singh off before she got the chance to scold him. "It's just a small headache. I'll go by Nurse Miller's office instead."

Principal Singh shifted her glass eyes between Jean and I, clearly connecting dots in her head. "See to it then, Miss Walsh."

I frowned, squeezing the keys now enclosed in my palm. I grabbed my bag up from the floor and quickly headed back out into the hallway. I couldn't think straight. I could barely walk straight. But I kept on going. Right outside and towards the parking lot. Following the honking sound of his key alarm. I finally noticed the blinking headlights of the gray truck sitting right there in the lot, and I'm not sure why, but I didn't hesitate. I guess I already saw it as a safer place than that building would ever be.

I got in.
Locked the doors.

And breathed.

Then I broke down. It surprised me how quickly it hit. But everything just opened up and poured out of me. And I hated it. I hated that I still had tears to cry. Each time I thought I had finally shed them all, they returned with a vengeance.

I shoved my face into my hands, trying to calm myself down, but Ethan had already appeared there in the dark. I knew eventually he would. I had gone much too long without seeing him at least once already. But I knew what had triggered my guilt.

I sniffled, picking up my head allowing my eyes to take in my surroundings. That initial comfort I had felt slowly disappeared and, in its place, a strong state of regret. Once again, I was suffocating.

I fell out of the passenger seat, nearly coughing up a lung as I stood hunched over outside. I swallowed down in between hacking. Nothing but gravel staring me back in my face.

"Hey—"

I gasped, flinching away from the hand that grasped my arm. Jean stood near me, hovering more like it, and my breath hitched. Feeling so tiny underneath his all-encompassing figure.

"What happened?" He looked vaguely concerned but also sort of amused by me.

I shook my head, pressing my hand to my forehead. "Nothing, I'm fine, I just needed air."

"Have you just been standing out here the whole time?" He laughed as he snatched his keys back from me. "The point was to hide out."

"I told you I'm not hiding from anyone."

He sighed, pulling a cigarette pack from his black jeans. "You make it sound so negative. I didn't mean it like that." He then held the pack out towards me. "Have a smoke. It'll calm you down."

"I quit."

He slipped one between the crack of his teeth. "Smoking is a language, Brynn. You can always brush up on your skills."

The sound of my name on his tongue stilled me. He said it with a softness I'd never heard before. As if it were always a part of his vocabulary.

"I shouldn't have listened to you."

He lit the end of the cigarette, eyes squinted as he took that first drag. "Because of your brother, right?"

I blinked, stunned at the sudden mention of him. "Don't talk about him."

"He told you to stay away from me, and now you don't know why." He plucked the cigarette out and tilted his head back, blowing skyward. "Maybe it's because you're as weird as I am now."

I couldn't help but grimace. "I'm nothing like you."

He brought the cigarette to his mouth again, taking a huge step towards me, forcing my body to become trapped between his and the truck. I still had a sliver of room to inch my way out from in front of him, but I had become fully paralyzed.

I should've listened.

Why didn't I just listen?

My gut screamed at me now. But I could only watch him closely. Not wanting to give him the satisfaction of my fear. His eyes traveled up my face, and my chest hiked as he brought his fingers to the stray curl hanging down my forehead.

"You used to wear those ribbons in your hair," he muttered, seemingly marveled by the absence of the accessory. "Like some sort of human doll."

I turned my face away, clenching my jaw tight, the same for my fist below. "Let me leave."

He exhaled, and I closed my eyes as the smoke swarmed my face. "You don't even know what you're afraid of."

"I'm not afraid. I just know where I belong."

"In there with all of them?"

"No." I eyed him, turning my head and raising my chin. "Far away from you."

He smiled for the first time since we'd begun talking, and it threw me off seeing him grinning down at me like that. Then he moved away, causing me to release the heaviest breath I hadn't been aware I'd been holding this whole time.

"Get in," he said as he opened up the door on his side.

I turned around again. "Excuse me?"

He hopped on the foot ledge and hung over the door. "You said far away, right?"

"I said far away from you."

"Don't tell me you'd rather go back in there." He took several quick drags of his cigarette before tossing it away. "They'll just smile in your face and offer you condolences all day. But if you come with me, I swear I'll treat you the way you want to be treated."

I crossed my arms over myself, though curious. "How would you know what I want?"

"Because it's the same thing that I want." He leaned forward, staring me down, dissecting me with his eyes. "I can promise you, you'll get no sympathy from me, Brynn Walsh."

I shook my head. "We are not the same, Jean Cohen."

"Maybe not before, but we are now."

My chest squeezed, and I gripped my arms to keep myself steady. I resented what he'd said, mainly because I knew it was the truth, but I hated the truth. I hated knowing Danielle had been right. I owed Allan just as much as, if not more than, I owed my mother. I hated knowing Ethan's heart was no longer hooked up to machines, that doctors weren't still fighting to keep him alive, and that he wouldn't be coming back home.

And I hated that today I'd fallen into the trap that is Jean. And that I saw myself in him now. I saw that beast because I had also become that beast. And everything I had ever been taught to hate had become me.

He was right.

We were now the same.

31

I didn't like the feeling of washing him off of me. Even as I stood beneath the warm stream, I could feel the leftover tingles of his lips melting off of my skin. He'd warned me that would happen. He'd even said it was bad luck in his teasing attempt to keep me in bed. Now I wish I had stayed, lying there underneath his warmth, letting him paint my collarbone with more kisses.

But that little self-conscious bug skittered it's way in again, forcing me to wrap the bed sheet around my exposed body and rush into the bathroom for a quick shower. Promising I'd be quick.

I turned the water off now.

There was no need to let all of those feelings go to waste.

I wished I could bottle them up and keep them as a memory. Spraying them on anytime, I wanted a taste of this moment. I smiled to myself as I stepped out of the tub onto the cold tile, reliving the best parts over again in my head. My cheeks flushed with heat, and I rushed over to the sink, staring at myself as I'd done when I came in. A stranger wouldn't be able to tell the difference, but I could see it. My aura had changed. Just as I knew it would. But, still, I couldn't believe it.

A knock sounded on the other side of the door just as I'd leaned over the sink edge to get a closer look.

"Is everything okay?" Jean's voice was low with concern.

"Everything's fine." I stepped over the abandoned sheet on the floor and reached for a towel, wrapping it around me.

"You're not hurt, are you?"

His words stilled me. "Of course not."

"Good." He sighed. "I just wanted to make sure."

I bit my lip to keep from grinning, and I rushed towards the door, though the reminder of the sheet still lying on the floor stopped me cold in my tracks. I hurried over to it, snatching it up and stuffing the stained thing into the laundry hamper, willing it to disappear altogether. Then I walked back out and joined him in the room. But I didn't make it but a few steps away from the door before I froze up again. My eyes widened as I noticed he still lay undressed in the bed then they dropped to my own clothes, still scattered on the floor. I quickly walked over and grabbed them.

"Are you leaving?" he asked suddenly.

I straightened, holding my clothes at my front, knitting my brow. "No, what makes you think that?"

He glanced down. "You're getting dressed again."

"I just thought—"

"We should?" he finished for me, one of his chuckles following after.

I was certain by now my cheeks would surely melt off. He appeared only amused as he grabbed the leather jacket that he'd retrieved from outside and got up..

"Turn around," he said.

And I did. Staring down at my wiggling toes to distract myself from his body standing so closely behind me. He placed the heavy material on my shoulders before guiding my hand away from the towel I still clinged onto. Everything fell to the floor, and I stood there wearing his jacket against my skin, wracking with a fresh wave of goosebumps.

I immediately faced him again. "Sorry. I have no clue how this goes."

"Don't worry, I'll try not to be too offended," he still teased.

I couldn't help but laugh along, pulling his jacket over my stomach as he led me back into bed.

The sky had grown dark, and the city lights had fully come on. I'd noticed that Jean had already switched on the lamps, flooding the room with a warm shade of brown-orange, setting me at ease again.

"Funny how it just swallows you whole," Jean mentioned, both hands comfortably underneath his head, just like the day in his courtyard.

I smiled, looking away from his relaxed posture and glancing down at his jacket. "I like it."

"I'll get you one that fits."

It was my turn to smirk as I turned onto my hip. "What makes you think I don't already own one?"

That made him laugh as he met my mischievous gaze, then he turned to me, holding his head up. "I'll believe it when I see it."

He stared at me long enough to make me blush, and I quickly glanced away. "M-maybe there's a good movie on TV…we should check."

He blew out a shallow sigh. "Movies are torture."

The smile on my lips faltered, although I was still convinced I'd heard wrong. "What?"

"I'm not really into them." His expression became reminiscent then he scoffed, "They're really bad at portraying real life anyway."

"But you always say we create our own reality."

"We do." He assured me with a simple chin nod. "And it's definitely not packed into an hour-and-a-half movie plot."

Still, I pulled at another straw. "Maybe that's their version."

"But why would anyone want someone else's version of reality?"

I swallowed down the painful throbbing in my throat, but it didn't go away. "I don't know."

"I guess if a person were into that sort of thing—" He finally looked back at me. "Are you?"

I forced my head to move. "No, I'm not really into them either."

He chuckled. "Just playing devil's advocate then?"

"Yea." I brought another smile to my face. "Devil's advocate."

His gaze swept down, landing on my curled legs, one of his hands simultaneously resting on top of my bare thighs. Again, he appeared to be thinking back to something. Normally, I wouldn't be able to catch all of these little cues, but I was slowly improving.

"How often do you do it?"

I let my eyes travel down to the old scars on my thighs, only just now realizing how exposed they were. I started to turn, but his finger deepened in my skin, stilling me in place.

"When we first met, I could still feel the scabs on some of them," he continued. "Have you done it since we met?"

"No."

He looked up at me, those eyes of his penetrating. "Neither have I."

I wanted to believe him. But I had already seen the fresh scars on his shoulder blades. I'd already felt them on his narrow hips. I didn't mention them. No matter how much I wanted to know why, he'd done it. What had made him need to do it?

"I know what Danielle brought up earlier hurt you," he said to me. "If I could take it back, I would. I wish we could've met differently."

I nodded, placing my hand on his. "It's okay."

"I've never met anyone like you, Elonie. I don't want to hurt you again."

"You won't." My hand moved up his arm and squeezed it, trying to convince him of my words. "You're my friend, Jean. The only friend I've ever had."

His eyes fluttered in disbelief. "That's not true."

"It is true."

He hooked his palm underneath my knee and pulled me closer to him. I rested my head on the pillow above us, and he did the same. "Tell me what it was like before me."

My eyes wandered below as my head was plagued with memories of what it was like. I didn't know how I could truly put everything into words. I didn't have the strength for it. If he knew just how difficult life had been before I met him then he'd be able to understand why I couldn't just simply tell him.

"With your eyes closed then," he muttered gently.

I stared into the black void behind my eyelids. Feeling his arm snake itself around me and, instinctively, I buried my face into his chest. At first, words fumbled out sloppily, stuttering over things I thought would be easier.

I'd shared the fact that it had been the first year I'd attempted to be a normal kid. I didn't want to be a homeschooled loner anymore. I wanted to experience what it was like to go to an actual school with actual friends in actual classrooms.

"My dad knew I wasn't ready," I explained. "He told me that I should wait until I was a little older." A small laugh left me as I recalled that conversation. "He'd been saying that since I was twelve."

"Why didn't he want you to go?"

"Because she never let me."

"Your mom."

I nodded. "He spent so much time trying to convince her to put me in school, but she never budged. Then she died, and he just—felt guilty, I guess."

"Why was she so against it?"

I slowly peeled my eyes open and looked up at him. "Please let me tell you about my dream instead."

"Elonie…"

"I really don't want to talk about her."

He took a deep breath. "Alright, tell me the dream, Mignonne."

I turned onto my back and stared up at the ceiling, starting a soft graze on the arm that still held me. All of a sudden, every detail whispered itself into my ear, and I grinned, looking up at him. "We were at your house, and the sun was shining so bright. It was the hottest day—summertime, I think."

He cracked a smile of his own. "Keep going."

"And we were both sitting out in the courtyard," I painted the picture again in my mind, "and you were playing with this ladybug that had landed on your finger. I told you how it was good luck." I giggled to myself. "You didn't buy it."

"Sounds like me."

"Then, all of a sudden, I heard a voice call my name, and when I looked over, I noticed your parents were out there with us. They were sitting at the tables, and your mom she asked me—" Jean's arm slowly slid off of my stomach, and I glanced up at him, realizing that his eyes were vacant and no longer on me. But I couldn't fight the strong urge to continue. "She asked me if we'd set a date…" I forced out a strangled laugh. "And the weirdest thing is she looked just like Madame Etienne."

A bitter chuckle escaped him as he rolled over. "You must've had a fever last night."

I lifted to my elbows and watched him reach down and pick up his discarded jeans from the floor, drawing out his cigarettes. He sat on the edge of the bed with his back to me as he smoked it. The silence that grew between us was thick enough to choke on. Even as I still lay blankly staring at him, I felt an uncomfortable tickle in my throat.

"Your dream is cute," he finally said after having taken several drags from the cigarette. "But unrealistic, to say the least."

"I agree." I sat up and crossed my ankles, gripping the jacket for some sort of comfort in the midst of the tension he'd created between us. "It was silly, but I figured I'd—"

"They'd never ask something like that." He leaned forward into a slouch as another thick cloud of smoke surrounded him. "They've never cared about a single thing I've ever done, and they definitely wouldn't care about that."

My breath hitched, and I swallowed roughly. "Jean…"

He slightly turned his head. "It's not your fault."

"But if I would've known…"

"Well, now you do."

But it wasn't enough. I craved to know the rest. I craved it like he craved to know me.

"What if we both…" My heart began palpitating before I could successfully get it out.

"Okay," he agreed and then looked over his shoulder. "Turn around then."

I held his stare for a few seconds more before I did what he said. Shifting to the other end of the bed and staring out at the city— sparkling so bright and standing so tall right outside of the terrace door windows.

Then I closed my eyes to it all. "Please go first."

I heard him exhale and soon after came that laugh of his that strangely comforted me right then.

"I don't know my parents," he told me with ease. "And I barely know the ones who adopted me."

Adopted?

The word stuck to me like glue. I bit my tongue to keep from asking him more.

"It's your turn," he soon reminded me.

I took a deep breath, placing both clenched fists on either side of me. "My mom was sick."

"Sick with what?"

"When were you adopted?"

He sighed. "I was thirteen."

"Where did they—"

"It's your go."

I brought my arm across and gripped my shoulder. "I can't remember what it was called…they never liked to talk about it around me."

"Why not?"

I lowered my head, feeling the pain behind my eyes as her voice filled my head. Mommy just feels everything a little too much sometimes. The dam broke and flooded my eyes. And I was helpless again.

"Hey, I'm right here," Jean's voice crept up behind me.

"It ate at her," I cried, folding down into myself. "I saw it. I saw it killing her, but I couldn't do anything to stop it."

Jean attempted to soothe me as he pulled me up into his body, bringing my legs onto the bed. "It's okay," he said.

"I couldn't make her stay."

"Maybe she wasn't meant to, Elonie."

"What do you mean?" I clung to his chest. Squeezing out more tears.

"You were meant to be here with me. And if she was still here… you wouldn't be."

I sniffled, thinking about what he'd said.

"It's not our fault." He gently caressed me with his tone. "It's not our fault they chose to leave us."

"But we won't leave each other, right?" I sniffled once more, pulling back and staring up at him. "I won't leave you, and you won't leave me."

He stroked the side of my face. "I would never leave you."

I held his wrist and closed my eyes, a sort of warmth settling throughout my body that I'd never known before. His lips put me in a trance. I was no longer here on earth. I was in the clouds…in heaven… transcending into another lifetime. But one with Jean. And no bad thing could ever happen to me there. Because I was with him. And deep down I knew I would always be with him.

I woke up the next morning remembering all that had happened. My body held all the details, and this time, I hadn't washed anything away. I felt his arms around me still as we both got dressed, and I frowned a bit as I returned his jacket.

"Thanks."

He stepped forward and took it, shrugging into it with ease. I turned to grab my bag from the floor, but he took my wrist and pulled me against him.

"Come back with me," he said.

I wanted to. Looking up at him right then, I couldn't think of being apart again. It didn't seem right. I knew him too well now.

"My dad wants me to meet her." I rested my cheek against his chest. "He'll kill me if I don't show up this time."

"Meet who?"

I rolled my eyes behind my closed lids. "Xandria."

He slightly pulled back. "Fabian?"

"Yes." I lifted my head, raising my brow. "You know her?"

"Famous for nothing socialite." He sucked his tooth and smirked. "My father's chairman of a real estate firm that both their grandfathers founded."

I could feel the confusion twisting my face. "She's an heiress?"

"And my father, an heir."

"Oh…"

He laughed, heading towards the door. "Maybe I will tag along. I haven't seen Xandie in a while."

I thought about what he'd just told me about his father, but there wasn't time to truly let it sink in. I would need to revisit it later.

"What do you say?"

My eyes fluttered as I climbed out of my head. "Sure."

I hadn't needed to give the suggestion much thought. It was Presley's fault we were even in this predicament. So, if he wanted to spring her onto me, then I would do the same.

I glanced over at Jean as we sat in another taxi, immersed in morning traffic. There were so many layers there that I hadn't peeled back yet. So much that I still didn't know. Now that I knew he felt the same way about me, too, I couldn't help but wonder if he still saw me as just entertainment. Maybe he didn't like movies because he had no control over the ending, but was I just a movie for him? He could find out everything he needed to know, and not like the ending. I wondered...is that what happened between him and Brynn?

I shook the fantastical thoughts out of my head. I couldn't let myself get too worried. We'd had the best night together. And I know he felt the same. I could hear those words still replaying in my head. I'll never leave you. I knew he meant every word.

"Don't answer it," Jean said as we climbed out of the cab and stood in front of the restaurant. "Surprise him."

I stared at the vibrating phone in my hand. It was the second phone call this morning. The first one had come after the text message I'd sent when I finally woke up. Informing Presley that I was alive and well and there was no need to worry. (Not as if he'd ever expressed worry). After those two phone calls yesterday, he'd given up, and I hadn't noticed the SUV parked outside this morning either. He'd picked up on exactly what I was doing. But he had no idea just how far I was willing to go to avoid being alone with them.

Although, by the expression he wore on his face now, something told me he had an inkling. I focused on counting my steps as we headed towards their reserved table, led by the host himself. I wanted Jean to hold my hand like he had before, but I was too nervous to reach for it myself. So I locked my fingers at my front and pretended they were his.

"Nice of you to finally join us," Presley greeted me with a hint of irritation in his tone as he stood up from the table.

I grinded my back teeth as I sat down across from her. Not once allowing our eyes to meet. Jean took a seat across from Presley. I glanced at him and noticed traces of humor on his face. It helped me relax, knowing he was unbothered. The last thing I wanted was for him to be uncomfortable.

"Xandria, I'd like you to meet my daughter, Elonie," Presley made introductions as soon as the host had left.

I reached for my water glass and took a deep sip just as she held out her hand towards me. But my eyes shot her daggers over the brim of the glass. And I held it long enough to prove a point. She retracted her hand and cleared her throat, taking up her orange juice with it now. She looked nothing like the retouched photos I'd seen. I noticed the little flaws on her face that made her more real and less for show. But I didn't let myself analyze for too long. It was better for me to think of her as unreal. Just another figment of my imagination.

"And your guest, Elonie?" Presley addressed me again.

I glanced over at Jean. Unsure of how to best introduce him.

"Jean Cohen." He reached across the table and shook my father's hand, taking it upon himself. "Pleased to meet you, sir."

Presley quickly nodded and released his hand. "The name sounds familiar."

"Ariel Cohen is my father."

"Ariel works with my father in real estate," Xandria mentioned as if to brush Presley's memory.

Presley slowly nodded, though his eyes narrowed a bit, causing my heart to pick up. "And what is it you're doing here with my daughter?"

"I wanted him here," I objected.

"Let him speak."

I looked over at Jean and shook my head. But he didn't seem at all phased by Presley's coldness.

"I heard an old family friend would be here," Jean simply replied. "I didn't plan on staying long."

Xandria gripped her glass now. "How are your parents, Jean?"

"I assume they're decent."

She nodded, seemingly unable to keep consistent eye contact with him. "And you?"

He smiled a little. "Well, I haven't really been the same since that thrilling afternoon."

Xandria blinked those dark eyes of hers away from him and pushed back from the table. "Please, excuse me."

I could see Presley's internal alarm going off. "Is it the baby?"

"No, don't worry, she's fine. I'll be…" A sort of ill expression crossed her face, and her eyes lowered in shame. "Oh, god, I'm so sorry, Presley."

"It's alright." Presley appeared to sweat bullets as he pulled at his collar. "It was an accident."

I, on the other hand, had completely stopped breathing. And by the way Presley and Jean stared at me, I was sure my face had turned all sorts of shades.

"We've been trying to tell you." Then, all of a sudden, he reached for my hand. "Elonie—"

"No, don't." My voice cracked and slipped past my trembling lips as I shifted back. "I don't want you to touch me."

"We were planning to tell you in a better way," Xandria attempted to placate me.

Tears spilled out of my eyes. "I don't care about your baby."

"Don't say that," Presley scolded me.

I glanced over at Jean, who sat speechless, though his eyes were speaking loudly at me. I nodded and watched him stand up from the table. I followed. Presley stood as well.

"You're not leaving," he said to me.

"You have everything you've ever wanted now."

"And what is that, Elonie?" He leaned towards me, fighting to keep his voice contained. "Do you even know what you're saying?"

I shook my head. "I hope she makes you happy."

"Elonie, don't do this. Don't walk out of here, Elonie!"

I ran off before he could come after me. Leaving behind even Jean. I felt every watching eye and the heaviness of the walls as they closed in.

But I was almost there.

Only a few more steps until I could disappear.

"Elonie!"

My arm dropped down from the cab I'd been hailing, and I turned around, watching Jean head towards me.

A huge, displaced grin on his face.

"Where were you headed without me?"

I let out a frustrated laugh, tears still raining down my cheeks. He took my face in both palms, using his thumbs to wipe them away, before pressing his lips to mine.

In the middle of the sidewalk. For everyone to see. It was even better than how I'd imagined it.

"Have you had enough of this city yet?" he asked.

I nodded with my eyes still closed. "I'm ready to go home."

32

"Honey, wake up."

I mumbled at the voice, pulling my pillow over my head as I turned
away.

"Brynn…honey…you're already late for school."

Now, there was no mistaking the voice belonged to my mother.
Her nails tickled my back as she lightly shook me. Sleep was pretty
much hopeless at this point. Not that I'd wanted to stay asleep. I just
didn't want to go back there.

"I'm sick," I said to her. "I can't go to school today."

Those claws transferred to my forehead, and I turned my face
further into the pillow.

"You feel fine, honey."

"It's cramps."

"Oh, Brynn." My mom sighed. "I'll get you a painkiller and a cup
of tea, but you've got to go to school."

I turned towards her, frowning up at her hovering face, which only
brought an identical frown to hers. It almost seemed strange to see it
there, judging by the way she'd been so happy lately. It reminded me
of how things used to be. But, although I was glad to see her happy, I
knew it would only be temporary. Good things never lasted. Soon, the

depression would return, and she'd be crawling back into bed again. I knew it for a fact.

"I don't have a ride there," I explained to her as I leaned back on my elbows. "And it's too late to ask anyone."

My mother's eyes perked up. "What if I take you?"

"No," I shot her down immediately.

"Well, why on earth not?"

My tired eyes fell to my lap, realizing that I couldn't give her a valid reason. "I just don't want to inconvenience you."

"Honey, your school is just down the street."

"Mom, please, can I just stay in bed?"

"Sweetie, I wish I could let you." She sighed, tilting her head still covered with a bonnet. "But your father has had to speak with your principal twice already this term. She says you're not doing well in any of your classes. Honey, he's just concerned about your grades, that's all."

"It's just been tough to stay focused." I tried not to let Jean's angry words seep in, but I could already feel my throat grow thick. "I told dad I couldn't do it. Why is he still making me go back there?"

"I didn't agree with sending you back, but that was your father's decision." She cupped her knees and glanced down at her lap, seemingly becoming uncomfortable with the topic. "He didn't want you seeing me like that any longer."

"But—"

"Your father means well, Brynn. He just wants to see you finish out the school year strong."

My eyes narrowed, and I turned my back towards her, staring a hole through the wall. "At this rate, I'll be in the eleventh grade forever."

My mother stood again. "I'll go get dressed now."

"Mom, I'll just walk to school."

"Oh, don't be ridiculous. My daughter is not walking to school."

If only she knew.

I threw the blankets off, growling under my breath, before scooting to the edge of the bed. It was strange how I didn't want to leave it. I'd gone months without sleeping in it, and now it physically hurt to part ways with the comfort of it. But I forced myself into the bathroom. Shoving my toothbrush around my mouth before jumping into the shower for a much needed rinse. I walked down the hallway as if I had weights on my ankles. Each step I took towards the front door reminded me of the horror that awaited me outdoors. But I couldn't have prepared myself for the gut wrenching sensation that awakened in my stomach as we walked into the garage that revealed the red eyesore of a car.

"Don't just stand there, Brynn," my mom said as she came around the vehicle. "Your father's going to kill us if your principal has to call home again."

I shook my head. "I'm going to throw up."

"Brynn Clarise." Her eyebrows arched at me, and she snapped her fingers towards the passenger seat. "Get your butt in this car."

I twisted my face and swallowed as I inched towards it.

Just breathe

I blew out a breath as soon as I heard his voice. "Ethan," I greeted him softly.

My mom got the engine started and I tucked myself inside, holding onto my bag that I'd placed in my lap.

"My god, it's been so long since I've driven anywhere."

I looked over at her, noticing her nervous smile. "Mom, maybe you shouldn't."

"Don't be silly," she laughed a little, bringing her hands to the wheel and gripping it like a long-lost friend. "It's not like I forgot how to drive. Mom still knows what she's doing."

I rested my head on the window and took another deep breath as she finally pulled out of the garage. I could avoid thinking about it. I just had to focus on anything else but that night.

"Angie and I visited the market on Saturday while you were napping," my mom started talking to me, making it hard to zone out. "Can you believe Mr. Culpepper still recognized me after all this time?"

I started gnawing on my fingernails.

"I just realized I didn't get the chance to ask him about his wife…"

A stoplight came up, and I watched with wide eyes as she drove through it. "Mom!"

"What's the matter?" She glanced over at me.

"It was red. You were supposed to stop."

She looked in the rearview, frowning as she spotted her mistake. "I'm sorry, I didn't even notice."

"Let's just focus on the road, okay?"

"You should hear yourself." She shook her curly head. "You treat me just like your father does." She scoffed. "As if I'm not capable of doing anything myself. It's insulting."

I rolled my eyes away. A few more minutes and I'd be out of this car. But then what? Could I really trust her to get home safely? The more I thought about it, the more irritated I became. Why had she felt the need to drive me? Why couldn't she have just let me stay home?

Don't blame her

I frowned at Ethan's voice, tucking my chin further.

"I sure hope Angela feels better…" My mom sighed as we drove down the narrow, winding road. "She had such a migraine on Sunday, the poor thing."

I wasn't even jealous of the unfair treatment she'd obviously given Angela versus her own daughter. I only wished she would stop bringing her up altogether.

"Anyway, she insisted on finishing preparing breakfast, but I had to send her home. She just seemed so down. Truly unlike herself—"

"Do we have to keep talking about her?"

She met my gaze, and I quickly looked away. "I won't put up with this behavior any longer, Brynn. What has that woman ever done to you?"

Besides ruining my life?

She did you a favor.

"Forget it," I grumbled.

"She's been a blessing to have around," she continued on. "I don't know what I'd do without her."

"You don't even need her help anymore. Dad said she was only supposed to be temporary."

"He's left it up to me to decide, and I've chosen to let her stay." She braked at the stop sign and turned to me. "Now you're going to stop with this attitude and learn to get along with her because she isn't going anywhere anytime soon."

I clenched my teeth and huffed, whipping my face back around. "Whatever."

We pulled into the school entrance moments later, and I already had my fingers curled around the door latch. Suddenly, I couldn't think of anything more pleasing than to finally be rid of this joyous car ride. But I hadn't expected anything less from the cursed vehicle. I would have loved to never have stepped foot inside of it again.

"Oh, look," my mom's voice caught my attention again, bringing me away from my remorseful thoughts. "It's your boyfriend."

I looked over and noticed the person she'd been referring to. Jean walked across the front grass and Elonie followed at his side. My fingers curled into themselves as I dropped my hand and slumped down into my seat. But the sudden honk of a horn made me flinch, and I quickly noticed that it had come from our car.

My eyes shot up. "Mom, no, don't!"

"Good morning, honey!" My mom called out to him with a wave of her hand.

I closed my eyes and fought the nauseating sensation sweeping over me, but it only worsened as I heard Jean reply back in greeting.

"How are you?" she continued.

My chest palpitated. I didn't know what to do. I'm sure I looked absolutely pitiful with my body sunken into the seat, but I couldn't move. I was frozen stiff. And, as if it could get any worse, Jean was heading over.

"Sit up, sweetie, don't be rude," my mom said to me as she swatted my arm, a bright and cheery smile painted on her warm features.

The heat of my anger rose up my neck, crawling underneath my cheeks and settling there.

Calm down, Brynn. She doesn't know!

But I didn't care. I hated her! She had no idea what she was doing.

"How are you doing, Mrs. Walsh?" Jean's cool tone poured into the car and brushed my skin, causing goosebumps to prickle up. "It's been a while."

"It certainly has." She placed her hand on my shoulder as she spoke to him. "I'm carrying Brynn to school this morning but she's not feeling too well. I think it's best if she goes by the nurse. Would you mind taking her?"

I cut my eyes at her.

"No, I don't mind."

My insides involuntarily warmed at his words, and finally, I met his gaze. "You don't have to take me."

He broke contact with me as he looked over his shoulder towards Elonie. "Maybe she should take you then."

"Oh, how rude of me." My mom's attention switched to the timid girl standing off to the side. "I don't believe we've met. I'm Sierra Walsh, Brynn's mother."

Elonie lifted her palm. "Nice to meet you, Mrs. Walsh. I'm Elonie Davis."

"It's so nice to meet you, Elonie. Are you friends with my Brynn?"

I gripped my bag tighter as I watched Elonie choke on her words. "She's new here," I sputtered out a reply.

"Oh, is she?" My mom's tone elevated a notch, and I closed my eyes again in embarrassment. "Well, welcome to our little town, Elonie. Where did you move here from?"

My fingers found the door latch again, my brain unable to take a single second more of this torture. Fresh air greeted my nose as soon as I got the door opened, and I nearly fell out of the car in an attempt to escape.

"Oh, Brynn, wait—"

I slammed the door shut. Ignoring her as I scurried around the back of the car.

"Make sure you see the nurse," my mom still called out of the window as I hurried up the sidewalk. "Okay, it was so nice seeing you two. Take care now…"

I hate you.

Stop saying that, Brynn!

But I do hate her!

No, you don't. She's our mother. Sure, she's embarrassing, but she means well.

I don't care. I—

"Brynn!"

My breath caught as I halted in my steps, clearly so overtaken by my anger that I'd forgotten who I'd left back there in my haste. I turned around just in time to catch that red car turning the roundabout, the woman inside waving at me one last time before driving away. My attention had quickly been gripped by Jean, though, as he walked towards me. I noticed Elonie remained put, and I was inwardly thankful for that.

Go inside, Brynn.I pulled my bag to my front, placing it as a barrier between Jean and I, but I couldn't walk away from him. My body wouldn't let me leave.

"Jean," My voice shook as I said his name, and I wanted to kick myself. "How have you—"

"Did you actually need the nurse?"

I blinked, confused at first, but suddenly remembered the only reason he was talking to me in the first place. I shook my head. "I just told her that because I didn't want to come today."

He sucked his tooth, patting his fist. "You're really good at that."

"What?"

"Lying."

My stomach turned, and a frown settled on my face. He looked over his shoulder and then back down at me.

"Alright, well—"

"Wait, just—" Brynn! I stepped towards him. "Please just talk to me, Jean." Don't! I winced, tilting my head away from Ethan's rising voice. "Please—"

The first bell rang right then. Shattering my heart with its piercing noise. Jean didn't seem phased by the noise, but then again, he'd never cared about rushing to class.

But he did turn and walk back over to Elonie who still stood there. Taking a bit of my hope with him.

Brynn, what are you doing? You know what he did to you!

"It was my fault I—"

It was his fault!

I shook my head, watching Jean and Elonie pinpricks in my eyes as he sent her off with a kiss to the lips.

He's hurting you, Brynn. Why can't you see that?

I tore my eyes away from them. "Just leave me alone, Ethan."

I can't just let you keep doing this to yourself…

The knob in my throat thickened as I turned to the side, pushing my fingers into the corners of my eyes. What hurt the most was knowing Ethan was right. Jean had hurt me and was still hurting me. But I'd hurt him, too. All of this was my fault, and I knew he wanted me to make it right.

"Come on," Jean called out to me.

I didn't hesitate.

I rushed over to him, taking that familiar spot by his side, but I couldn't ignore the fact that he didn't put his arm around my shoulders or take my hand in his. He didn't try to touch me at all. He barely looked at me as we walked off towards the parking lot.

I reached up and scratched my neck, relieving the tension that had built up there, but it only temporarily helped.

The headlights of the truck blinked as we approached it, and I walked up to the back door, hurrying inside to avoid being spotted by patrolling security. Jean got in on the other side, and I barely got a word out before he'd yanked me towards him by the neck. Smashing our lips. Suffocating me instantly. But I didn't stop him. I couldn't stop him. Not if I wanted things to go back to normal. Not if I wanted him to trust me again.

I let my eyes become clouded with tears, refusing to watch my hands undress myself, but I still felt his hands—rough and filled with anger. That anger grabbed my shaking limbs, gripped at my skin, and pulled at the root of my hair. Searching for anything that would receive its pain. But as soon as my hands hesitated to participate, he'd taken me by the wrist, pinning me with the ugliest glare I'd ever seen him give me.

"You're not even trying!"

I dropped my head and sobbed. "I'm sorry."

"Just get off."

"Jean—"

"I said get off."

I sniffled, staring at him as I took my weight off of his lap and pushed myself against the door. Tears trickling down my sweaty cheeks.

He tilted his head back and closed his eyes, letting out a robust sigh. "It's not going to work out, Brynn."

"We can try again." I tried my best to convince him. "I'll do it right this time, I promise."

"No, it's not—" He shook his head and sighed again. "It's just different. I know you're not mine."

"I am—"

"No, you're not," he said, finally opening his eyes raising his head up again. "Don't you get it, Brynn? You and him…you'll always be connected to each other."

"No," I bit.

He shook his head and started fastening his jeans. "You just don't get it. You never did."

My chest heaved in panic. "Jean, please don't—"

"Just stop already. It's over, Brynn."

"Why?" I cried, but they were frustrated tears as my own anger reared its ugly head. "Because of her? Because now you've slept with her?"

He grabbed my face and slammed my head against the window. "Don't!" I closed my eyes to the terrifying look on his face, my voice becoming caught in my throat as he covered my mouth as if to shut it. "You don't get to throw your stones at me."

I tried releasing myself from his grip, but he held me in place, pushing himself closer and trapping me further.

"Look at me!"

I peeled my eyes open, cowering under his glare.

"Funny how quick you are to judge when a few short months ago you were in the exact same spot as she is right now," he continued. "Ready and willing to give me everything. And you did, didn't you?" His hand tightened on my jaw when I failed to answer. "Didn't you?"

I nodded as best I could.

He chuckled, shaking his head. "There you go, lying again." He brought his face closer, so close that I could feel the warmth of his breath on my cheeks. "You took everything away from me, girl." He watched more tears slip out of my eyes and slide down my face. "Do you think it's been easy for me to see your face every day?"

I squeezed my eyes shut as he brought his mouth next to my ear. My heart pounded violently in my chest, and my hands gripped the seat.

"I wanted to kill you for what you did to me," he said to me, and my chin trembled as his words left permanent wounds on me. "I still want to…and I will if you don't stay away from me."

He let go of my mouth and pushed himself off of me, but my body was still in shock, and my head throbbed with a headache that was on the brink of making me vomit. Despite all of this, I couldn't look away from Jean. His eyes were sharp underneath narrowed eyelids, and those lips were set in a firm line. Not a trace of regret on his face.

He looked done with me.

And my heart officially broke in two.

I slipped out of his truck, standing on weak legs, attempting to keep myself from falling apart again. Jean came around on my side and stood in front of me. Both of us caring less about the patrol car now. I looked down at my feet to avoid his gaze.

"Maybe I'll just go ahead and do it then," I softly uttered.

"Don't threaten me, girl," he said with a dry chuckle. "It actually wouldn't be the worst thing at this point."

I looked up at him, becoming upset again. "You hate me that much."

"I hate you more than I've ever hated anyone in my life, Brynn." He stepped towards me and gently took my face in his hands now. "I opened up to you. I shared more with you than I've shared with anyone. And the whole time, you weren't even mine. You weren't even deserving of any of it."

My eyes glazed over again. "I'm sorry I lied to you, Jean."

"You know you should do it." His fingers slid down to my chin and pinched it. "Spare me the torture of seeing your face every day, okay?"

I bowed my head.

"Go now."

I knit my brows. "Jean—"

"Just like I showed you in France. Smooth and easy…"

I swallowed and closed my eyes as I remembered France.

The rain.

The dark hotel room.

The smile on Jean's face…the face that no longer smiled for me.

And never would again.

33

Brynn looked just like her mother.

I envied that a little.

I'd gotten everything from Presley. Our eyes resembled the darkest shade of a mood ring. Our faces both lacked those sharp, mature angles. The dimple that indented only our right cheek was even the same.

If I didn't see his face every time I looked in the mirror then I would know for sure I wasn't his. I would no longer be confused by how I felt inside. The feeling that I didn't belong to him at all.

Sometimes, I felt that way about mom, too.

She'd been so different from me. She knew things, she'd explored places, she'd gotten more out of life. She would tell me how Presley ruined that for her. How he'd forced her to slow down. She'd get so upset talking about it. She'd resented him for the longest.

She hadn't wanted the same for me. She'd planned to take me away. As soon as I came out of her belly, we'd both leave. She hadn't wanted this life for us. She'd wanted me to grow up on warm sand by the beach underneath a hot sun. She'd wanted me to know her parents. She'd wanted me to have everything she didn't have growing up. But Presley… he wouldn't let her leave. They'd fought and made love, and she'd decided to stay for him.

He'd convinced her we were her family now.

Mom had resented that, too.

But she was in love. From the first time she laid her eyes on me. I was her baby doll, she'd said.

Her little cabbage.

I wish I saw what she saw. Maybe if I looked a little more like her then I wouldn't miss her so much. If I had her amber eyes. Her angular jaw. Her pretty braids… She left before she could finish teaching me. She left before she could do a lot of things.

"Begin working on your assignments quietly," Mr. Jones's voice trickled into my thoughts, causing me to focus on him at his spot behind his desk.

"Hey." Liam settled into his seat next to me. "How was your weekend?"

I blinked my eyes, clearing my hazy vision. "H-hey."

"Hey…" Liam parted his lips in an amused smile. "Everything alright?"

"Yes."

"Are you sure? You seem off."

I nodded, giving him a small smile. "I'm fine." Then I shifted to face him. "How was your weekend?"

He laughed suddenly. "I asked you first."

"Oh." My eyes widened, but I couldn't help but giggle. "Sorry, I didn't hear you. My weekend was good. I finished my book."

"Wait, you just bought it last weekend, didn't you?"

"Sometimes I can't sleep, so I just read."

He looked confused.

"But I guess it doesn't really make me sleepy like it does other people," I said with a laugh of my own.

"Crazy girl," he said.

My grin stayed, that nice fuzzy feeling stirring the pit of my stomach. "What did you do this weekend?"

"We had a scrimmage out of town."

Now, it was my turn to look confused. "A what?"

"It's a fake game," he explained to me. "We play against another school for practice for the next game."

"Oh." I nodded, grabbing my bag up from the floor. "Was it fun?"

He looked reminiscent as he chuckled. "Yea, I can be a little competitive, so the guys didn't take the loss too well."

My eyes lit up. "You won?"

"You say that as if we aren't running champs," he said, leaning towards me, brown eyes squinted. "We're undefeated, okay?"

I laughed. "Pardon me."

I still felt his eyes on me as I slipped out my French textbook and a pencil to write.

"Elonie, I uh…"

I glanced at him, noticing his eyes had lowered to the floor and his lips had twisted to the side. The search for a pencil became the least of my concern as I swallowed.

"I'm sorry." He looked at me with those sincere eyes. "I didn't mean to make you feel bad about…" He scratched the side of his jaw. "Well, I shouldn't have gotten mad at you. It wasn't right."

I could tell he was fighting something on his tongue. Something he'd done when we'd gotten into the argument before. But I hadn't wanted to know then. I'd wanted to hold onto the image of Jean that lived in my head. But now my body ached with that familiar urge. I wondered if what sat on the tip of his tongue had something to do with Brynn.

This morning's events had conjured up that uncomfortable feeling again. The same feeling I'd had when I saw that waitress smile. The same feeling I'd had when I'd spied on Cole and Lana that day after school. Just to confirm what I'd already known. Hurting my own feelings as I watched them kiss inside of the pool building…for everyone to see.

Liam still stared at me with that same look on his face, and I had to force myself not to pry. "It's okay," I said.

He shook his head, finally allowing that serious expression to let up. "My dad says never say that after someone apologizes."

My brows mended. "Why not?"

"Because it tells the other person what they did wrong is okay."

My eyes wandered in meditation. "I guess I never thought about it like that before."

"Trust me, no one has." He grabbed his backpack and unzipped the front.

I slid my hand underneath my curls and leaned on my elbow, watching him take out his assignment. I admired Liam for having the guts to do what I couldn't. If left up to me, who knows when we would've made up? I smiled to myself, realizing that now everything could go back to normal.

"I'm sorry, too." The words fell out of my mouth before I could catch them.

He looked over, shaking his head. "You shouldn't be sorry for anything."

My lips parted again as I searched his face. "I just felt like I should apologize, too."

"You were just defending yourself, Elonie."

"Well, I said some things I shouldn't have."

He shrugged his shoulders. "Maybe I deserved it. Somehow, I'm always getting in the middle of things that don't concern me."

I'd heard that before. "What do you mean by that?"

I could tell I'd caught him off guard with my sudden interest, and he quickly shook his head as if to brush it off. But I couldn't let it go this time. I really wanted to know.

"You can trust me, Liam," I insisted, bringing us closer as I leaned in.

He tapped his pencil against the edge of his desk, dropping his gaze to his lap. "I just meant...I have a history of making things worse..."

"Are you talking about Ethan?" I didn't know why his name came to mind, but it did. I could always tell when he was thinking about him. "You know, you never told me how the car accident happened."

He avoided my eyes, which was odd, but I knew this topic still caused him so much pain.

"Can you tell me more about him?" I suggested instead.

Liam smiled, and it relieved me. "Ethan was the only one who could whoop my butt in soccer." He shook his head fondly. "He was a beast on the field."

"I didn't know he played soccer, too."

"He was our best midfielder." He chuckled and glanced at me with a smirk. "Besides me, of course."

"Of course," I giggled.

"We actually got accepted into the same university," he went on, tapping away at the desk again. "We were planning to drive cross country together after graduation."

"I bet he was smart at math like Brynn."

"Oh yea. They were both huge nerds." Liam chuckled. "But they never had that sibling rivalry thing. Not like Danielle and Allan."

"Really?" I asked this as if I hadn't witnessed it for myself.

"Well, it's mostly Danielle who makes a big deal out of anything she does better. But, then again, she's that way with everyone. She likes to intimidate."

"Is that why people are so afraid of her?"

Liam raised a dark brow. "I'm not afraid of her. I just stay away from her."

"I now know why."

"There's something wrong with that girl." He appeared to think something over before his eyes fluttered up. "Did Brynn ever tell you about what happened last year?"

I sucked my lips in as I nodded, knowing it wasn't the truth but desperate to keep this conversation going. "I didn't know you knew about that, too."

"The whole school knows about it, thanks to Danielle." Liam frowned this time as he thought back. "She threw Brynn under the bus."

"How?" I asked quickly.

"The only reason Brynn started doing it is because Danielle used to."

"Started doing what?"

"The—" He appeared uneasy as he motioned his finger to the back of his throat. "You know…"

Just like that, I had already forgotten that I was supposed to know all of this information. Liam hadn't noticed the slip up though. I swallowed as I realized what he'd told me. Suddenly, I was reminded of mornings at the café. Brynn almost never ate. Then, I remembered all the times I'd watched Danielle's lunch go untouched.

It all made sense now.

"She made it look like Brynn was the only one with a problem," he said.

"Why would she do that to her?"

"She got jealous of Brynn."

"Jealous," I muttered—half to myself.

"Brynn was easier to get along with. A perfectionist, too, but at least she wasn't mean."

It was strange to hear that. It's as if he were talking about a completely different Brynn. One that I hadn't gotten the privilege of meeting.

"Plus, she was Ethan's little sister," Liam told me. "And everyone loved Ethan."

"Everyone?"

Liam chuckled. "Everyone."

"Even Singh?"

The smile faltered as he rubbed his jaw again. "I think she favored him a little too much."

I drew my eyebrows in again and waited.

"I mean, you see how she treats Allan and Danielle…like her little…minions or something."

"Was Ethan one, too?"

"No." He sat up and pointed the pencil towards the door, accusing her from afar. "She tried to get him to do it, though. She wanted him to report on everyone like they do, but he wouldn't stand for it."

My heart began to pound. I saw Danielle's face in my head again. Then, Principal Singh. And I began to wonder about that day in the office. Had Singh already known the truth beforehand?

"Singh threatened his letter of recommendation a few times just to scare him into cooperating," Liam commented.

I shook my head, wide-eyed. "That's so unfair."

"That woman is a tyrant. My dad says the staff here knows how she is, too. They're scared of—"

The door of our classroom opened up, crumbling the imaginary walls I'd built around us and snatching my attention away from Liam.

Allan stood in the doorway, staring at me in the same way he had that first day we'd met: impatiently.

"Miss Davis—"

"Huh?"

Mr. Jones reclined in his seat, extending his arm towards the door, indicating no other choice but to go with him. I blinked down and began gathering my things. Allan's razor-sharp glare cut as I passed by him into the hallway, causing me so much discomfort I'd begun to walk as soon as I heard the door close behind us. But he'd hindered me, blocking my path.

"Where's Brynn?" He immediately started an interrogation.

I was shaken, visibly lost for words.

"I know you know," he continued. "I saw you with her this morning. I watched you leave her out there with him."

"I—"

"Did he upset her? Is that why she left school?"

"I don't know." It was the truth. I had no idea what had happened after I went inside, leaving them alone to talk. "I didn't even know she left."

Allan breathed heavily through his nose and shook his head at me. "Something is wrong. I know he did something to her."

"He didn't." Once again, I was overwhelmed by the need to defend Jean. "She only wanted to talk—"

"Because he's ignoring her!" Allan stepped towards me, and I flinched. "I knew this would happen. I knew he would drop her as soon as he found another toy to play with."

"Stop," I uttered, unable to look at him any longer.

"He used her up and threw her away like a piece of trash. And you think he won't do the same thing to you?"

"You don't know anything about—"

"I know more than you do."

I clenched my jaw. "Well, I know things, too." Fire stung my tongue, surprising us both. "I've heard about you and your sister."

He turned his back to me. "I don't care what you've heard about me."

"Where are you taking me?"

"Principal Singh needs to have a word with you."

"I'm sure whatever she needs to know, you'd be able to inform her."

Allan froze. And so did I. All of the nerve shedding from me. He turned and walked back towards me.

"Our sophomore year," Allan said, his voice causing my hair to stand on edge. "Ask Cohen why Jasmine Tavares had to transfer in the middle of it."

My eyes fluttered and fell to the floor.

"Come on."

I silently followed behind him all the way to Principal Singh's office. Confusion still wreaking havoc on my mind. But that confusion only worsened when I noticed Jean. He sat in the chair that Danielle had that day. The day she tried to ruin my life. I had a strange feeling that whatever this was, it was going to be much worse.

"Come in and sit down, Elonie." Principal Singh stood in front of that familiar window with the half-open blinds. That stern expression never failed to make my stomach twist.

I avoided that hard stare of hers, keeping my eyes on Jean as I released the door, letting it close behind me.

His eyes spoke to me. The same way they'd spoken to me after he'd come out of the office that first day we'd met. Even through my shivering state I'd been able to read those eyes loud and clear. They said the same thing right now. They begged me to lie.

I sat down next to him. "Hi."

"Hey girl," he whispered, then smiled a little.

"Miss Davis," Principal Singh alerted me, bringing my attention to her. "This isn't a social hour. I've called you in here for a reason."

"What reason?" I asked timidly.

"It's been brought to my attention that you may know Brynn Walsh's whereabouts." Singh left her post near the window and stepped forward. "Her mother says she dropped her off at school this morning, and now she's gone missing."

I slowly shook my head. "I don't."

"Miss Davis, is it true you were with Brynn Walsh this morning when she was dropped off by her mother?"

"I told you she wasn't there," Jean muttered.

"I'm speaking to her, Mr. Cohen."

My palms grew moist as I brought my hands to my upper arms and gripped tight. "I went to get breakfast as soon as I arrived." The lie easily slipped out. "I haven't seen Brynn since last week."

Jean adjusted himself, angling himself toward me as he rested his cheek on his fist. I watched him to see if I could spot any hints he attempted to give me, though Singh was not finished with me yet.

"Allan Turner said that he saw you in front of the school building right before the bell rang," she said, straightening the glass paper mache on her desk. "You were speaking with Brynn, and she seemed upset."

"I never said anything to her—"

"She wasn't there," Jean threw out again, a harshness that hadn't been present before added to his tone.

I realized that I'd made a mistake, and immediately, the walls closed in. My chest began to heave as I dug my nails into my arms.

"I was the only one with Brynn," Jean continued as he shifted to the edge of his seat. "She told me she wanted to leave. She said she couldn't stop thinking about her brother and how he would've been graduating soon. I tried to convince her to stay, but she wouldn't listen."

"But she didn't return home as per her mother's statement, so you must know where she is, Jean," Principal Singh said.

I turned my head, gluing my lips shut, refusing to make matters worse. Jean held the arms of the chair as a chuckle left him.

"I told you already," he answered. "I have no idea."

"Very well." Singh nodded, bringing both hands to her front, those lips taut again. "You'll both be placed in detention for the remainder of the week."

My eyes grew in size. "But why?"

"You can't give us detention," Jean said, though he still wore an amused grin. "We didn't do anything wrong. Brynn is the one who left."

"And I believe you're the reason why," Principal Singh spoke frankly.

"What does it matter what you believe?"

"Would you like a week of suspension instead, Mr. Cohen? I can't imagine what that would do to your academic record. The odds of you graduating are beginning to look very slim at this point."

Jean suddenly rose up from the chair. "Why don't you just go ahead and expel me then? I know that's what you've been dying to do since that day."

Singh turned her back to him. "Miss Davis, you have my permission to leave—"

"She doesn't deserve detention." Jean still fought Singh on my behalf. "She hasn't done anything wrong."

Singh only shook her head as she sat down. "That's where you're wrong." She locked her fingers and placed her hands on her desk, giving me a cock of her eyebrow. "I warned her about you, Jean Cohen. These are the consequences for not heeding those warnings."

I was fully heaving at this point, both eyes fixed on Singh, unable to look away from the grimace she wore now. I'd never seen her expression become so deeply disgusted. It was evident that she disliked Jean—for whatever reason—but judging by the look on his face, I could see the feeling was mutual.

"Return to your classes, Miss Davis," Singh finished. "Your father will receive a notice in the mail regarding your detention. Be sure to have it signed and returned back to me by the end of the week."

I hated leaving Jean behind. But for some reason, Principal Singh no longer wanted me there. Whatever threats she had saved up for him, she clearly didn't want me to hear. It was hard for me to focus on anything else, though. Even as I sat in math class, staring at Brynn's empty seat while attempting to avoid Allan's looming eyes, I thought about Jean. I left class early, offering Mr. Leech the menstruation excuse, heading straight for Jean's truck in the parking lot.

The millions of questions crowding my head helped my feet move down those brick steps faster, and I wouldn't have stopped if I hadn't heard a familiar voice calling my name. Making me pause and turn towards the voice as soon as I reached the sidewalk. Liam walked from the opposite direction and, beside him, a man who stood about the same height but a lot stockier in size. I knew right away that he was Liam's father. Those similar brown eyes and strong jawline only confirmed it as they neared closer.

"Hey, where are you headed?" Liam asked, gripping a duffel bag at his side.

I almost choked as I attempted to catch my breath from the brisk walk. "I…I just needed to…get some air."

Liam's face shifted to a look of concern. "What's wrong?"

"Nothing, I just felt a little lightheaded in class." My eyes quickly shot over to his dad. "I was on my way back, though."

"Ah, the bell's nearly ringing for lunch," he replied, waving his hand over his shoulder. "I figured I'd pull him out of class a few minutes early, too."

"Oh yea." Liam motioned towards the man. "This is my dad."

"Coach Ackert."

I shook his hand, forcing my facial muscles to smile. "Nice to meet you, I'm Elonie Davis."

"I know…" Coach Ackert grinned over at Liam. "My son might have mentioned you once or twice."

Liam gave his dad's shoulder a punch, though he genuinely laughed, clearly unbothered by the exposure.

"Anyway, it's nice to finally put a pretty face to the famous Elonie Davis."

My face warmed at his compliment. "Liam's told me a lot about you, too."

"Has he?" Coach Ackert smirked and folded his arms. "Then you know I taught him everything he knows—soccer, girls, the whole shebang."

I giggled, realizing they both shared the same teasing humor. It instantly made me comfortable around him and even helped the leftover nerves I'd had from earlier dissolve.

"I will neither confirm or deny that." Liam chuckled, pulling his duffel further onto his shoulder. "Anyway, we better head to the field." He then looked down at me. "Do you want to come?"

The question was simple, but for some reason, I drew a blank, and nothing came out. Liam seemed to realize my dilemma, but the bell made its presence known before he could jump in and save me. I was back underneath the water. Drowning. Although I still stood there with them, I was being pulled further down. And that pull only became stronger until I was forced to look over my shoulder. Noticing Jean stood at the bottom of the brick stairwell. Only then did sound return, and I gasped for air, reminded of the only thing that mattered to me at the moment.

"I'm sorry, Liam," I said, though my voice couldn't have been any louder than a whisper, and I swiftly turned towards his father. "It was very nice to meet you, sir."

I didn't stay a second longer. Not even to hear what he'd said in return. I walked away from Liam and over to that brick stairwell.

Back to Jean.

His attention remained on Liam as I walked up to him. Those eyes looking straight over my head. I don't think he would've noticed me if I hadn't said his name. And, even then, I'm surprised my fragile tone had been able to bring him out of his trance. But I almost wished it hadn't. The stare he gave me brought me right back to that hallway. I hadn't seen it since that day. And I thought, for sure, I'd never see it again.

He slowly lowered down until he was seated on the steps. I swallowed the knob in my throat as he pressed his face into his palms and heavily sighed.

"Jean, what's…" My voice became trapped as I watched him shake his head and look up at me again, noticing his eyes were red with tears.

"I have to tell you something," he said.

I nodded. "Tell me."

"Not right now. Not here."

"Let's leave then," I suggested urgently.

He shook his head. "I've gotten you into enough trouble."

"I don't care about that, Jean."

He squeezed his eyes with his fingers and stood up, towering over me once again. "Come on."

I followed closely behind him, gripping my arms and keeping my face down until we were safely in his truck, away from any spying eyes. I looked over, waiting for him to start the engine, but he remained still.

"Jean?"

He didn't say anything. He just stared forward, seemingly watching as our peers shuffled out of the building to enjoy their lunch period. But I could only watch him. I wished I could read his mind. Know his thoughts. Burrow myself inside of his body to feel how he felt. On impulse, I reached out to touch him, but he flinched away, shocking me to the core. Leaving me cold and confused.

He looked at me, startled. "I'm leaving, Elonie."

I blinked. Unable to fully comprehend what he'd just said. I needed more. I pleaded for more with my eyes.

He gripped the steering wheel and leaned up towards it. Whatever he needed to say looked painful. I could see it all on his face. For the first time, I could read his emotions perfectly.

"Soon…" He continued with his eyes closed. "And I want you to come with me."

"Yes."

He peeled his eyes open, looking quite irritated. "You don't know what I mean."

"What do you mean, Jean?"

"I mean, I'm going to do it." He raised his head and glared at me, making me shiver. "I'm going to finally end this."

My breath hitched, and I froze. "What?"

"I've been planning it for years," he said, his tone deadpan. "Don't try and talk me out of it."

My eyebrows fastened as a flood of tears spilled down my cheeks. This time, I hadn't even felt them come. They rushed in and blinded my view of him. But it didn't matter. I refused to look at him.

I couldn't.

He was breaking my heart.

"Elonie," he said my name again, and I knew exactly what he wanted to know before he asked. "Will you come with me?"

I trembled, staring down at my lap. "I want…I want to stay here with you."

"There is no me here, Elonie."

I looked up at the ceiling, taking deep breaths, although I felt like my heart was pushing through my throat. "Oh, god."

"God has nothing to do with it," he snapped all of a sudden. Staring me directly in the eye. "This is my choice, and I'm not backing out of it."

"Why?" I asked through gritted teeth.

"Why?" He slowly leaned up, resting both arms on the compartment between us. "Do you really want to know?"

I nodded with a heaving chest, anticipating his answer, though my frown returned as he began shaking his head.

"You can't know," he said, then he brought his face closer to mine, close enough to hear his heart pounding below. "You can't know until you promise me you'll come."

I turned my face away, hiding it with my palm as I sobbed, feeling my body convulse as he ripped me in half. Part of me shriveled up on the floor like a baby, refusing to have no part in this scheme. The other part…folded into his embrace, allowing his fingers to caress my scalp, comforting me in that familiar way.

I closed my eyes. Ignoring that sad little girl as she cried on the floor. Shaking back and forth. I ignored her like Presley had ignored me. Watching mom slip away in that bathtub. Unable to save her last breath.

"I promise," I cried, wrapping my arms tight around Jean's neck as if he were going away right now. "Please don't leave me, Jean."

"I told you I won't." He brought my forehead to his and looked me square in the eye. "You're mine forever, Mignonne."

I shivered beneath the weight of his words, feeling the chill seep into my bones as I clung to him, desperate for warmth that seemed just out of reach. His breath brushed against my skin, heavy with the promise of something I couldn't quite understand, yet I knew it held the power to change everything. The world outside felt distant, the echoes of my past fading into a blur as his voice tethered me to the present, to this moment where only we existed. The pull of his gaze drew me deeper into the darkness we shared, a place where light dared not enter. And in that abyss, I found my answer, though it frightened me more than the unknown ever could.

"Forever," I whispered, but the word hung in the air, unfinished, as the reality of what forever might mean settled in—a truth I wasn't sure I was ready to face. The silence between us grew thick, and I wondered if there was still time to turn back, to choose another path. But the choice was no longer mine to make. It had been made the moment I let him in, and now, there was only one way forward.

And so, with a heart heavy with fear and something that might have been hope, I closed my eyes, surrendering to the inevitability of what was to come...

Author's Note

This book contains discussions of death, suicide, self-harm, trauma, anxiety/depression, miscarriage, eating disorders, and dating violence. I pray I've done these topics justice and mean no offense to anyone who has faced any of these challenges.

Thank you!

Milton Keynes UK
Ingram Content Group UK Ltd.
UKHW032321121024
449589UK00010B/443